POKÉMON™

ADVENTURES

BLACK & WHITE

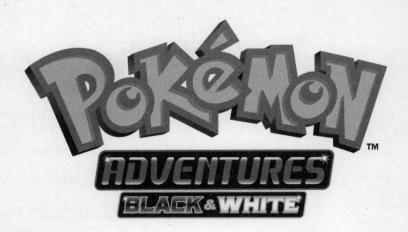

**Pokémon ADVENTURES
BLACK AND WHITE**
Volume 3
Perfect Square Edition

Story by **HIDENORI KUSAKA**
Art by **SATOSHI YAMAMOTO**

© 2014 Pokémon.
© 1995–2014 Nintendo/Creatures Inc./GAME FREAK inc.
TM, ®, and character names are trademarks of Nintendo.
POCKET MONSTERS SPECIAL Vol. 45
by Hidenori KUSAKA, Satoshi YAMAMOTO
© 1997 Hidenori KUSAKA, Satoshi YAMAMOTO
All rights reserved.
Original Japanese edition published by SHOGAKUKAN.
English translation rights in the United States of America, Canada,
the United Kingdom and Ireland arranged with SHOGAKUKAN.

Translation/Tetsuichiro Miyaki
English Adaptation/Annette Roman
Touch-up & Lettering/Susan Daigle-Leach
Design/Shawn Carrico
Editor/Annette Roman

Printed in the U.S.A.

Published by VIZ Media, LLC
P.O. Box 77010
San Francisco, CA 94107

10 9 8 7 6 5 4 3 2 1
First printing, March 2014

www.perfectsquare.com

www.viz.com

POKÉMON™
ADVENTURES
BLACK & WHITE

3

VOLUME THREE

Story by
Hidenori Kusaka

Art by
Satoshi Yamamoto

& WHITE

SOME PLACE IN SOME TIME...
A YOUNG TRAINER NAMED BLACK, WHO DREAMS OF WINNING THE POKÉMON LEAGUE, RECEIVES A POKÉDEX FROM PROFESSOR JUNIPER AND SETS OFF ON HIS TRAINING JOURNEY TO COLLECT THE GYM BADGES HE NEEDS TO ENTER NEXT YEAR'S POKÉMON LEAGUE. ON THE WAY, HE MEETS WHITE, THE OWNER OF A POKÉMON TALENT AGENCY, AND ENDS UP WORKING FOR HER.

BLACK IS ATTACKED BY N, THE KING OF TEAM PLASMA, WHOSE IDEAL IS TO "LIBERATE" POKÉMON FROM THEIR TRAINERS. BLACK WINS HIS FIRST GYM BADGE. AND THEN, IN ORDER TO FULFILL BOTH THEIR DREAMS, BLACK AND WHITE SET OUT FOR THEIR NEXT DESTINATION...

A STORY ABOUT YOUNG PEOPLE ENTRUSTED WITH POKÉDEXES BY THE WORLD'S LEADING POKÉMON RESEARCHERS. TOGETHER WITH THEIR POKÉMON, THEY TRAVEL, BATTLE, AND EVOLVE!

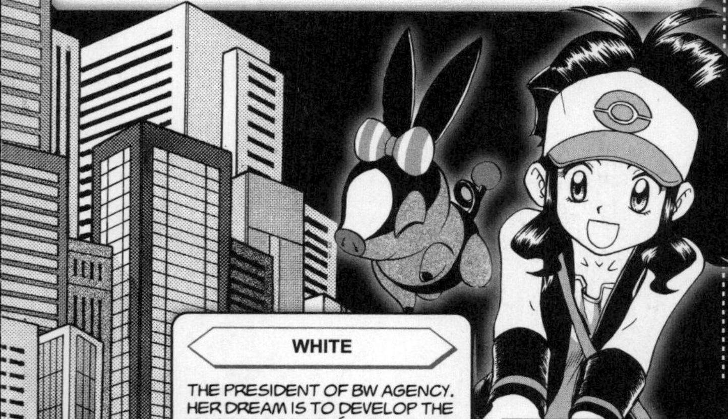

WHITE

THE PRESIDENT OF BW AGENCY. HER DREAM IS TO DEVELOP THE CAREERS OF POKÉMON STARS. SHE TAKES HER WORK VERY SERIOUSLY AND WILL DO ANYTHING TO SUPPORT HER POKÉMON ACTORS.

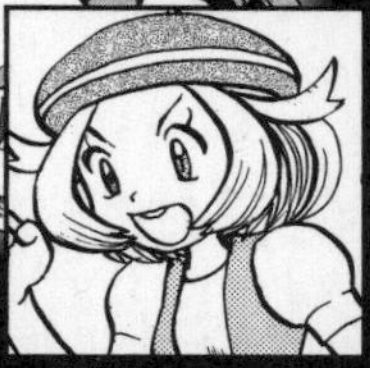

BIANCA

BLACK'S CHILDHOOD FRIEND WHO LIKES TO TAKE THINGS AT HER OWN PACE. SHE DEPARTS ON HER TRAINING JOURNEY WITH OSHAWOTT!

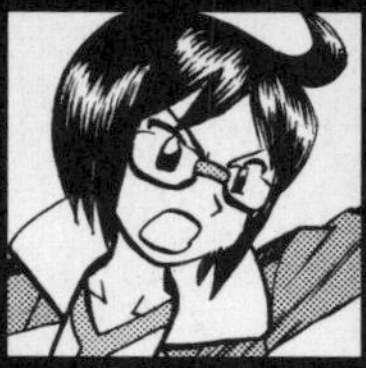

CHEREN

BLACK'S CHILDHOOD FRIEND. A KIND, SERIOUS BOY. HE HEADS OUT ON HIS POKÉMON JOURNEY WITH SNIVY!

POKÉMON ADVENTURES The Tenth Chapter 10 BLACK

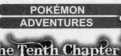

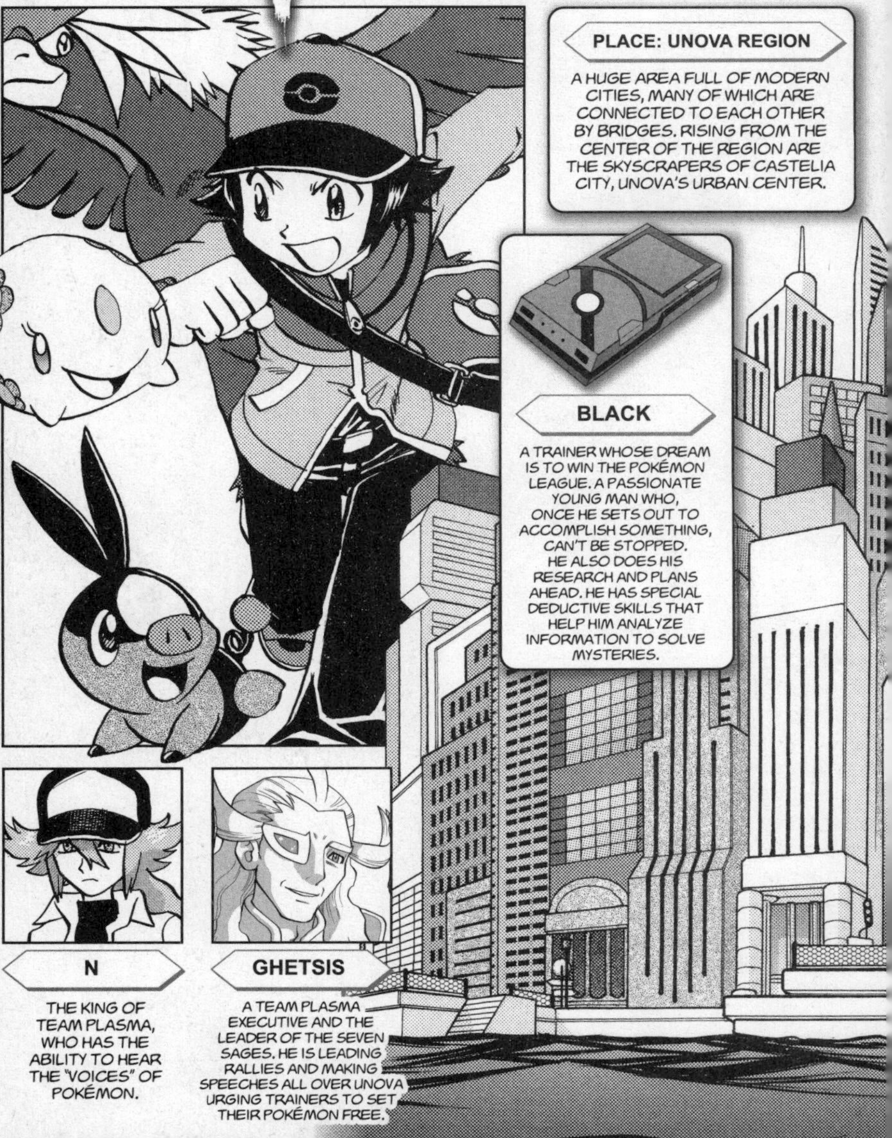
PLACE: UNOVA REGION
A HUGE AREA FULL OF MODERN CITIES, MANY OF WHICH ARE CONNECTED TO EACH OTHER BY BRIDGES. RISING FROM THE CENTER OF THE REGION ARE THE SKYSCRAPERS OF CASTELIA CITY, UNOVA'S URBAN CENTER.
BLACK
A TRAINER WHOSE DREAM IS TO WIN THE POKÉMON LEAGUE. A PASSIONATE YOUNG MAN WHO, ONCE HE SETS OUT TO ACCOMPLISH SOMETHING, CAN'T BE STOPPED. HE ALSO DOES HIS RESEARCH AND PLANS AHEAD. HE HAS SPECIAL DEDUCTIVE SKILLS THAT HELP HIM ANALYZE INFORMATION TO SOLVE MYSTERIES.
GHETSIS
A TEAM PLASMA EXECUTIVE AND THE LEADER OF THE SEVEN SAGES. HE IS LEADING RALLIES AND MAKING SPEECHES ALL OVER UNOVA URGING TRAINERS TO SET THEIR POKÉMON FREE.
N
THE KING OF TEAM PLASMA, WHO HAS THE ABILITY TO HEAR THE "VOICES" OF POKÉMON.

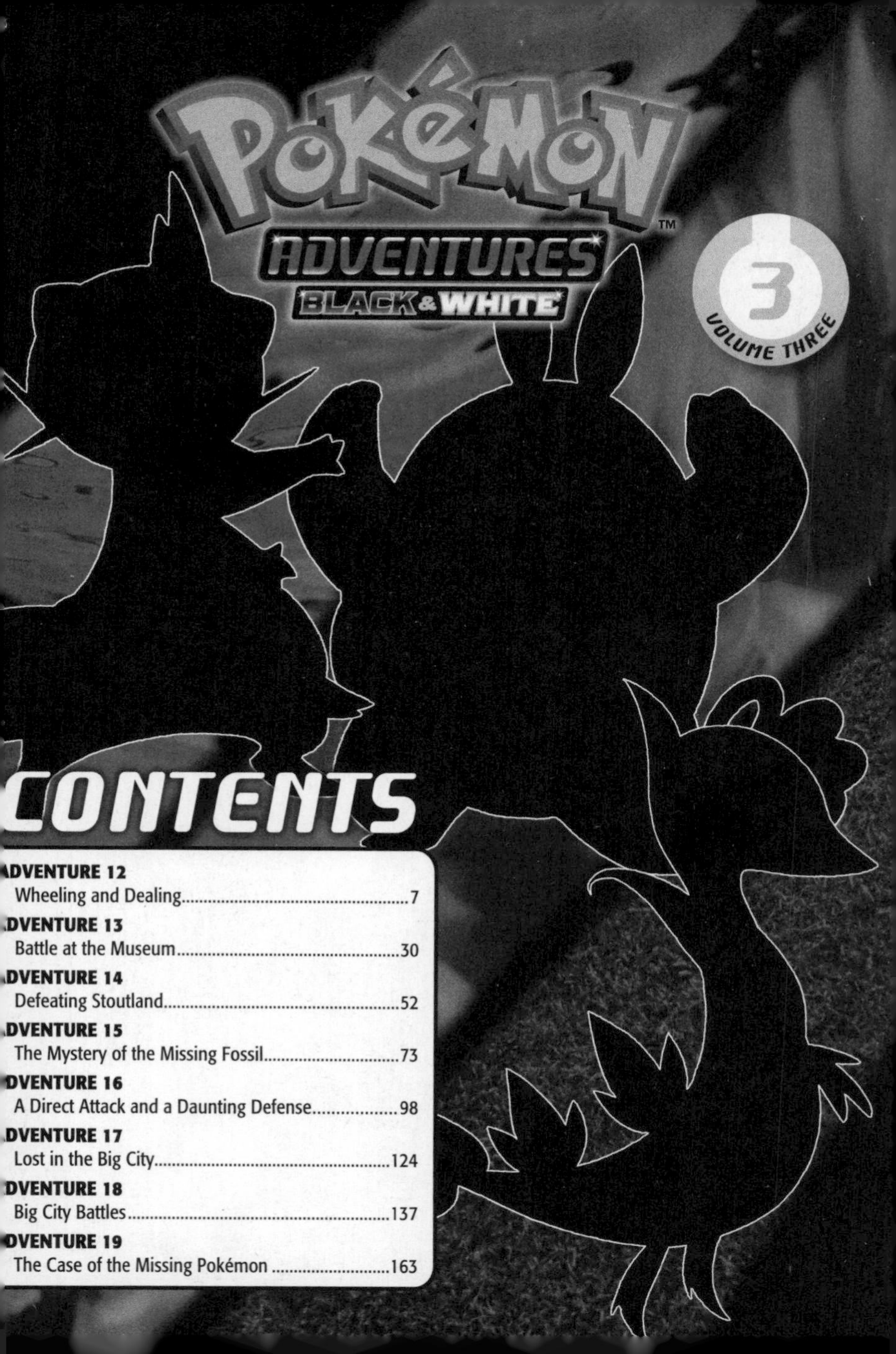
POKéMON ADVENTURES BLACK & WHITE
3
VOLUME THREE

CONTENTS

POKÉMON ADVENTURES BLACK & WHITE

SCRAGGY

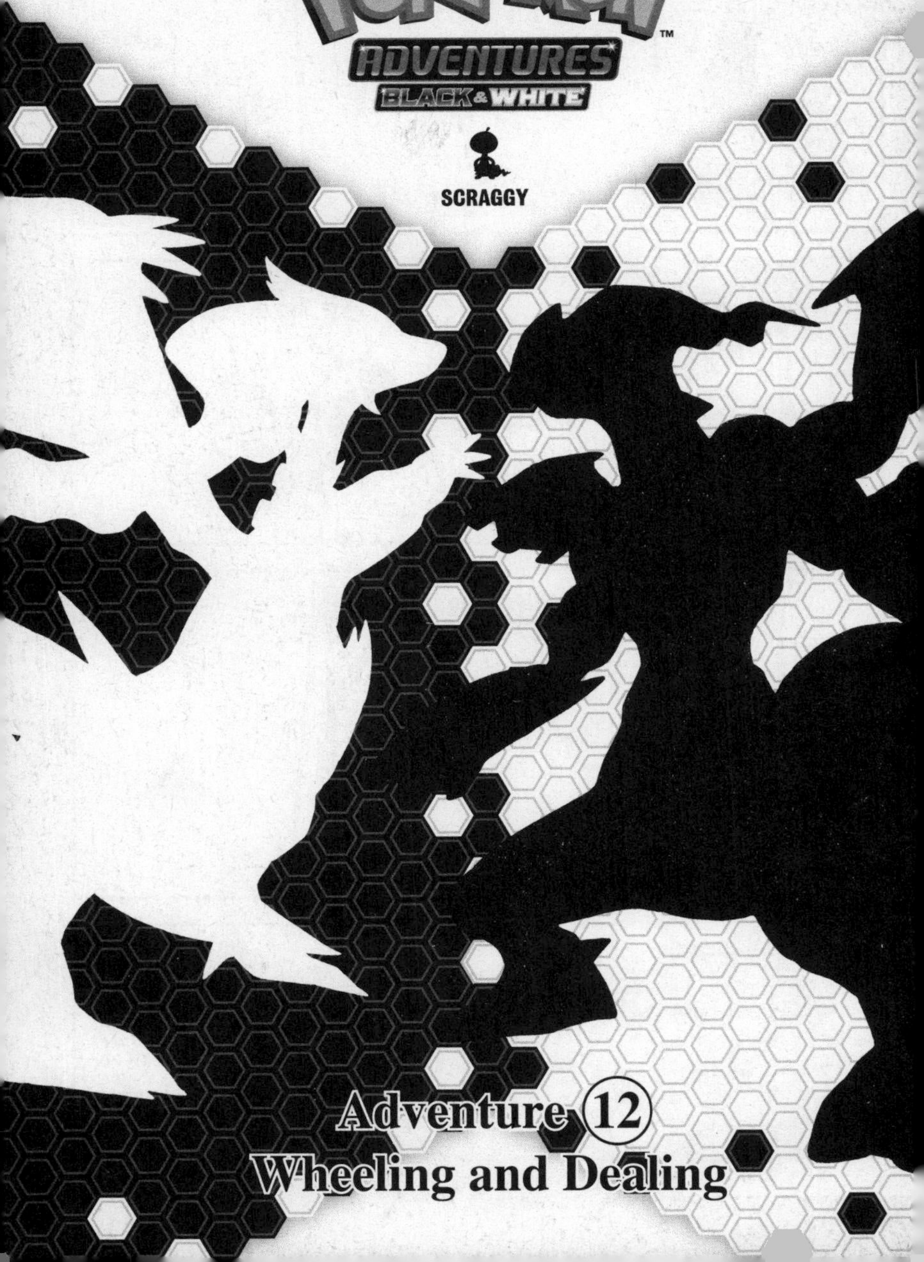

Adventure 12
Wheeling and Dealing

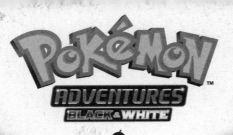

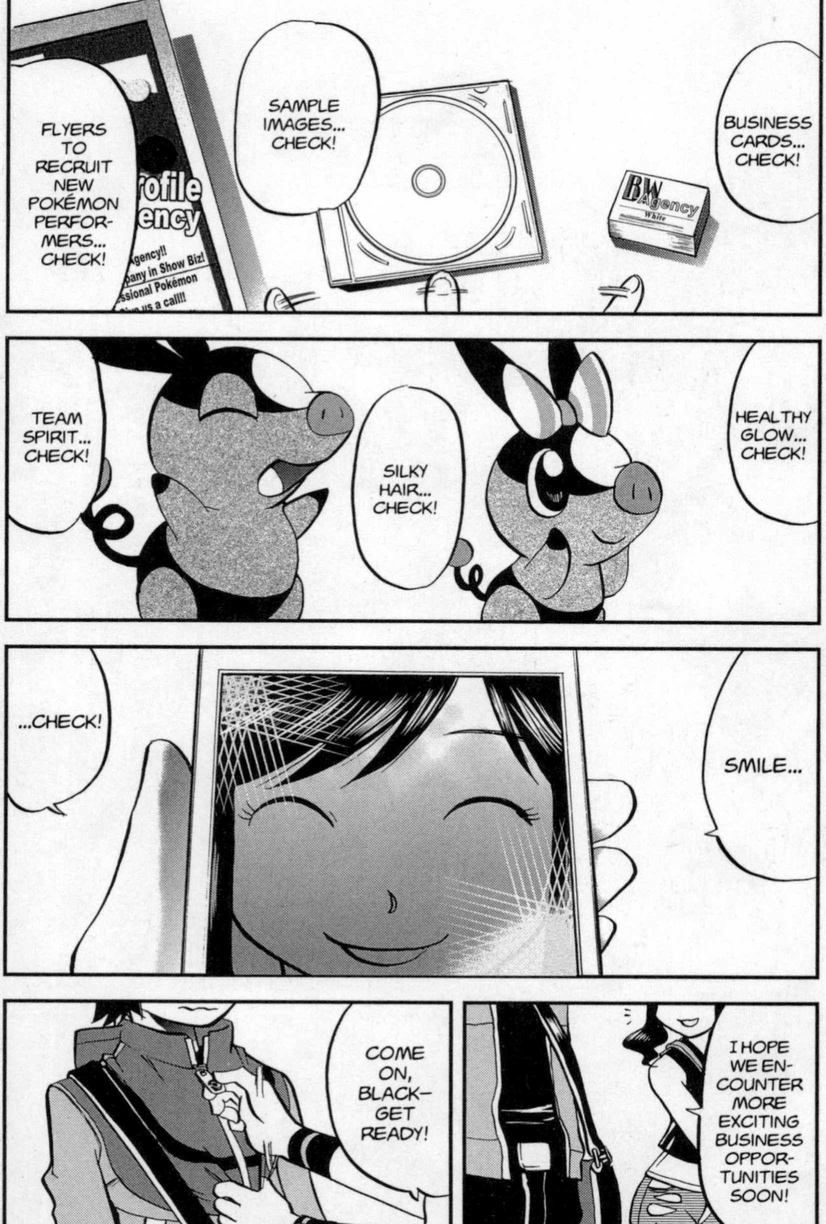
BUSINESS CARDS... CHECK!
BW Agency White
SAMPLE IMAGES... CHECK!
FLYERS TO RECRUIT NEW POKÉMON PERFORMERS... CHECK!
HEALTHY GLOW... CHECK!
SILKY HAIR... CHECK!
TEAM SPIRIT... CHECK!
SMILE...
...CHECK!
I HOPE WE ENCOUNTER MORE EXCITING BUSINESS OPPORTUNITIES SOON!
COME ON, BLACK—GET READY!

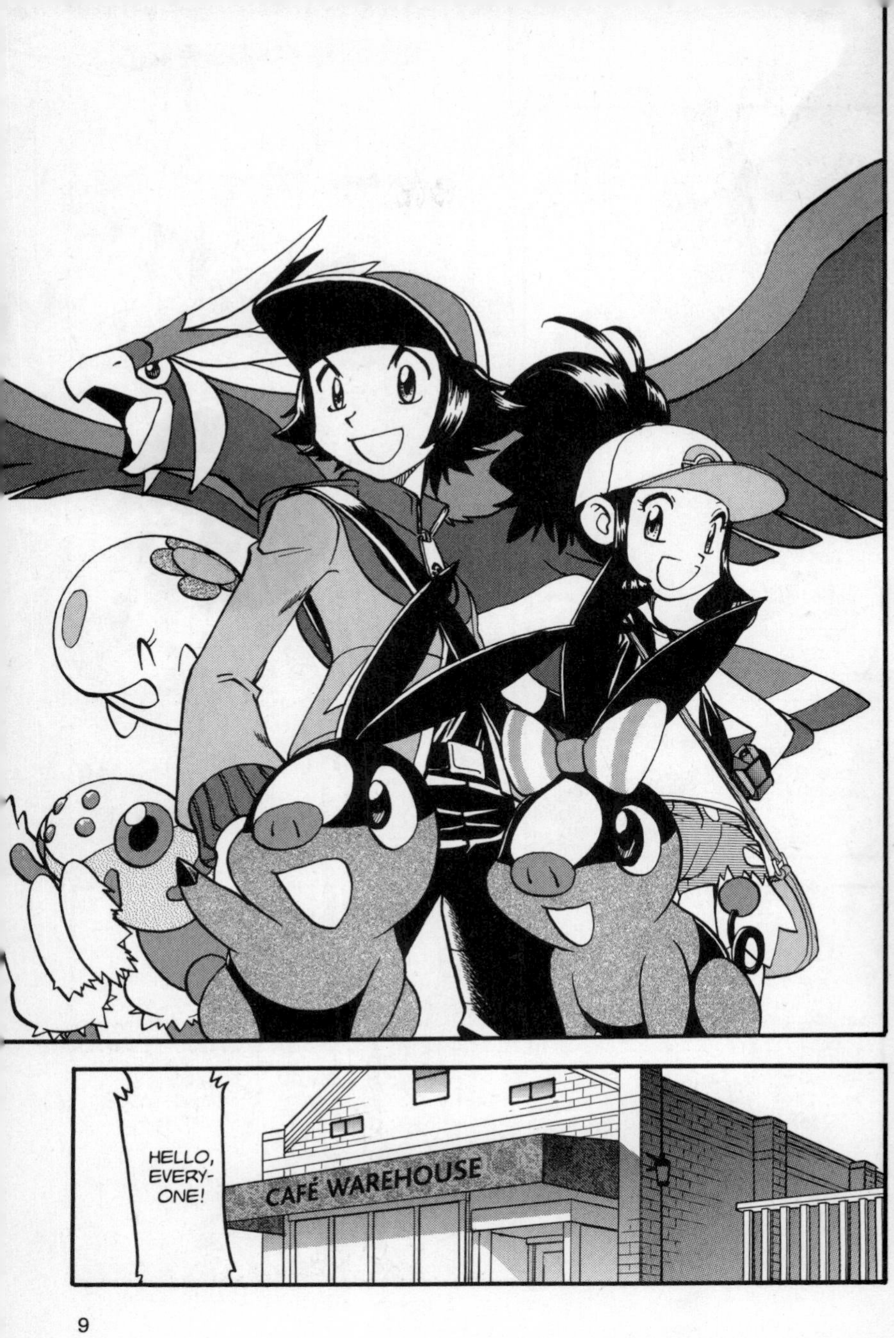
CAFÉ WAREHOUSE
HELLO, EVERY-ONE!

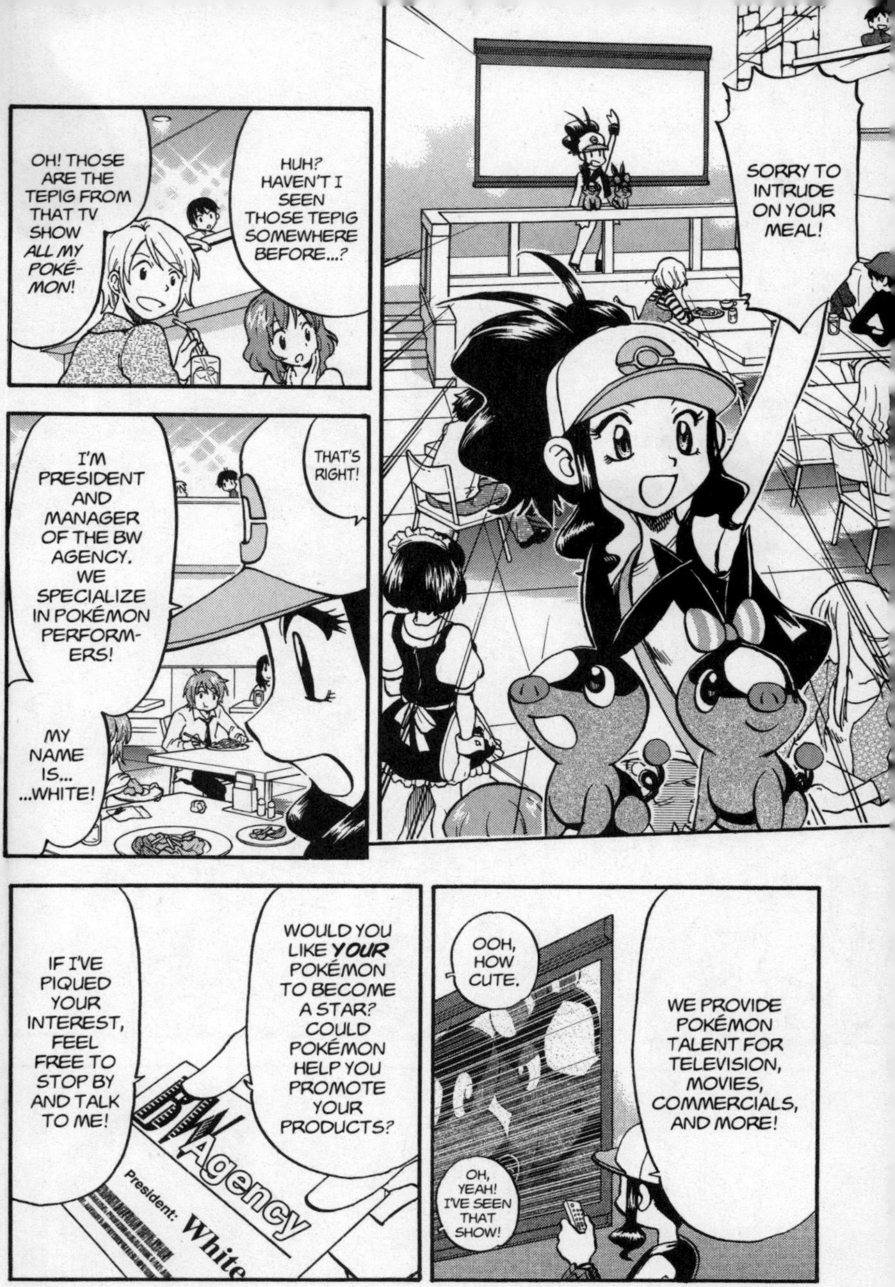
SORRY TO INTRUDE ON YOUR MEAL!
HUH? HAVEN'T I SEEN THOSE TEPIG SOMEWHERE BEFORE...?
OH! THOSE ARE THE TEPIG FROM THAT TV SHOW *ALL MY POKÉMON*!
THAT'S RIGHT!
I'M PRESIDENT AND MANAGER OF THE BW AGENCY. WE SPECIALIZE IN POKÉMON PERFORMERS!
MY NAME IS... ...WHITE!
WE PROVIDE POKÉMON TALENT FOR TELEVISION, MOVIES, COMMERCIALS, AND MORE!
OOH, HOW CUTE.
OH, YEAH! I'VE SEEN THAT SHOW!
WOULD YOU LIKE ***YOUR*** POKÉMON TO BECOME A STAR? COULD POKÉMON HELP YOU PROMOTE YOUR PRODUCTS?
IF I'VE PIQUED YOUR INTEREST, FEEL FREE TO STOP BY AND TALK TO ME!
BW Agency
President: White

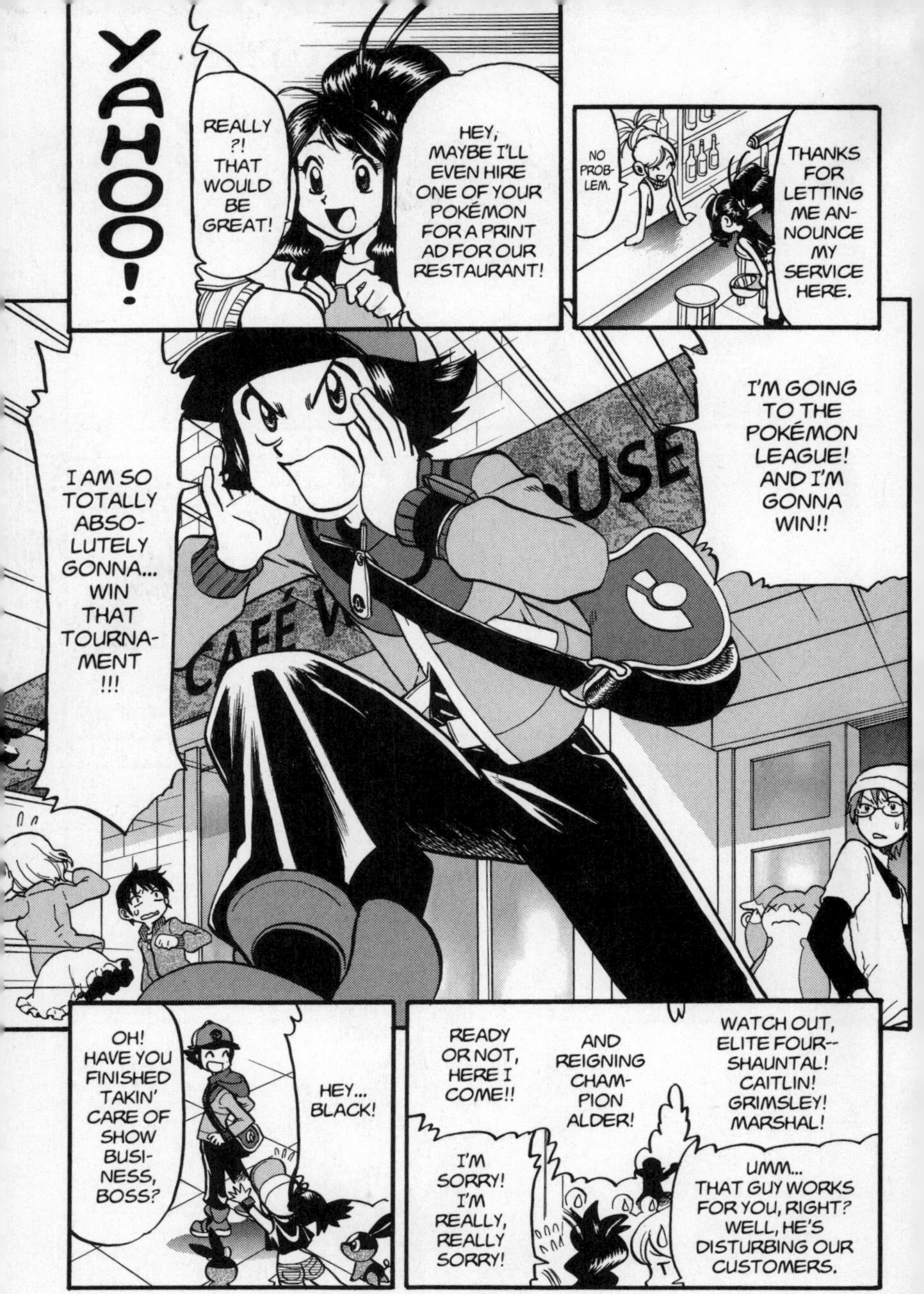
THANKS FOR LETTING ME ANNOUNCE MY SERVICE HERE.
NO PROBLEM.
HEY, MAYBE I'LL EVEN HIRE ONE OF YOUR POKÉMON FOR A PRINT AD FOR OUR RESTAURANT!
REALLY?! THAT WOULD BE GREAT!
YAHOO!
I'M GOING TO THE POKÉMON LEAGUE! AND I'M GONNA WIN!!
I AM SO TOTALLY ABSOLUTELY GONNA... WIN THAT TOURNAMENT!!!
WATCH OUT, ELITE FOUR-- SHAUNTAL! CAITLIN! GRIMSLEY! MARSHAL!
AND REIGNING CHAMPION ALDER!
READY OR NOT, HERE I COME!!
UMM... THAT GUY WORKS FOR YOU, RIGHT? WELL, HE'S DISTURBING OUR CUSTOMERS.
I'M SORRY! I'M REALLY, REALLY SORRY!
HEY... BLACK!
OH! HAVE YOU FINISHED TAKIN' CARE OF SHOW BUSINESS, BOSS?

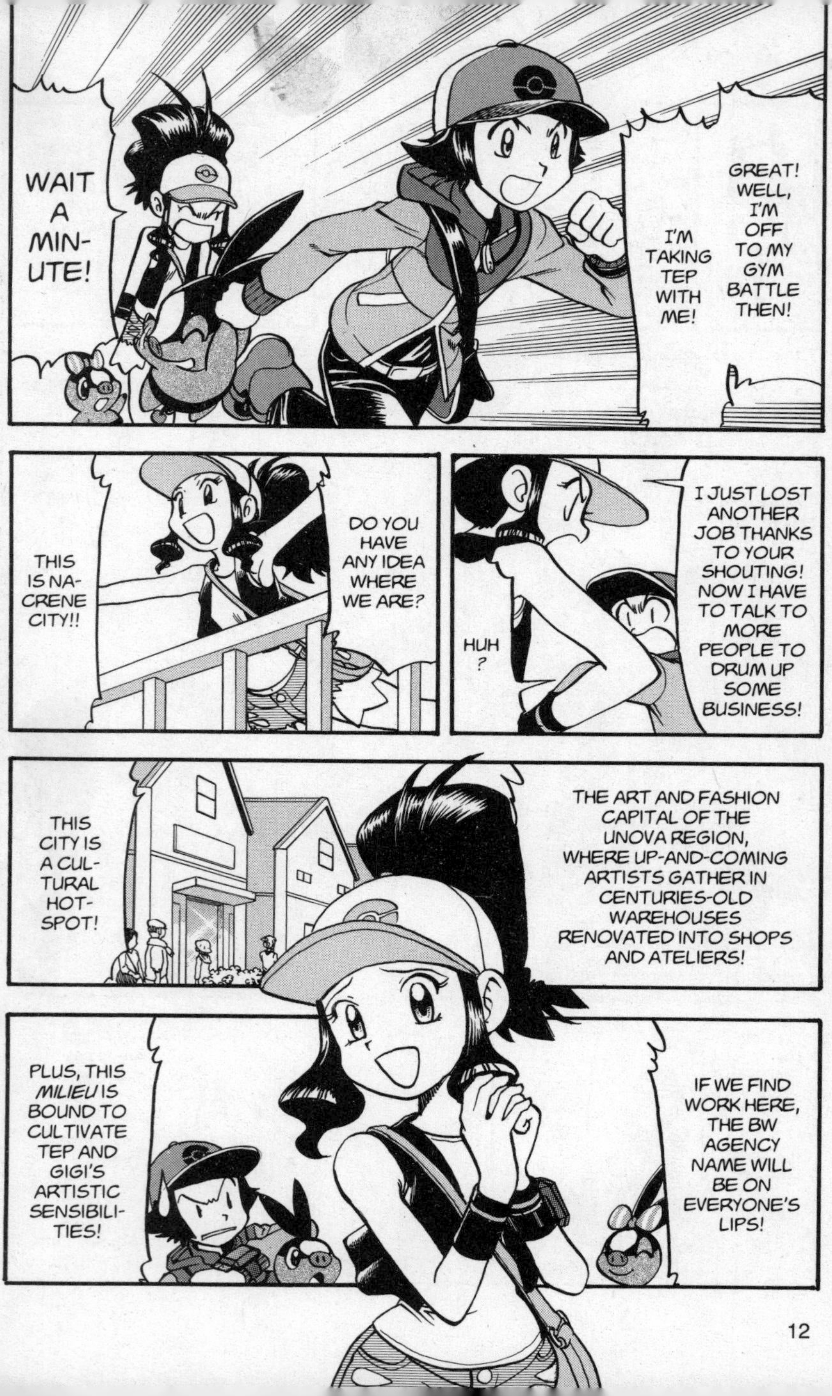
GREAT! WELL, I'M OFF TO MY GYM BATTLE THEN!
I'M TAKING TEP WITH ME!
WAIT A MIN-UTE!
I JUST LOST ANOTHER JOB THANKS TO YOUR SHOUTING! NOW I HAVE TO TALK TO MORE PEOPLE TO DRUM UP SOME BUSINESS!
HUH?
DO YOU HAVE ANY IDEA WHERE WE ARE?
THIS IS NA-CRENE CITY!!
THE ART AND FASHION CAPITAL OF THE UNOVA REGION, WHERE UP-AND-COMING ARTISTS GATHER IN CENTURIES-OLD WAREHOUSES RENOVATED INTO SHOPS AND ATELIERS!
THIS CITY IS A CUL-TURAL HOT-SPOT!
IF WE FIND WORK HERE, THE BW AGENCY NAME WILL BE ON EVERYONE'S LIPS!
PLUS, THIS *MILIEU* IS BOUND TO CULTIVATE TEP AND GIGI'S ARTISTIC SENSIBILI-TIES!

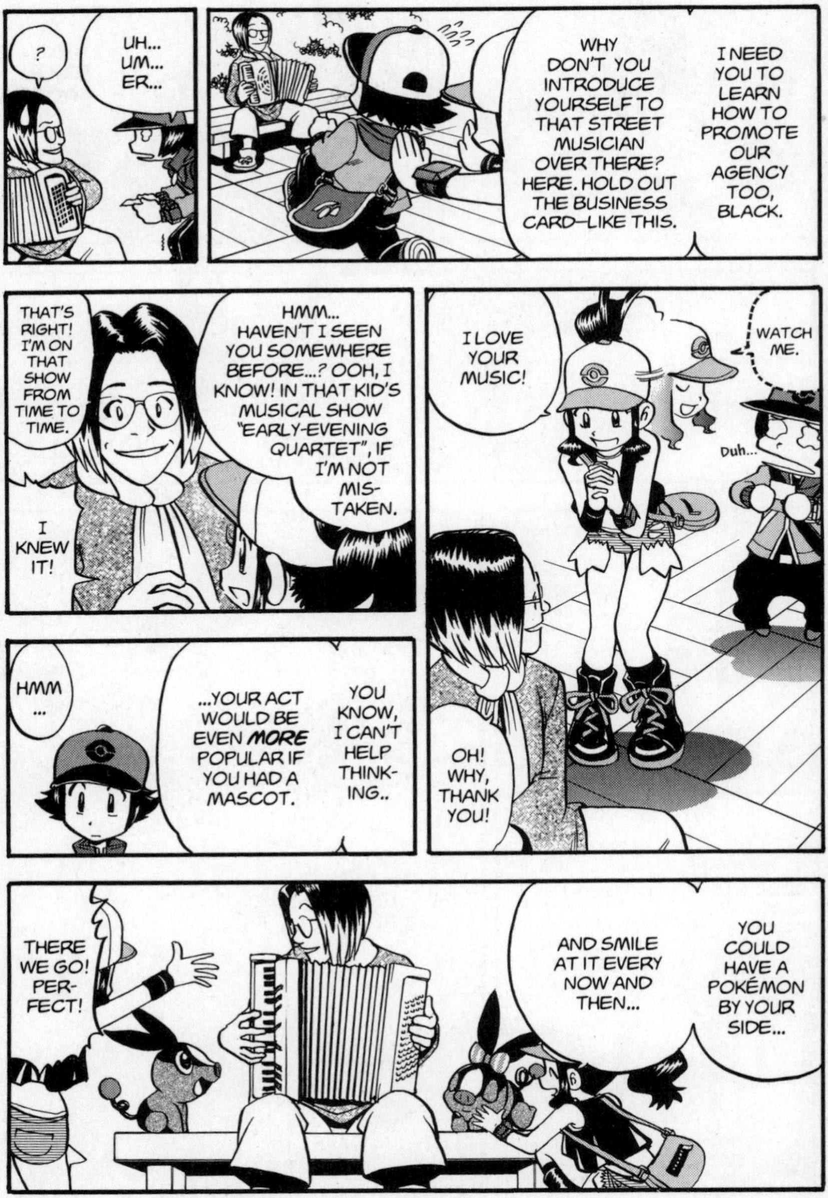
I NEED YOU TO LEARN HOW TO PROMOTE OUR AGENCY TOO, BLACK.
WHY DON'T YOU INTRODUCE YOURSELF TO THAT STREET MUSICIAN OVER THERE? HERE. HOLD OUT THE BUSINESS CARD—LIKE THIS.
UH... UM... ER...
?
WATCH ME.
I LOVE YOUR MUSIC!
Duh...
OH! WHY, THANK YOU!
HMM... HAVEN'T I SEEN YOU SOMEWHERE BEFORE...? OOH, I KNOW! IN THAT KID'S MUSICAL SHOW "EARLY-EVENING QUARTET", IF I'M NOT MIS-TAKEN.
THAT'S RIGHT! I'M ON THAT SHOW FROM TIME TO TIME.
I KNEW IT!
YOU KNOW, I CAN'T HELP THINK-ING..
...YOUR ACT WOULD BE EVEN ***MORE*** POPULAR IF YOU HAD A MASCOT.
HMM ...
YOU COULD HAVE A POKÉMON BY YOUR SIDE...
AND SMILE AT IT EVERY NOW AND THEN...
THERE WE GO! PER-FECT!

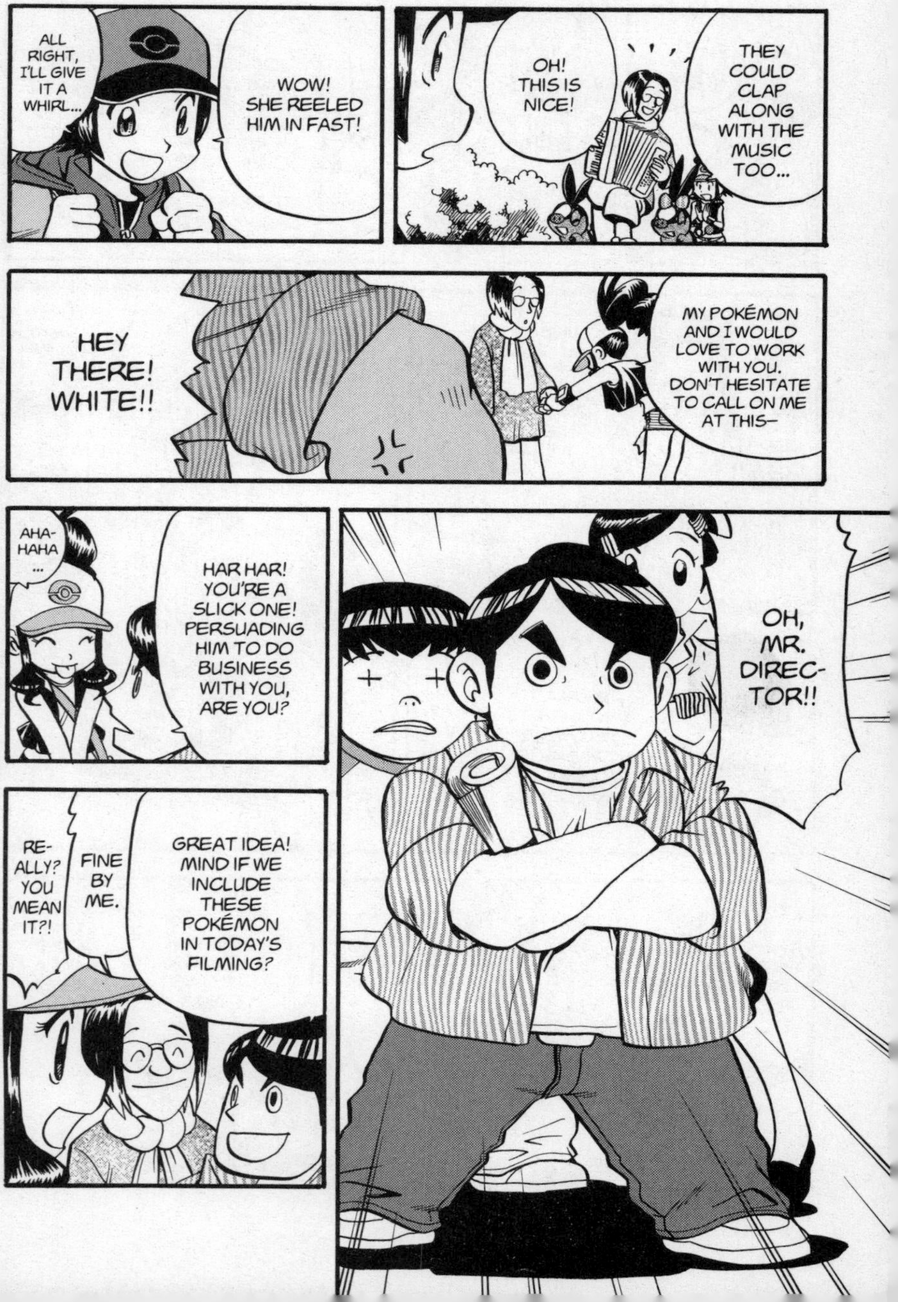
THEY COULD CLAP ALONG WITH THE MUSIC TOO...
OH! THIS IS NICE!
WOW! SHE REELED HIM IN FAST!
ALL RIGHT, I'LL GIVE IT A WHIRL...
MY POKÉMON AND I WOULD LOVE TO WORK WITH YOU. DON'T HESITATE TO CALL ON ME AT THIS—
HEY THERE! WHITE!!
OH, MR. DIRECTOR!!
HAR HAR! YOU'RE A SLICK ONE! PERSUADING HIM TO DO BUSINESS WITH YOU, ARE YOU?
AHA-HAHA...
GREAT IDEA! MIND IF WE INCLUDE THESE POKÉMON IN TODAY'S FILMING?
FINE BY ME.
RE-ALLY? YOU MEAN IT?!

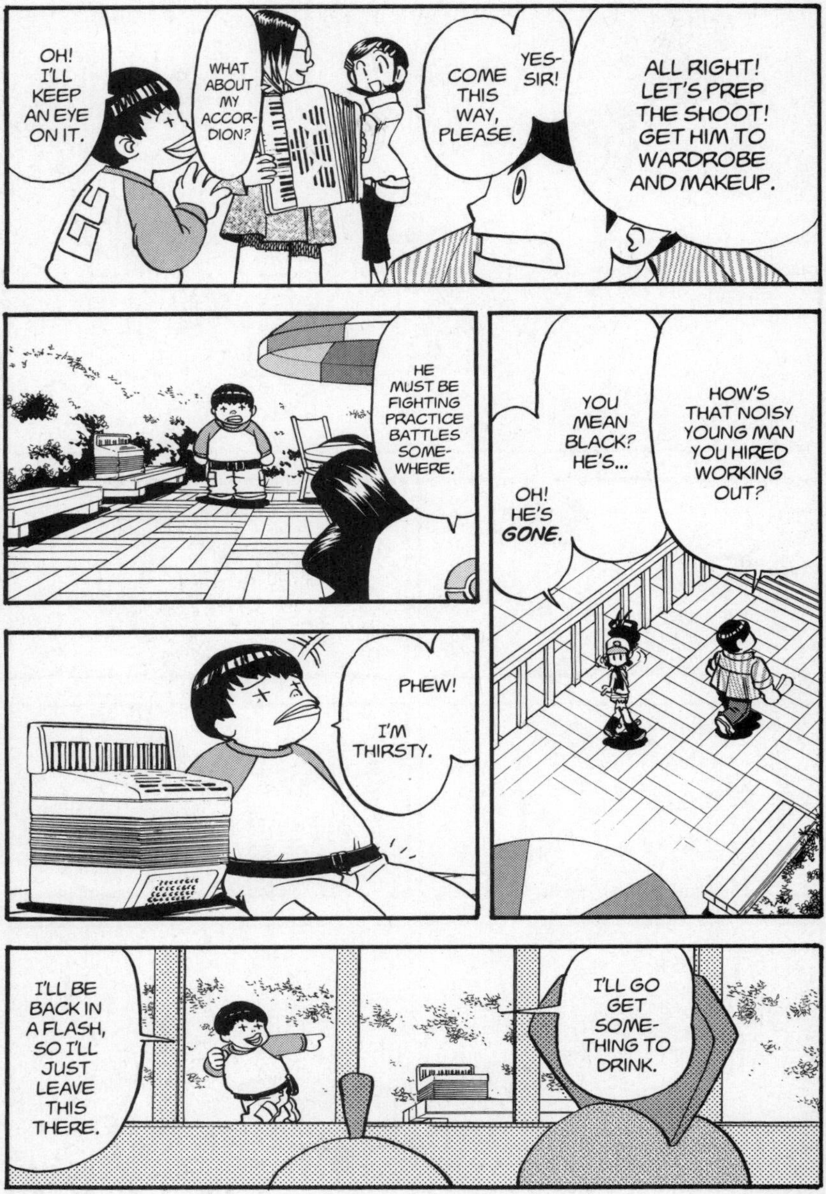
ALL RIGHT! LET'S PREP THE SHOOT! GET HIM TO WARDROBE AND MAKEUP.
YES-SIR!
COME THIS WAY, PLEASE.
WHAT ABOUT MY ACCORDION?
OH! I'LL KEEP AN EYE ON IT.
HOW'S THAT NOISY YOUNG MAN YOU HIRED WORKING OUT?
YOU MEAN BLACK? HE'S...
OH! HE'S *GONE*.
HE MUST BE FIGHTING PRACTICE BATTLES SOMEWHERE.
PHEW!
I'M THIRSTY.
I'LL GO GET SOMETHING TO DRINK.
I'LL BE BACK IN A FLASH, SO I'LL JUST LEAVE THIS THERE.

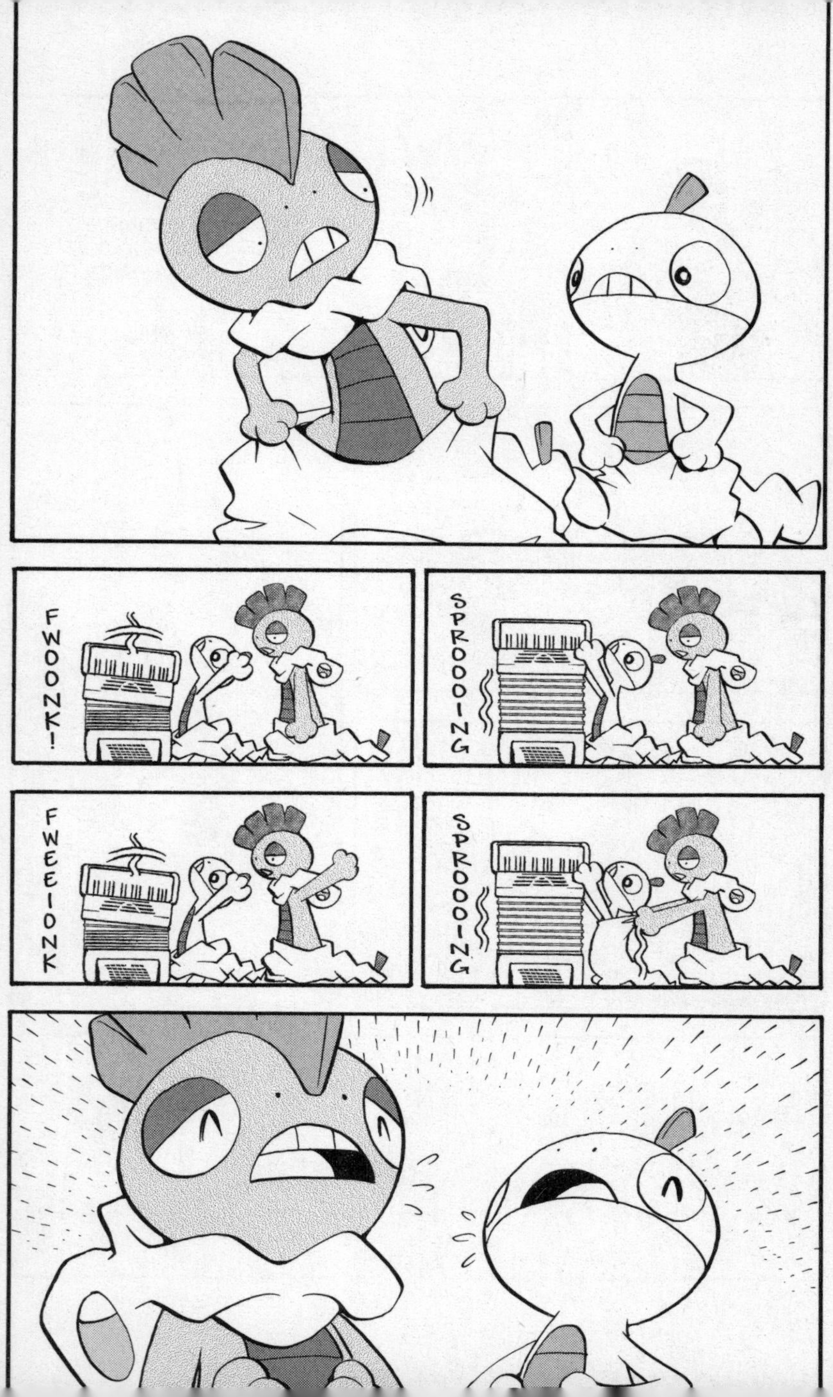
SPROOOING
FWOONK!
SPROOOING
FWEEIONK

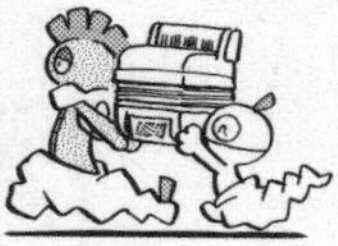

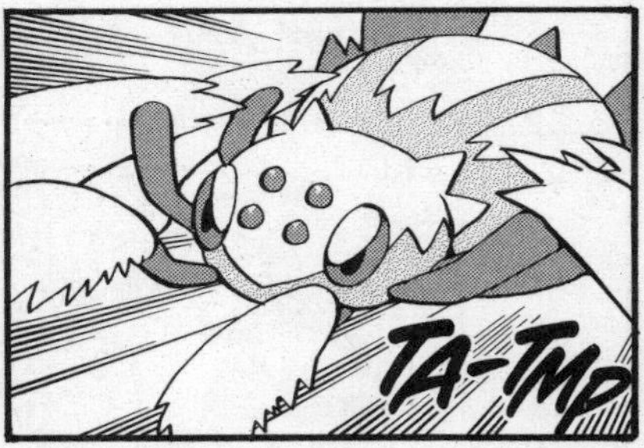
TA-TMP

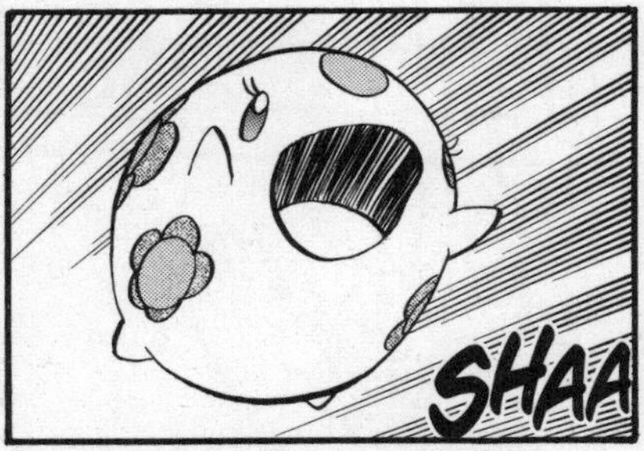
SHAA

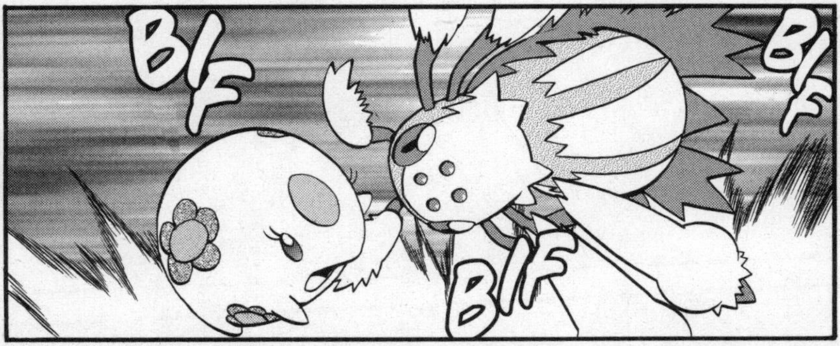
BIF
BIF
BIF

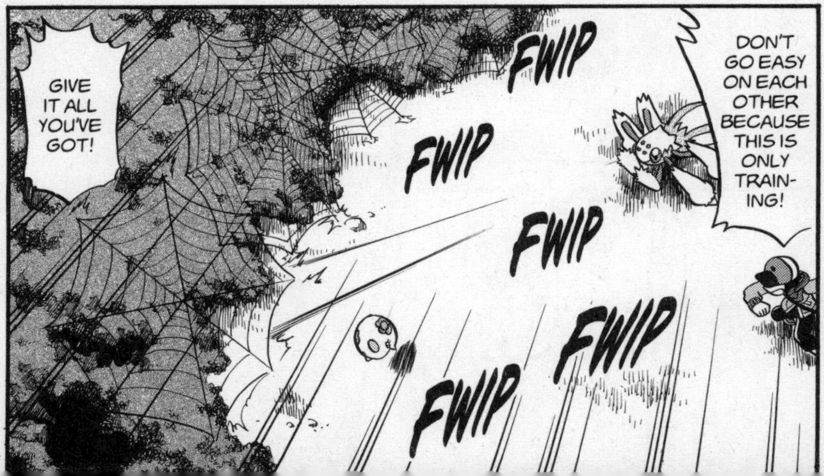
DON'T GO EASY ON EACH OTHER BECAUSE THIS IS ONLY TRAIN-ING!
FWIP
FWIP
FWIP
FWIP
FWIP
GIVE IT ALL YOU'VE GOT!

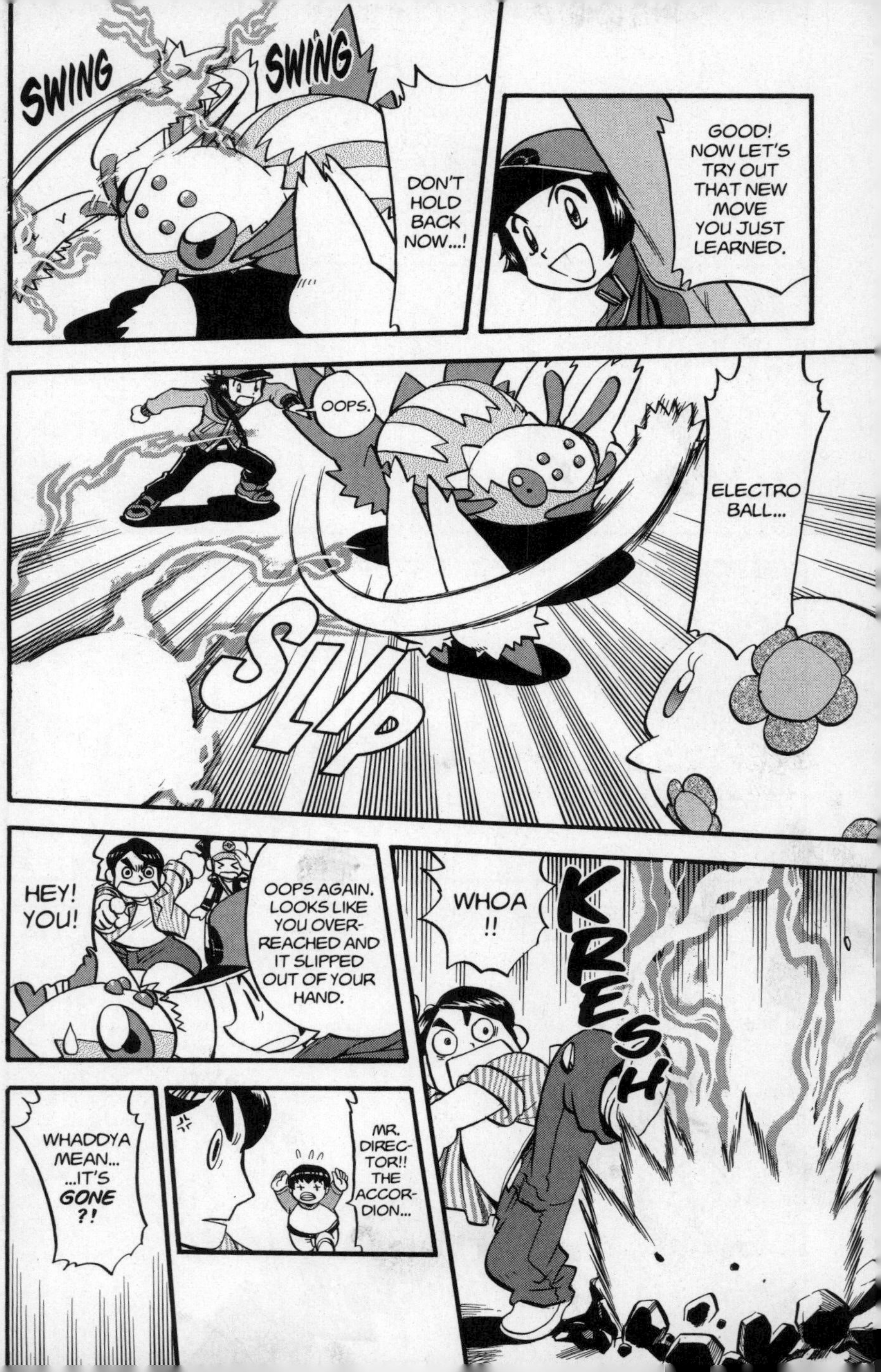
GOOD! NOW LET'S TRY OUT THAT NEW MOVE YOU JUST LEARNED.
DON'T HOLD BACK NOW...!
SWING
SWING
ELECTRO BALL...
SLIP
OOPS.
WHOA!!
KRESH
OOPS AGAIN. LOOKS LIKE YOU OVER-REACHED AND IT SLIPPED OUT OF YOUR HAND.
HEY! YOU!
MR. DIRECTOR!! THE ACCORDION...
WHADDYA MEAN... ...IT'S *GONE*?!

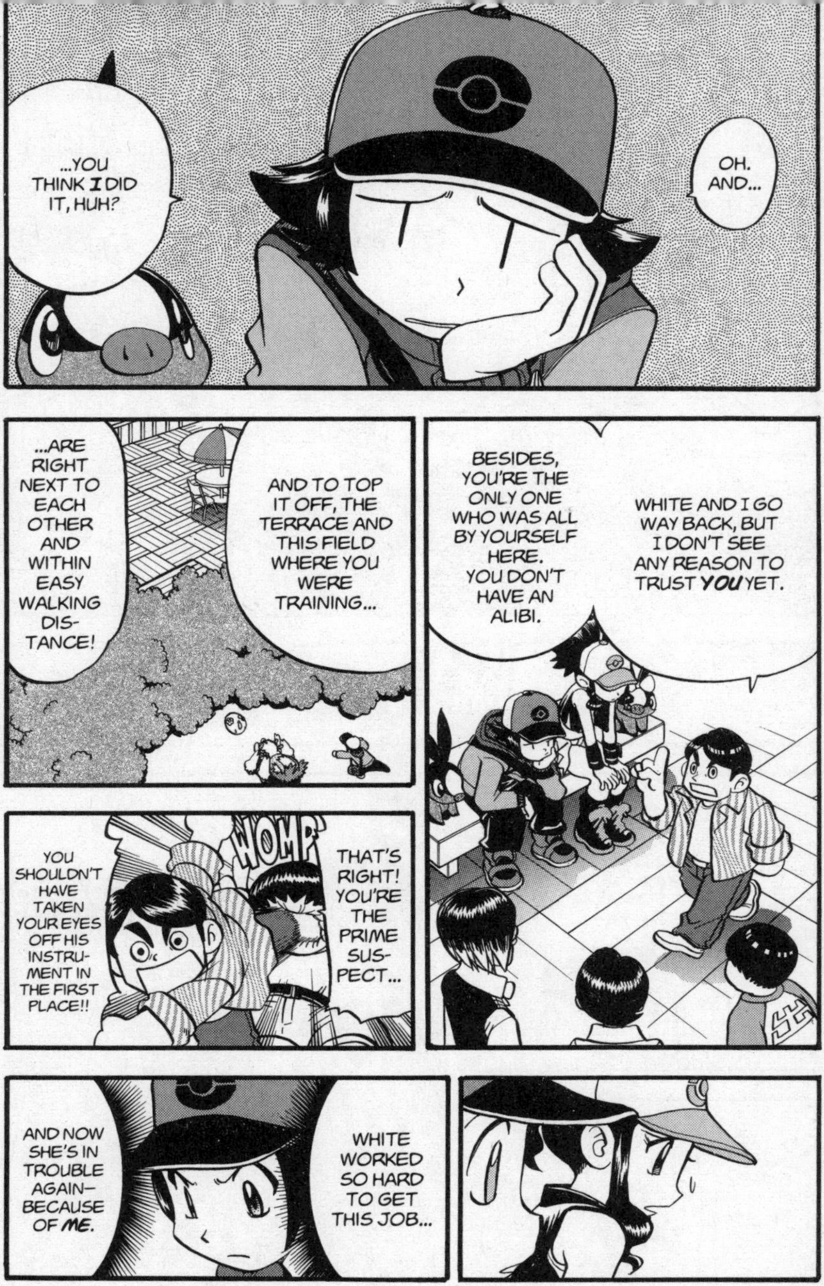
OH. AND...
...YOU THINK I DID IT, HUH?
WHITE AND I GO WAY BACK, BUT I DON'T SEE ANY REASON TO TRUST YOU YET.
BESIDES, YOU'RE THE ONLY ONE WHO WAS ALL BY YOURSELF HERE. YOU DON'T HAVE AN ALIBI.
AND TO TOP IT OFF, THE TERRACE AND THIS FIELD WHERE YOU WERE TRAINING...
...ARE RIGHT NEXT TO EACH OTHER AND WITHIN EASY WALKING DIS-TANCE!
THAT'S RIGHT! YOU'RE THE PRIME SUS-PECT...
WOMP
YOU SHOULDN'T HAVE TAKEN YOUR EYES OFF HIS INSTRU-MENT IN THE FIRST PLACE!!
WHITE WORKED SO HARD TO GET THIS JOB...
AND NOW SHE'S IN TROUBLE AGAIN—BECAUSE OF ME.

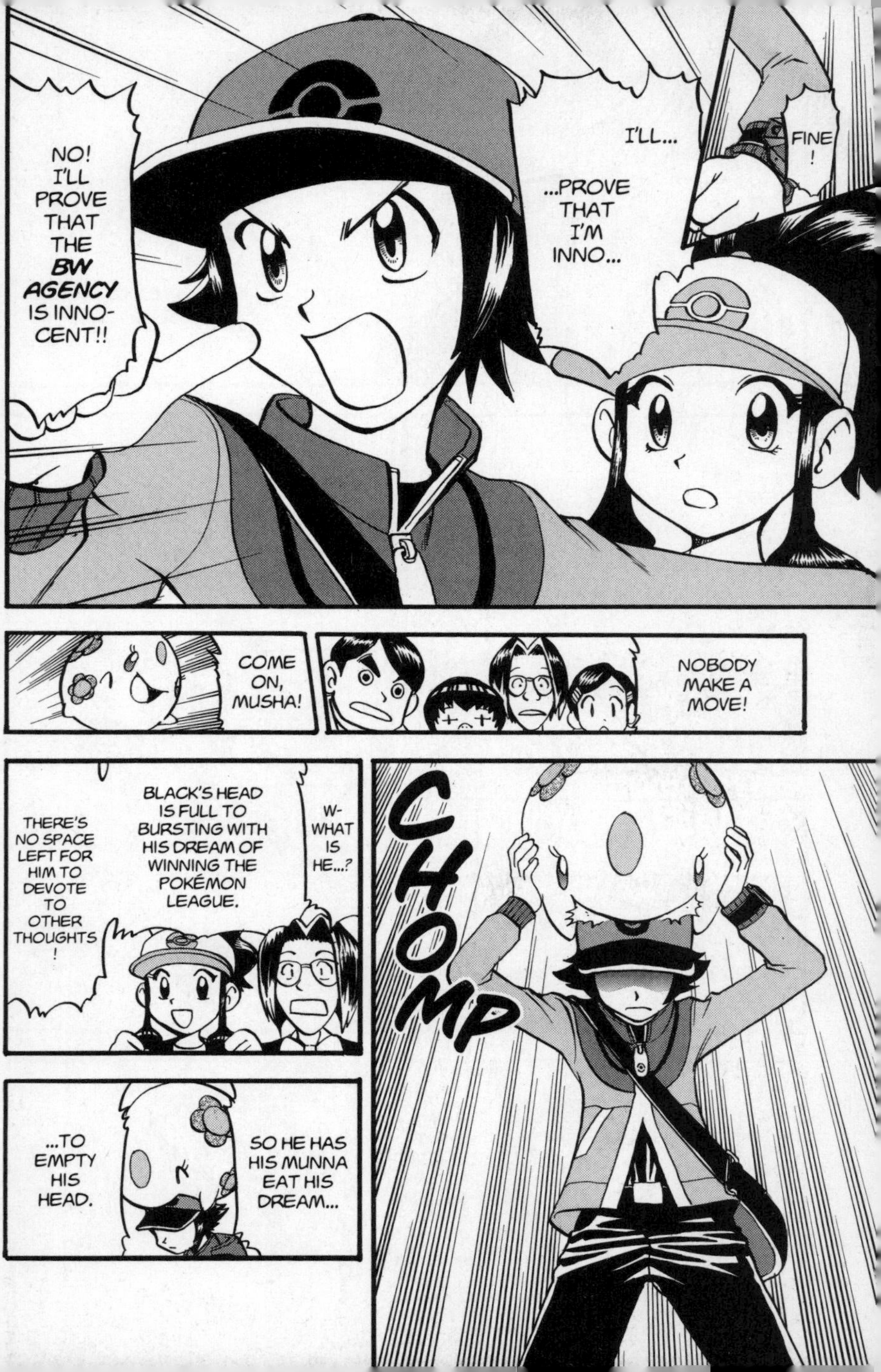
FINE!
I'LL...
...PROVE THAT I'M INNO...
NO! I'LL PROVE THAT THE ***BW AGENCY*** IS INNOCENT!!
NOBODY MAKE A MOVE!
COME ON, MUSHA!
CHOMP
W-WHAT IS HE...?
BLACK'S HEAD IS FULL TO BURSTING WITH HIS DREAM OF WINNING THE POKÉMON LEAGUE.
THERE'S NO SPACE LEFT FOR HIM TO DEVOTE TO OTHER THOUGHTS!
SO HE HAS HIS MUNNA EAT HIS DREAM...
...TO EMPTY HIS HEAD.

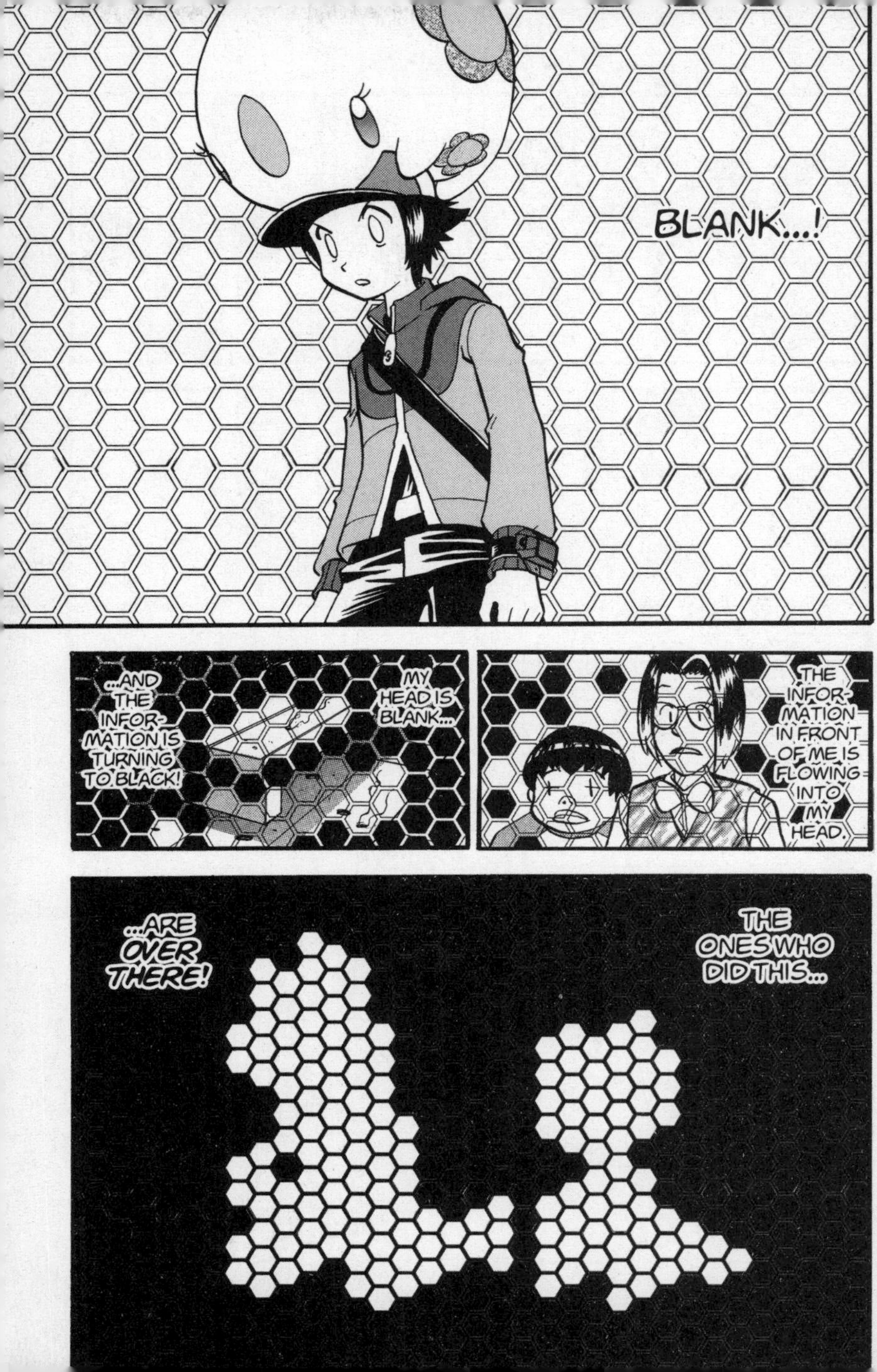
BLANK...!
THE INFORMATION IN FRONT OF ME IS FLOWING INTO MY HEAD.
MY HEAD IS BLANK...
...AND THE INFORMATION IS TURNING TO BLACK!
THE ONES WHO DID THIS...
...ARE OVER THERE!

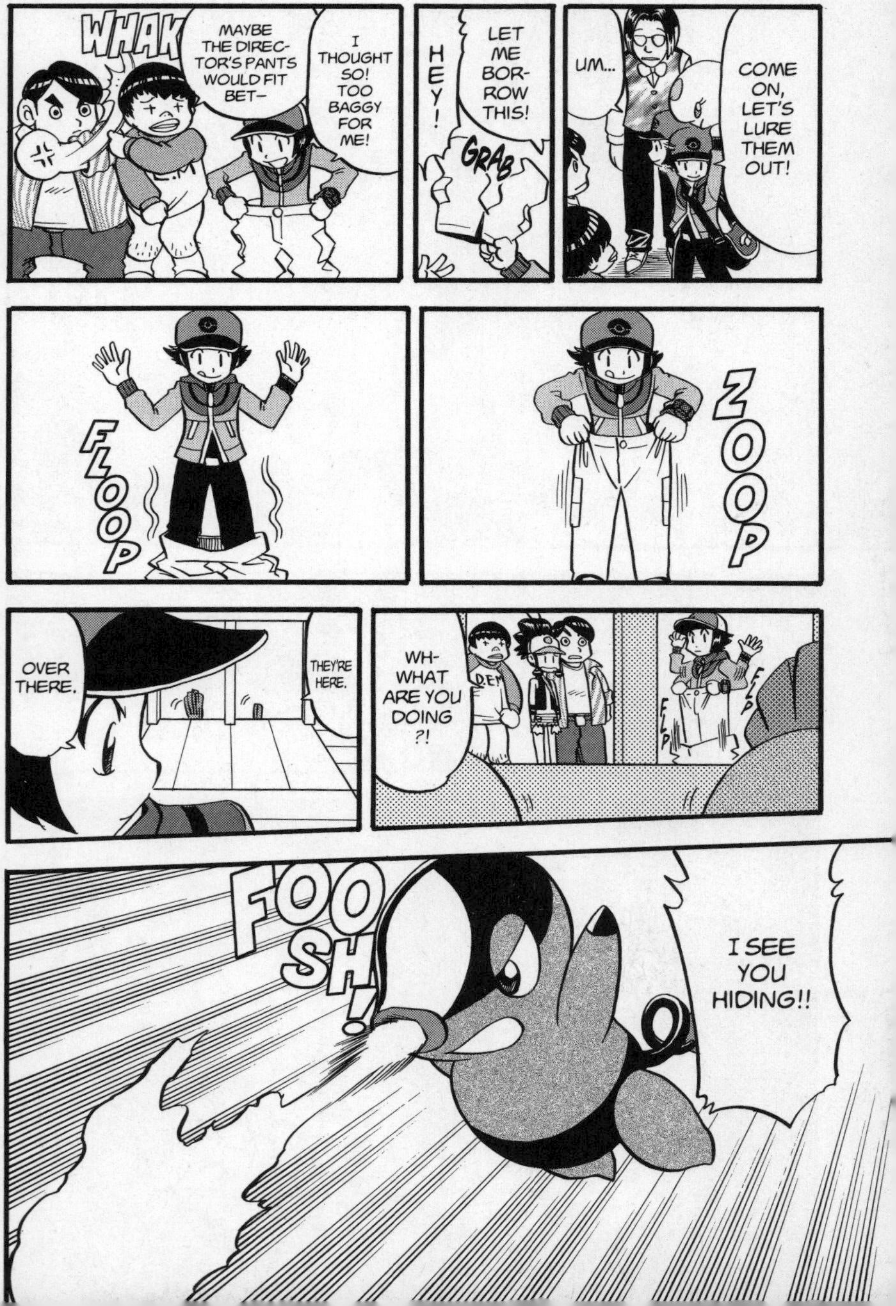
COME ON, LET'S LURE THEM OUT!
UM...
LET ME BORROW THIS!
HEY!
GRAB
I THOUGHT SO! TOO BAGGY FOR ME!
MAYBE THE DIRECTOR'S PANTS WOULD FIT BET–
WHAK
ZOOP
FLOOP
FLP
FLP
WH- WHAT ARE YOU DOING ?!
THEY'RE HERE.
OVER THERE.
I SEE YOU HIDING!!
FOOSH!

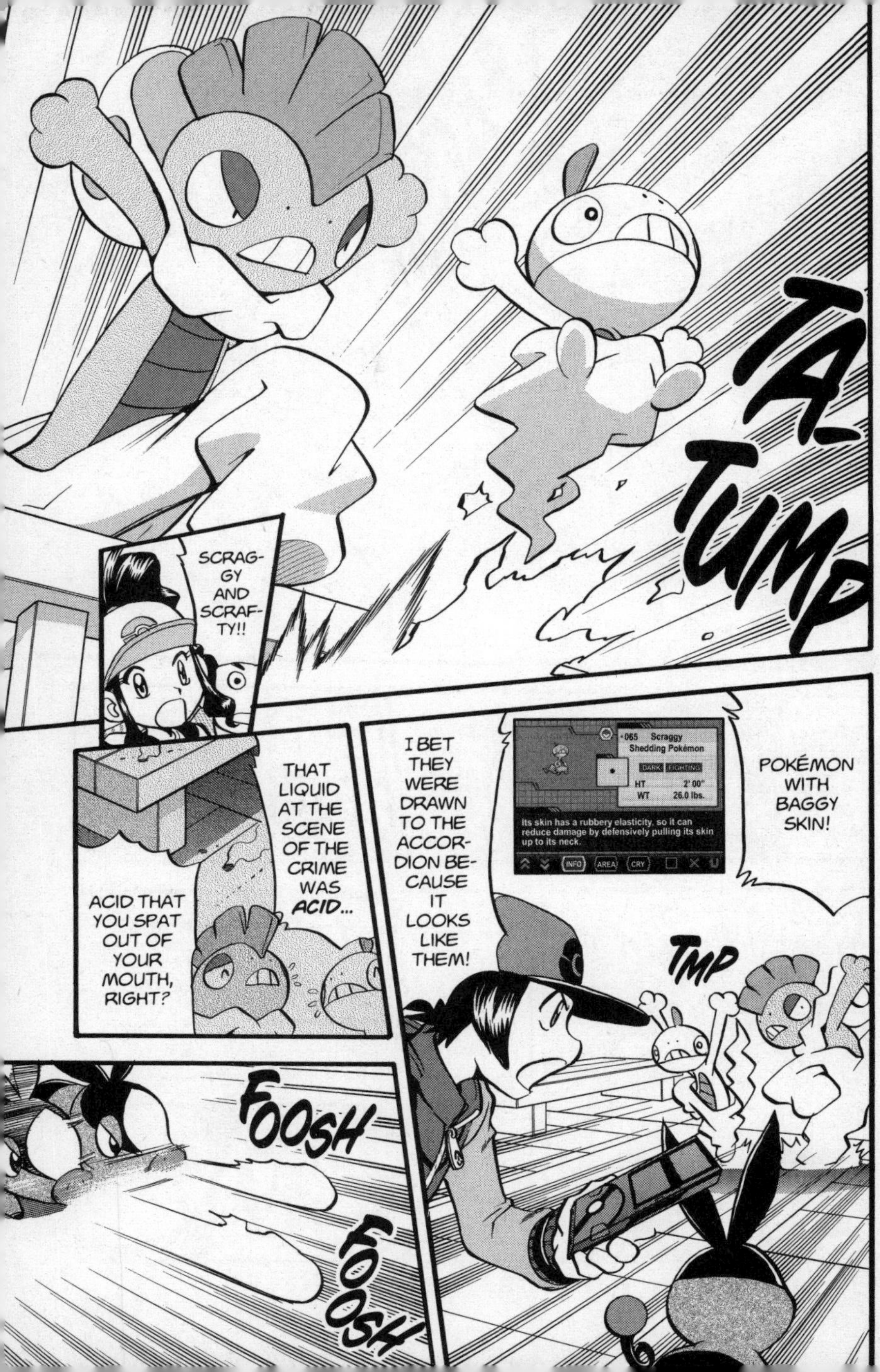
TA-TUMP
SCRAGGY AND SCRAFTY!!
POKÉMON WITH BAGGY SKIN!
065 Scraggy
Shedding Pokémon
DARK FIGHTING
HT 2' 00"
WT 26.0 lbs.
Its skin has a rubbery elasticity, so it can reduce damage by defensively pulling its skin up to its neck.
INFO AREA CRY
I BET THEY WERE DRAWN TO THE ACCORDION BECAUSE IT LOOKS LIKE THEM!
TMP
THAT LIQUID AT THE SCENE OF THE CRIME WAS *ACID*...
ACID THAT YOU SPAT OUT OF YOUR MOUTH, RIGHT?
FOOSH
FOOSH

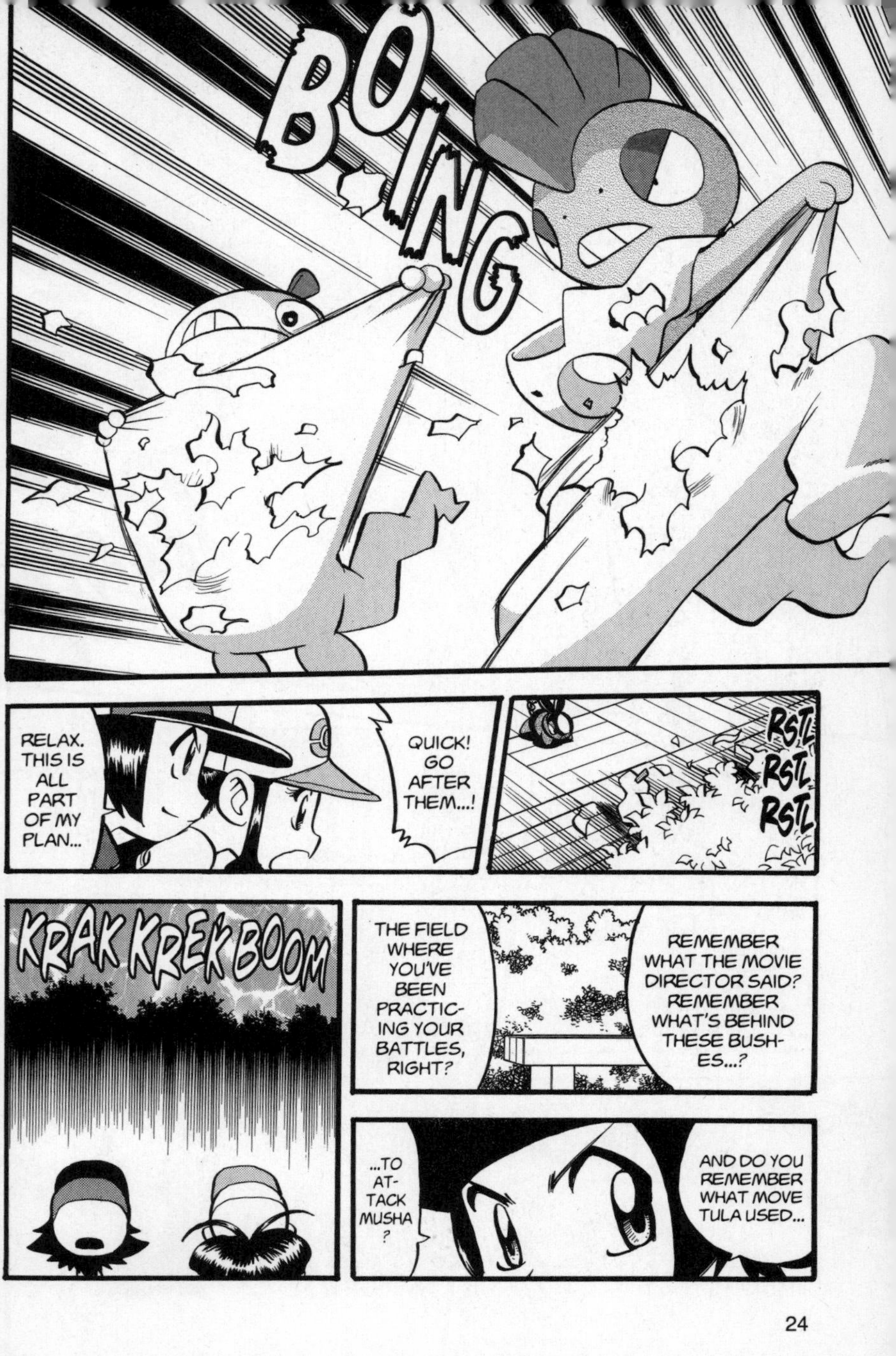
BOING
RSTL RSTL RSTL
QUICK! GO AFTER THEM...!
RELAX. THIS IS ALL PART OF MY PLAN...
REMEMBER WHAT THE MOVIE DIRECTOR SAID? REMEMBER WHAT'S BEHIND THESE BUSH-ES...?
THE FIELD WHERE YOU'VE BEEN PRACTIC-ING YOUR BATTLES, RIGHT?
AND DO YOU REMEMBER WHAT MOVE TULA USED...
...TO AT-TACK MUSHA?
KRAK KREK BOOM

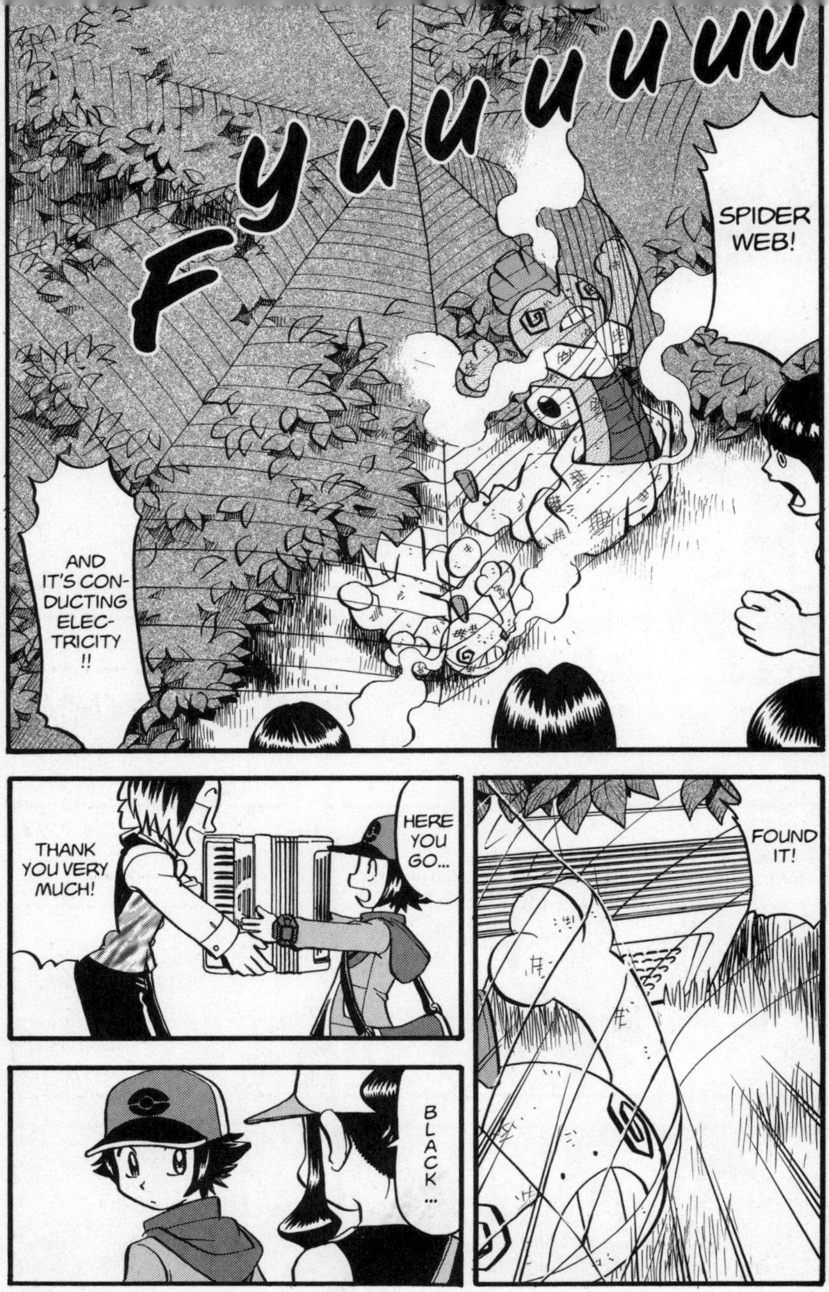
Fyuuuuuuu
SPIDER WEB!
AND IT'S CONDUCTING ELECTRICITY!!
FOUND IT!
HERE YOU GO...
THANK YOU VERY MUCH!
BLACK...

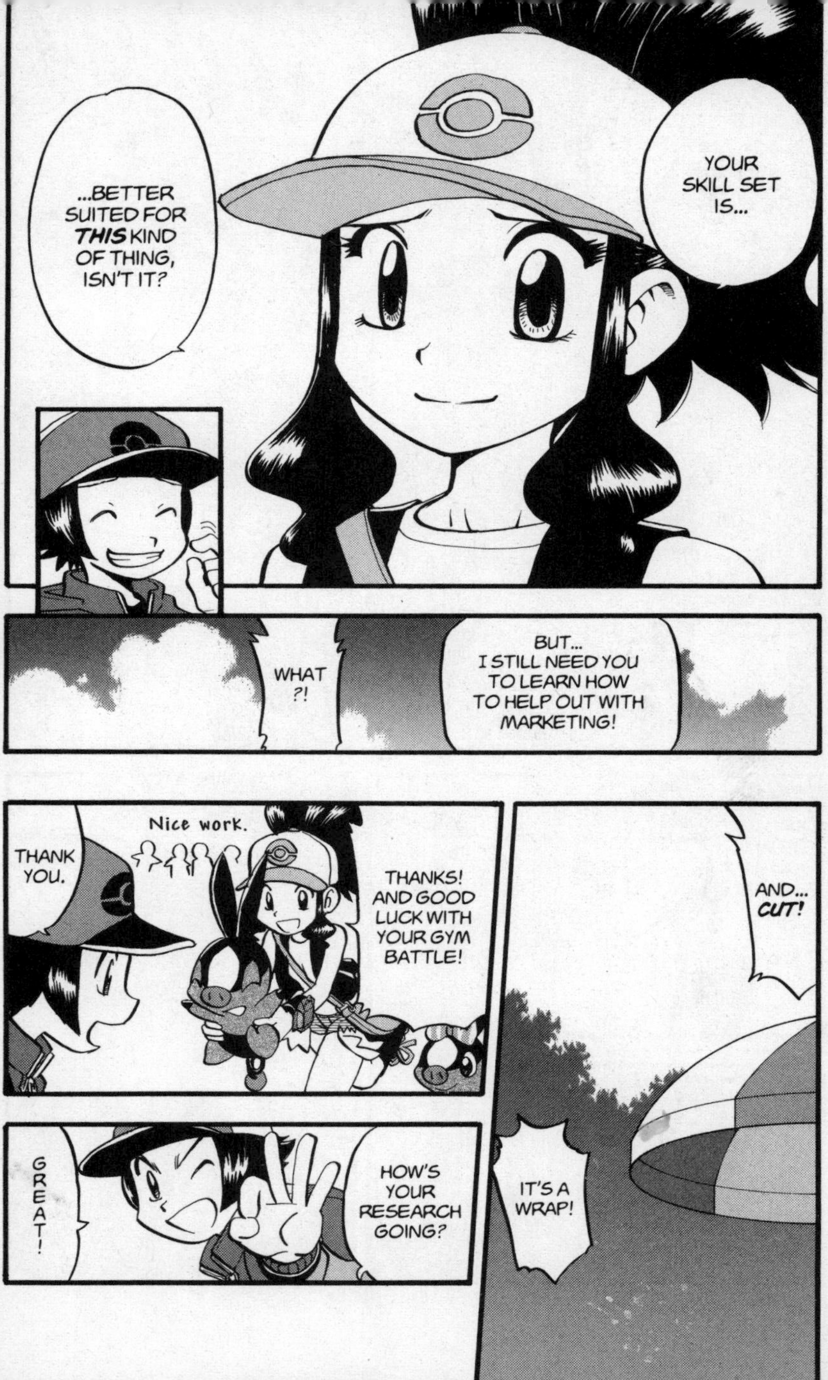
YOUR SKILL SET IS...
...BETTER SUITED FOR THIS KIND OF THING, ISN'T IT?
BUT... I STILL NEED YOU TO LEARN HOW TO HELP OUT WITH MARKETING!
WHAT?!
AND... CUT!
IT'S A WRAP!
Nice work.
THANKS! AND GOOD LUCK WITH YOUR GYM BATTLE!
THANK YOU.
HOW'S YOUR RESEARCH GOING?
GREAT!

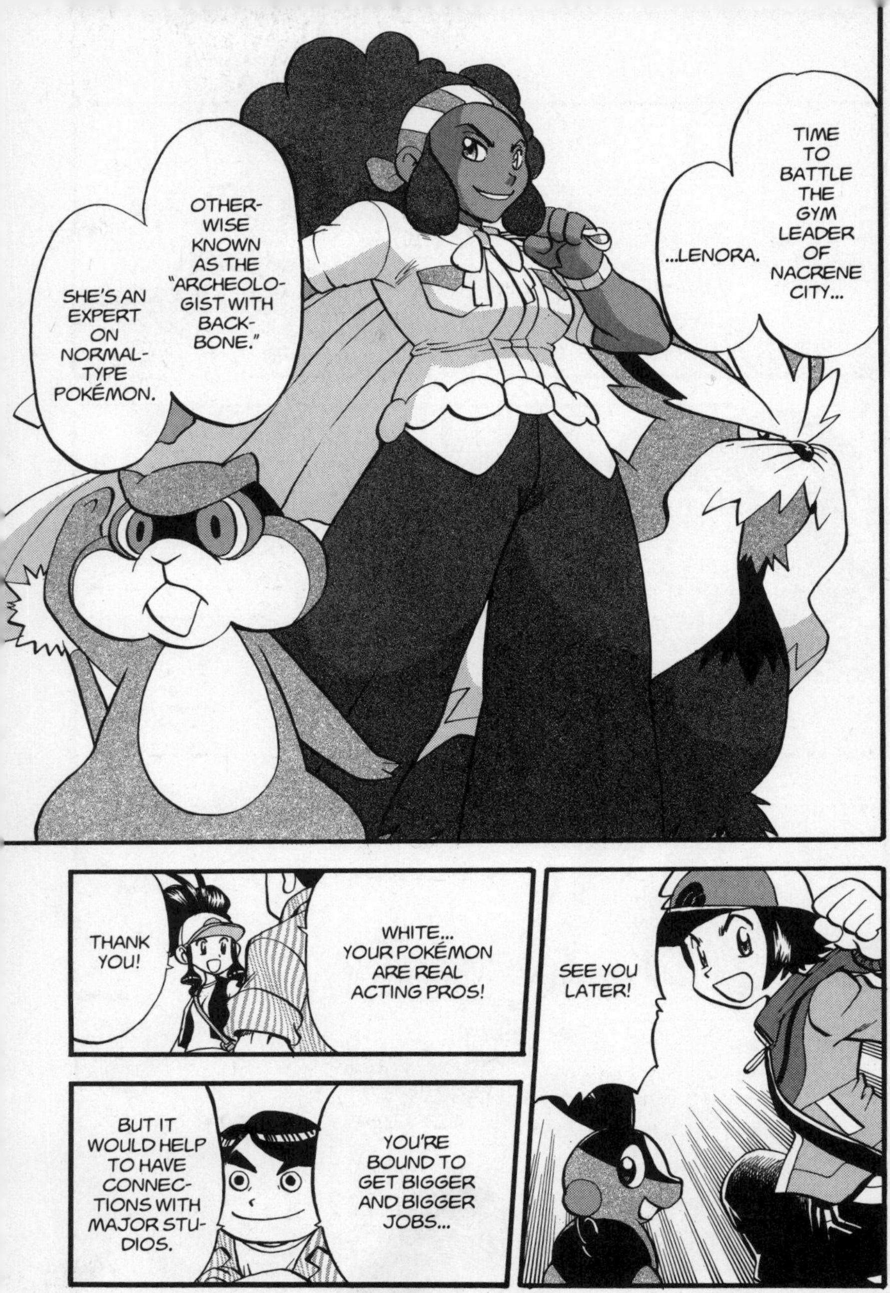

TIME TO BATTLE THE GYM LEADER OF NACRENE CITY...
...LENORA.
OTHER-WISE KNOWN AS THE "ARCHEOLO-GIST WITH BACK-BONE."
SHE'S AN EXPERT ON NORMAL-TYPE POKÉMON.
SEE YOU LATER!
WHITE... YOUR POKÉMON ARE REAL ACTING PROS!
THANK YOU!
YOU'RE BOUND TO GET BIGGER AND BIGGER JOBS...
BUT IT WOULD HELP TO HAVE CONNEC-TIONS WITH MAJOR STU-DIOS.

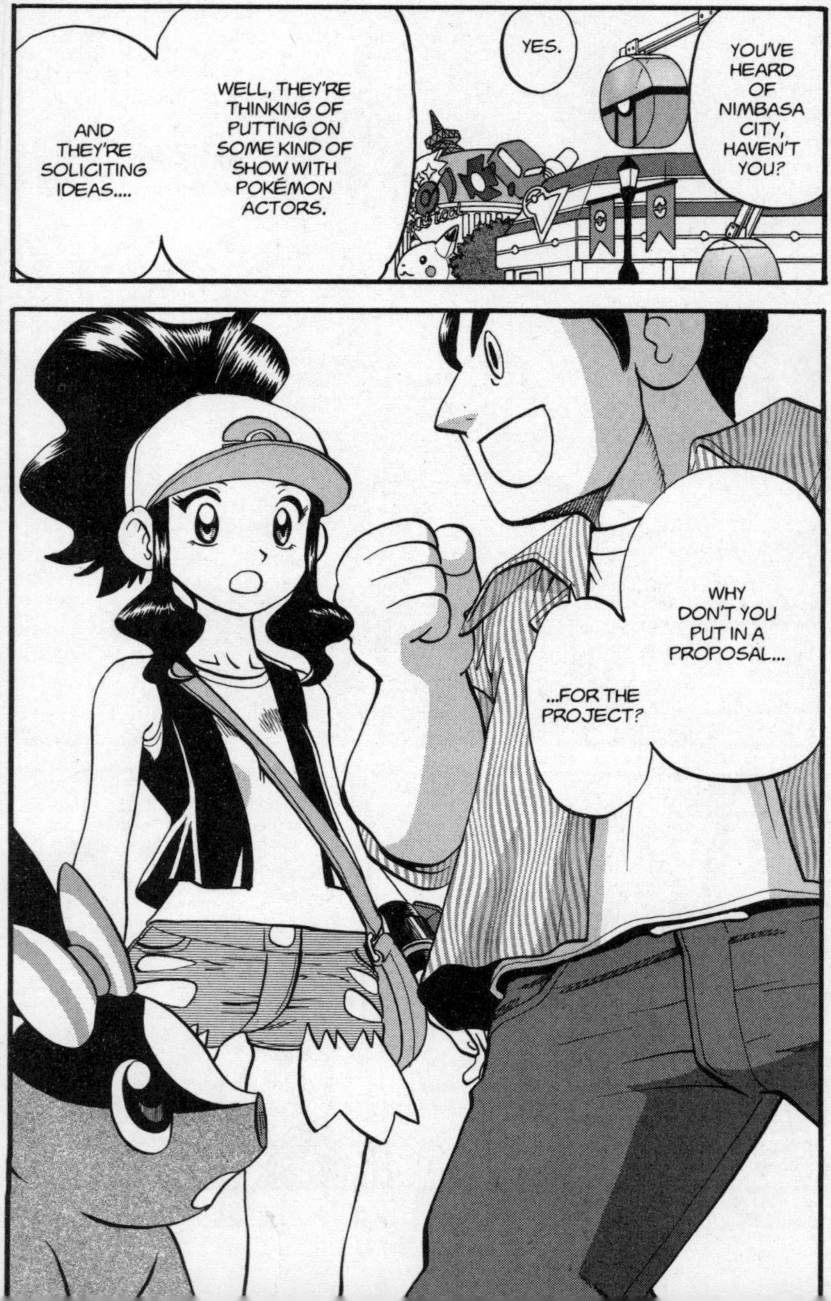
YOU'VE HEARD OF NIMBASA CITY, HAVEN'T YOU?
YES.
WELL, THEY'RE THINKING OF PUTTING ON SOME KIND OF SHOW WITH POKÉMON ACTORS.
AND THEY'RE SOLICITING IDEAS....
WHY DON'T YOU PUT IN A PROPOSAL...
...FOR THE PROJECT?

ADVENTURE MAP

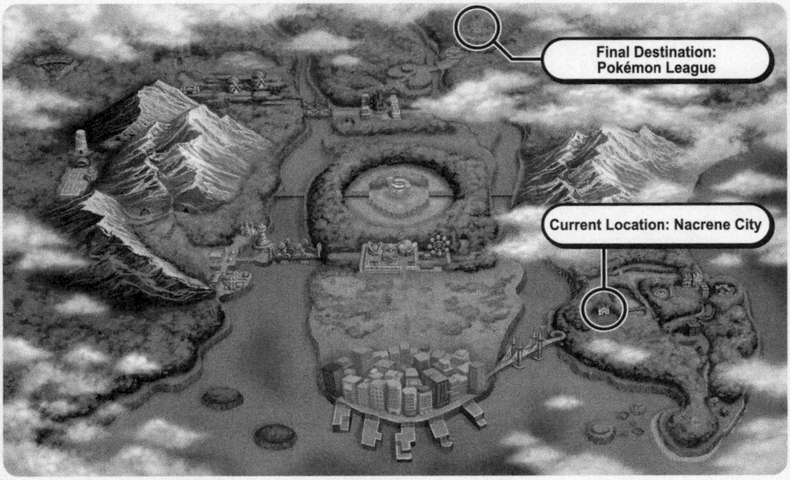

Final Destination:
Pokémon League
Current Location: Nacrene City

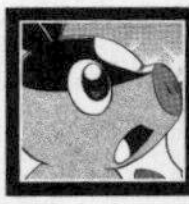

Fire Pig Pokémon **Tep**
Tepig ♂ | Fire
Lv.15 Ability: Blaze

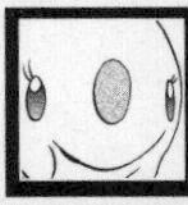

Dream Eater Pokémon **Musha**
Munna ♂ | Psychic
Lv.37 Ability: Forewarn

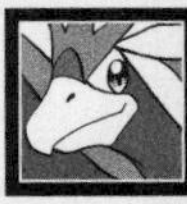

Valiant Pokémon **Brav**
Braviary ♂ | Normal | Flying
Lv.54 Ability: Sheer Force

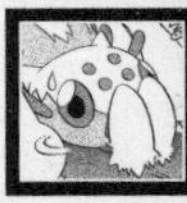

EleSpider Pokémon **Tula**
Galvantula ♂ | Bug | Electric
Lv.38 Ability: Unnerve

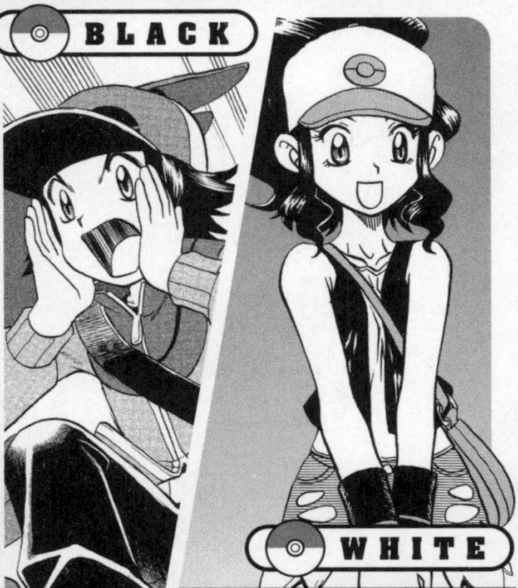

BLACK
WHITE

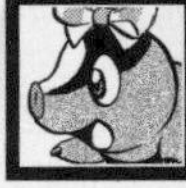

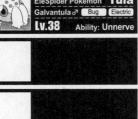

Fire Pig Pokémon **Gigi**
Tepig ♀ | Fire
Lv.05 Ability: Blaze

TRIO BADGE ? ? ? ? ? ? ?

Pokémon™ Adventures Black & White

PATRAT

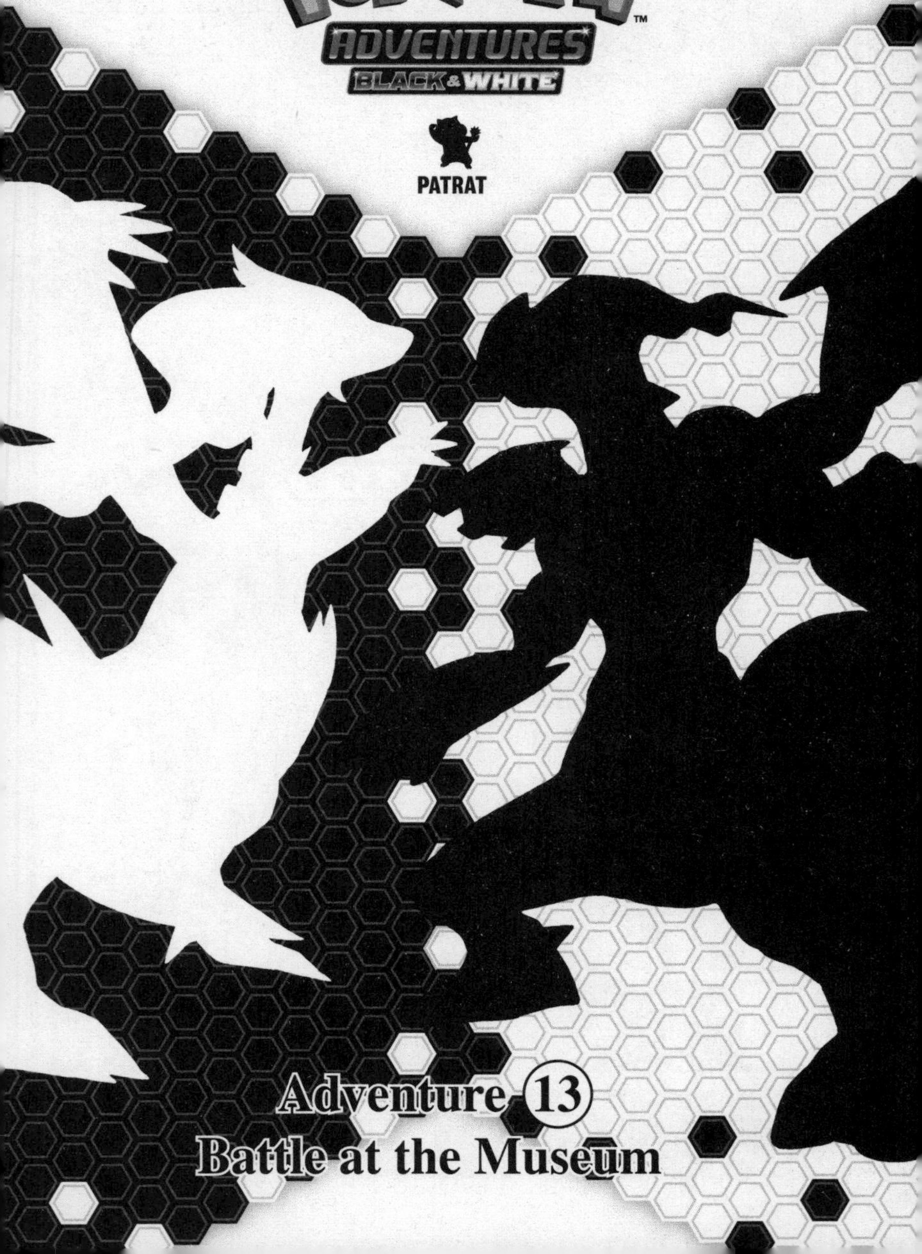

Adventure 13
Battle at the Museum

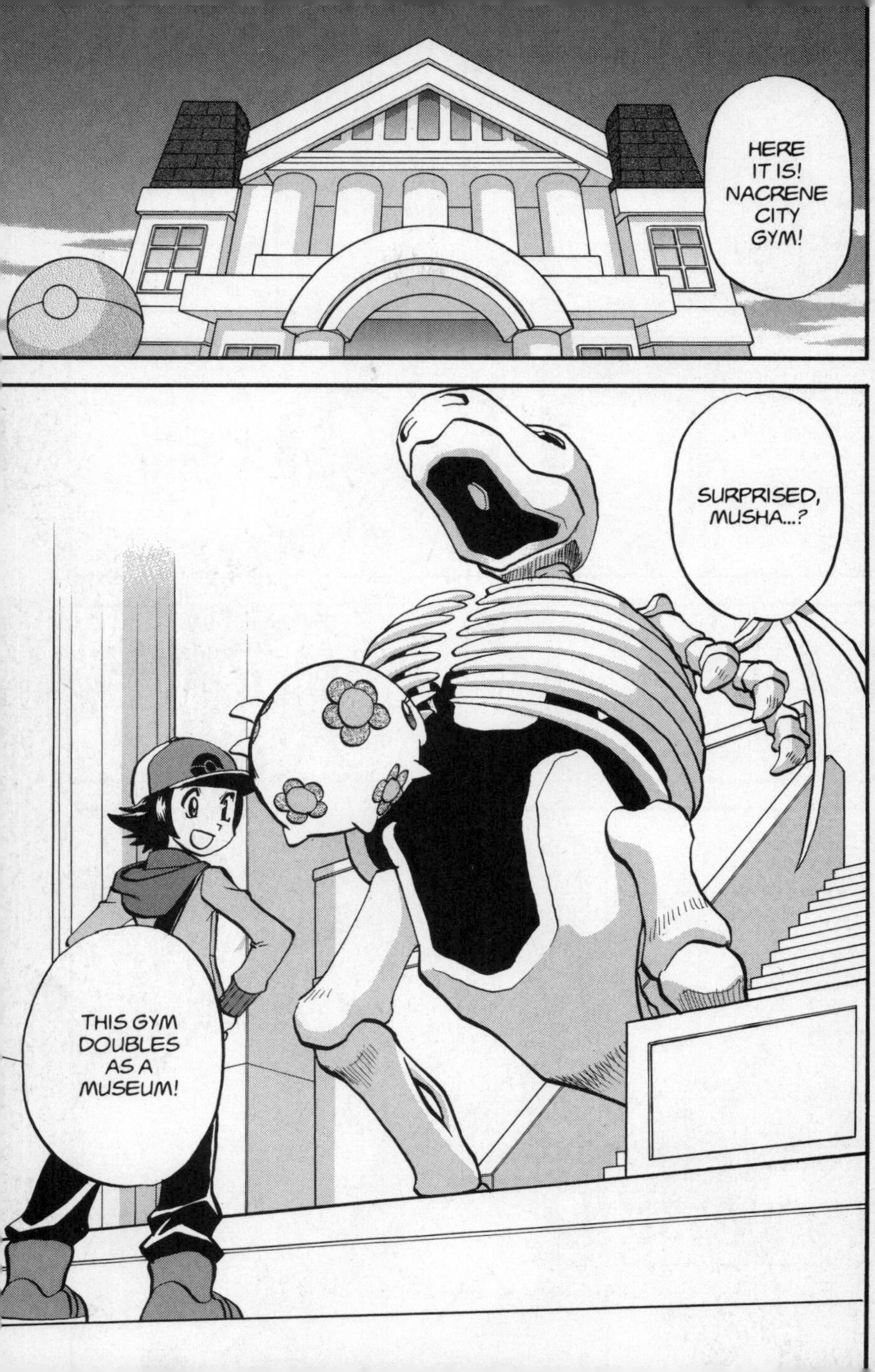
HERE IT IS! NACRENE CITY GYM!
SURPRISED, MUSHA...?
THIS GYM DOUBLES AS A MUSEUM!

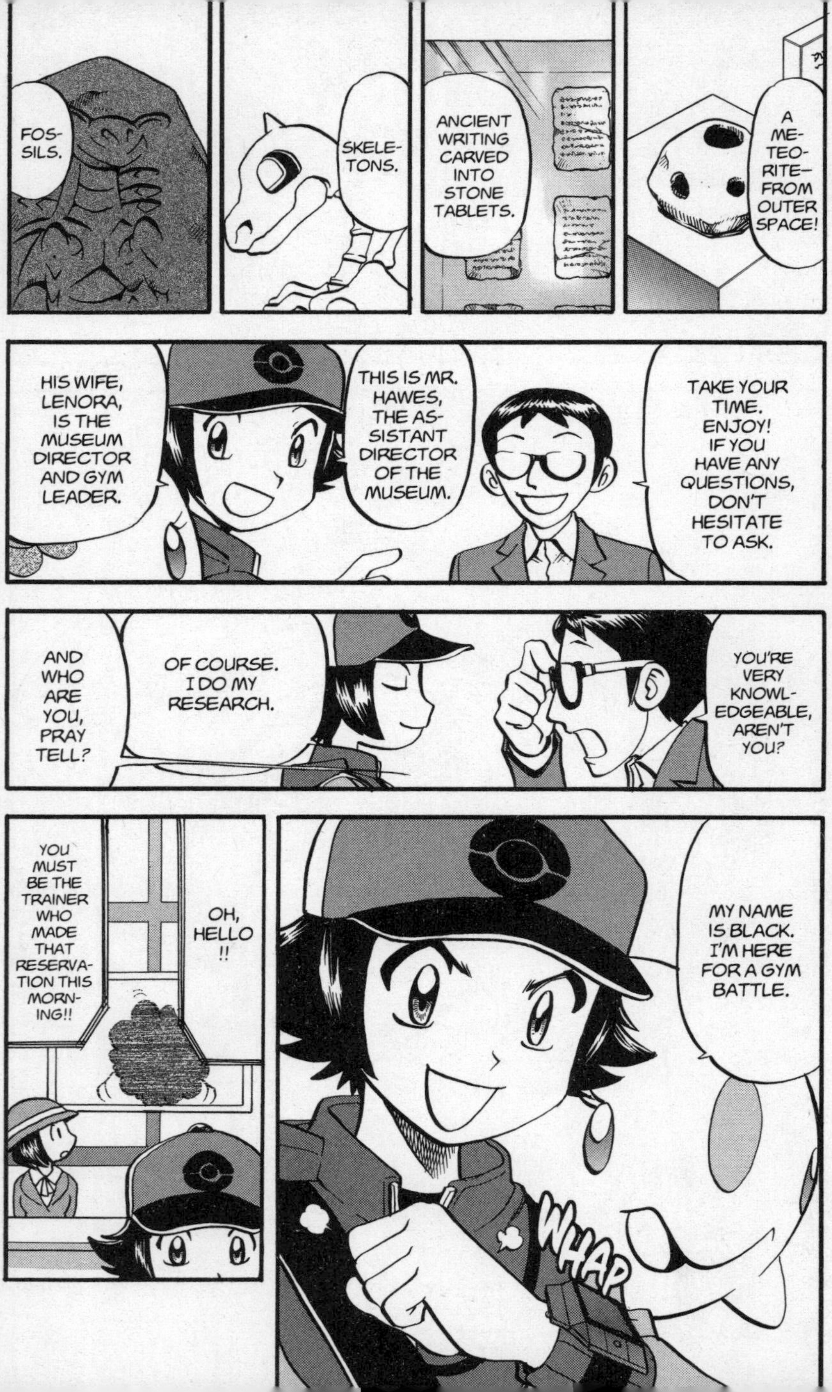
A METEORITE—FROM OUTER SPACE!
ANCIENT WRITING CARVED INTO STONE TABLETS.
SKELETONS.
FOSSILS.
TAKE YOUR TIME. ENJOY! IF YOU HAVE ANY QUESTIONS, DON'T HESITATE TO ASK.
THIS IS MR. HAWES, THE ASSISTANT DIRECTOR OF THE MUSEUM.
HIS WIFE, LENORA, IS THE MUSEUM DIRECTOR AND GYM LEADER.
YOU'RE VERY KNOWLEDGEABLE, AREN'T YOU?
OF COURSE. I DO MY RESEARCH.
AND WHO ARE YOU, PRAY TELL?
MY NAME IS BLACK. I'M HERE FOR A GYM BATTLE.
WHAP
OH, HELLO !!
YOU MUST BE THE TRAINER WHO MADE THAT RESERVATION THIS MORNING!!

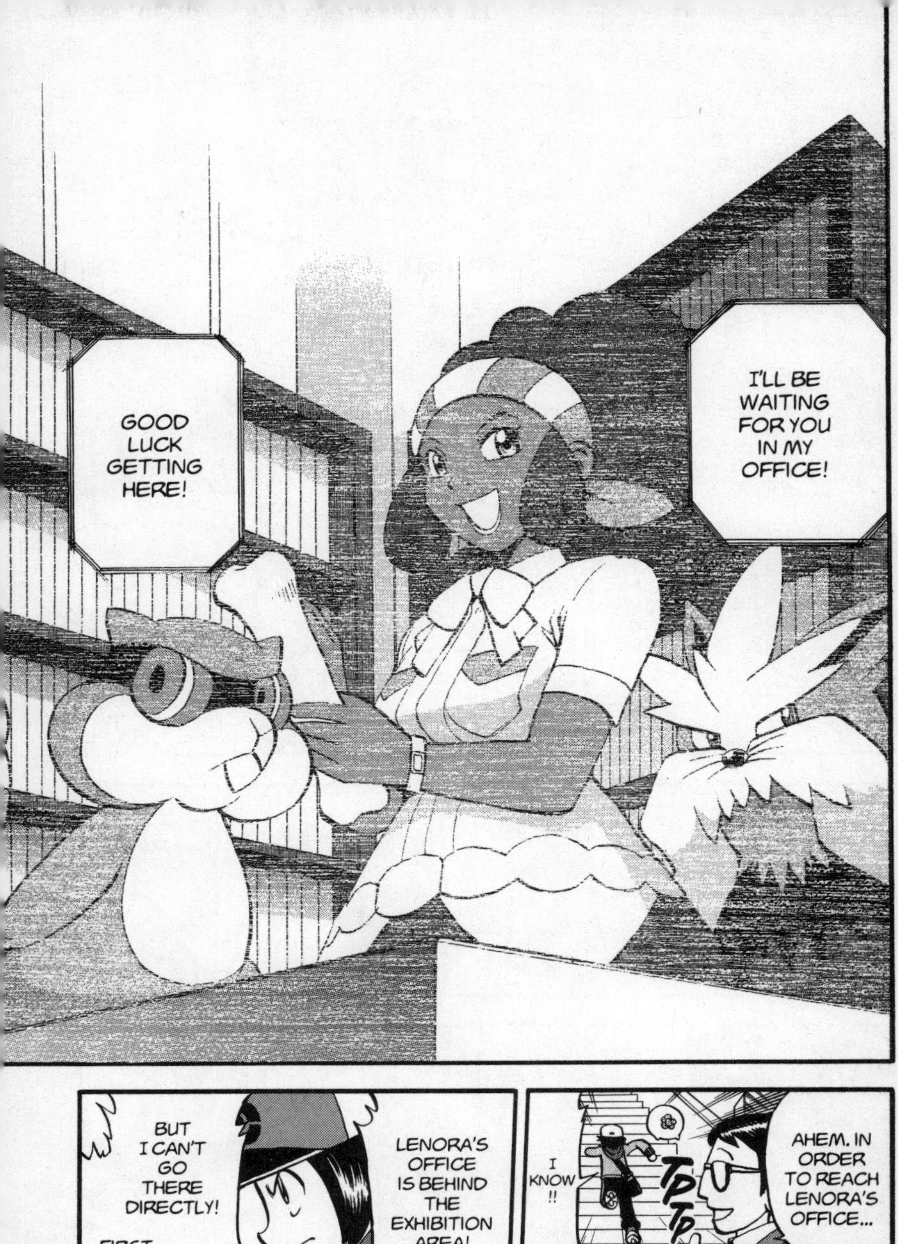
I'LL BE WAITING FOR YOU IN MY OFFICE!
GOOD LUCK GETTING HERE!
AHEM. IN ORDER TO REACH LENORA'S OFFICE...
TPTP
I KNOW!!
LENORA'S OFFICE IS BEHIND THE EXHIBITION AREA!
BUT I CAN'T GO THERE DIRECTLY!
FIRST...

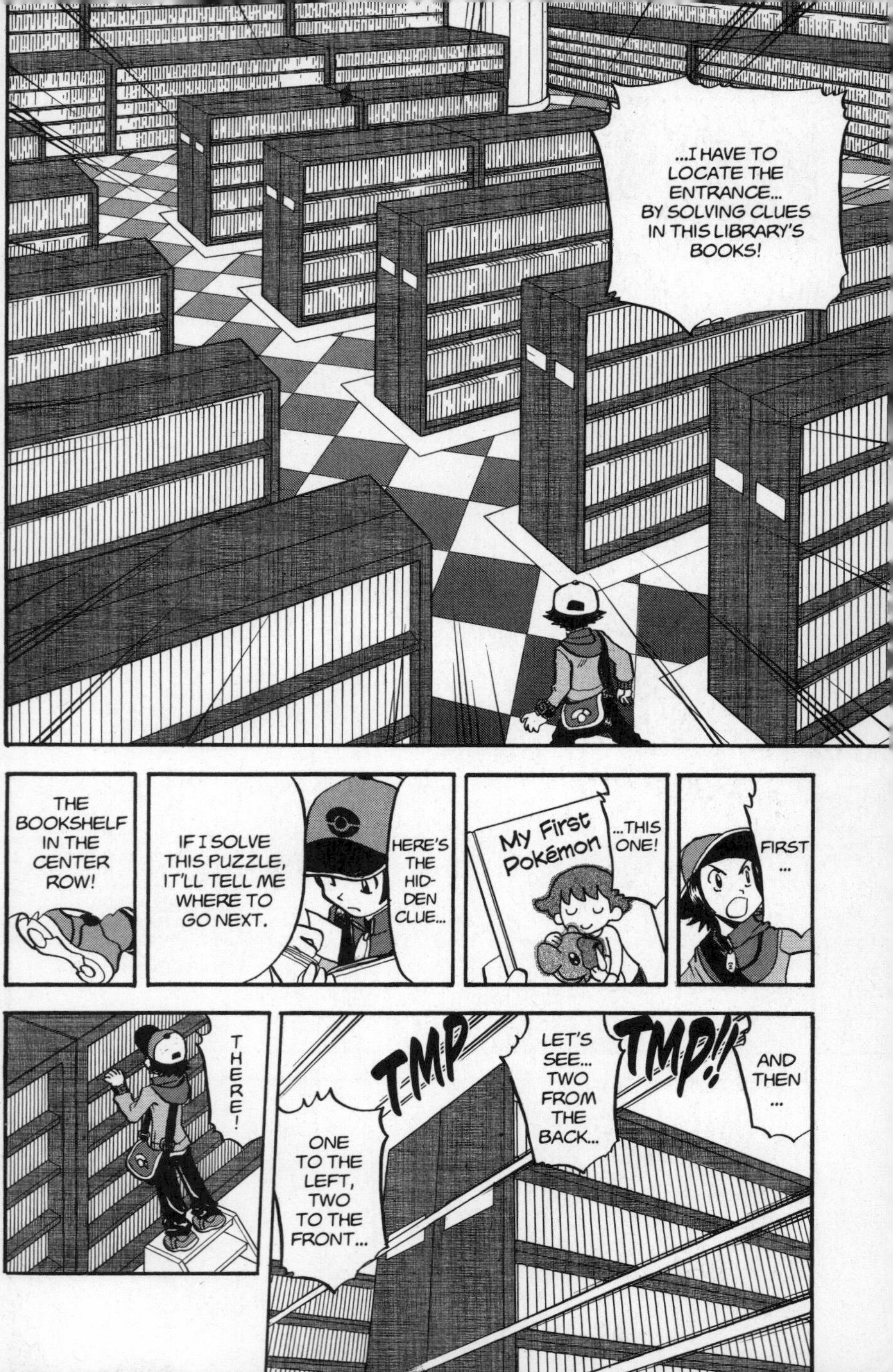
...I HAVE TO LOCATE THE ENTRANCE... BY SOLVING CLUES IN THIS LIBRARY'S BOOKS!
FIRST ...
...THIS ONE!
My First Pokémon
HERE'S THE HID-DEN CLUE...
IF I SOLVE THIS PUZZLE, IT'LL TELL ME WHERE TO GO NEXT.
THE BOOKSHELF IN THE CENTER ROW!
AND THEN ...
TMP!!
LET'S SEE... TWO FROM THE BACK...
TMP
ONE TO THE LEFT, TWO TO THE FRONT...
THERE!

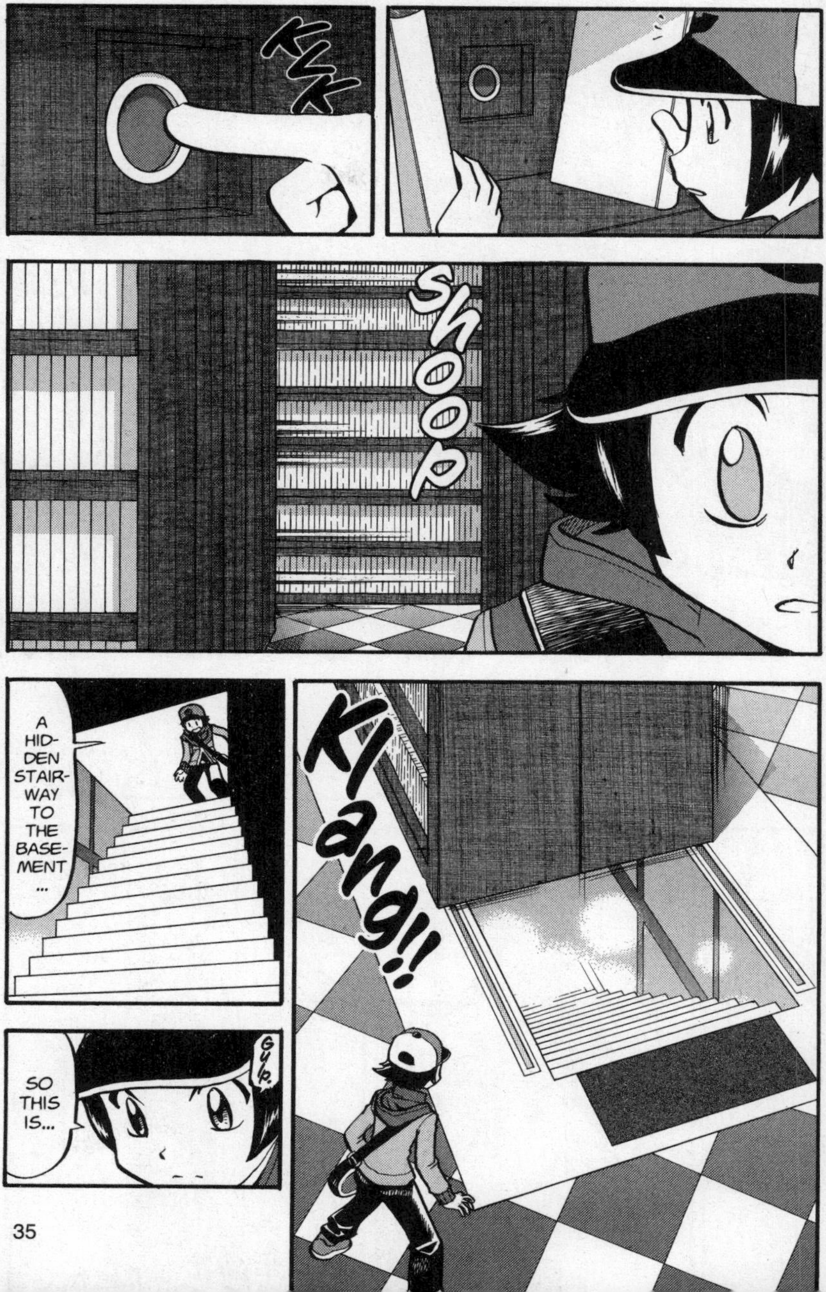
KLK
SHOOP
Klang!!
A HIDDEN STAIRWAY TO THE BASEMENT...
Gulp.
SO THIS IS...

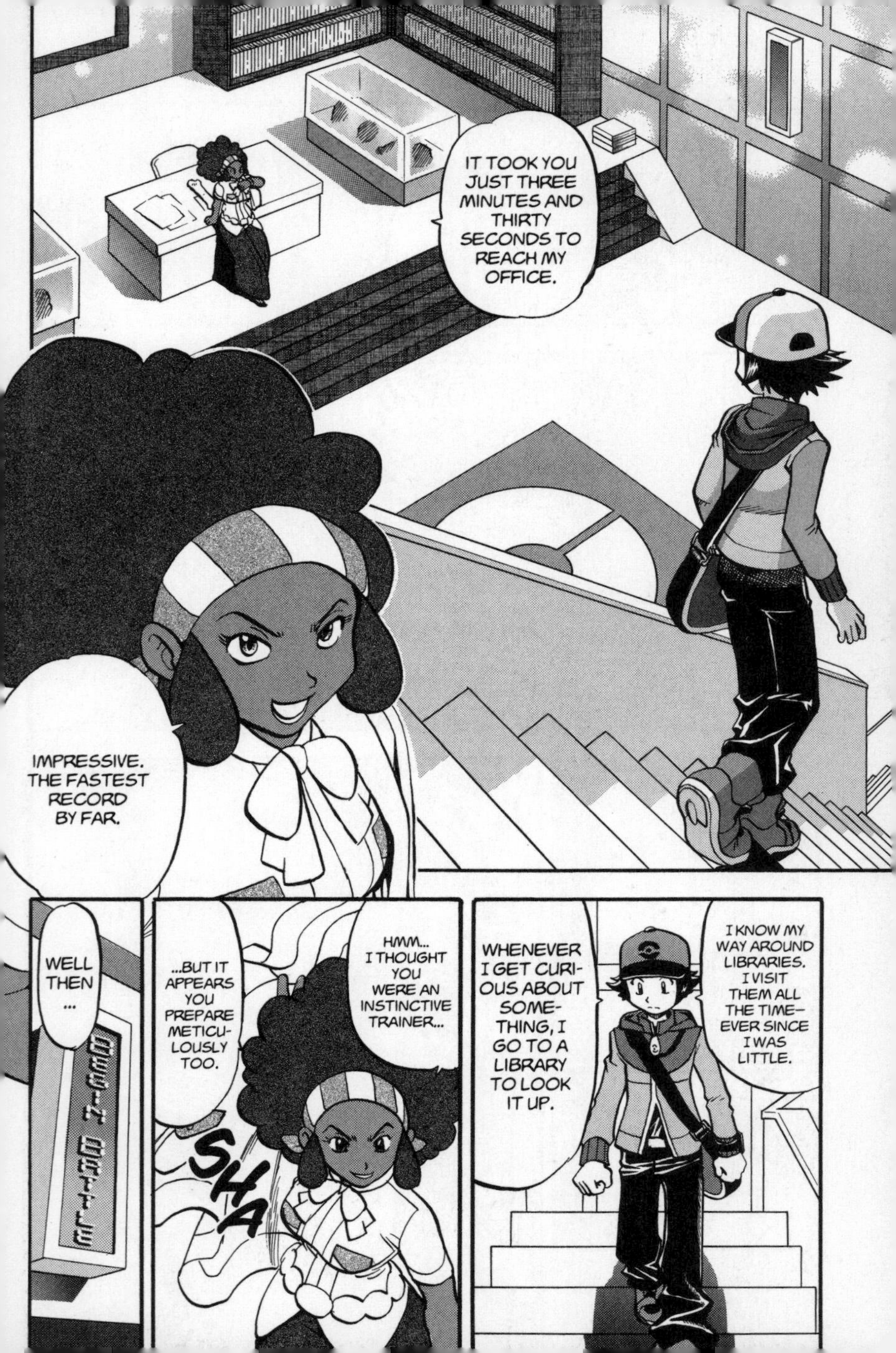
IT TOOK YOU JUST THREE MINUTES AND THIRTY SECONDS TO REACH MY OFFICE.
IMPRESSIVE. THE FASTEST RECORD BY FAR.
I KNOW MY WAY AROUND LIBRARIES. I VISIT THEM ALL THE TIME—EVER SINCE I WAS LITTLE.
WHENEVER I GET CURIOUS ABOUT SOMETHING, I GO TO A LIBRARY TO LOOK IT UP.
HMM... I THOUGHT YOU WERE AN INSTINCTIVE TRAINER...
...BUT IT APPEARS YOU PREPARE METICULOUSLY TOO.
SHA
WELL THEN ...

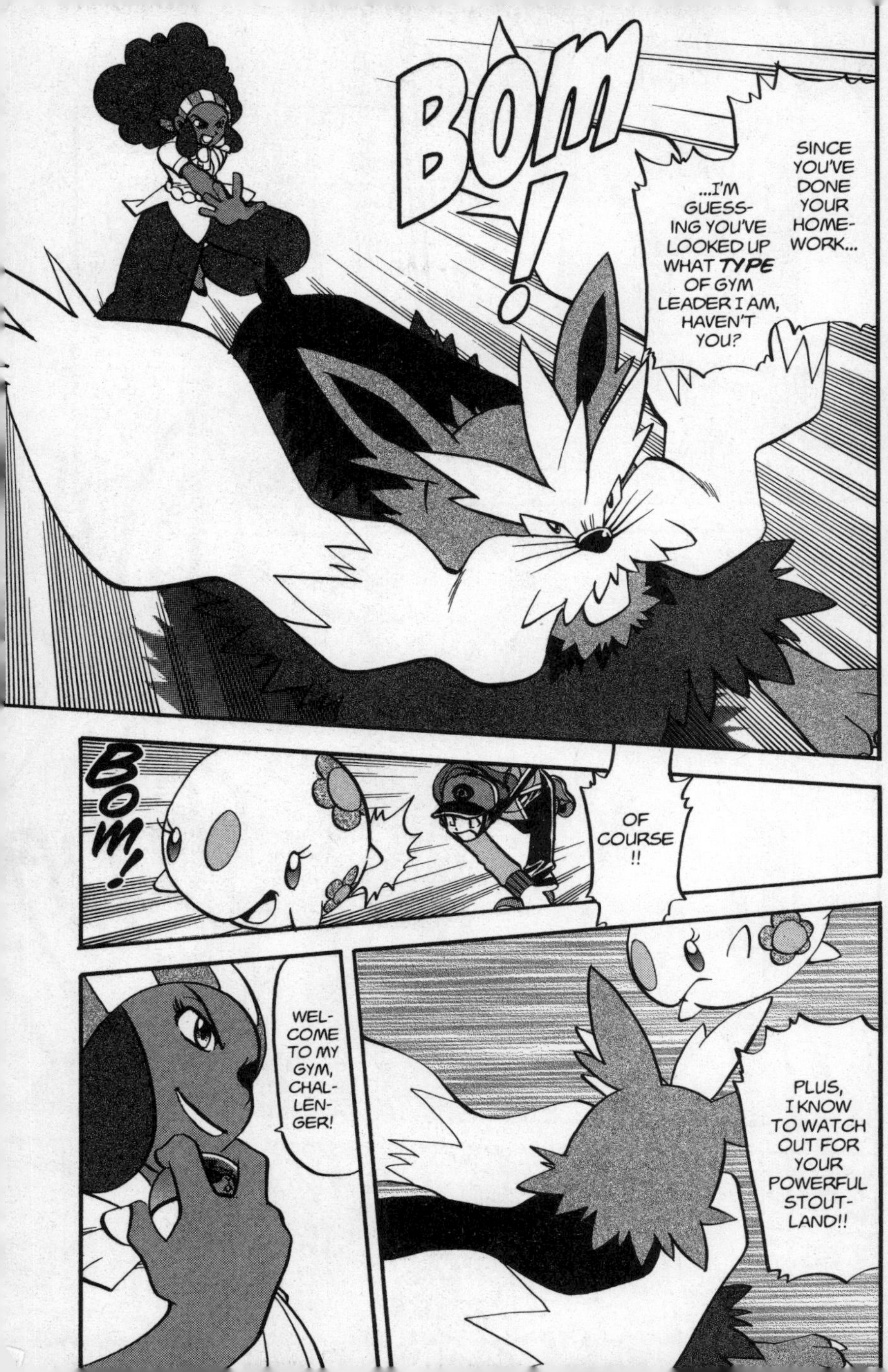
BOM!
SINCE YOU'VE DONE YOUR HOMEWORK...
...I'M GUESSING YOU'VE LOOKED UP WHAT *TYPE* OF GYM LEADER I AM, HAVEN'T YOU?
OF COURSE!!
BOM!
PLUS, I KNOW TO WATCH OUT FOR YOUR POWERFUL STOUTLAND!!
WELCOME TO MY GYM, CHALLENGER!

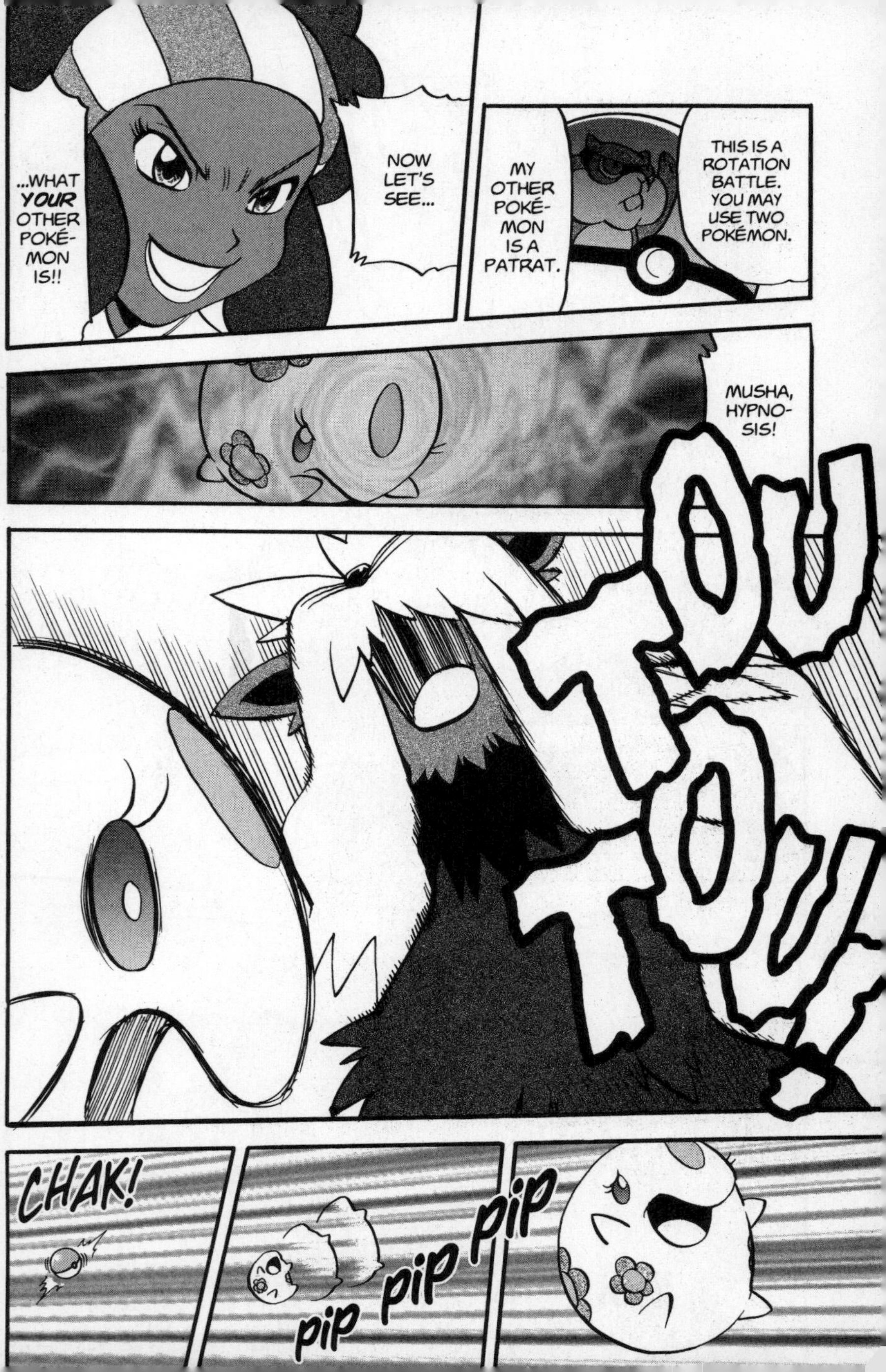
THIS IS A ROTATION BATTLE. YOU MAY USE TWO POKÉMON.
MY OTHER POKÉ-MON IS A PATRAT.
NOW LET'S SEE...
...WHAT **YOUR** OTHER POKÉ-MON IS!!
MUSHA, HYPNO-SIS!
TOU TOU!
pip pip pip
CHAK!

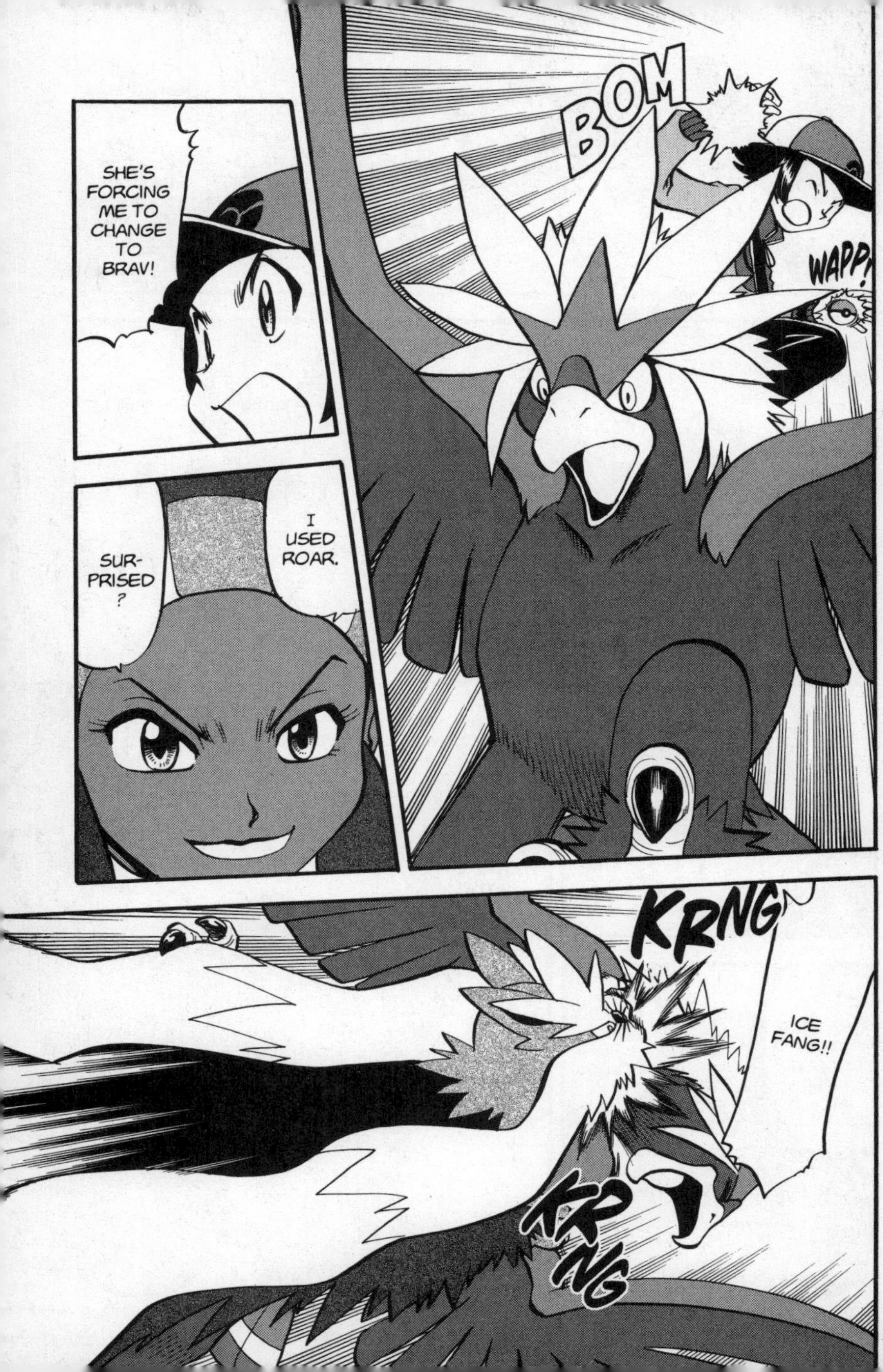
BOM
WAPP!
SHE'S FORCING ME TO CHANGE TO BRAV!
I USED ROAR.
SUR-PRISED?
KRNG
ICE FANG!!
KRNG

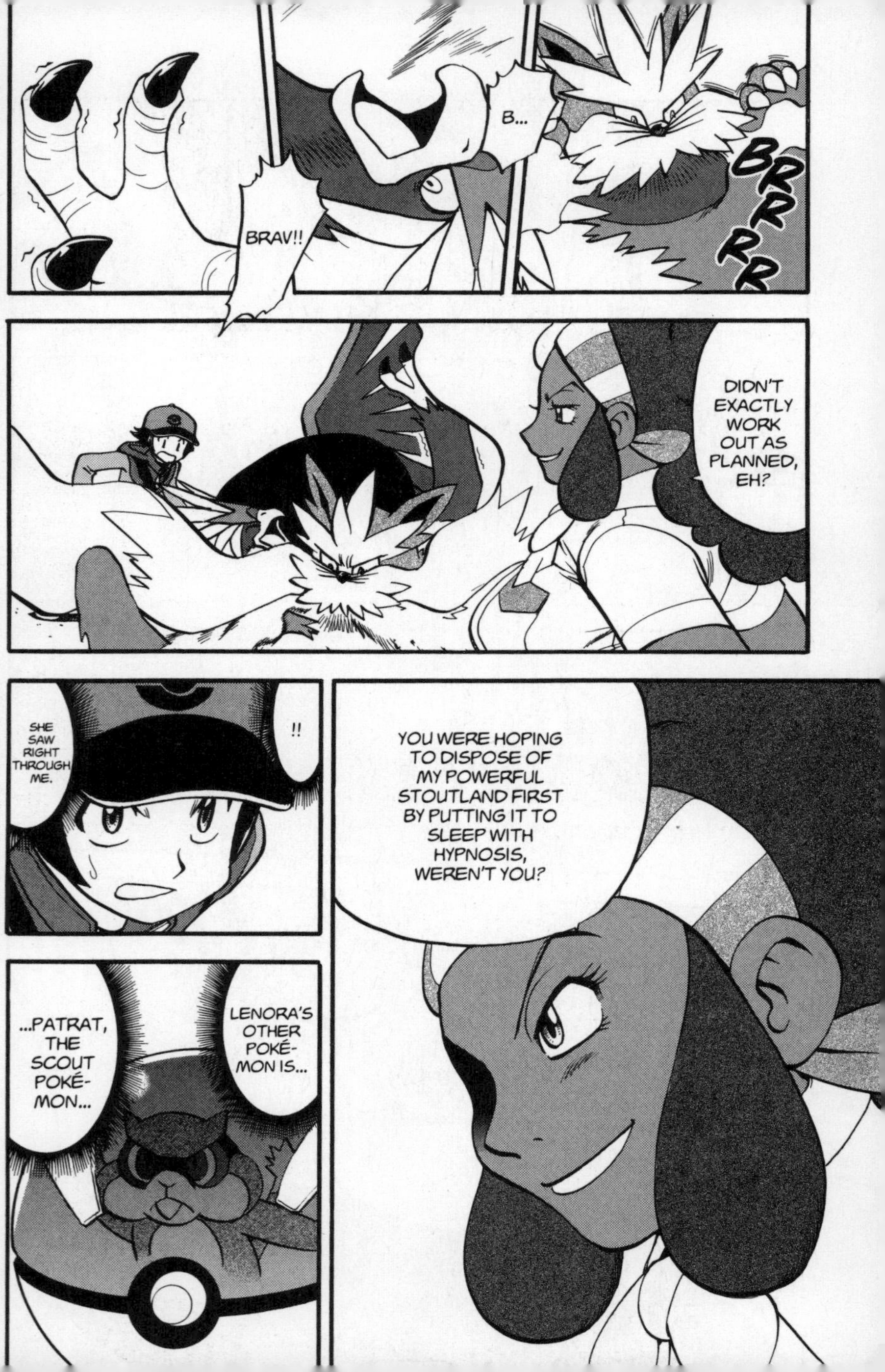
B...
BRRRR
BRAV!!
DIDN'T EXACTLY WORK OUT AS PLANNED, EH?
YOU WERE HOPING TO DISPOSE OF MY POWERFUL STOUTLAND FIRST BY PUTTING IT TO SLEEP WITH HYPNOSIS, WEREN'T YOU?
!!
SHE SAW RIGHT THROUGH ME.
LENORA'S OTHER POKÉ-MON IS...
...PATRAT, THE SCOUT POKÉ-MON...

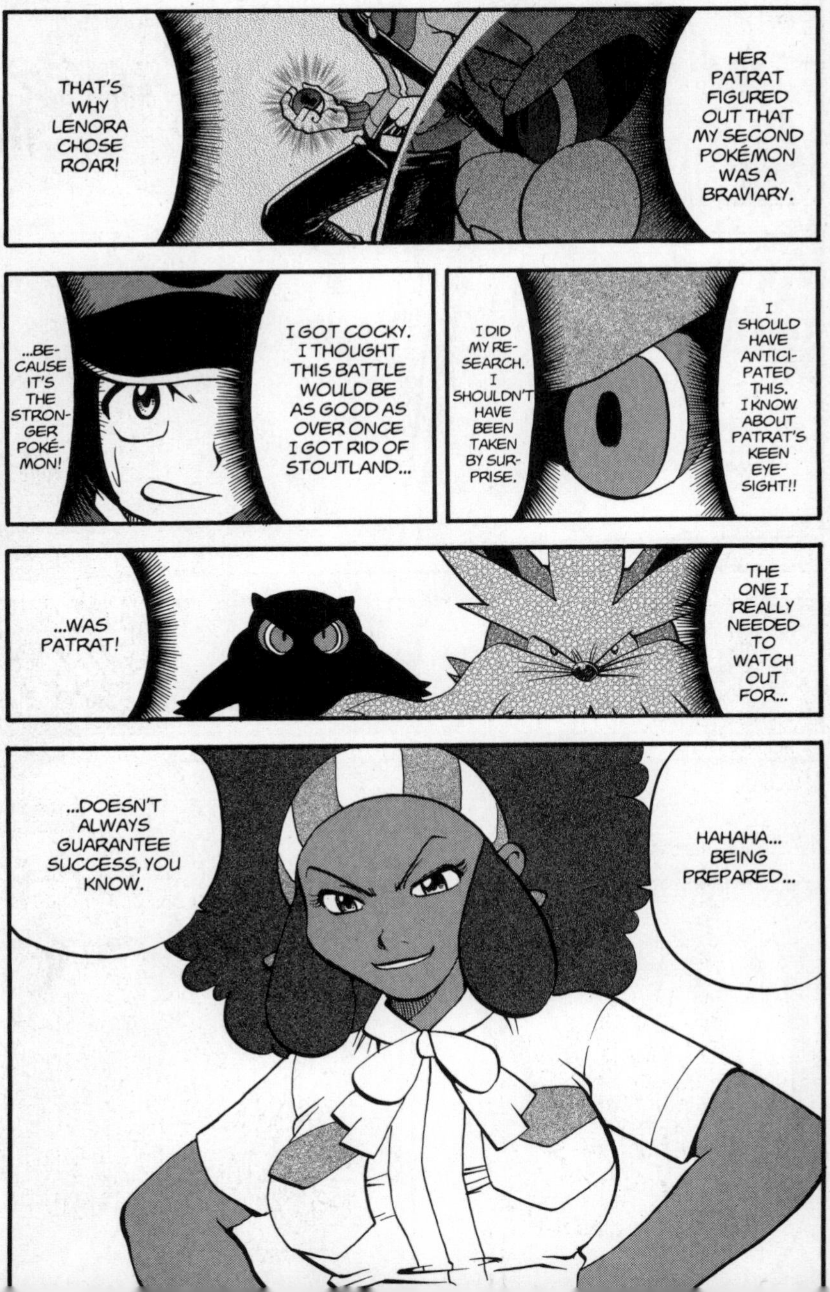
HER PATRAT FIGURED OUT THAT MY SECOND POKÉMON WAS A BRAVIARY.
THAT'S WHY LENORA CHOSE ROAR!
I SHOULD HAVE ANTICIPATED THIS. I KNOW ABOUT PATRAT'S KEEN EYESIGHT!!
I DID MY RESEARCH. I SHOULDN'T HAVE BEEN TAKEN BY SURPRISE.
I GOT COCKY. I THOUGHT THIS BATTLE WOULD BE AS GOOD AS OVER ONCE I GOT RID OF STOUTLAND...
...BECAUSE IT'S THE STRONGER POKÉMON!
THE ONE I REALLY NEEDED TO WATCH OUT FOR...
...WAS PATRAT!
HAHAHA... BEING PREPARED...
...DOESN'T ALWAYS GUARANTEE SUCCESS, YOU KNOW.

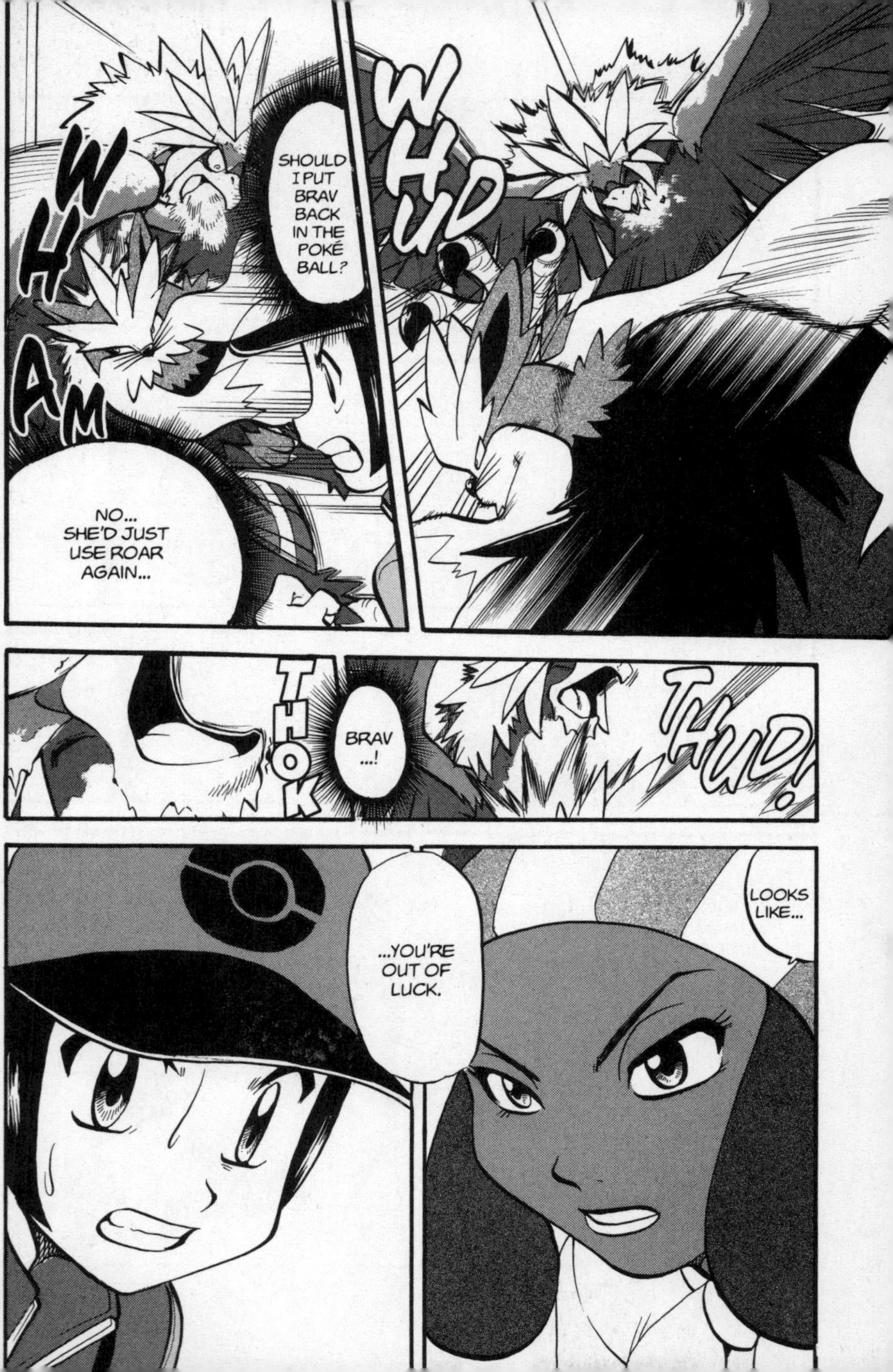
WHUD
WHAM
SHOULD I PUT BRAV BACK IN THE POKÉ BALL?
NO... SHE'D JUST USE ROAR AGAIN...
THUD!
BRAV ...!
THOK
LOOKS LIKE...
...YOU'RE OUT OF LUCK.

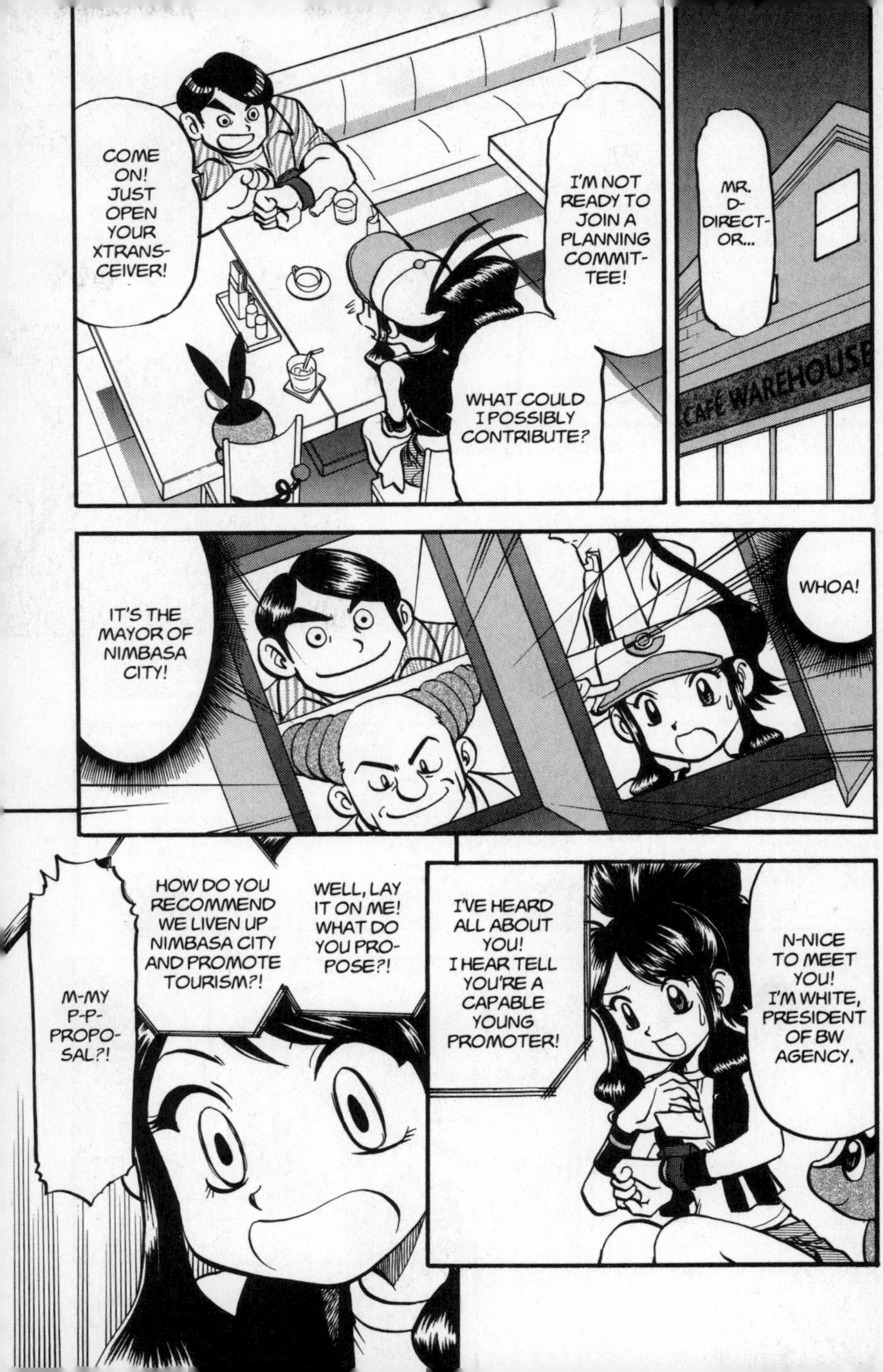
MR. D-DIRECTOR...
CAFÉ WAREHOUSE
I'M NOT READY TO JOIN A PLANNING COMMITTEE!
WHAT COULD I POSSIBLY CONTRIBUTE?
COME ON! JUST OPEN YOUR XTRANSCEIVER!
WHOA!
IT'S THE MAYOR OF NIMBASA CITY!
N-NICE TO MEET YOU! I'M WHITE, PRESIDENT OF BW AGENCY.
I'VE HEARD ALL ABOUT YOU! I HEAR TELL YOU'RE A CAPABLE YOUNG PROMOTER!
WELL, LAY IT ON ME! WHAT DO YOU PROPOSE?!
HOW DO YOU RECOMMEND WE LIVEN UP NIMBASA CITY AND PROMOTE TOURISM?!
M-MY P-P-PROPOSAL?!

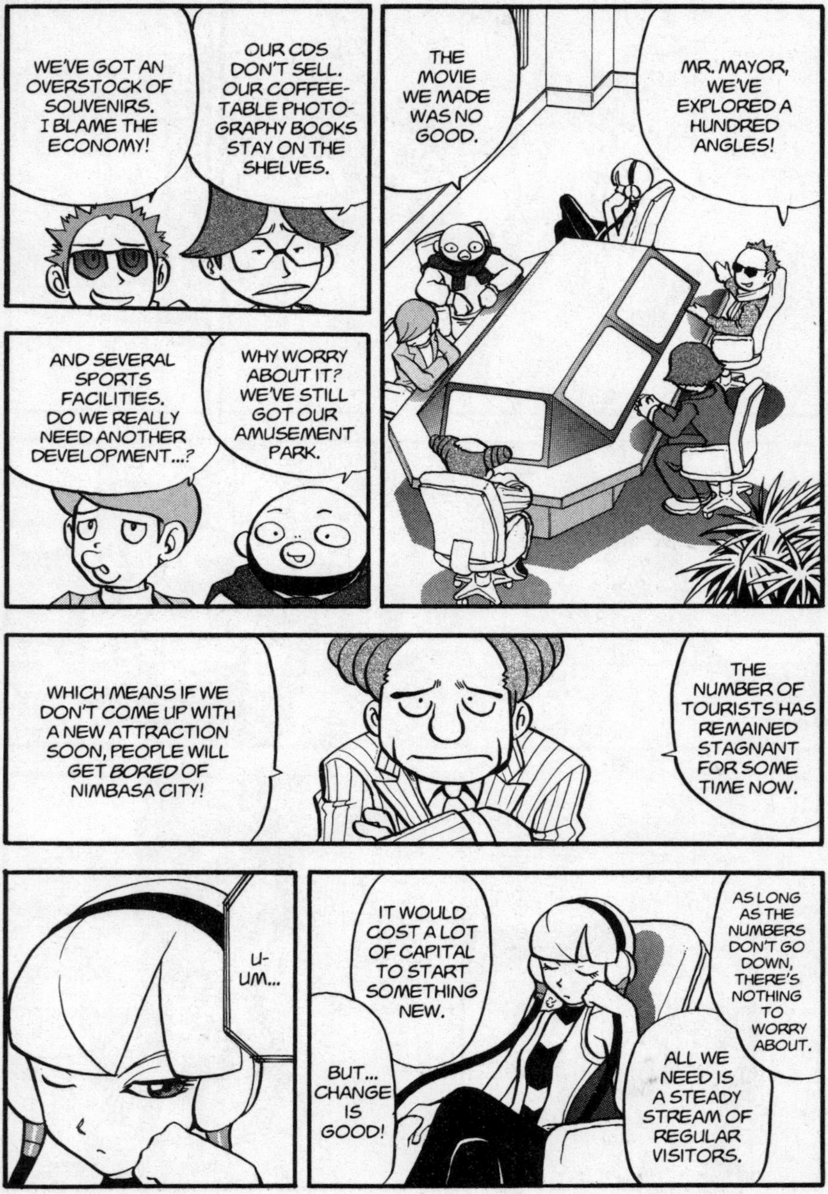
MR. MAYOR, WE'VE EXPLORED A HUNDRED ANGLES!
THE MOVIE WE MADE WAS NO GOOD.
OUR CDS DON'T SELL. OUR COFFEE-TABLE PHOTOGRAPHY BOOKS STAY ON THE SHELVES.
WE'VE GOT AN OVERSTOCK OF SOUVENIRS. I BLAME THE ECONOMY!
WHY WORRY ABOUT IT? WE'VE STILL GOT OUR AMUSEMENT PARK.
AND SEVERAL SPORTS FACILITIES. DO WE REALLY NEED ANOTHER DEVELOPMENT...?
THE NUMBER OF TOURISTS HAS REMAINED STAGNANT FOR SOME TIME NOW.
WHICH MEANS IF WE DON'T COME UP WITH A NEW ATTRACTION SOON, PEOPLE WILL GET *BORED* OF NIMBASA CITY!
AS LONG AS THE NUMBERS DON'T GO DOWN, THERE'S NOTHING TO WORRY ABOUT.
IT WOULD COST A LOT OF CAPITAL TO START SOMETHING NEW.
ALL WE NEED IS A STEADY STREAM OF REGULAR VISITORS.
BUT... CHANGE IS GOOD!
U-UM...

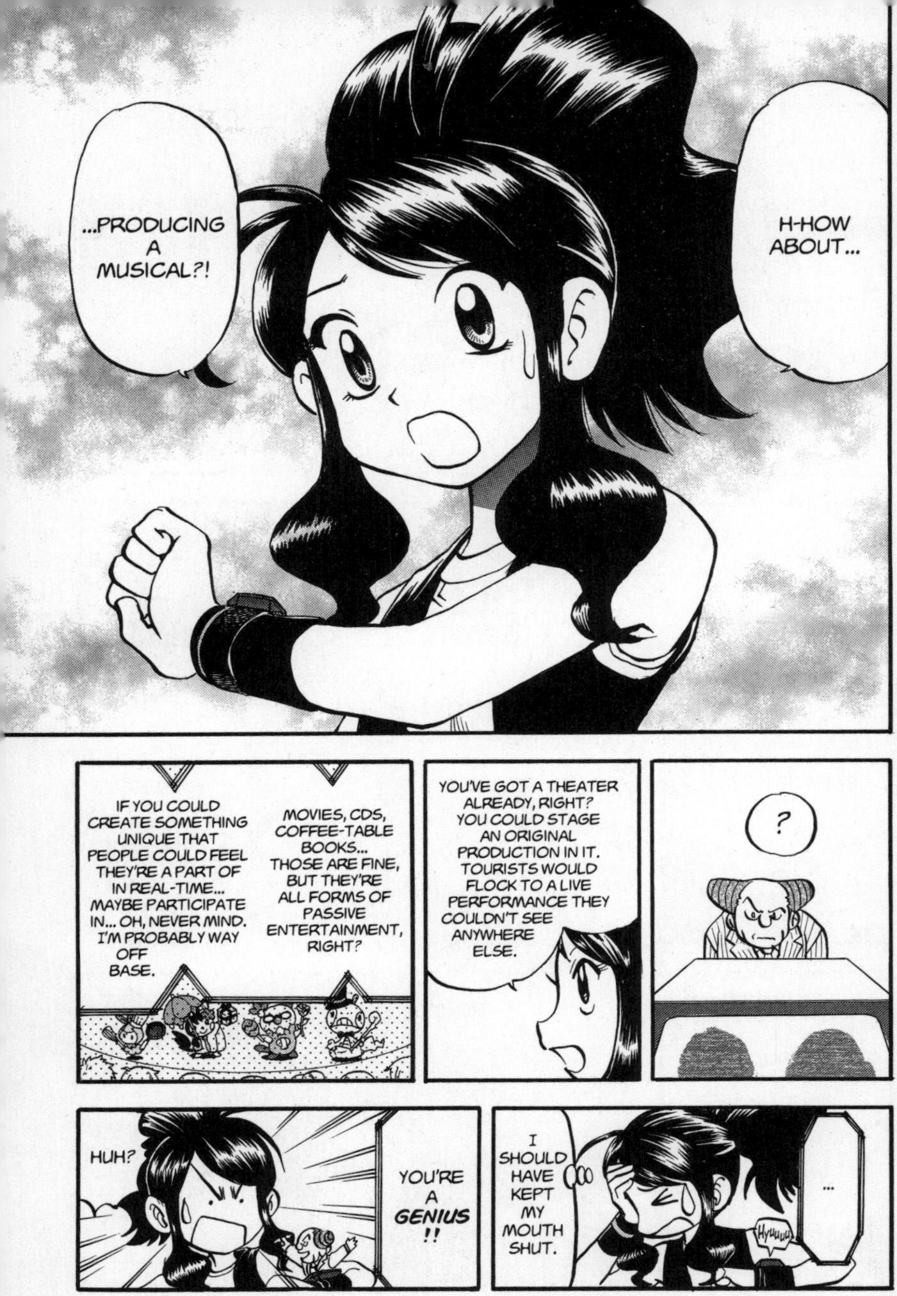

H-HOW ABOUT...
...PRODUCING A MUSICAL?!
?
YOU'VE GOT A THEATER ALREADY, RIGHT? YOU COULD STAGE AN ORIGINAL PRODUCTION IN IT. TOURISTS WOULD FLOCK TO A LIVE PERFORMANCE THEY COULDN'T SEE ANYWHERE ELSE.
MOVIES, CDS, COFFEE-TABLE BOOKS... THOSE ARE FINE, BUT THEY'RE ALL FORMS OF PASSIVE ENTERTAINMENT, RIGHT?
IF YOU COULD CREATE SOMETHING UNIQUE THAT PEOPLE COULD FEEL THEY'RE A PART OF IN REAL-TIME... MAYBE PARTICIPATE IN... OH, NEVER MIND. I'M PROBABLY WAY OFF BASE.
...
Hyuuu
I SHOULD HAVE KEPT MY MOUTH SHUT.
YOU'RE A GENIUS!!
HUH?

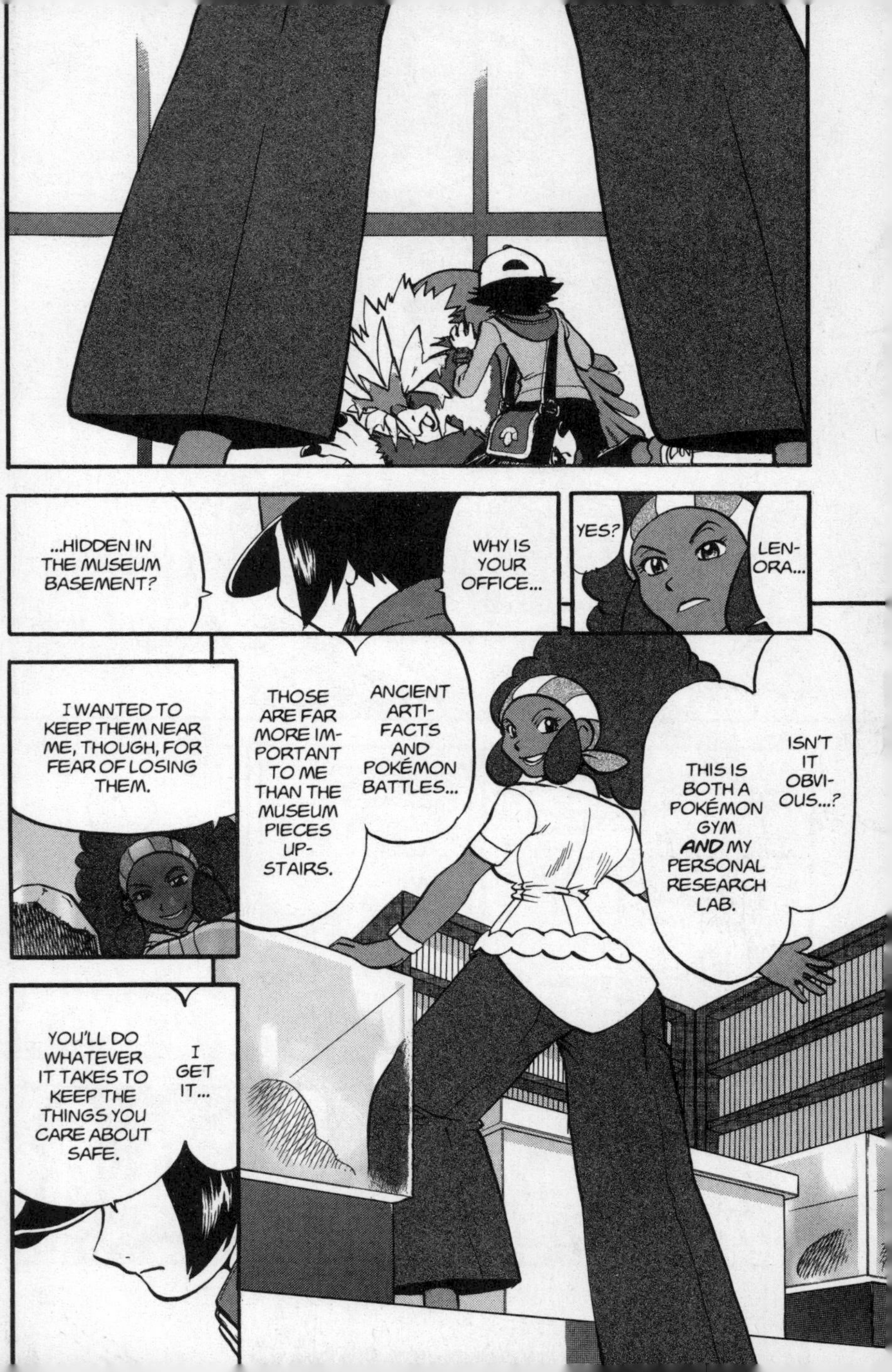
LENORA...
YES?
WHY IS YOUR OFFICE...
...HIDDEN IN THE MUSEUM BASEMENT?
ISN'T IT OBVIOUS...?
THIS IS BOTH A POKÉMON GYM AND MY PERSONAL RESEARCH LAB.
ANCIENT ARTIFACTS AND POKÉMON BATTLES...
THOSE ARE FAR MORE IMPORTANT TO ME THAN THE MUSEUM PIECES UPSTAIRS.
I WANTED TO KEEP THEM NEAR ME, THOUGH, FOR FEAR OF LOSING THEM.
I GET IT...
YOU'LL DO WHATEVER IT TAKES TO KEEP THE THINGS YOU CARE ABOUT SAFE.

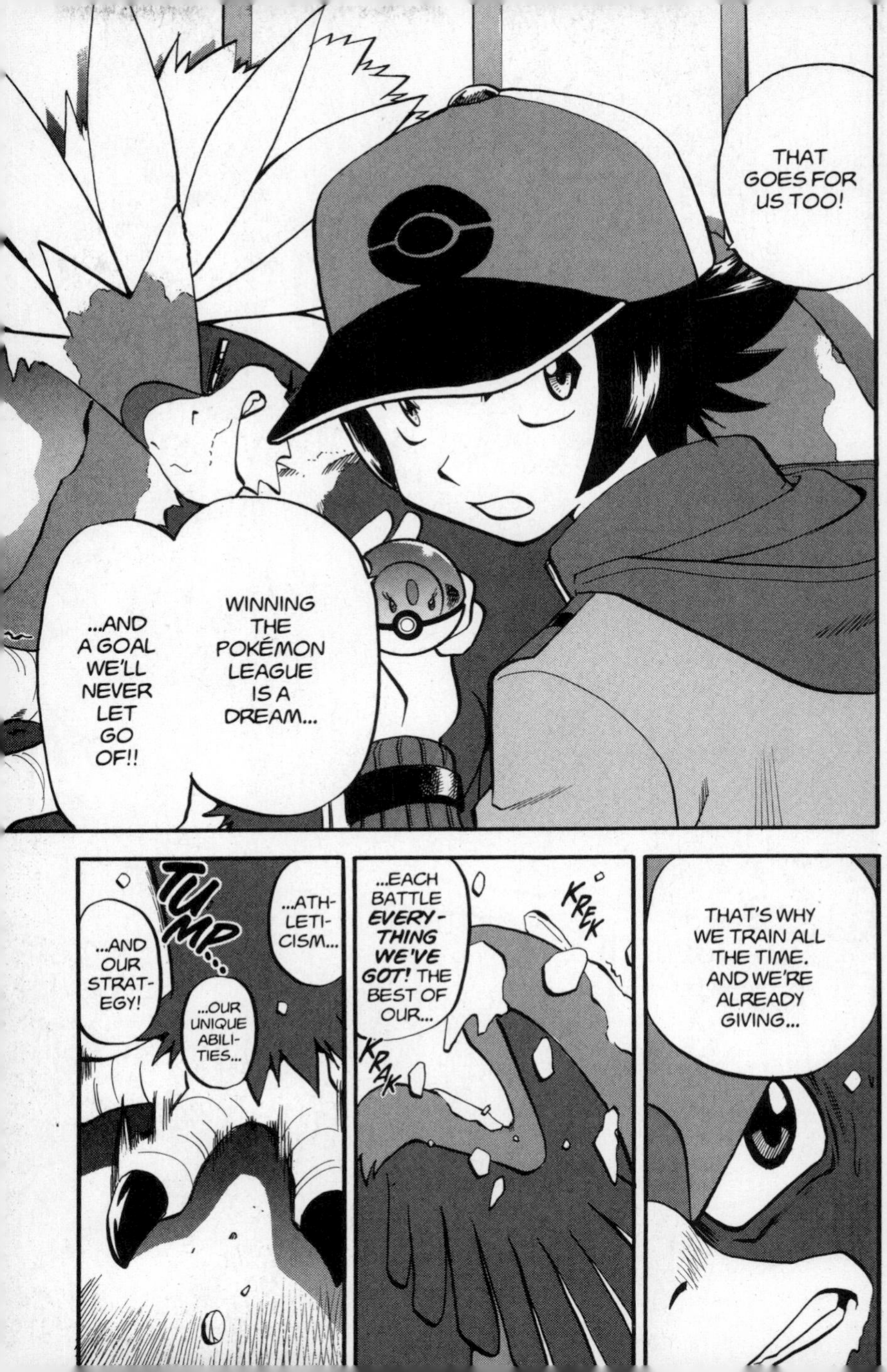
THAT GOES FOR US TOO!
WINNING THE POKÉMON LEAGUE IS A DREAM...
...AND A GOAL WE'LL NEVER LET GO OF!!
THAT'S WHY WE TRAIN ALL THE TIME. AND WE'RE ALREADY GIVING...
KREK
...EACH BATTLE ***EVERYTHING WE'VE GOT!*** THE BEST OF OUR...
KRAK
...ATHLETICISM...
TUMP...
...OUR UNIQUE ABILITIES...
...AND OUR STRATEGY!

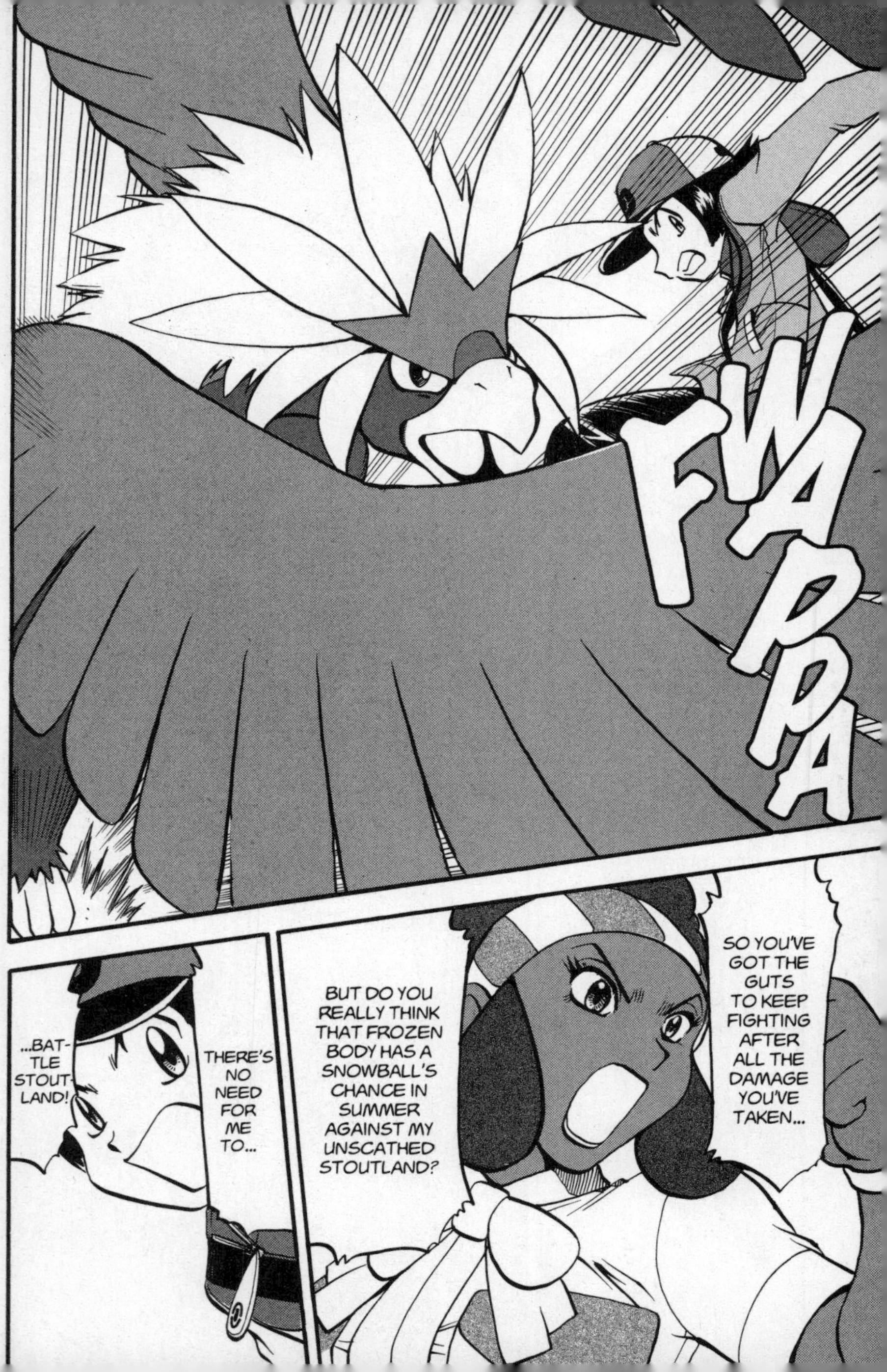
FWAPPA
SO YOU'VE GOT THE GUTS TO KEEP FIGHTING AFTER ALL THE DAMAGE YOU'VE TAKEN...
BUT DO YOU REALLY THINK THAT FROZEN BODY HAS A SNOWBALL'S CHANCE IN SUMMER AGAINST MY UNSCATHED STOUTLAND?
THERE'S NO NEED FOR ME TO...
...BATTLE STOUTLAND!

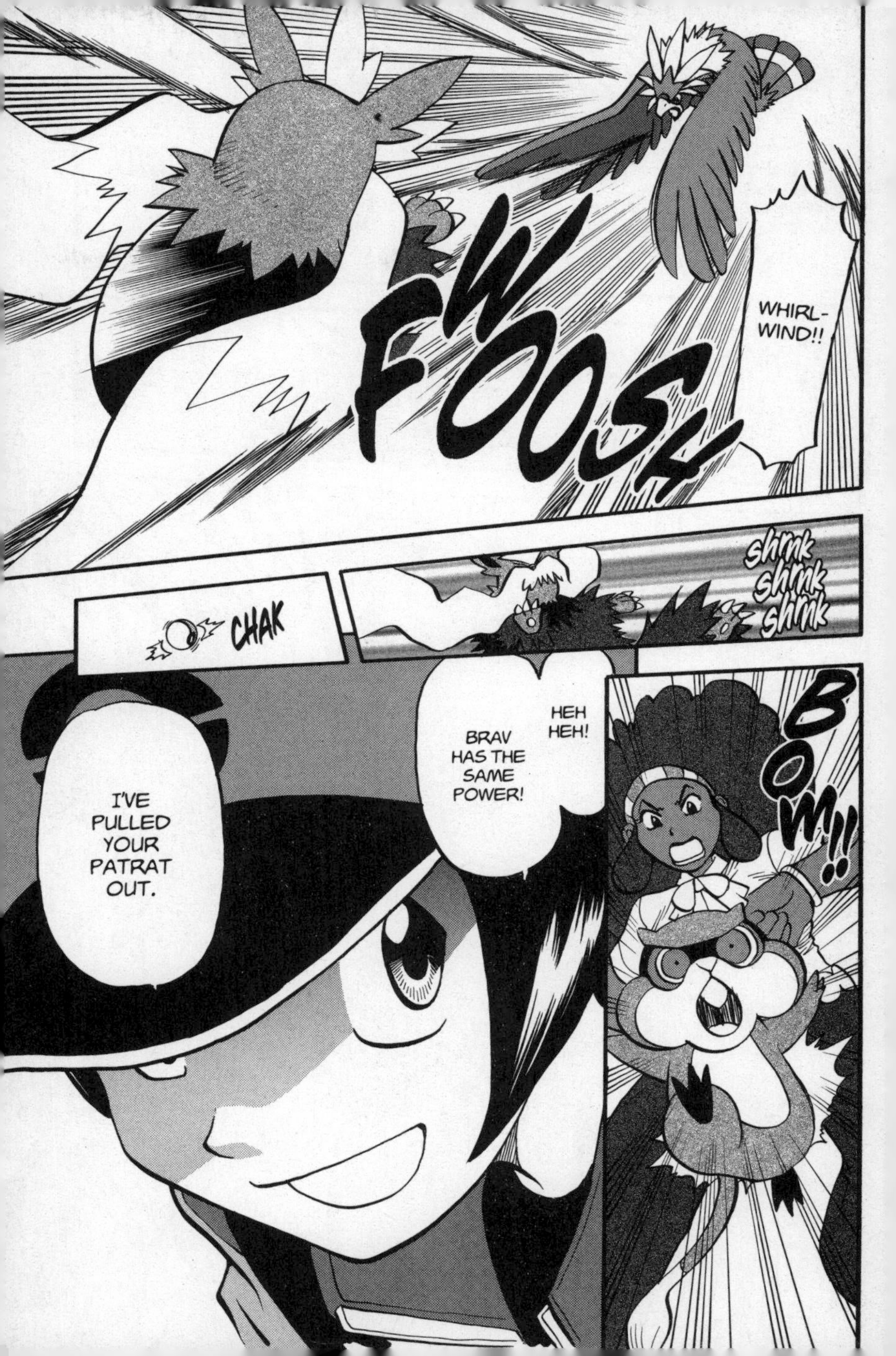
WHIRL-WIND!!
FWOOSH
shrnk shrnk shrnk
CHAK
BOOM!!
HEH HEH!
BRAV HAS THE SAME POWER!
I'VE PULLED YOUR PATRAT OUT.

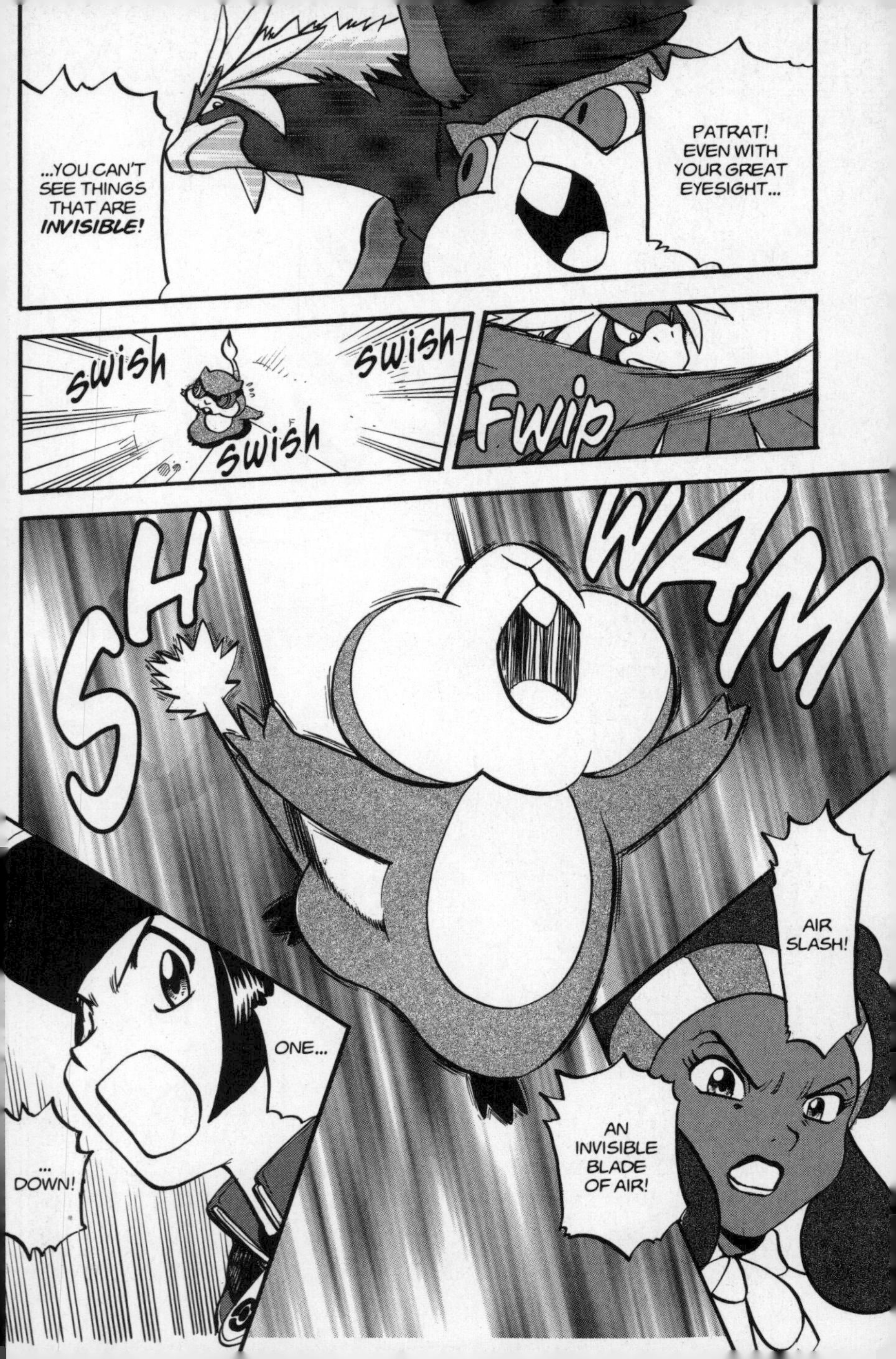
PATRAT! EVEN WITH YOUR GREAT EYESIGHT...
...YOU CAN'T SEE THINGS THAT ARE *INVISIBLE!*
Fwip
swish
swish
swish
WAM
SH
AIR SLASH!
AN INVISIBLE BLADE OF AIR!
ONE...
... DOWN!

Final Destination:
Pokémon League

Current Location:
Nacrene City Gym

BLACK

WHITE

Fire Pig Pokémon **Tep**
Tepig ♂ — Fire
Lv.16 Ability: Blaze

Dream Eater Pokémon **Musha**
Munna ♂ — Psychic
Lv.37 Ability: Forewarn

Valiant Pokémon **Brav**
Braviary ♂ — Normal / Flying
Lv.54 Ability: Sheer Force

EleSpider Pokémon **Tula**
Galvantula ♂ — Bug / Electric
Lv.38 Ability: Unnerve

Fire Pig Pokémon **Gigi**
Tepig ♀ — Fire
Lv.05 Ability: Blaze

TRIO BADGE

POKÉMON ADVENTURES BLACK & WHITE

STOUTLAND

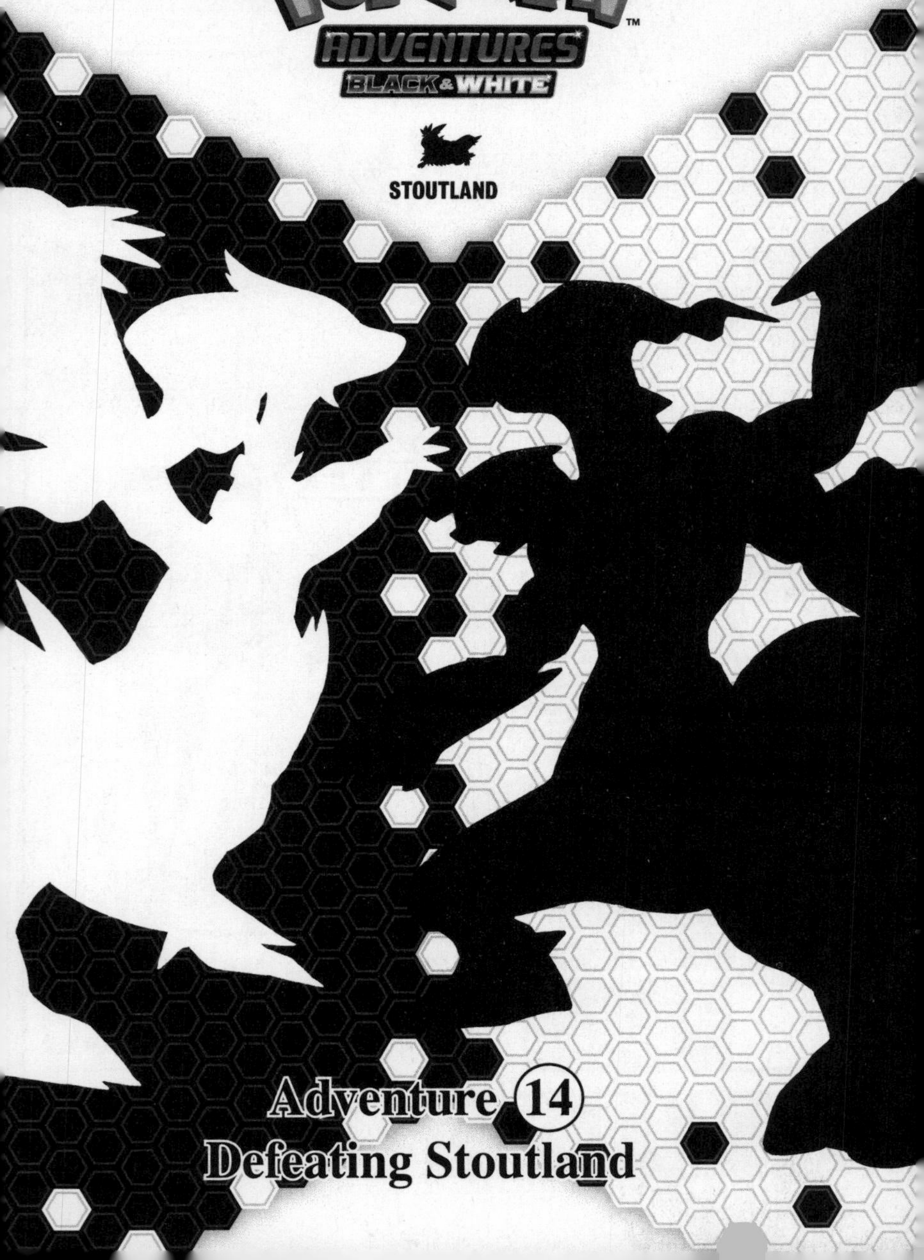

Adventure 14
Defeating Stoutland

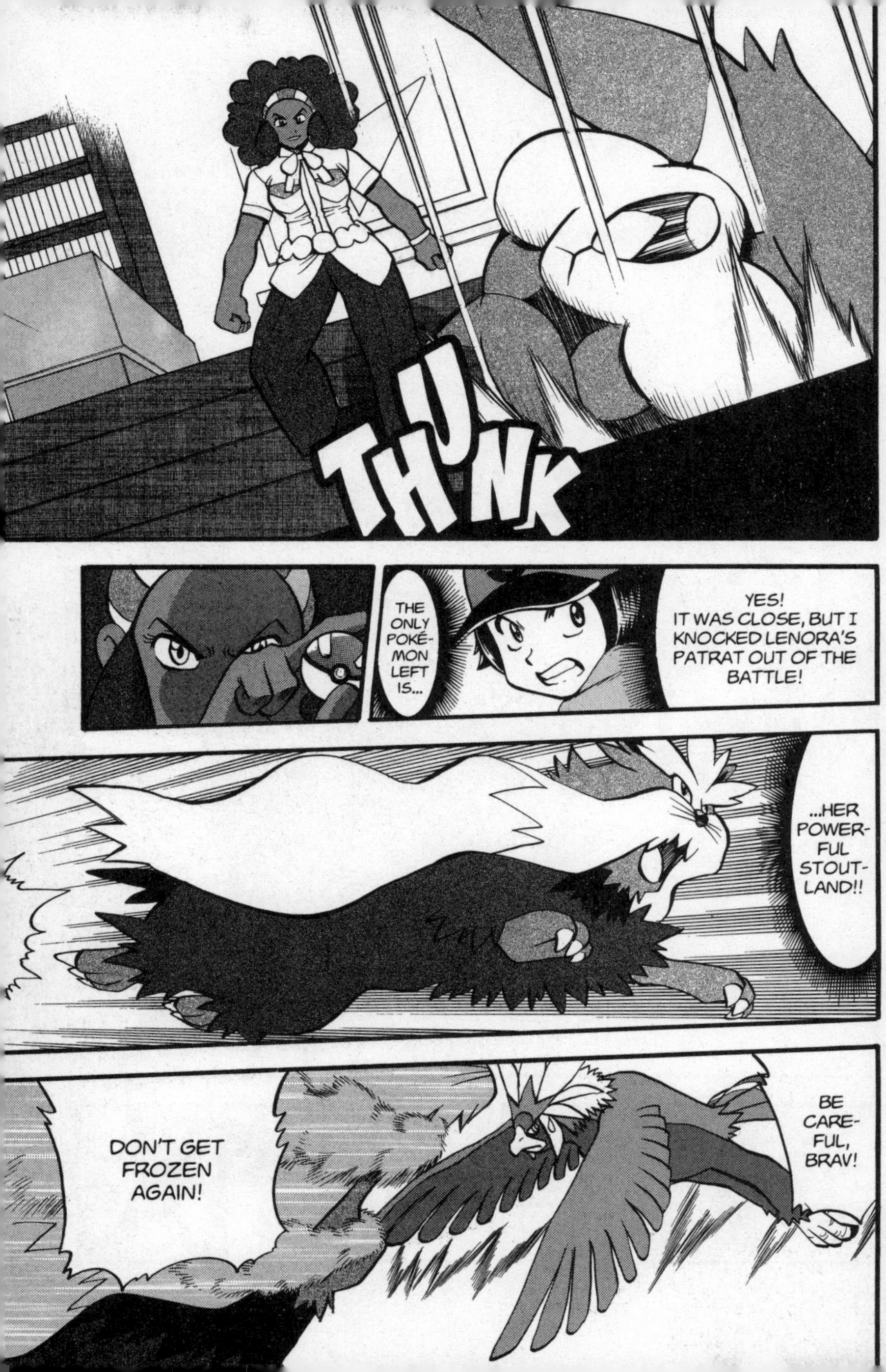
THUNK
YES! IT WAS CLOSE, BUT I KNOCKED LENORA'S PATRAT OUT OF THE BATTLE!
THE ONLY POKÉ-MON LEFT IS...
...HER POWER-FUL STOUT-LAND!!
BE CARE-FUL, BRAV!
DON'T GET FROZEN AGAIN!

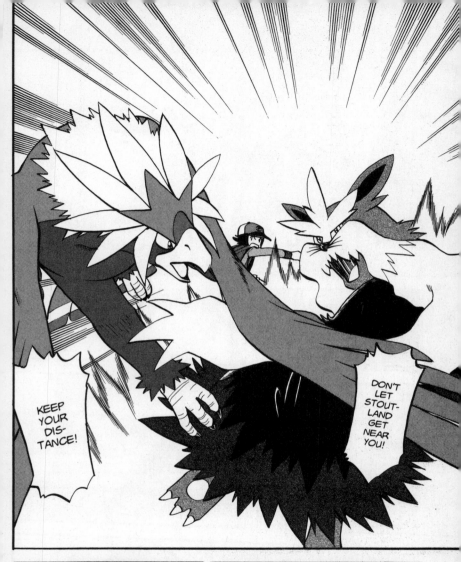

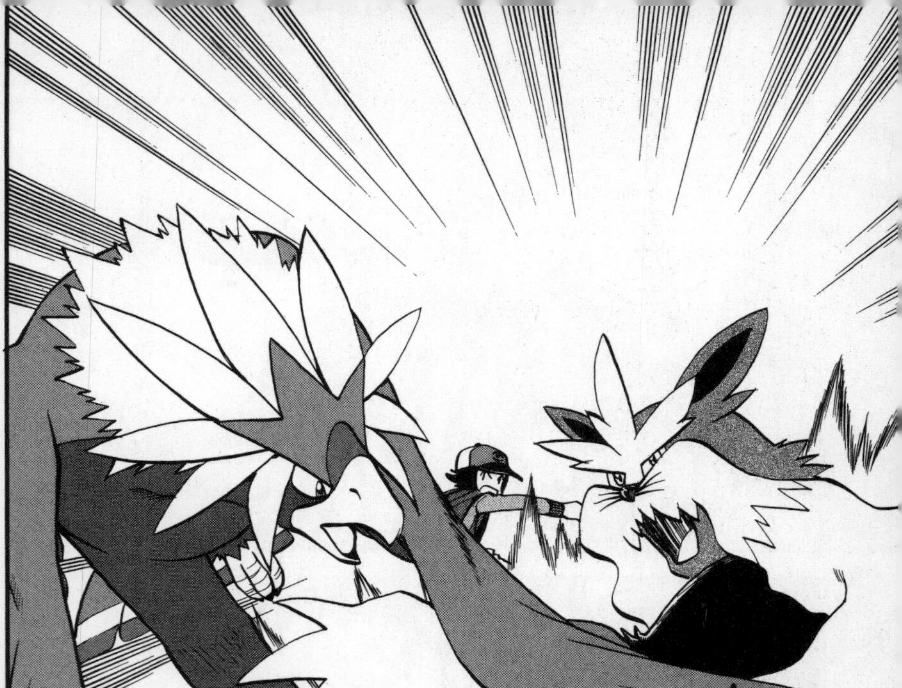
DON'T LET STOUT-LAND GET NEAR YOU!
KEEP YOUR DIS-TANCE!

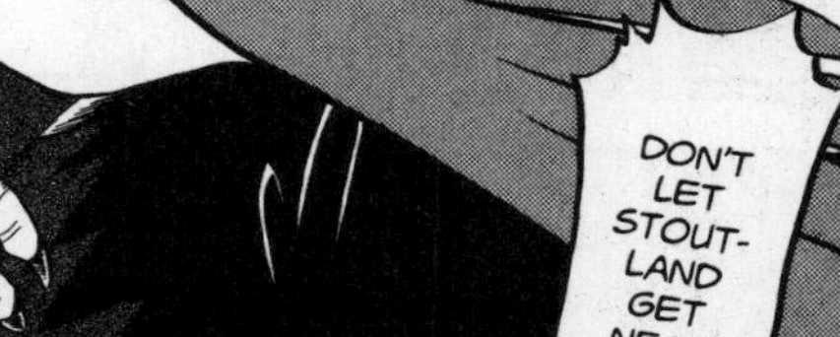
MEAN-WHILE, I GOT-TA...
...DO SOME THINKING!! I NEED A BRIGHT IDEA!

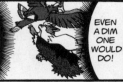

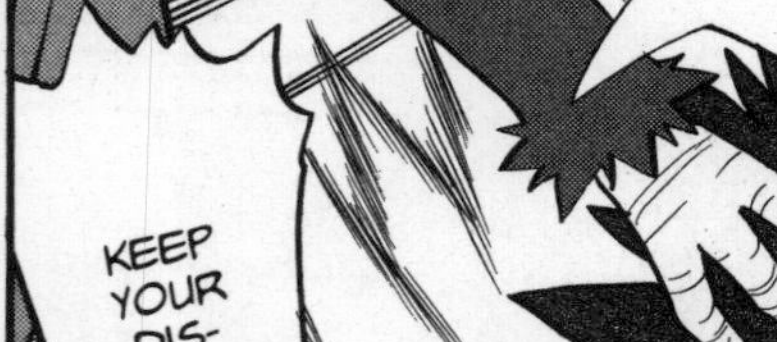
EVEN A DIM ONE WOULD DO!
I'VE GOT TO COOK UP A PLAN TO DEFEAT STOUT-LAND!

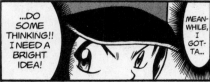

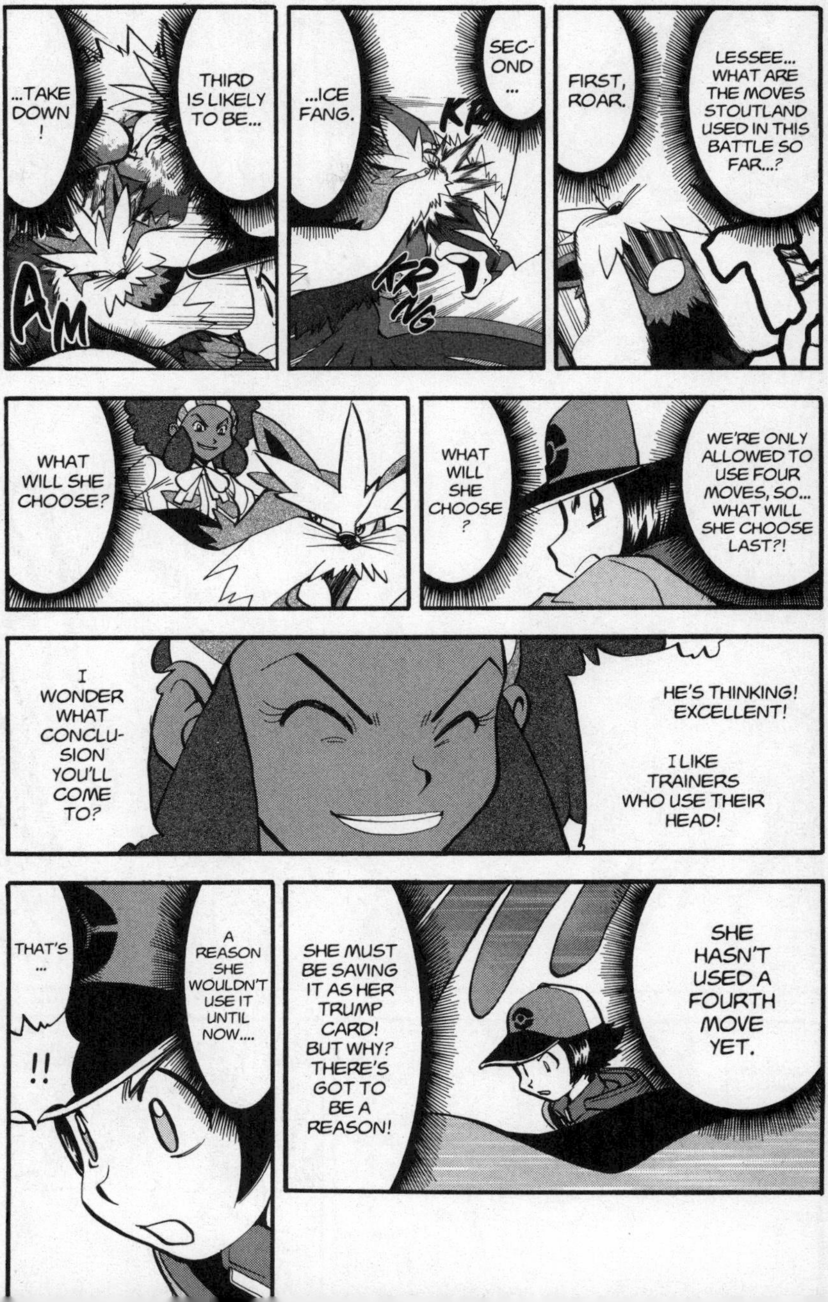
LESSEE... WHAT ARE THE MOVES STOUTLAND USED IN THIS BATTLE SO FAR...?
FIRST, ROAR.
SEC-OND ...
KR
...ICE FANG.
KRRNG
THIRD IS LIKELY TO BE...
...TAKE DOWN!
AM
WE'RE ONLY ALLOWED TO USE FOUR MOVES, SO... WHAT WILL SHE CHOOSE LAST?!
WHAT WILL SHE CHOOSE?
WHAT WILL SHE CHOOSE?
HE'S THINKING! EXCELLENT!
I LIKE TRAINERS WHO USE THEIR HEAD!
I WONDER WHAT CONCLUSION YOU'LL COME TO?
SHE HASN'T USED A FOURTH MOVE YET.
SHE MUST BE SAVING IT AS HER TRUMP CARD! BUT WHY? THERE'S GOT TO BE A REASON!
A REASON SHE WOULDN'T USE IT UNTIL NOW....
THAT'S ...
!!

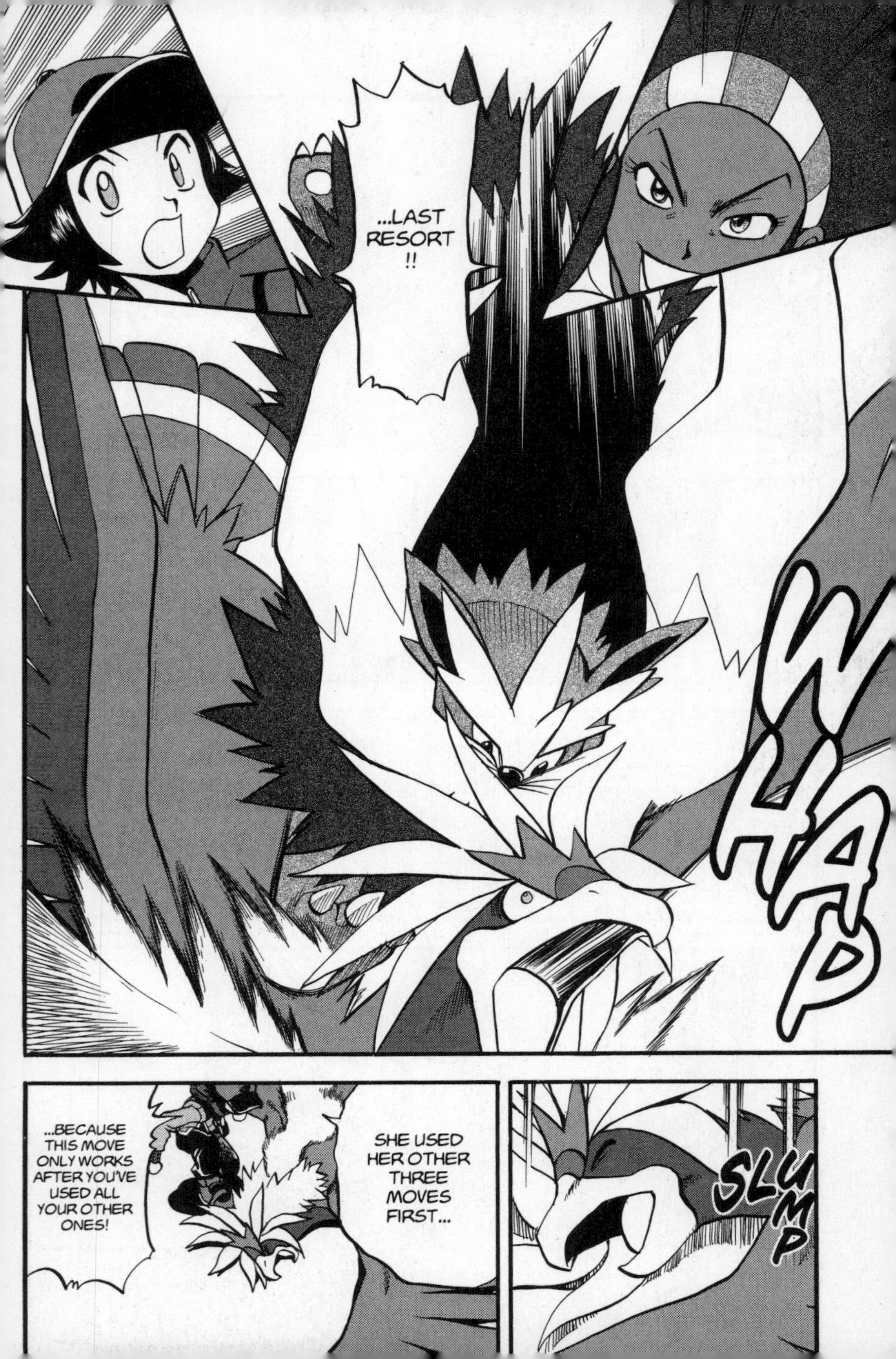
...LAST RESORT !!
WHAP
SLUMP
SHE USED HER OTHER THREE MOVES FIRST...
...BECAUSE THIS MOVE ONLY WORKS AFTER YOU'VE USED ALL YOUR OTHER ONES!

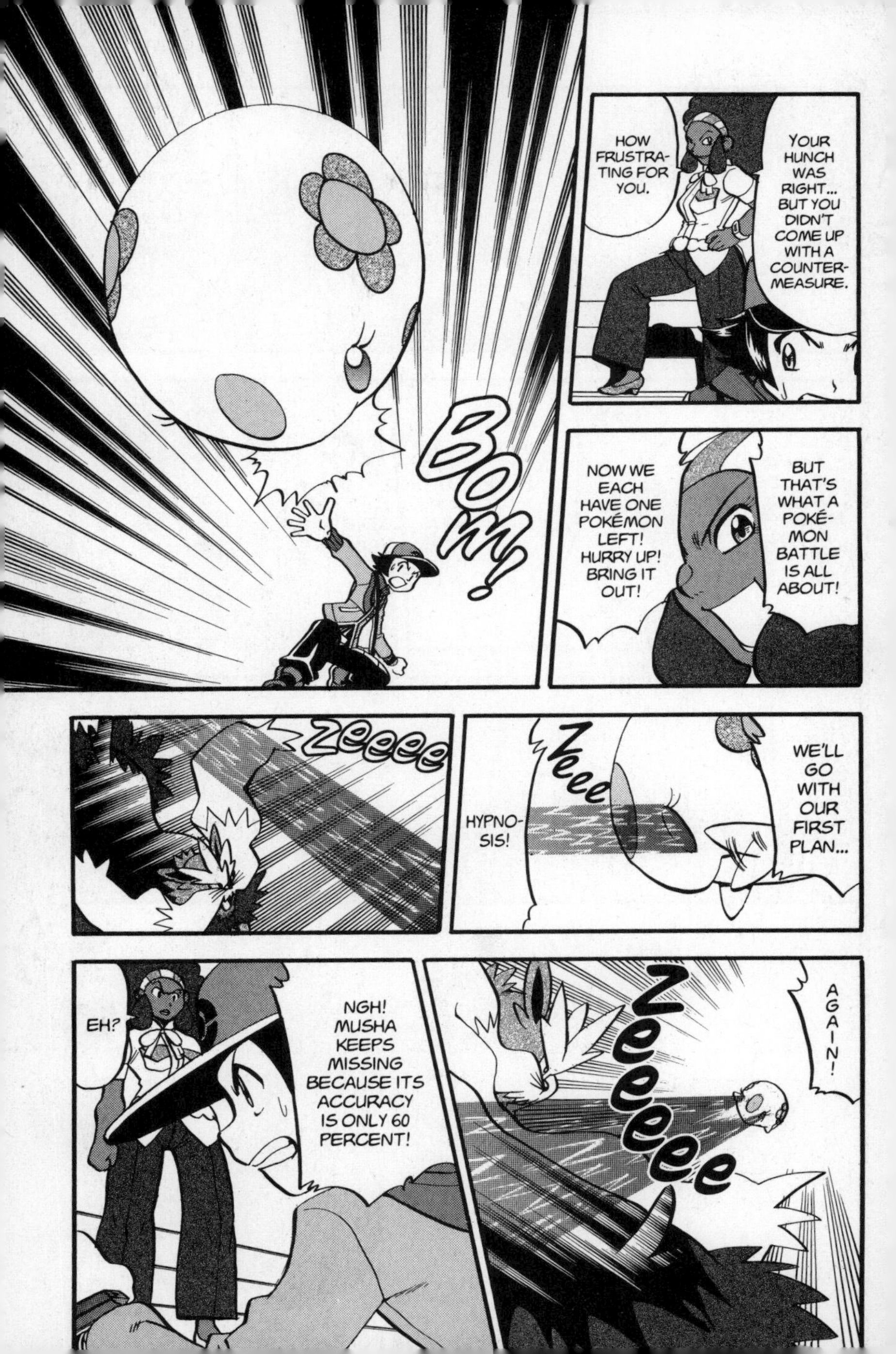
YOUR HUNCH WAS RIGHT... BUT YOU DIDN'T COME UP WITH A COUNTER-MEASURE.
HOW FRUSTRATING FOR YOU.
BUT THAT'S WHAT A POKÉMON BATTLE IS ALL ABOUT!
NOW WE EACH HAVE ONE POKÉMON LEFT! HURRY UP! BRING IT OUT!
BOOM!
WE'LL GO WITH OUR FIRST PLAN...
Zeee
HYPNOSIS!
Zeeee
AGAIN!
Zeeeeee
NGH! MUSHA KEEPS MISSING BECAUSE ITS ACCURACY IS ONLY 60 PERCENT!
EH?

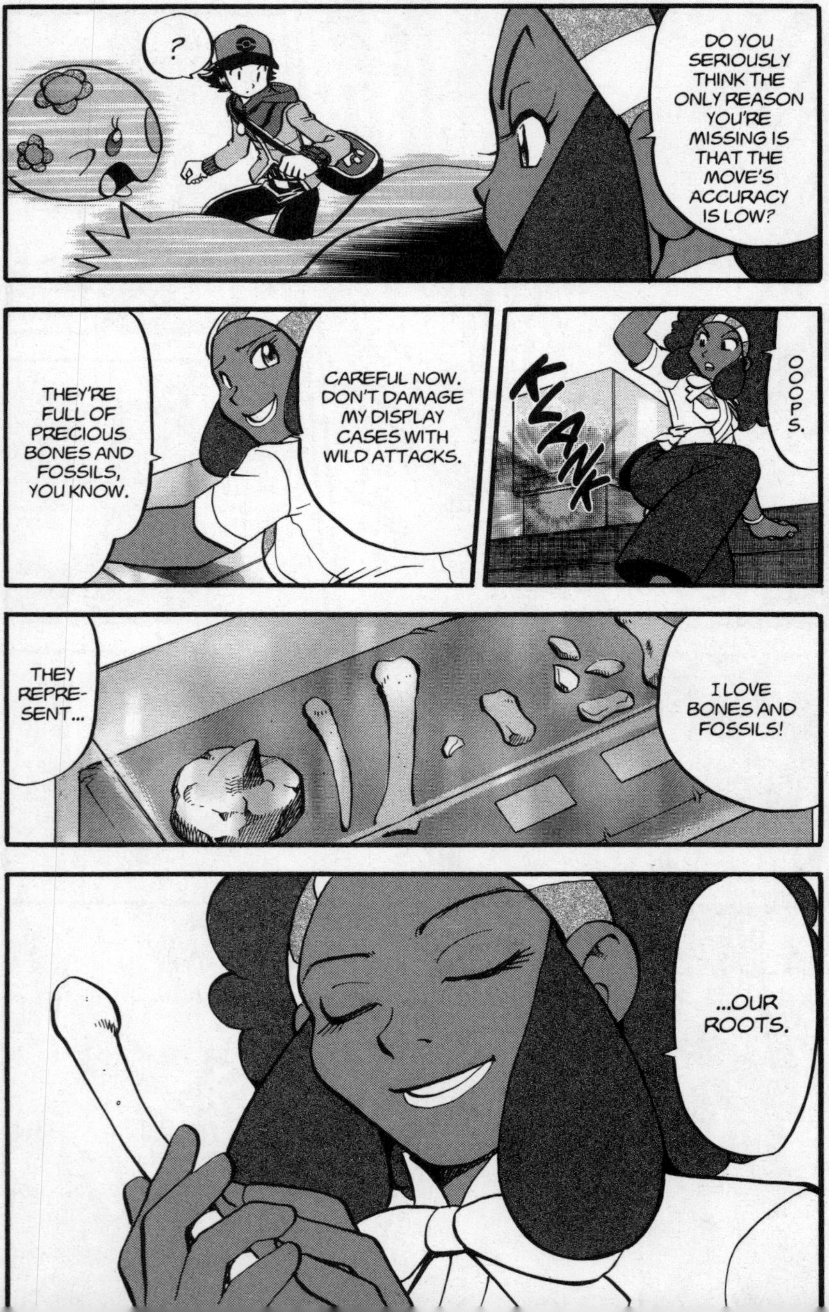
DO YOU SERIOUSLY THINK THE ONLY REASON YOU'RE MISSING IS THAT THE MOVE'S ACCURACY IS LOW?
?
KLANK
OOOPS.
CAREFUL NOW. DON'T DAMAGE MY DISPLAY CASES WITH WILD ATTACKS.
THEY'RE FULL OF PRECIOUS BONES AND FOSSILS, YOU KNOW.
I LOVE BONES AND FOSSILS!
THEY REPRE-SENT...
...OUR ROOTS.

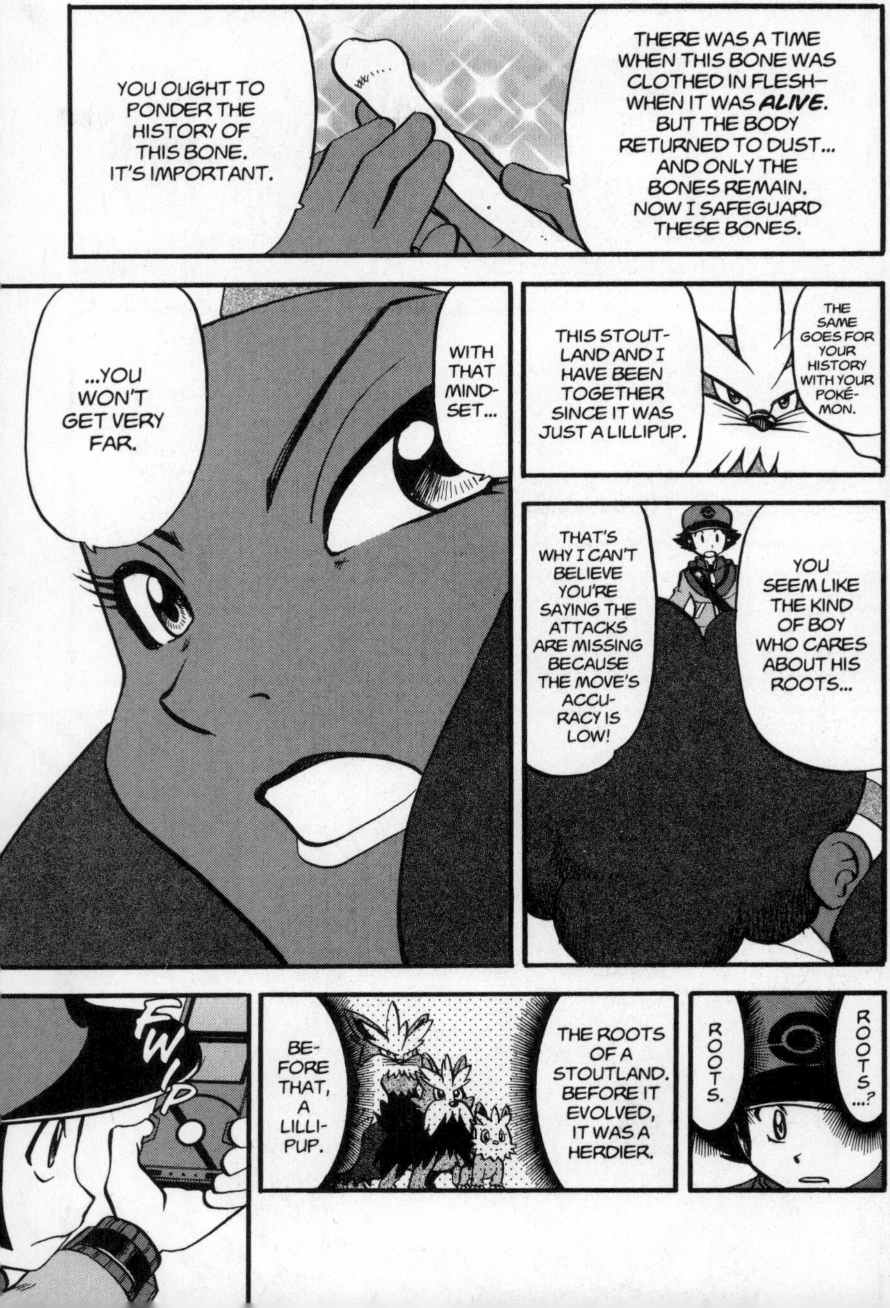
THERE WAS A TIME WHEN THIS BONE WAS CLOTHED IN FLESH— WHEN IT WAS **ALIVE**. BUT THE BODY RETURNED TO DUST... AND ONLY THE BONES REMAIN. NOW I SAFEGUARD THESE BONES.
YOU OUGHT TO PONDER THE HISTORY OF THIS BONE. IT'S IMPORTANT.
THE SAME GOES FOR YOUR HISTORY WITH YOUR POKÉ-MON.
THIS STOUT-LAND AND I HAVE BEEN TOGETHER SINCE IT WAS JUST A LILLIPUP.
YOU SEEM LIKE THE KIND OF BOY WHO CARES ABOUT HIS ROOTS...
THAT'S WHY I CAN'T BELIEVE YOU'RE SAYING THE ATTACKS ARE MISSING BECAUSE THE MOVE'S ACCU-RACY IS LOW!
WITH THAT MIND-SET...
...YOU WON'T GET VERY FAR.
ROOTS...?
ROOTS.
THE ROOTS OF A STOUTLAND. BEFORE IT EVOLVED, IT WAS A HERDIER.
BE-FORE THAT, A LILLI-PUP.
FWIP

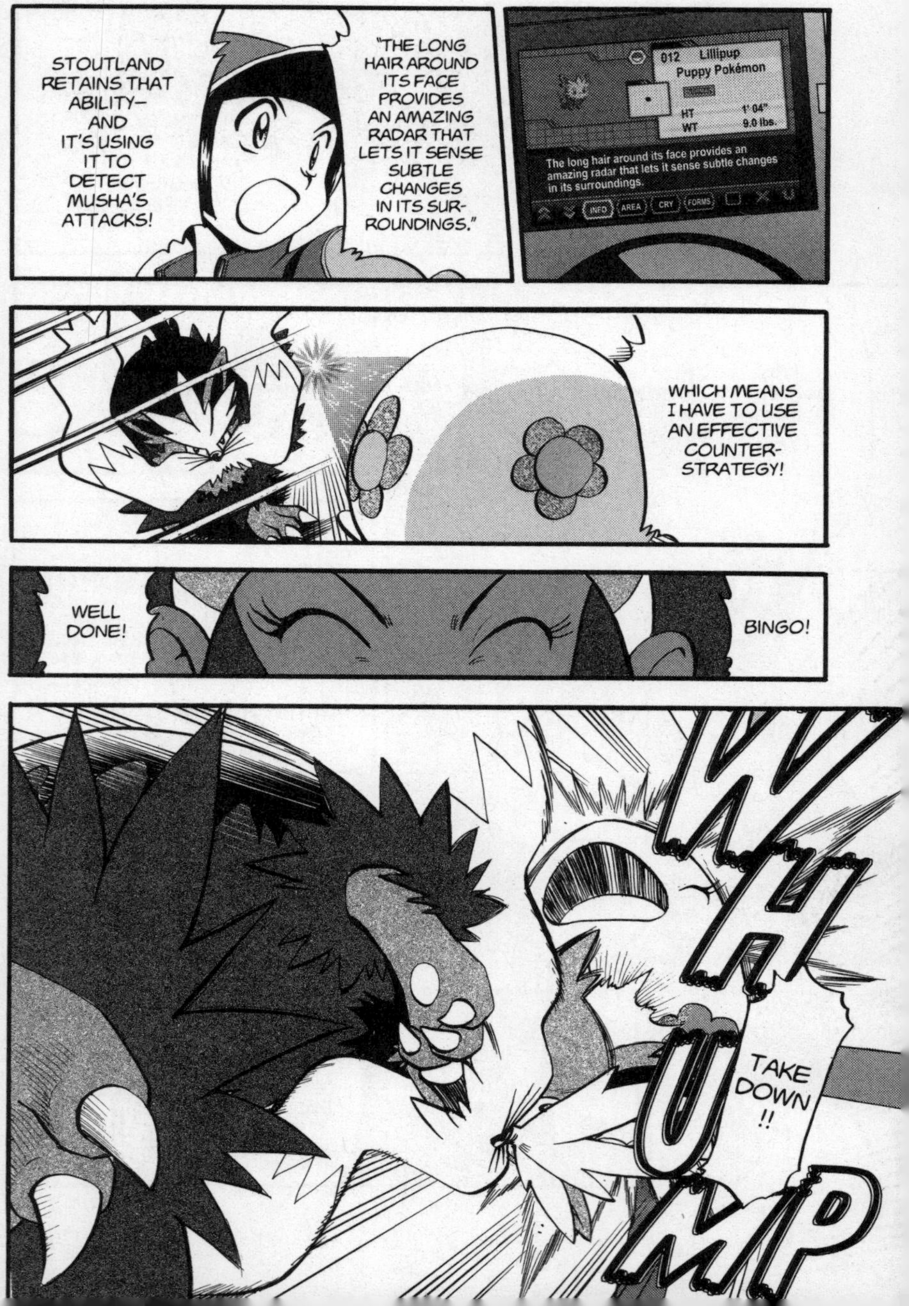
012 Lillipup
Puppy Pokémon
HT 1' 04"
WT 9.0 lbs.
The long hair around its face provides an amazing radar that lets it sense subtle changes in its surroundings.
INFO AREA CRY FORMS
"THE LONG HAIR AROUND ITS FACE PROVIDES AN AMAZING RADAR THAT LETS IT SENSE SUBTLE CHANGES IN ITS SURROUNDINGS."
STOUTLAND RETAINS THAT ABILITY—AND IT'S USING IT TO DETECT MUSHA'S ATTACKS!
WHICH MEANS I HAVE TO USE AN EFFECTIVE COUNTER-STRATEGY!
BINGO!
WELL DONE!
WHUMP
TAKE DOWN!!

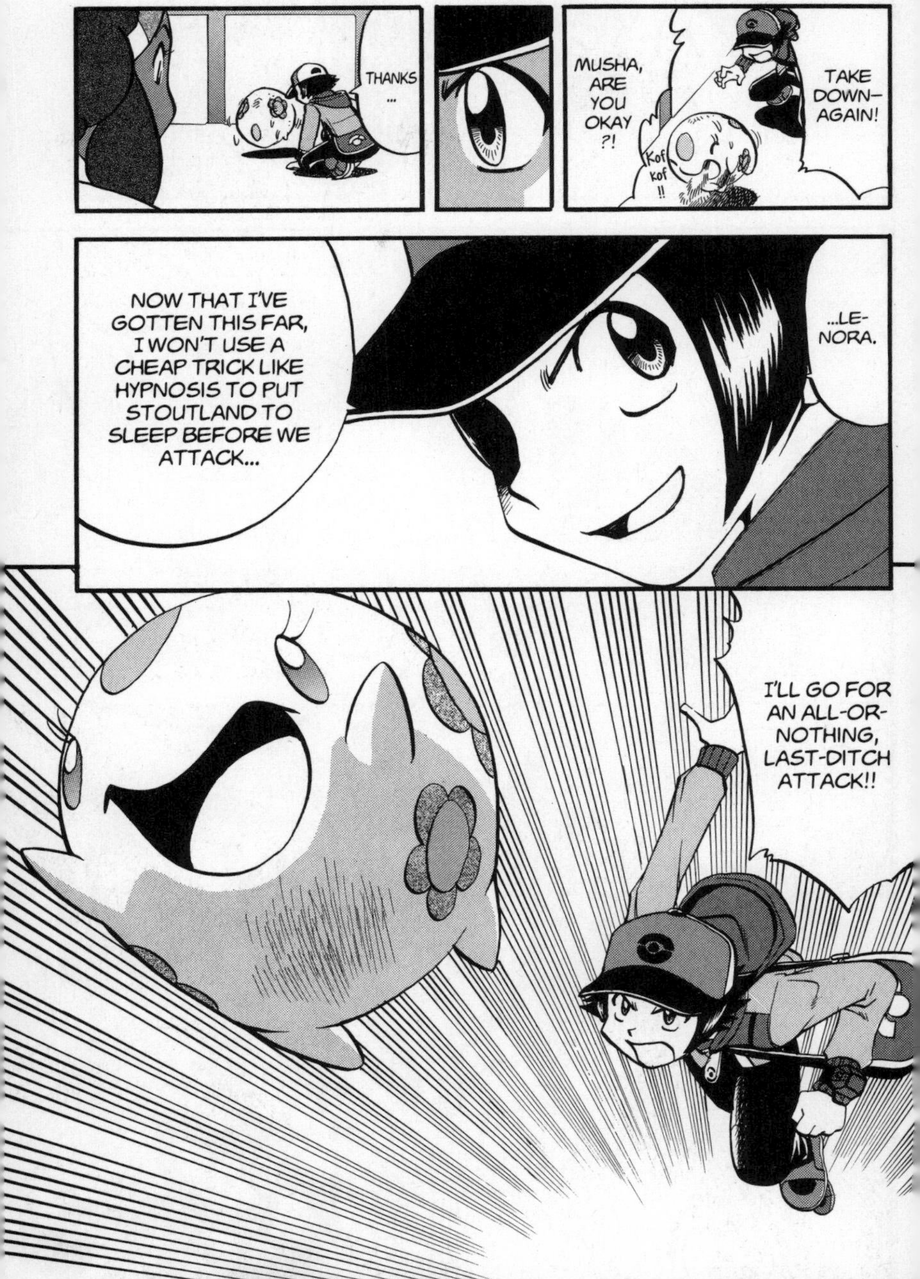
TAKE DOWN— AGAIN!
MUSHA, ARE YOU OKAY ?!
Kof kof !!
THANKS ...
...LE- NORA.
NOW THAT I'VE GOTTEN THIS FAR, I WON'T USE A CHEAP TRICK LIKE HYPNOSIS TO PUT STOUTLAND TO SLEEP BEFORE WE ATTACK...
I'LL GO FOR AN ALL-OR-NOTHING, LAST-DITCH ATTACK!!

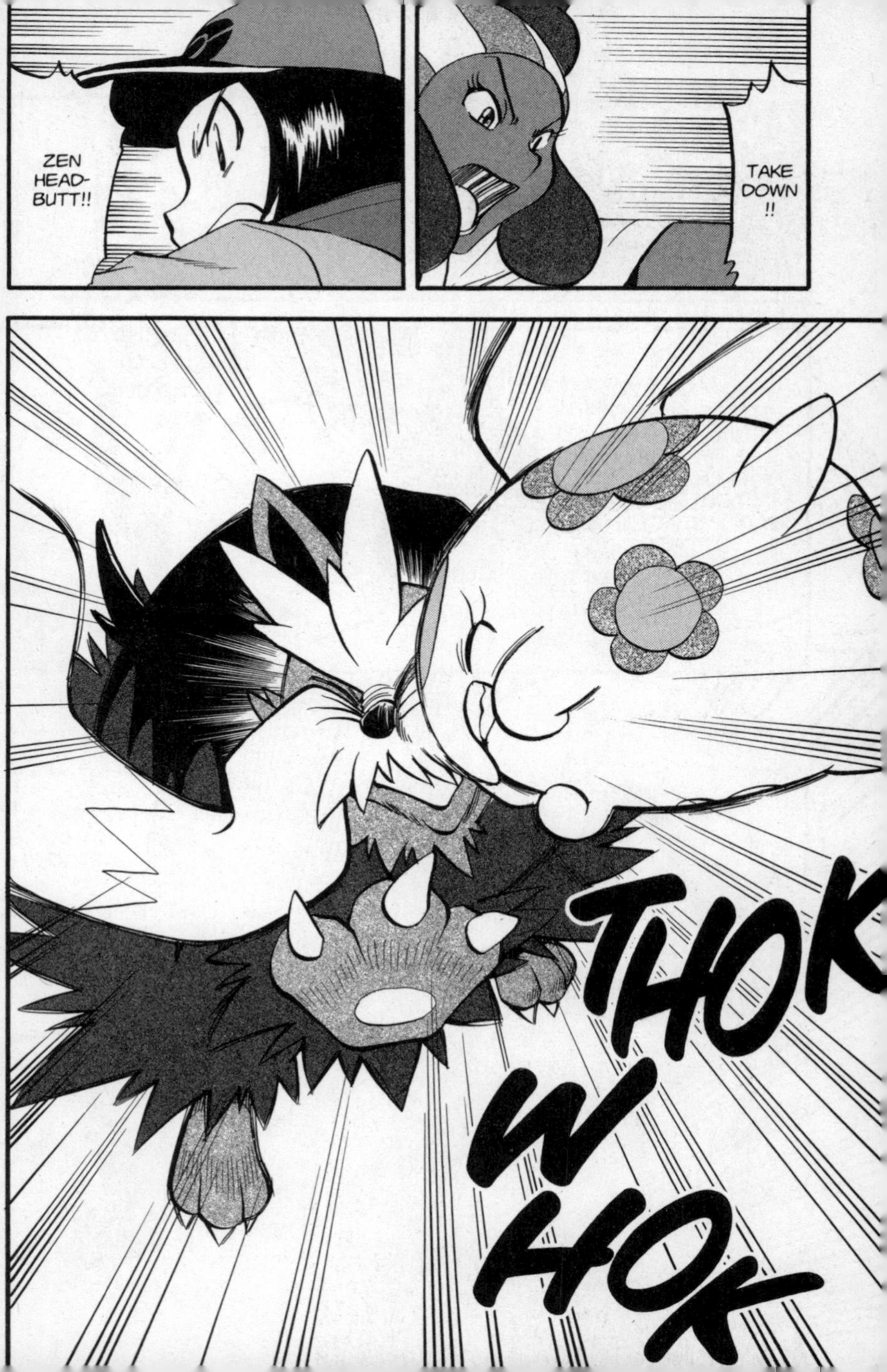
TAKE DOWN!!
ZEN HEAD-BUTT!!
THOK WHOK

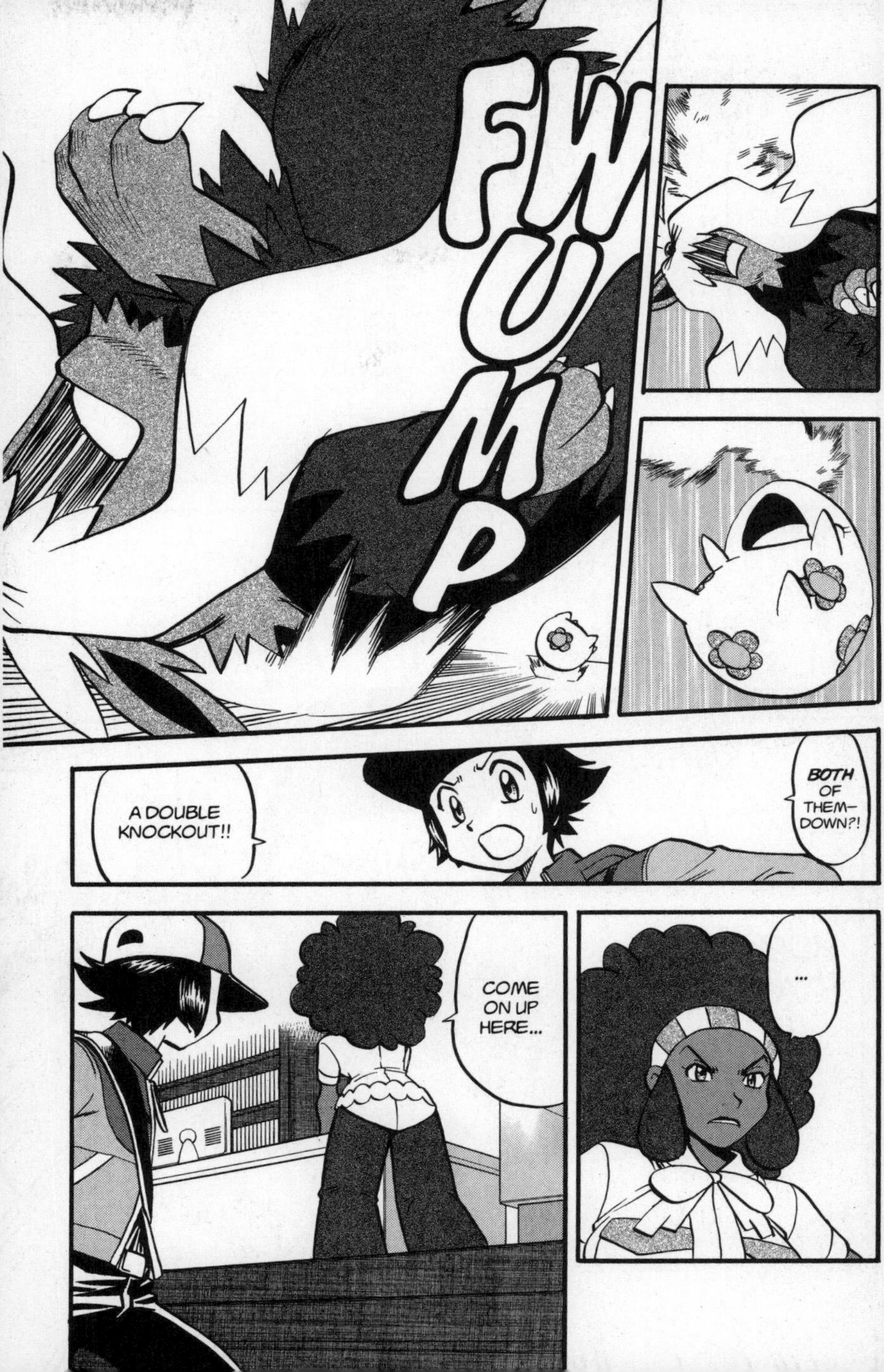
FWUMP
BOTH OF THEM— DOWN?!
A DOUBLE KNOCKOUT!!
...
COME ON UP HERE...

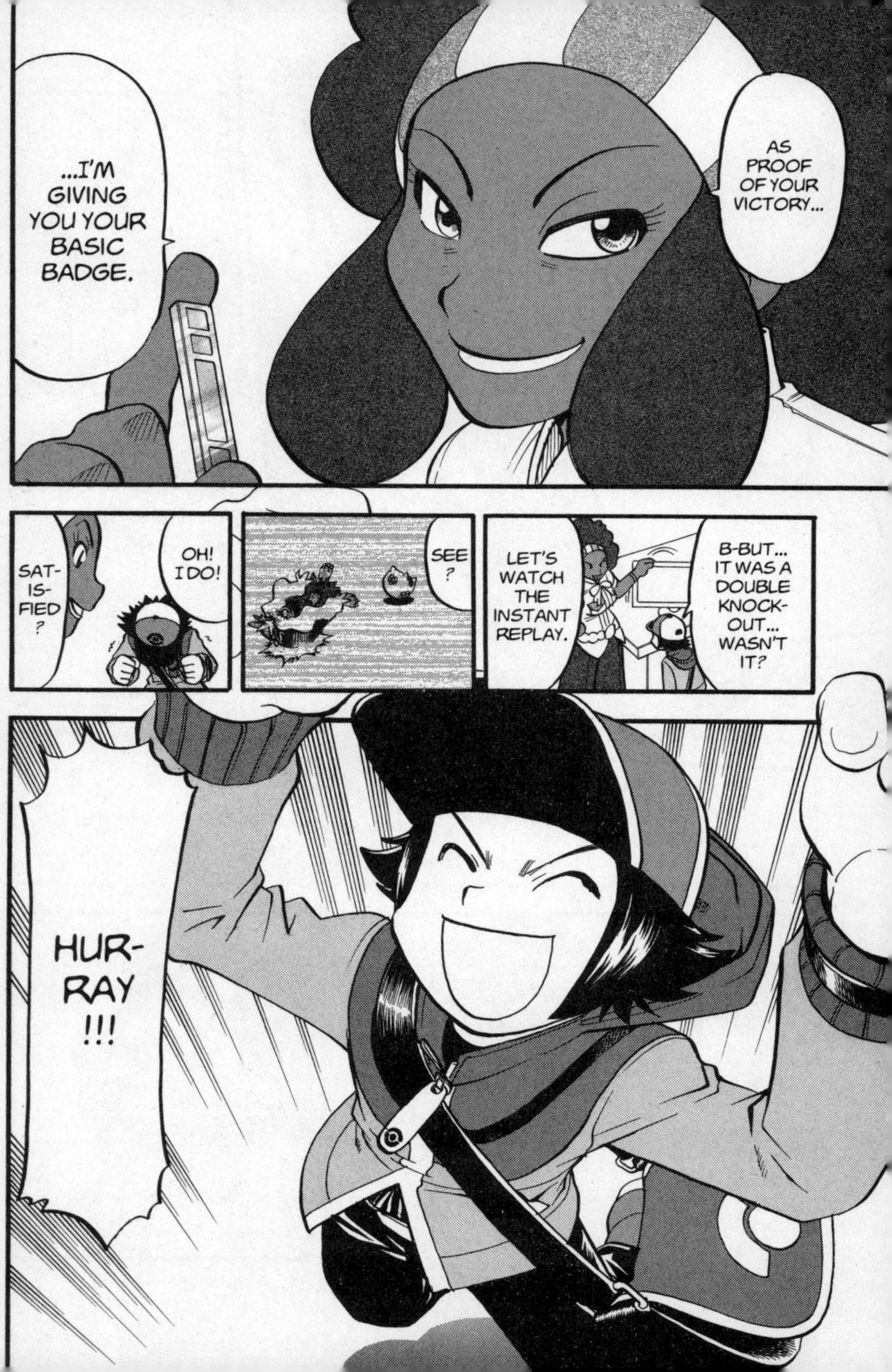
AS PROOF OF YOUR VICTORY...
...I'M GIVING YOU YOUR BASIC BADGE.
B-BUT... IT WAS A DOUBLE KNOCK-OUT... WASN'T IT?
LET'S WATCH THE INSTANT REPLAY.
SEE?
OH! I DO!
SAT-IS-FIED?
HUR-RAY!!!

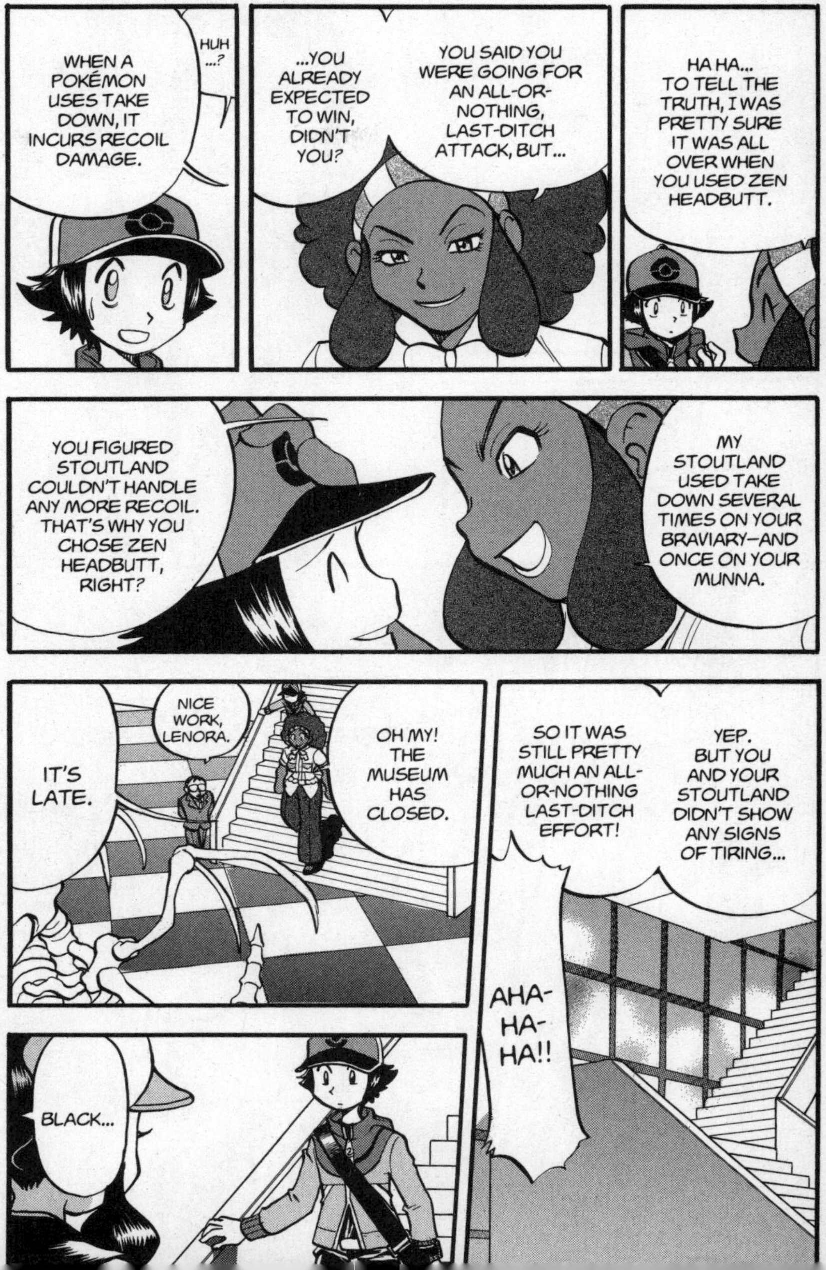
HA HA... TO TELL THE TRUTH, I WAS PRETTY SURE IT WAS ALL OVER WHEN YOU USED ZEN HEADBUTT.
YOU SAID YOU WERE GOING FOR AN ALL-OR-NOTHING, LAST-DITCH ATTACK, BUT...
...YOU ALREADY EXPECTED TO WIN, DIDN'T YOU?
HUH ...?
WHEN A POKÉMON USES TAKE DOWN, IT INCURS RECOIL DAMAGE.
MY STOUTLAND USED TAKE DOWN SEVERAL TIMES ON YOUR BRAVIARY—AND ONCE ON YOUR MUNNA.
YOU FIGURED STOUTLAND COULDN'T HANDLE ANY MORE RECOIL. THAT'S WHY YOU CHOSE ZEN HEADBUTT, RIGHT?
YEP. BUT YOU AND YOUR STOUTLAND DIDN'T SHOW ANY SIGNS OF TIRING...
SO IT WAS STILL PRETTY MUCH AN ALL-OR-NOTHING LAST-DITCH EFFORT!
AHA-HA-HA!!
OH MY! THE MUSEUM HAS CLOSED.
NICE WORK, LENORA.
IT'S LATE.
BLACK...

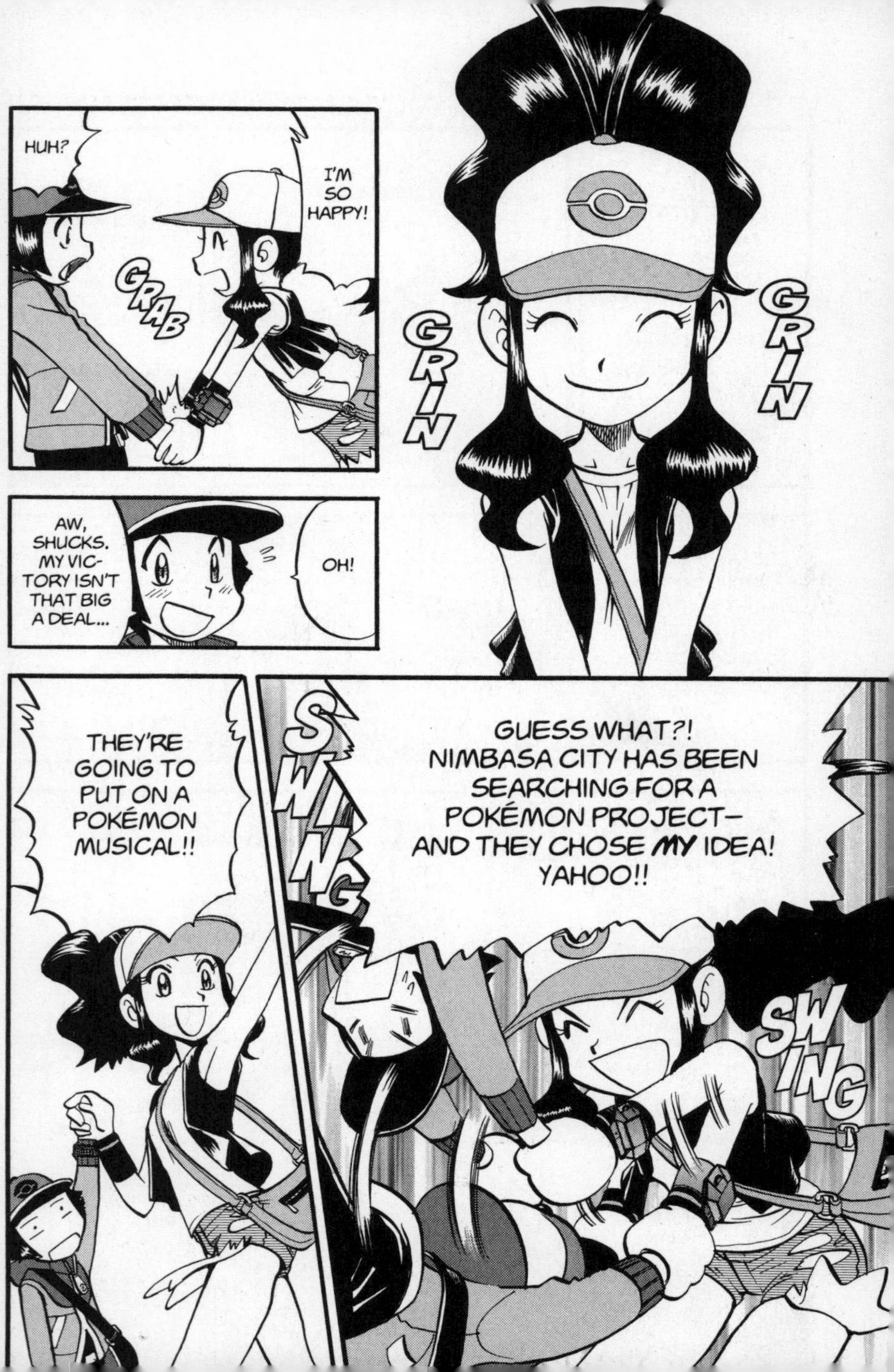

GRIN
GRIN
I'M SO HAPPY!
HUH?
GRAB
OH!
AW, SHUCKS. MY VICTORY ISN'T THAT BIG A DEAL...
GUESS WHAT?! NIMBASA CITY HAS BEEN SEARCHING FOR A POKÉMON PROJECT—AND THEY CHOSE *MY* IDEA! YAHOO!!
SWING
SWING
THEY'RE GOING TO PUT ON A POKÉMON MUSICAL!!

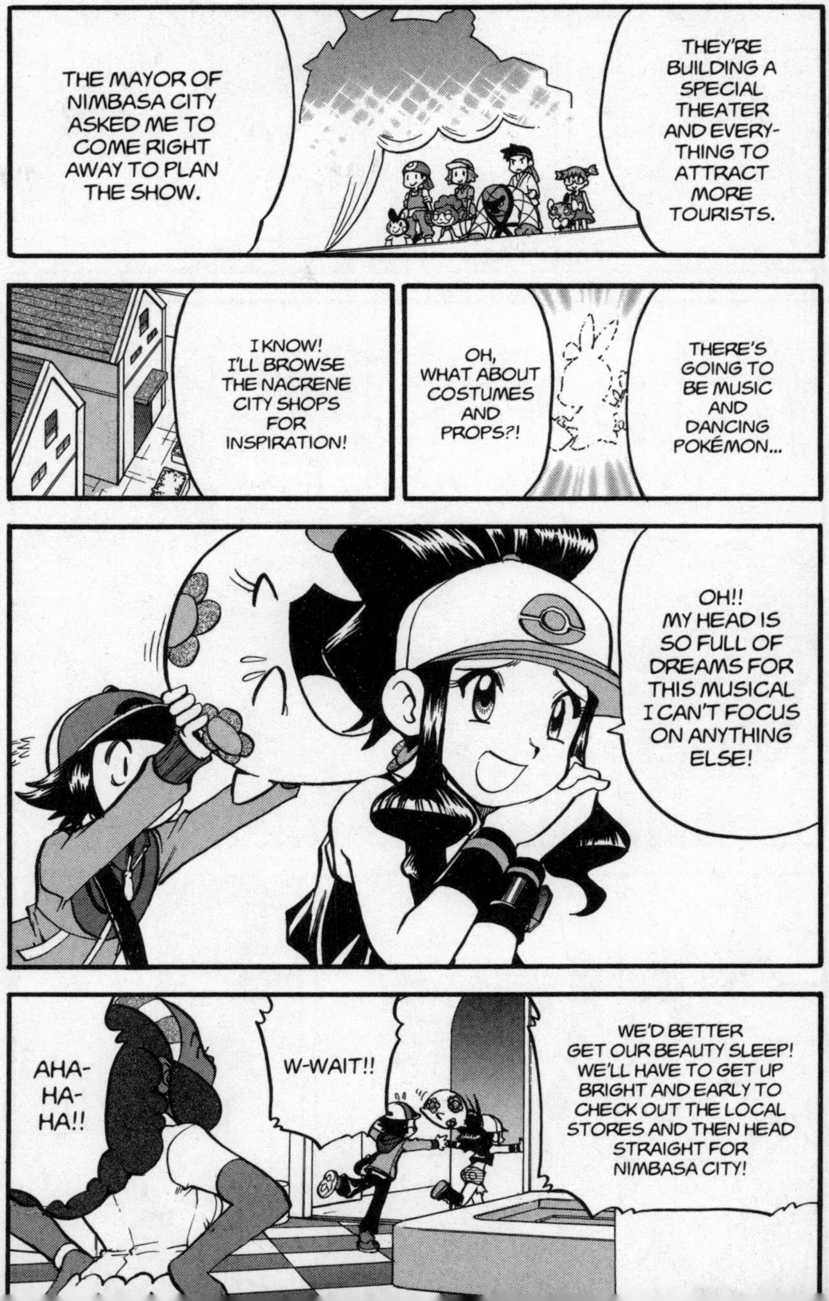
THEY'RE BUILDING A SPECIAL THEATER AND EVERY-THING TO ATTRACT MORE TOURISTS.
THE MAYOR OF NIMBASA CITY ASKED ME TO COME RIGHT AWAY TO PLAN THE SHOW.
THERE'S GOING TO BE MUSIC AND DANCING POKÉMON...
OH, WHAT ABOUT COSTUMES AND PROPS?!
I KNOW! I'LL BROWSE THE NACRENE CITY SHOPS FOR INSPIRATION!
OH!! MY HEAD IS SO FULL OF DREAMS FOR THIS MUSICAL I CAN'T FOCUS ON ANYTHING ELSE!
WE'D BETTER GET OUR BEAUTY SLEEP! WE'LL HAVE TO GET UP BRIGHT AND EARLY TO CHECK OUT THE LOCAL STORES AND THEN HEAD STRAIGHT FOR NIMBASA CITY!
W-WAIT!!
AHA-HA-HA!!

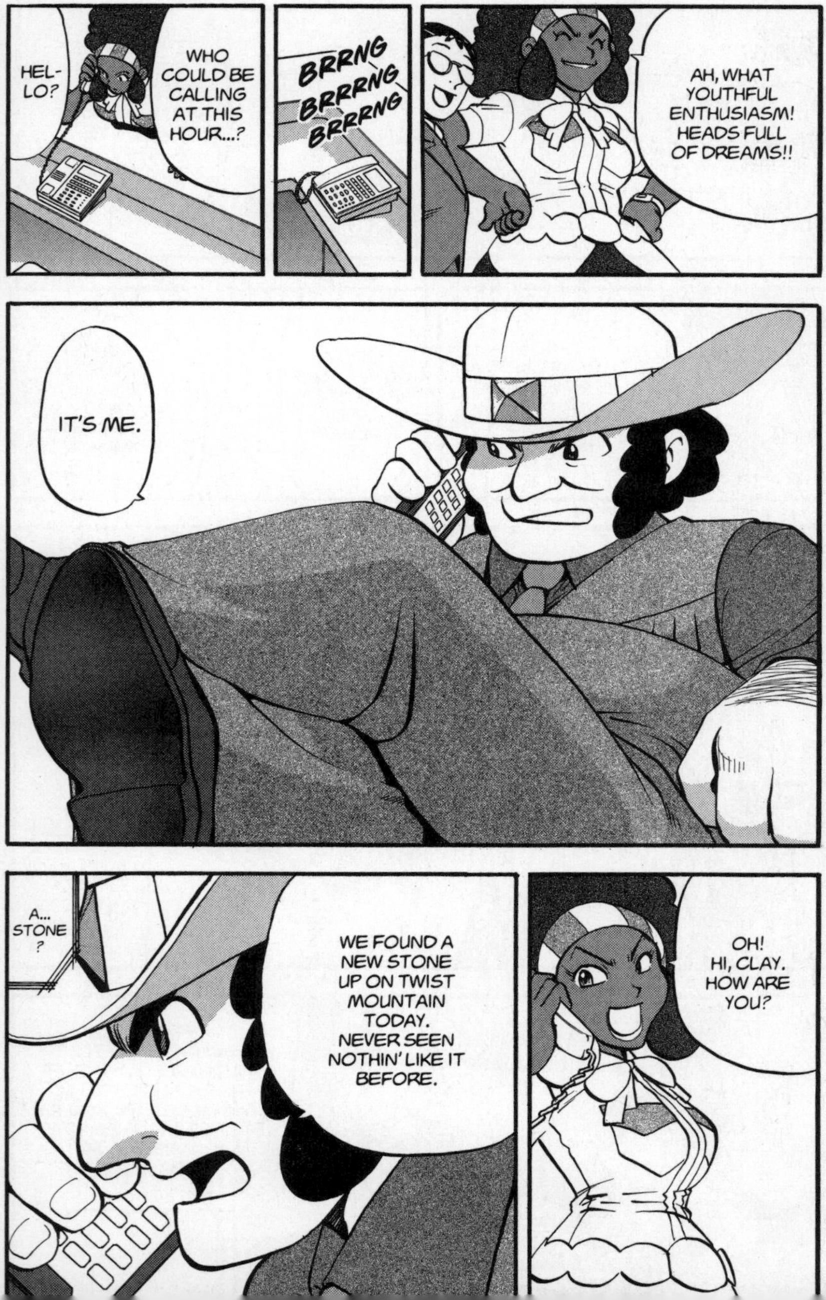
AH, WHAT YOUTHFUL ENTHUSIASM! HEADS FULL OF DREAMS!!
BRRNG
BRRRNG
BRRRNG
WHO COULD BE CALLING AT THIS HOUR...?
HEL-LO?
IT'S ME.
OH! HI, CLAY. HOW ARE YOU?
WE FOUND A NEW STONE UP ON TWIST MOUNTAIN TODAY. NEVER SEEN NOTHIN' LIKE IT BEFORE.
A... STONE?

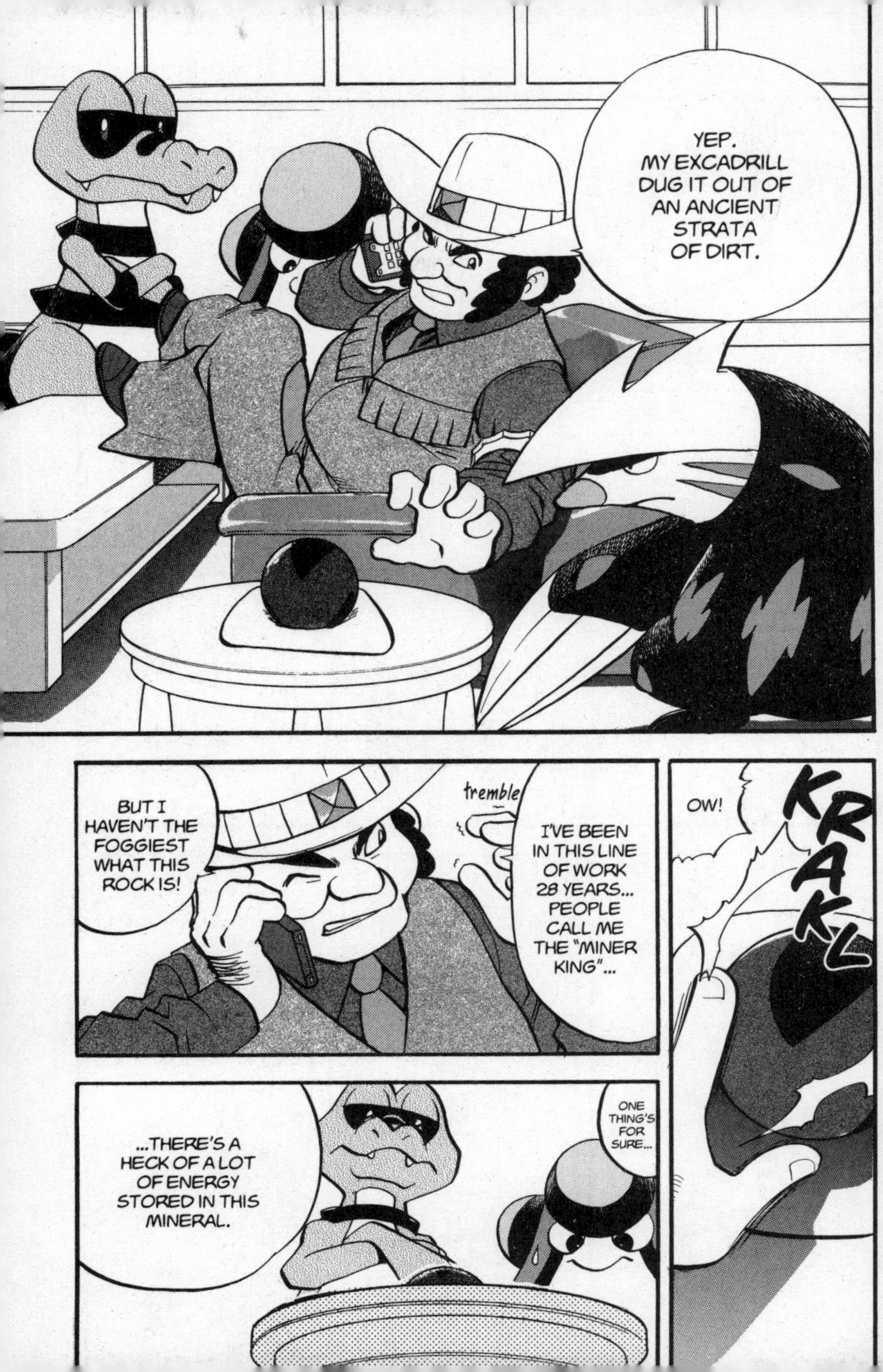
YEP. MY EXCADRILL DUG IT OUT OF AN ANCIENT STRATA OF DIRT.
OW!
KRAKL
tremble
I'VE BEEN IN THIS LINE OF WORK 28 YEARS... PEOPLE CALL ME THE "MINER KING"...
BUT I HAVEN'T THE FOGGIEST WHAT THIS ROCK IS!
ONE THING'S FOR SURE...
...THERE'S A HECK OF A LOT OF ENERGY STORED IN THIS MINERAL.

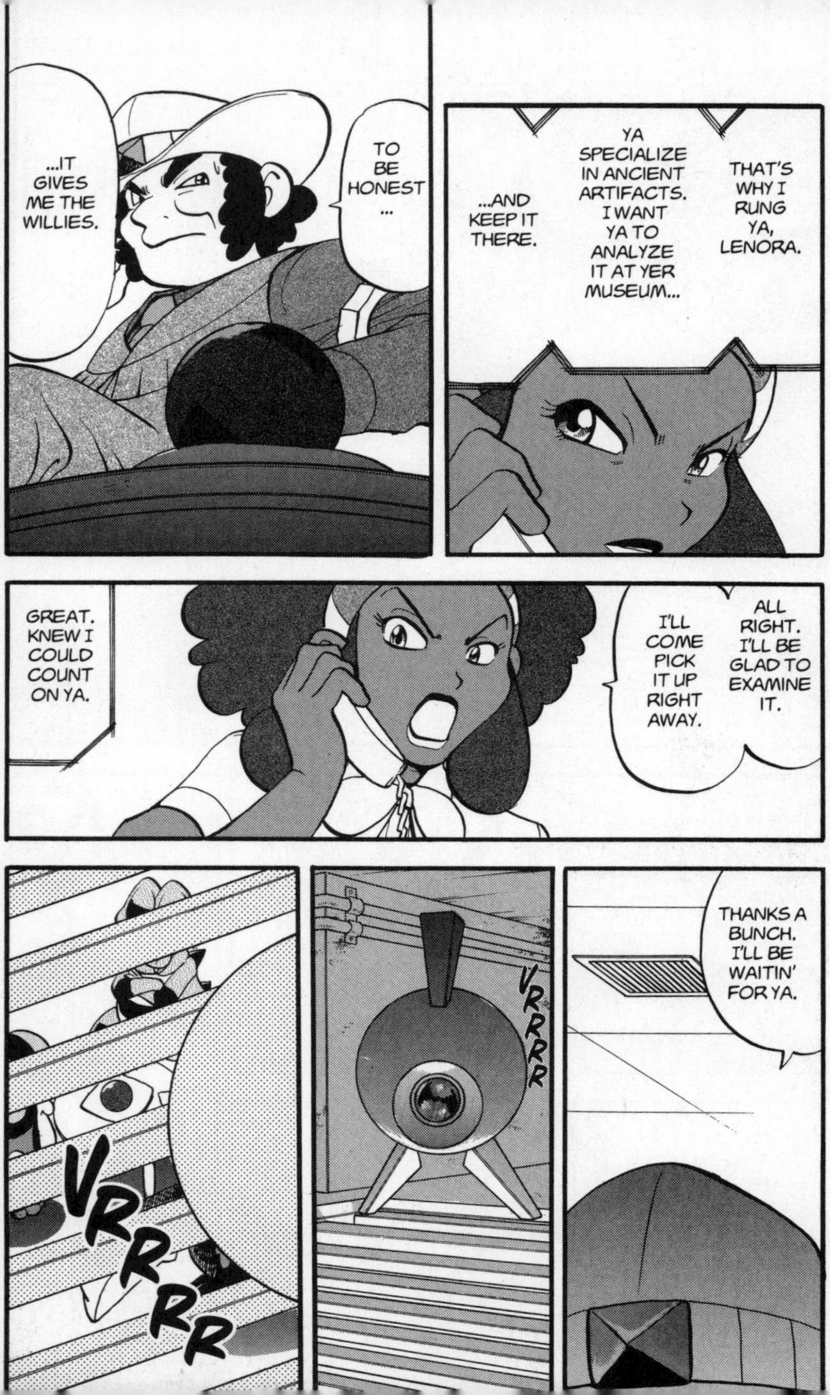
THAT'S WHY I RUNG YA, LENORA.
YA SPECIALIZE IN ANCIENT ARTIFACTS. I WANT YA TO ANALYZE IT AT YER MUSEUM...
...AND KEEP IT THERE.
TO BE HONEST...
...IT GIVES ME THE WILLIES.
ALL RIGHT. I'LL BE GLAD TO EXAMINE IT.
I'LL COME PICK IT UP RIGHT AWAY.
GREAT. KNEW I COULD COUNT ON YA.
THANKS A BUNCH. I'LL BE WAITIN' FOR YA.
VRRRR
VRRRRR

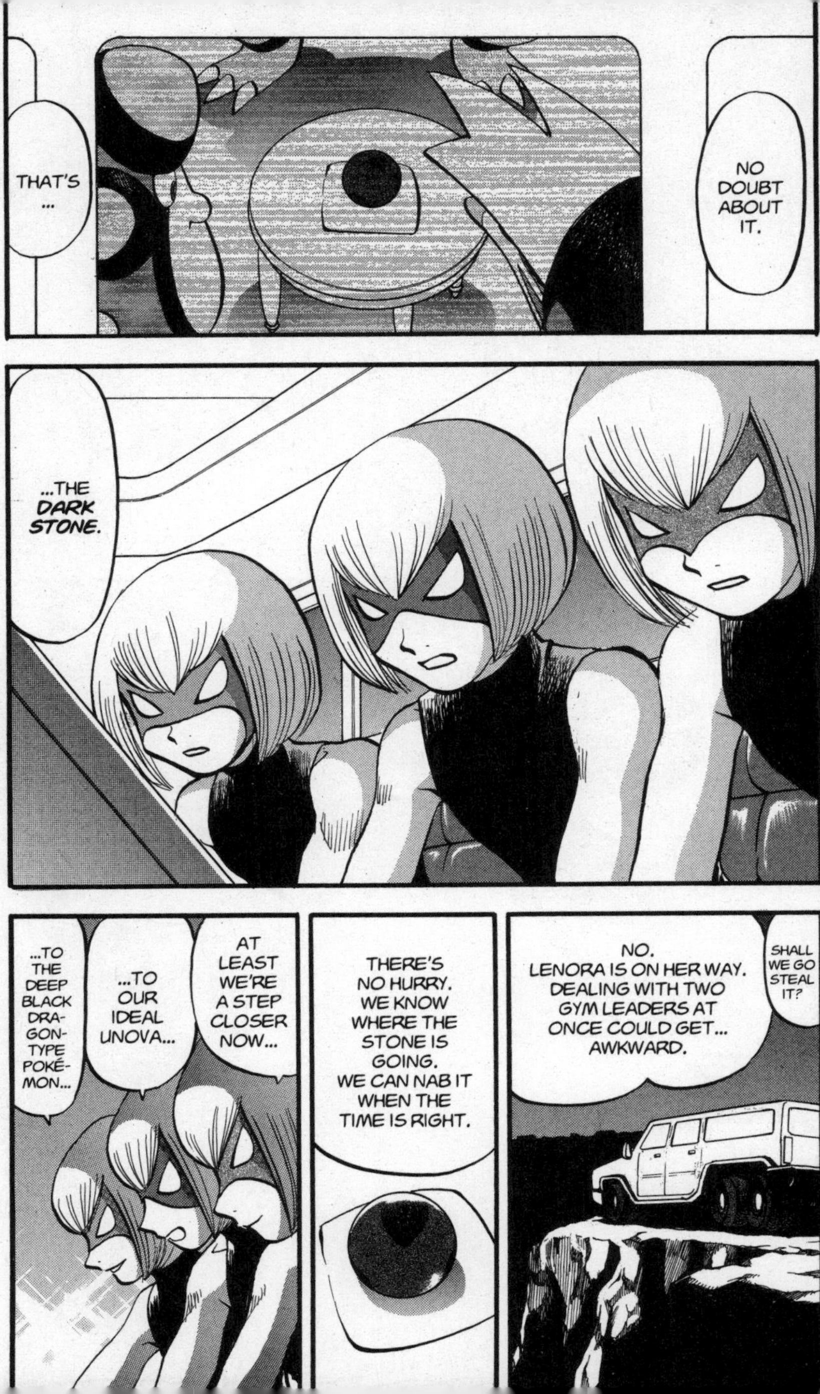
NO DOUBT ABOUT IT.
THAT'S ...
...THE *DARK STONE*.
SHALL WE GO STEAL IT?
NO. LENORA IS ON HER WAY. DEALING WITH TWO GYM LEADERS AT ONCE COULD GET... AWKWARD.
THERE'S NO HURRY. WE KNOW WHERE THE STONE IS GOING. WE CAN NAB IT WHEN THE TIME IS RIGHT.
AT LEAST WE'RE A STEP CLOSER NOW...
...TO OUR IDEAL UNOVA...
...TO THE DEEP BLACK DRAGON-TYPE POKÉMON...

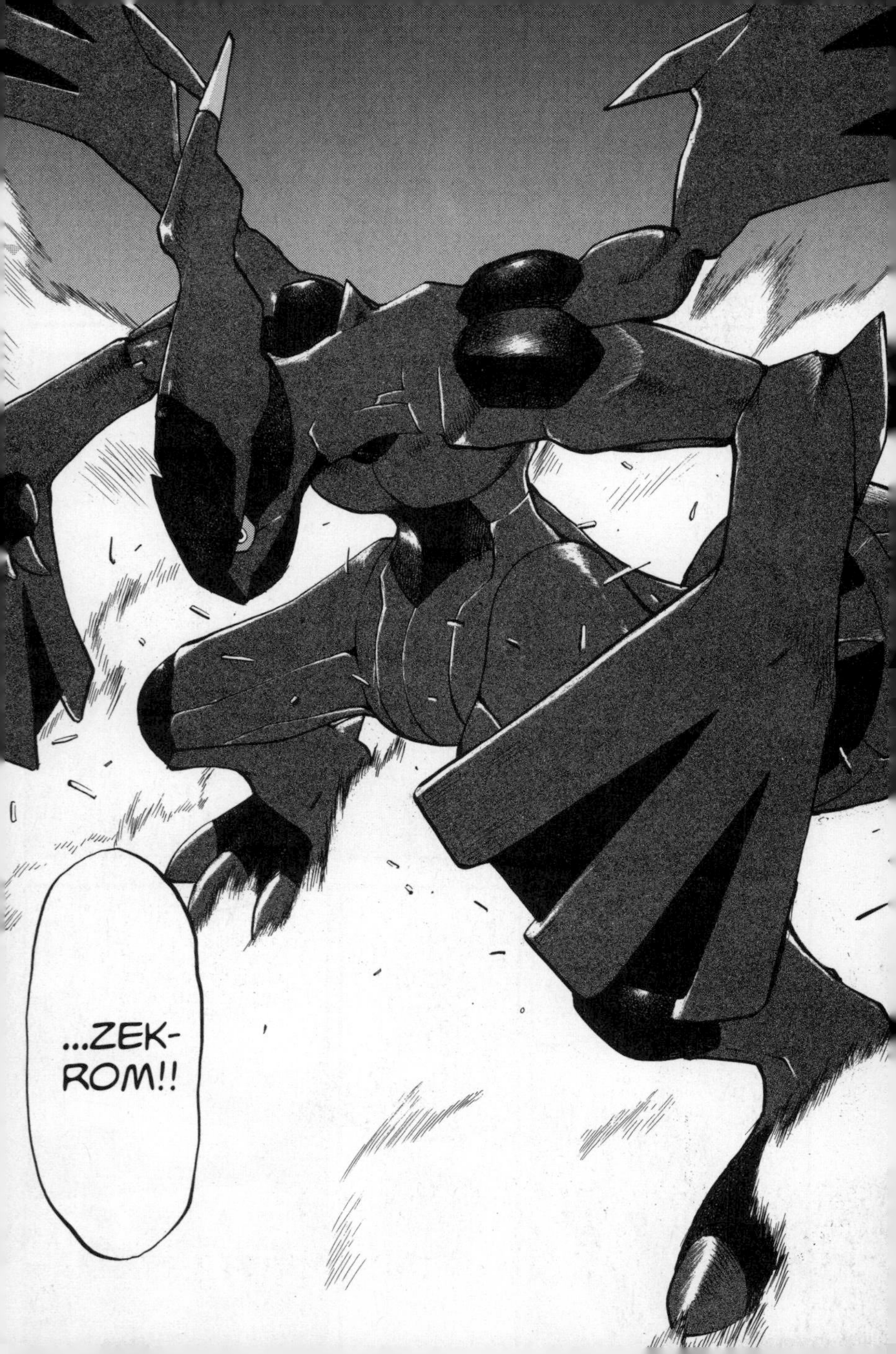
...ZEK-
ROM!!

Pokémon™ Adventures Black & White

COFAGRIGUS

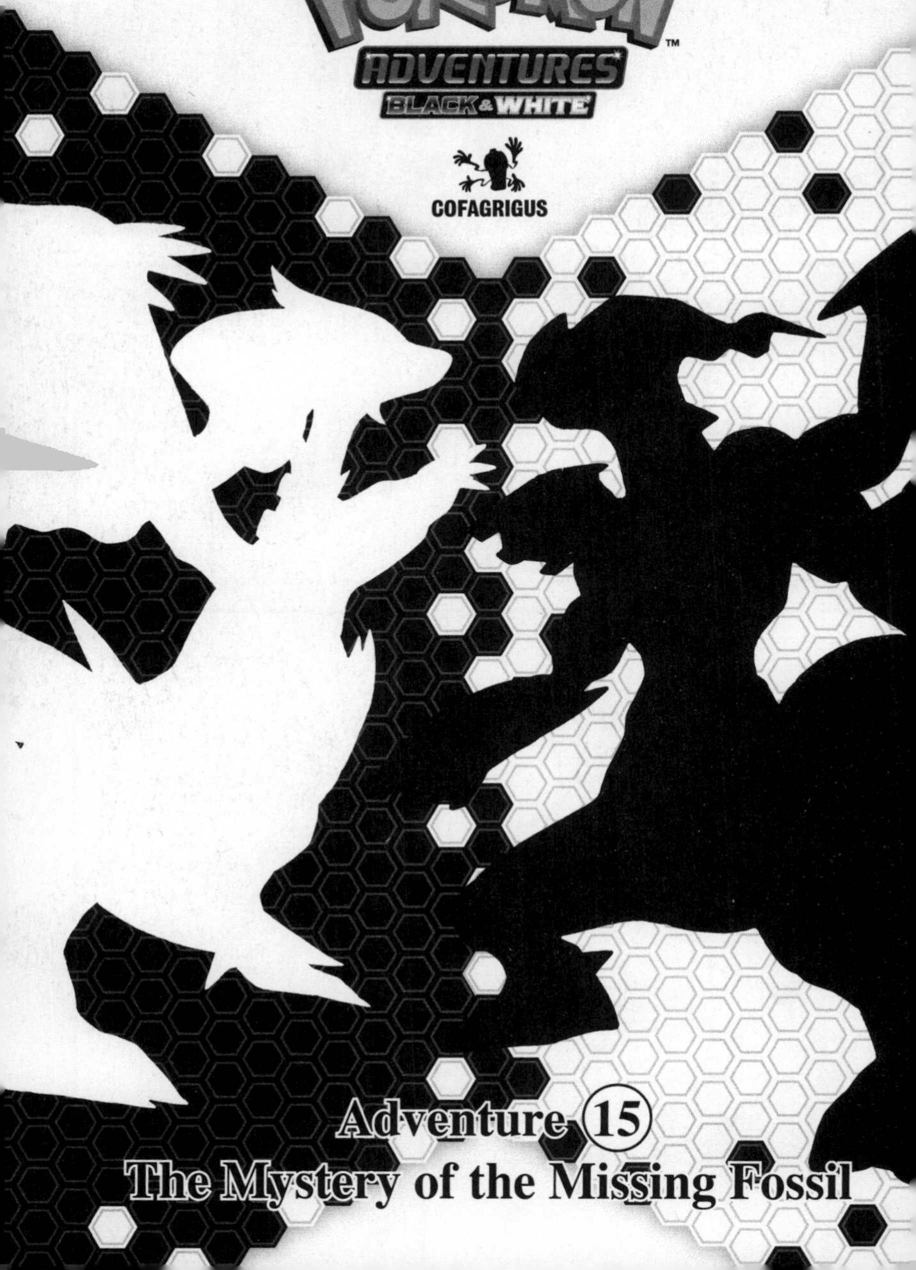

Adventure 15
The Mystery of the Missing Fossil

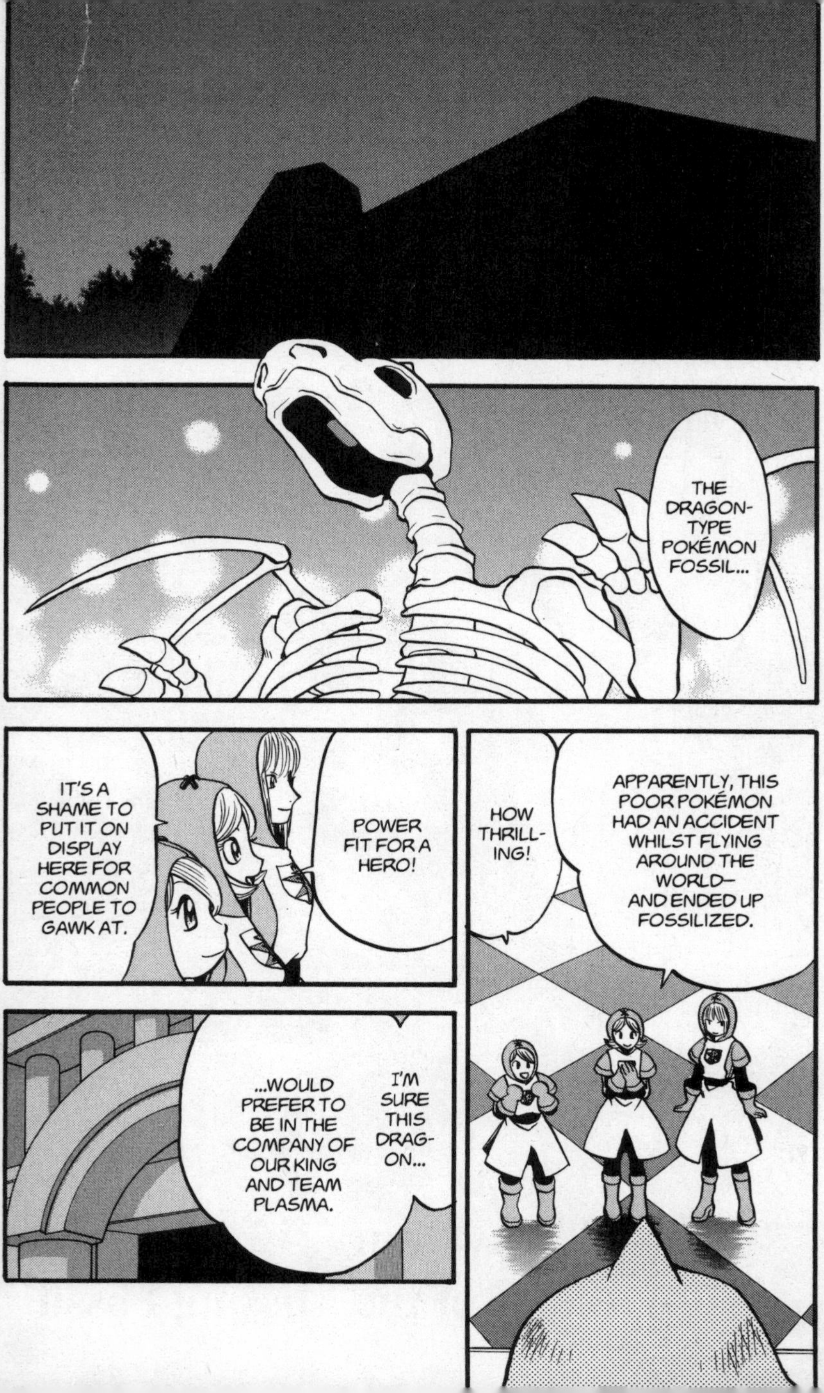
THE DRAGON-TYPE POKÉMON FOSSIL...
APPARENTLY, THIS POOR POKÉMON HAD AN ACCIDENT WHILST FLYING AROUND THE WORLD— AND ENDED UP FOSSILIZED.
HOW THRILLING!
POWER FIT FOR A HERO!
IT'S A SHAME TO PUT IT ON DISPLAY HERE FOR COMMON PEOPLE TO GAWK AT.
I'M SURE THIS DRAGON...
...WOULD PREFER TO BE IN THE COMPANY OF OUR KING AND TEAM PLASMA.

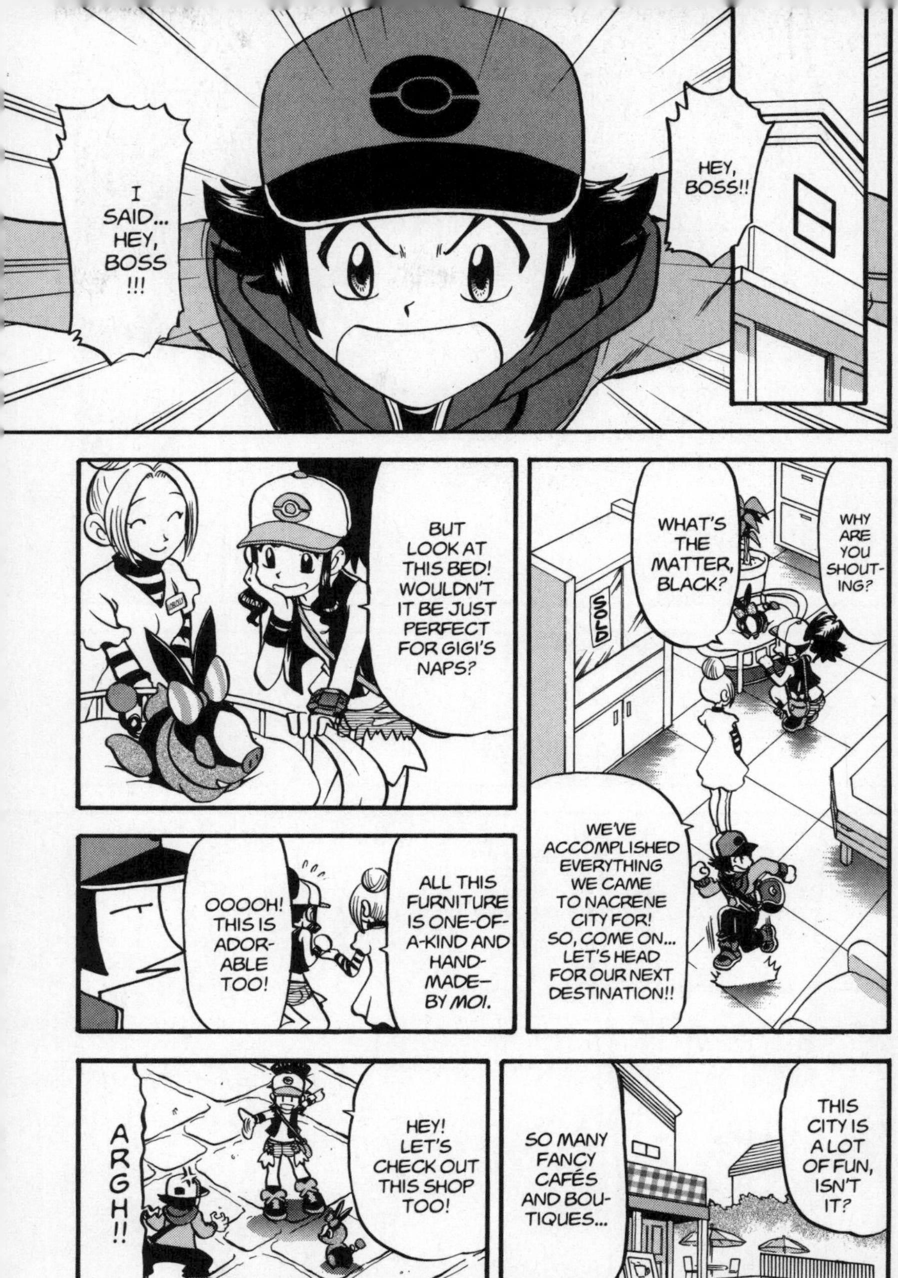
HEY, BOSS!!
I SAID... HEY, BOSS!!!
WHY ARE YOU SHOUTING?
WHAT'S THE MATTER, BLACK?
WE'VE ACCOMPLISHED EVERYTHING WE CAME TO NACRENE CITY FOR! SO, COME ON... LET'S HEAD FOR OUR NEXT DESTINATION!!
BUT LOOK AT THIS BED! WOULDN'T IT BE JUST PERFECT FOR GIGI'S NAPS?
SOLD
ALL THIS FURNITURE IS ONE-OF-A-KIND AND HAND-MADE—BY *MOI*.
OOOOH! THIS IS ADOR-ABLE TOO!
THIS CITY IS A LOT OF FUN, ISN'T IT?
SO MANY FANCY CAFÉS AND BOUTIQUES...
HEY! LET'S CHECK OUT THIS SHOP TOO!
ARGH!!

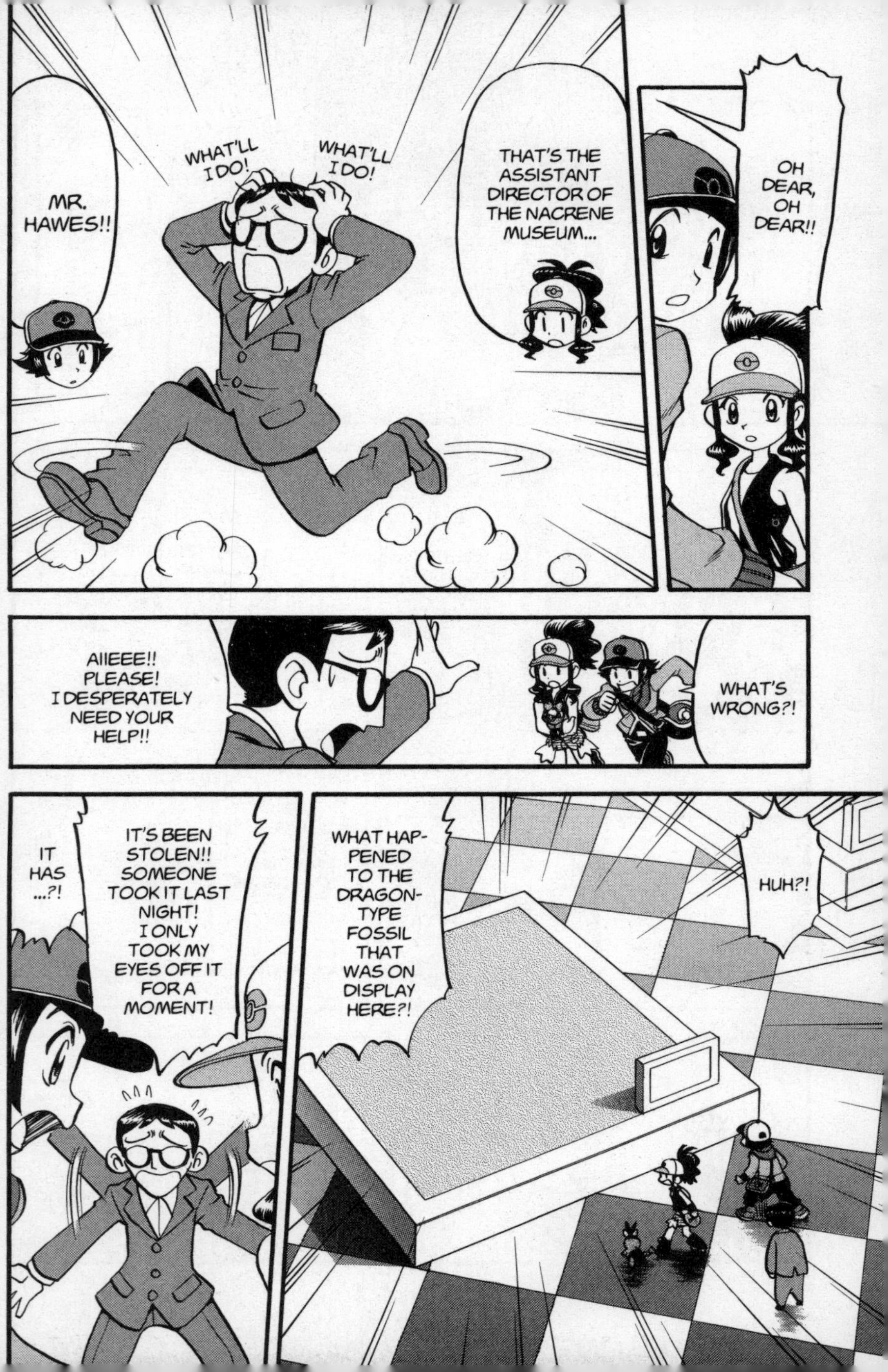
OH DEAR, OH DEAR!!
THAT'S THE ASSISTANT DIRECTOR OF THE NACRENE MUSEUM...
WHAT'LL I DO!
WHAT'LL I DO!
MR. HAWES!!
WHAT'S WRONG?!
AIIEEE!! PLEASE! I DESPERATELY NEED YOUR HELP!!
HUH?!
WHAT HAP-PENED TO THE DRAGON-TYPE FOSSIL THAT WAS ON DISPLAY HERE?!
IT'S BEEN STOLEN!! SOMEONE TOOK IT LAST NIGHT! I ONLY TOOK MY EYES OFF IT FOR A MOMENT!
IT HAS ...?!

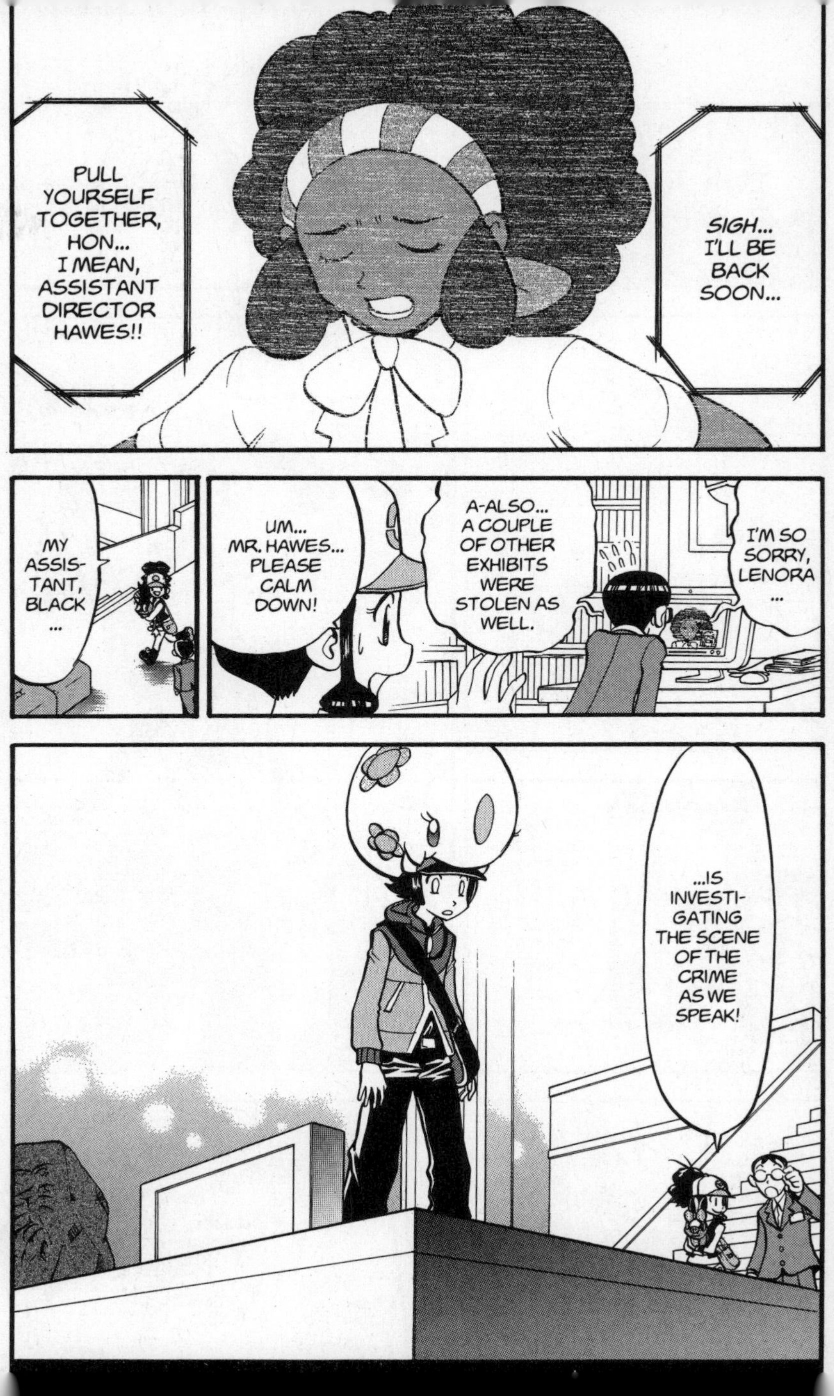
SIGH... I'LL BE BACK SOON...
PULL YOURSELF TOGETHER, HON... I MEAN, ASSISTANT DIRECTOR HAWES!!
I'M SO SORRY, LENORA ...
A-ALSO... A COUPLE OF OTHER EXHIBITS WERE STOLEN AS WELL.
UM... MR. HAWES... PLEASE CALM DOWN!
MY ASSIS-TANT, BLACK ...
...IS INVESTI-GATING THE SCENE OF THE CRIME AS WE SPEAK!

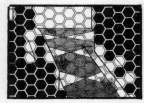

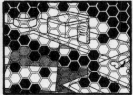

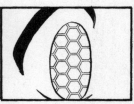

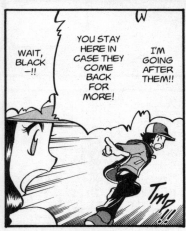

THE THIEVES ARE HEADED WEST. AND THEY HAVEN'T GOTTEN VERY FAR.
UN-CHOMP
R... REALLY ?!
I'M GOING AFTER THEM!!
YOU STAY HERE IN CASE THEY COME BACK FOR MORE!
WAIT, BLACK —!!
TMP!!
IF THEY DO COME BACK... WHAT COULD THE TWO OF US POSSIBLY DO ABOUT IT?
HEY... YOU THERE!
YOU'RE IN AN AWFUL HURRY.
MAYBE THIS WILL SLOW YOU DOWN.

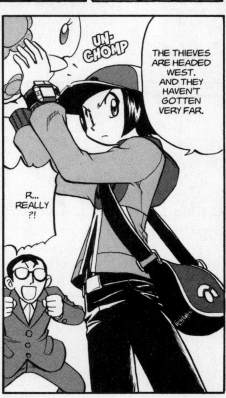

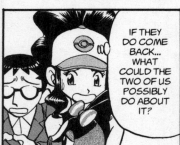

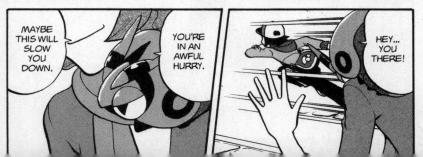

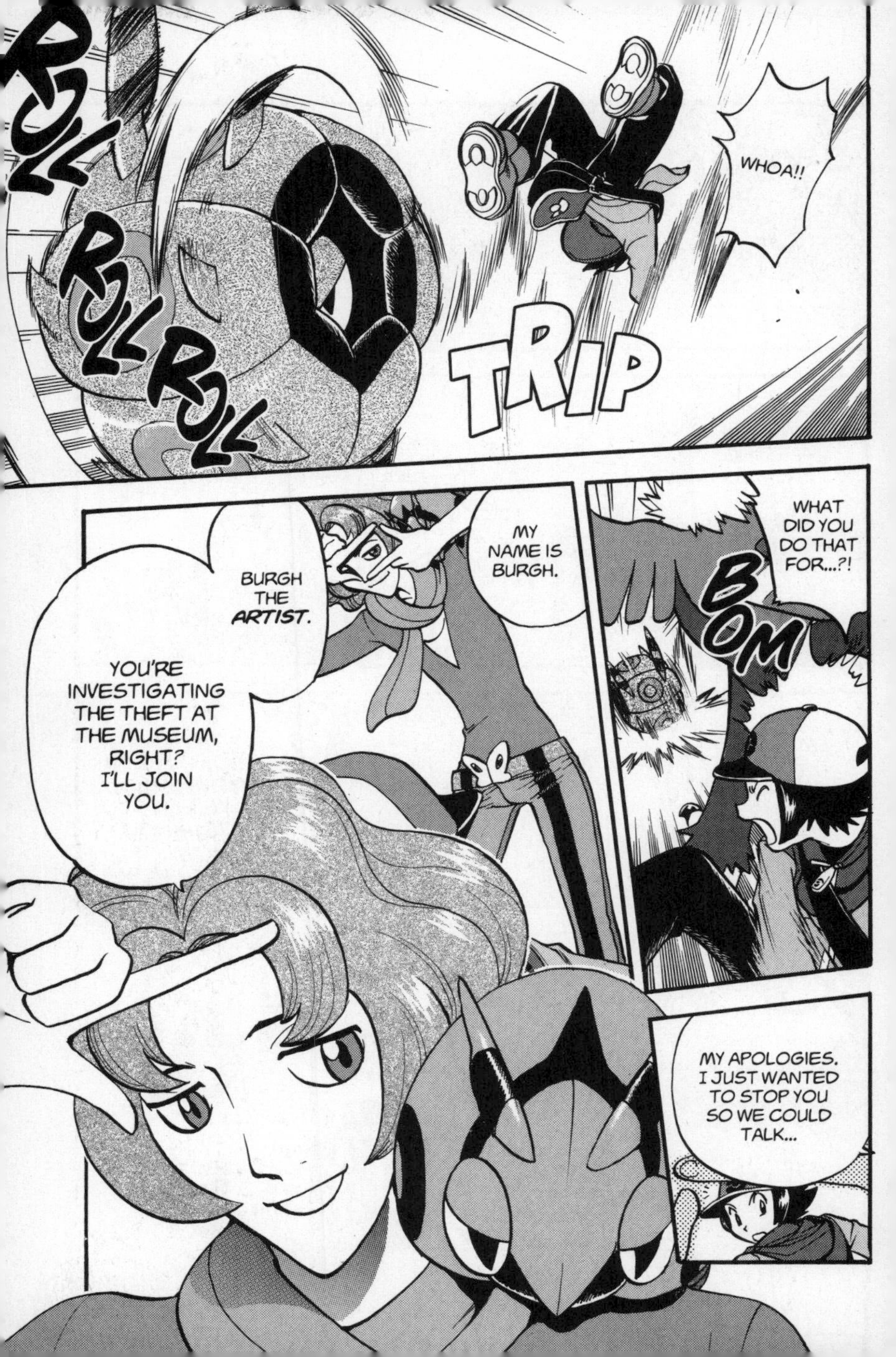
WHOA!!
TRIP
ROLL ROLL ROLL
WHAT DID YOU DO THAT FOR...?!
BOM
MY APOLOGIES. I JUST WANTED TO STOP YOU SO WE COULD TALK...
MY NAME IS BURGH.
BURGH THE *ARTIST*.
YOU'RE INVESTIGATING THE THEFT AT THE MUSEUM, RIGHT? I'LL JOIN YOU.

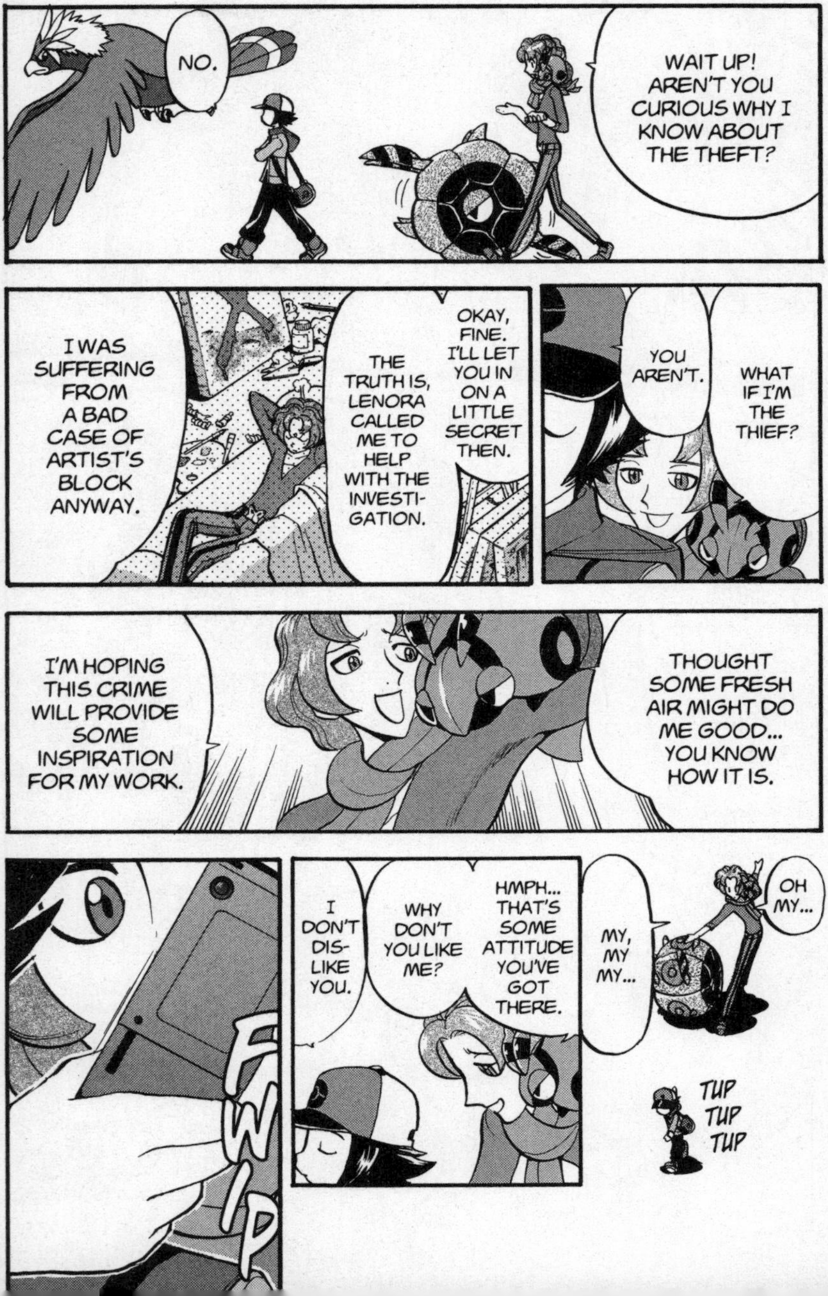
WAIT UP! AREN'T YOU CURIOUS WHY I KNOW ABOUT THE THEFT?
NO.
WHAT IF I'M THE THIEF?
YOU AREN'T.
OKAY, FINE. I'LL LET YOU IN ON A LITTLE SECRET THEN.
THE TRUTH IS, LENORA CALLED ME TO HELP WITH THE INVESTI-GATION.
I WAS SUFFERING FROM A BAD CASE OF ARTIST'S BLOCK ANYWAY.
THOUGHT SOME FRESH AIR MIGHT DO ME GOOD... YOU KNOW HOW IT IS.
I'M HOPING THIS CRIME WILL PROVIDE SOME INSPIRATION FOR MY WORK.
OH MY...
MY, MY MY...
TUP TUP TUP
HMPH... THAT'S SOME ATTITUDE YOU'VE GOT THERE.
WHY DON'T YOU LIKE ME?
I DON'T DIS-LIKE YOU.
FWIP

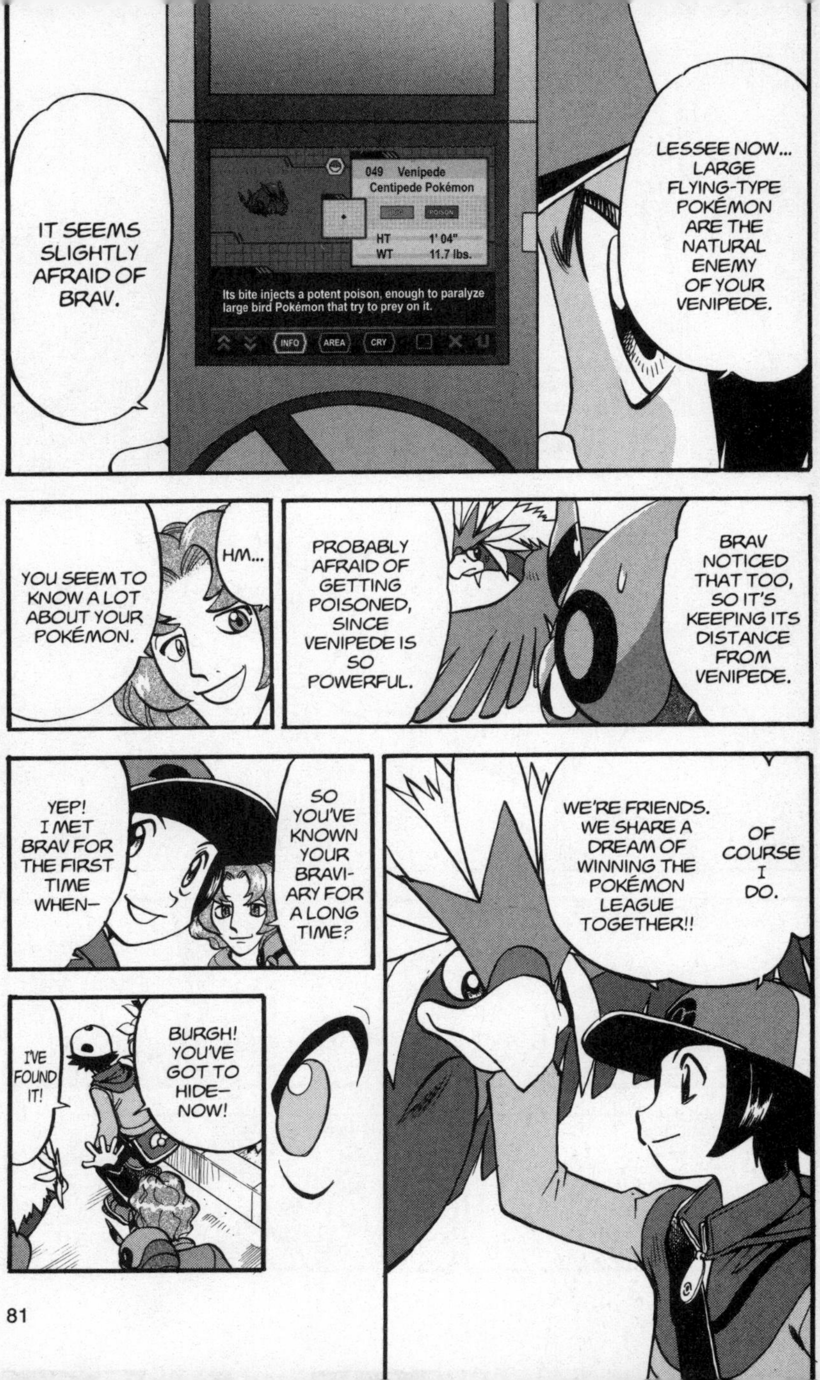
LESSEE NOW... LARGE FLYING-TYPE POKÉMON ARE THE NATURAL ENEMY OF YOUR VENIPEDE.
049 Venipede
Centipede Pokémon
POISON
HT 1' 04"
WT 11.7 lbs.
Its bite injects a potent poison, enough to paralyze large bird Pokémon that try to prey on it.
INFO
AREA
CRY
IT SEEMS SLIGHTLY AFRAID OF BRAV.
BRAV NOTICED THAT TOO, SO IT'S KEEPING ITS DISTANCE FROM VENIPEDE.
PROBABLY AFRAID OF GETTING POISONED, SINCE VENIPEDE IS SO POWERFUL.
HM...
YOU SEEM TO KNOW A LOT ABOUT YOUR POKÉMON.
OF COURSE I DO.
WE'RE FRIENDS. WE SHARE A DREAM OF WINNING THE POKÉMON LEAGUE TOGETHER!!
SO YOU'VE KNOWN YOUR BRAVIARY FOR A LONG TIME?
YEP! I MET BRAV FOR THE FIRST TIME WHEN—
BURGH! YOU'VE GOT TO HIDE— NOW!
I'VE FOUND IT!

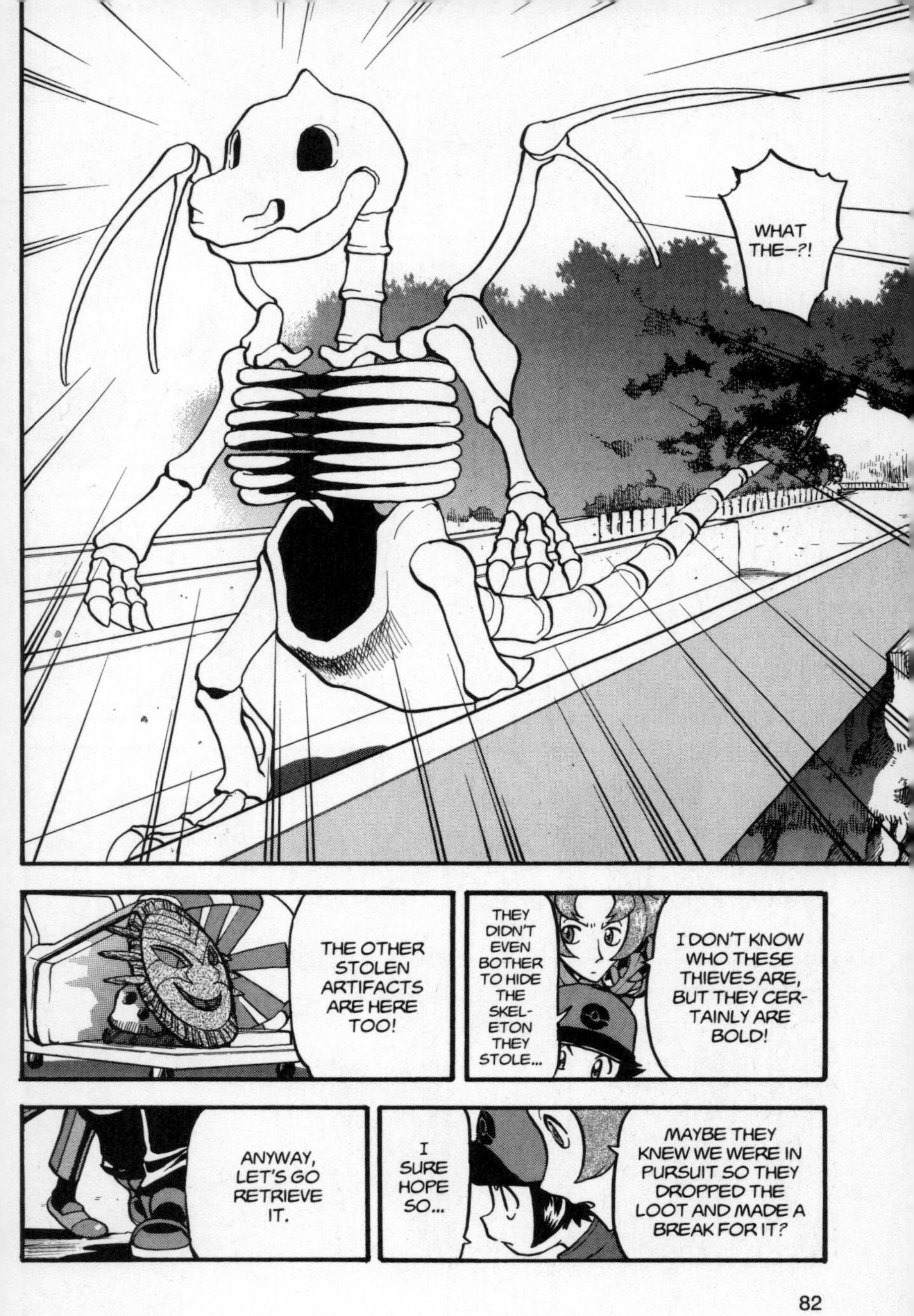
WHAT THE—?!
I DON'T KNOW WHO THESE THIEVES ARE, BUT THEY CERTAINLY ARE BOLD!
THEY DIDN'T EVEN BOTHER TO HIDE THE SKELETON THEY STOLE...
THE OTHER STOLEN ARTIFACTS ARE HERE TOO!
MAYBE THEY KNEW WE WERE IN PURSUIT SO THEY DROPPED THE LOOT AND MADE A BREAK FOR IT?
I SURE HOPE SO...
ANYWAY, LET'S GO RETRIEVE IT.

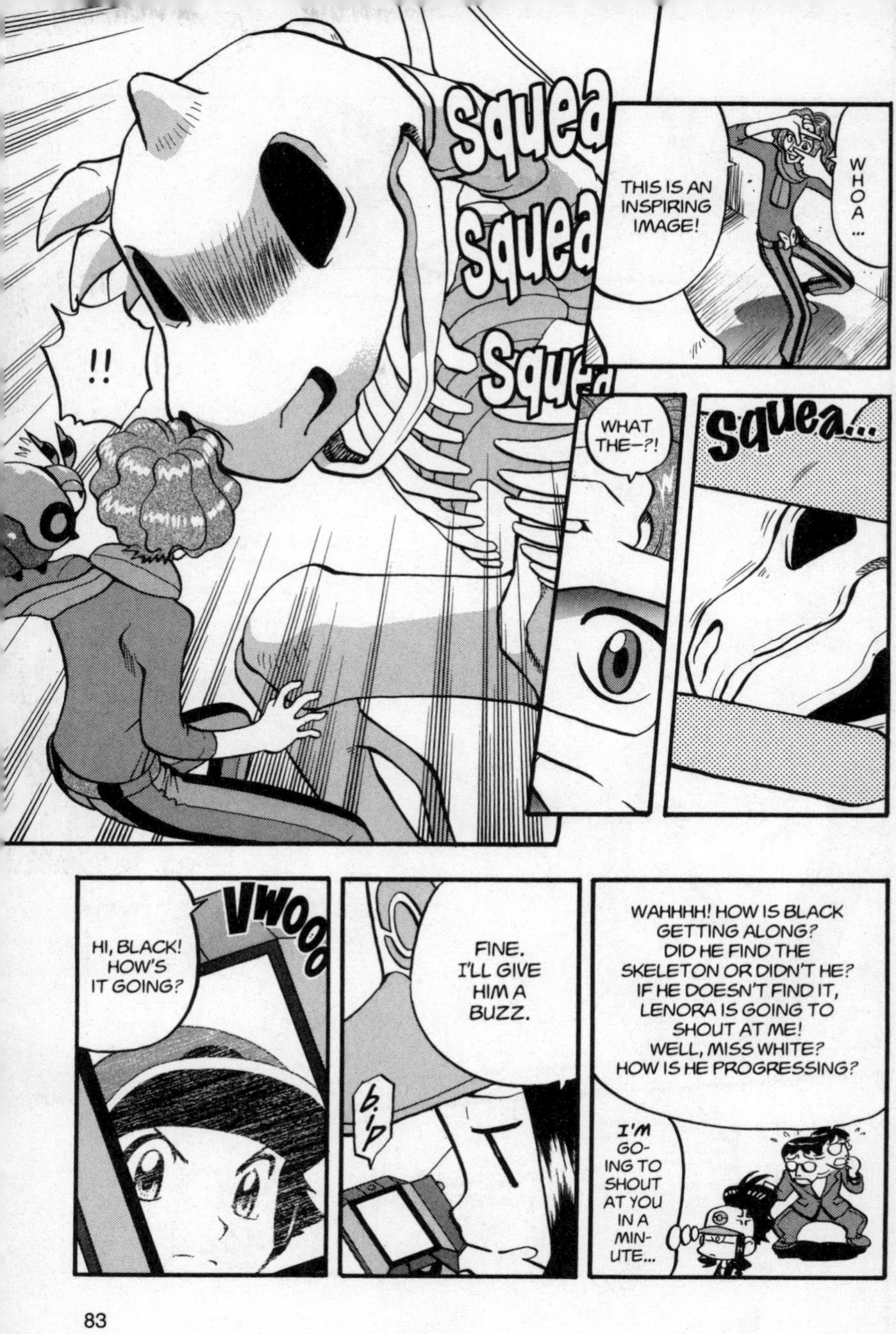
WHOA...
THIS IS AN INSPIRING IMAGE!
Squea...
WHAT THE–?!
Squea
Squea
Squea
!!
WAHHHH! HOW IS BLACK GETTING ALONG? DID HE FIND THE SKELETON OR DIDN'T HE? IF HE DOESN'T FIND IT, LENORA IS GOING TO SHOUT AT ME! WELL, MISS WHITE? HOW IS HE PROGRESSING?
I'M GOING TO SHOUT AT YOU IN A MINUTE...
FINE. I'LL GIVE HIM A BUZZ.
bip
VWOOO
HI, BLACK! HOW'S IT GOING?

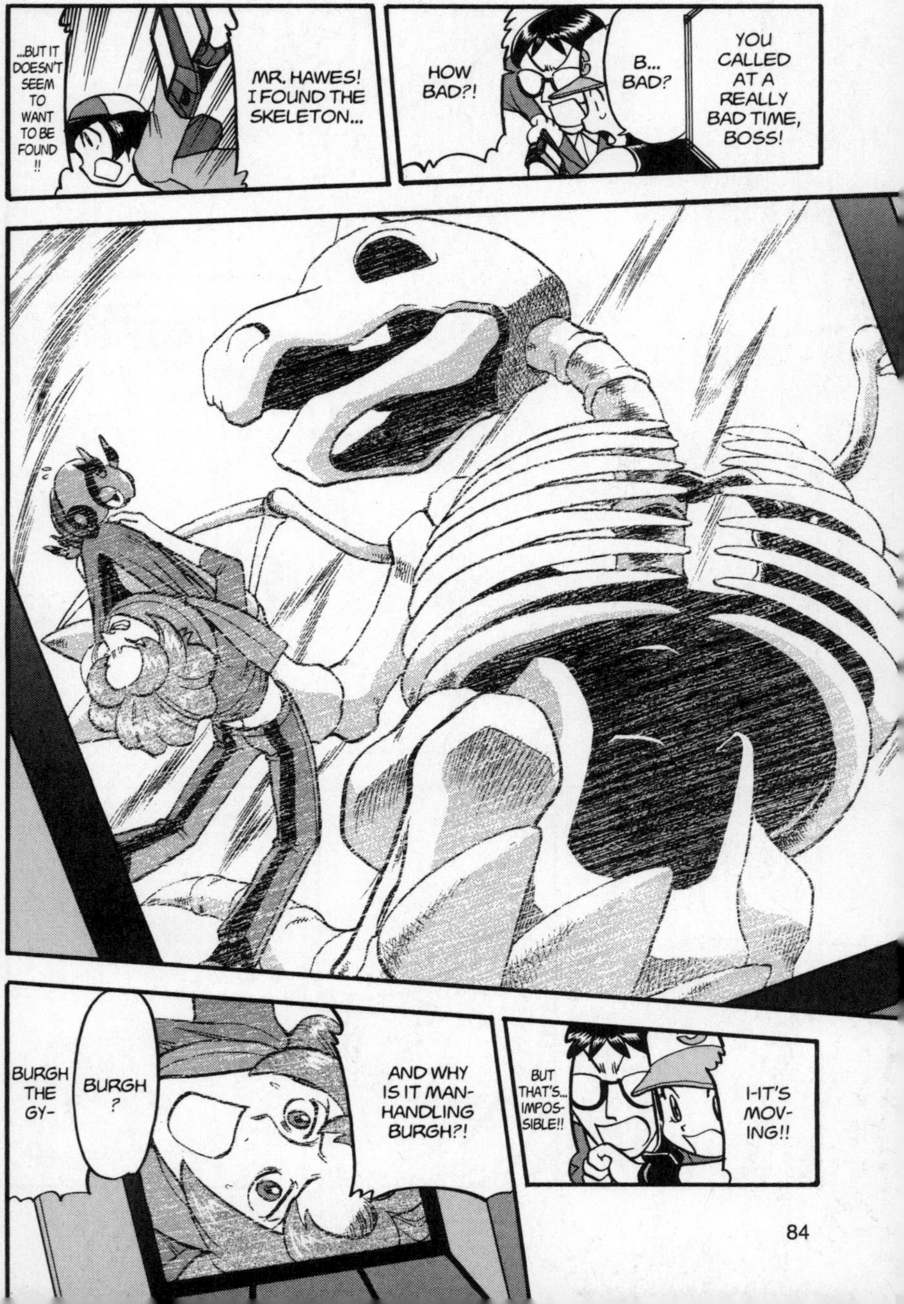
YOU CALLED AT A REALLY BAD TIME, BOSS!
B... BAD?
HOW BAD?!
MR. HAWES! I FOUND THE SKELETON...
...BUT IT DOESN'T SEEM TO WANT TO BE FOUND !!
I-IT'S MOV-ING!!
BUT THAT'S... IMPOS-SIBLE!!
AND WHY IS IT MAN-HANDLING BURGH?!
BURGH ?
BURGH THE GY-

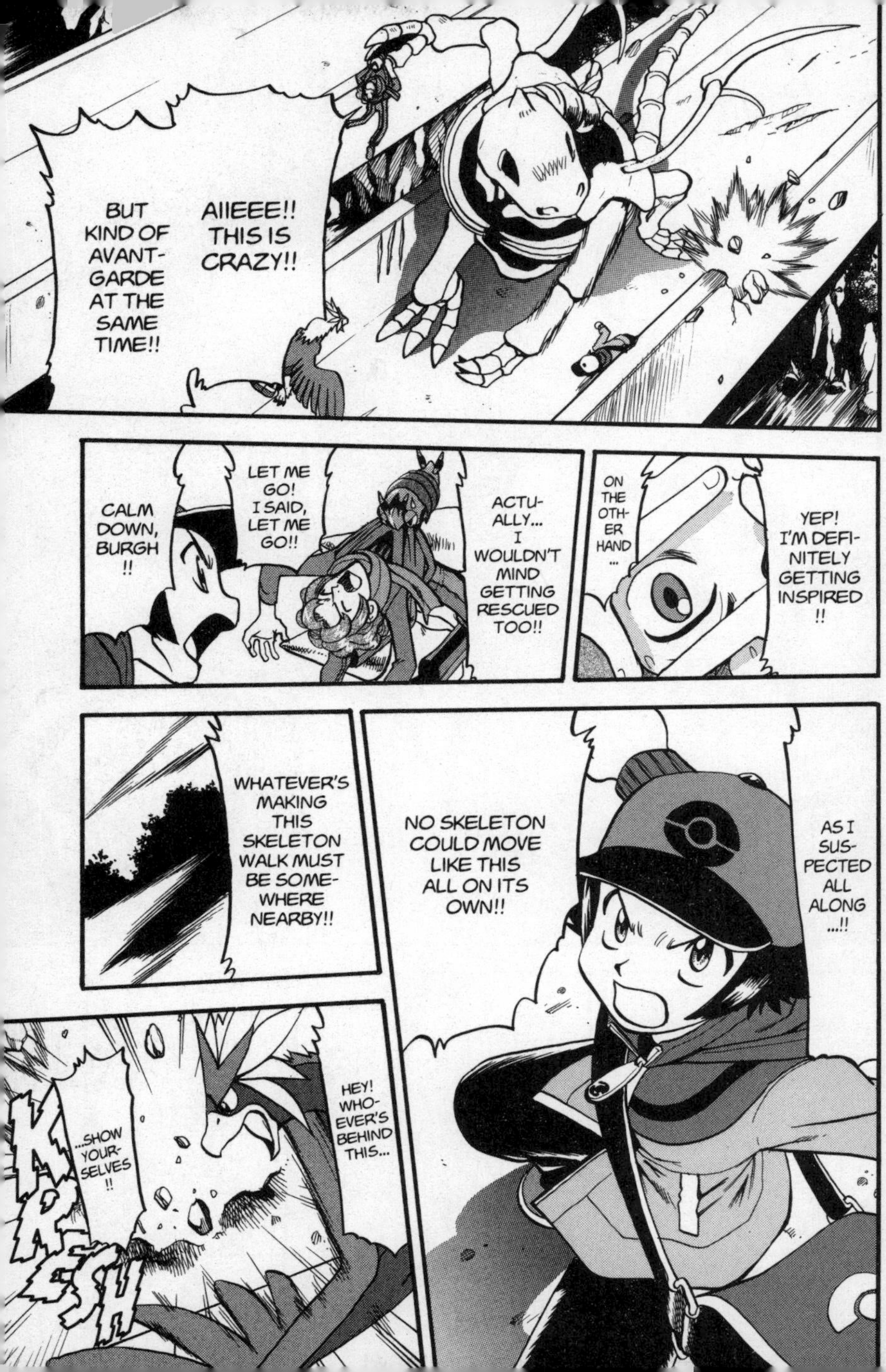
AIIEEE!! THIS IS CRAZY!!
BUT KIND OF AVANT-GARDE AT THE SAME TIME!!
YEP! I'M DEFINITELY GETTING INSPIRED!!
ON THE OTHER HAND...
ACTUALLY... I WOULDN'T MIND GETTING RESCUED TOO!!
LET ME GO! I SAID, LET ME GO!!
CALM DOWN, BURGH!!
AS I SUSPECTED ALL ALONG...!!
NO SKELETON COULD MOVE LIKE THIS ALL ON ITS OWN!!
WHATEVER'S MAKING THIS SKELETON WALK MUST BE SOMEWHERE NEARBY!!
HEY! WHOEVER'S BEHIND THIS...
...SHOW YOURSELVES!!
KRESH

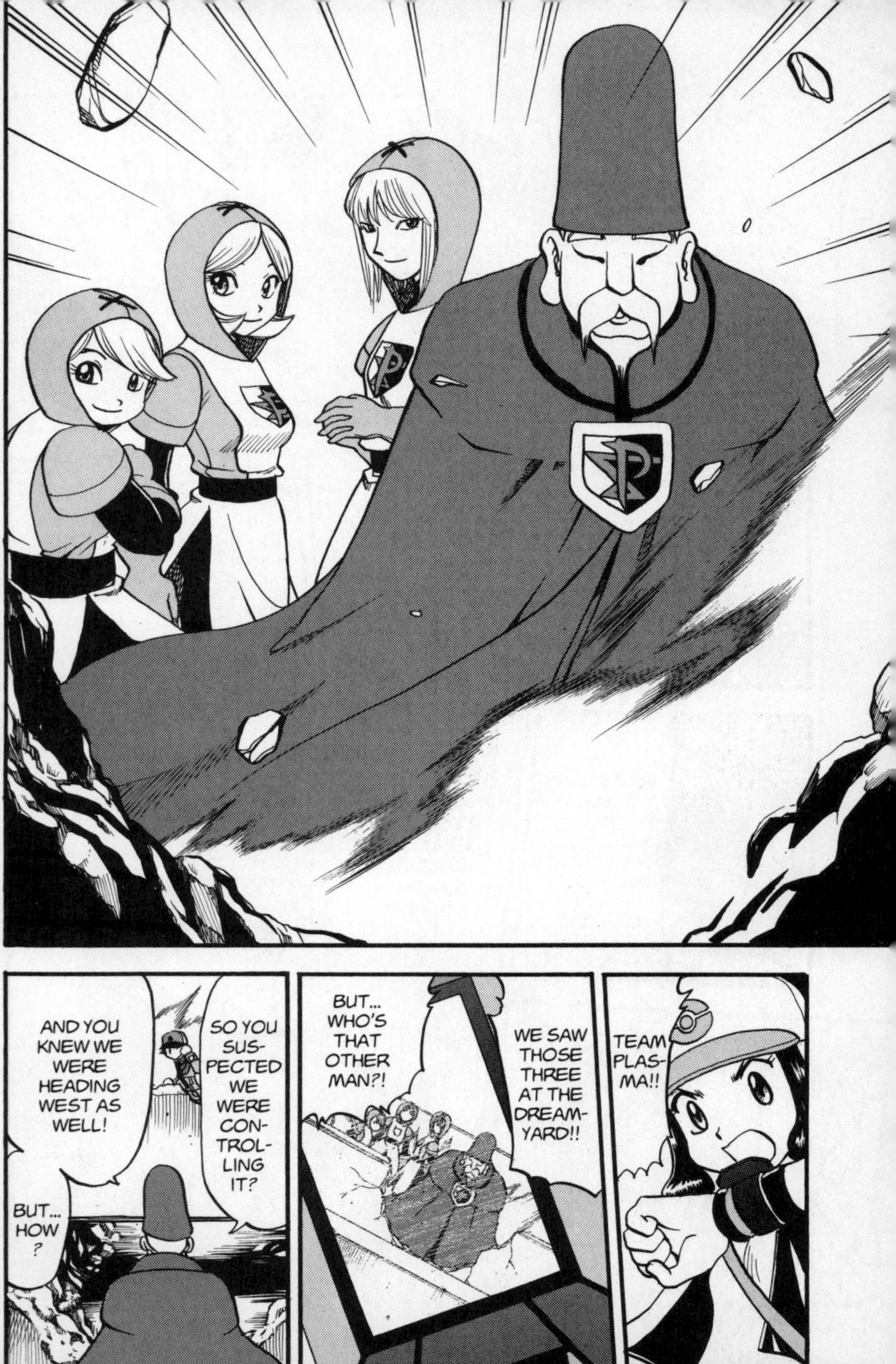
TEAM PLAS-MA!!
WE SAW THOSE THREE AT THE DREAM-YARD!!
BUT... WHO'S THAT OTHER MAN?!
SO YOU SUS-PECTED WE WERE CON-TROL-LING IT?
AND YOU KNEW WE WERE HEADING WEST AS WELL!
BUT... HOW?

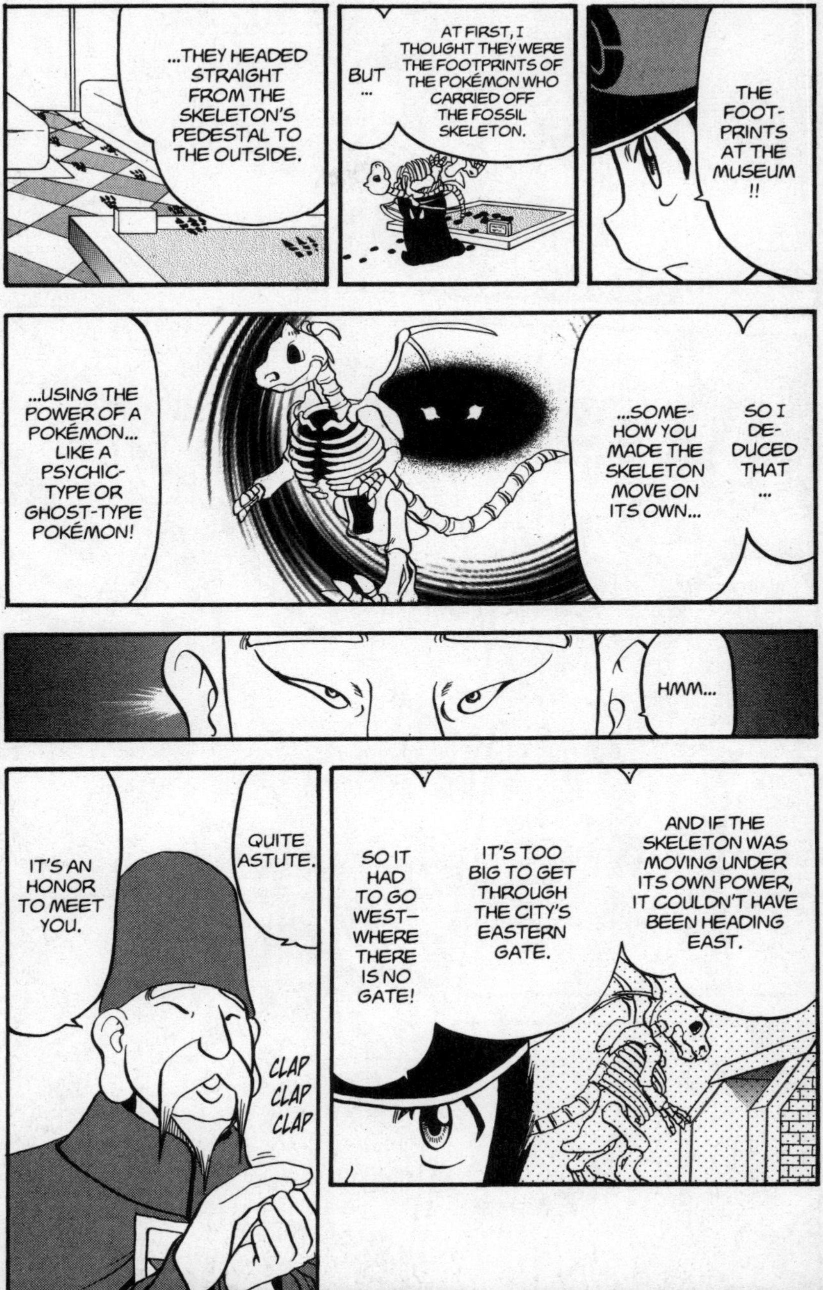
THE FOOT-PRINTS AT THE MUSEUM !!
AT FIRST, I THOUGHT THEY WERE THE FOOTPRINTS OF THE POKÉMON WHO CARRIED OFF THE FOSSIL SKELETON.
BUT ...
...THEY HEADED STRAIGHT FROM THE SKELETON'S PEDESTAL TO THE OUTSIDE.
SO I DE-DUCED THAT ...
...SOME-HOW YOU MADE THE SKELETON MOVE ON ITS OWN...
...USING THE POWER OF A POKÉMON... LIKE A PSYCHIC-TYPE OR GHOST-TYPE POKÉMON!
HMM...
AND IF THE SKELETON WAS MOVING UNDER ITS OWN POWER, IT COULDN'T HAVE BEEN HEADING EAST.
IT'S TOO BIG TO GET THROUGH THE CITY'S EASTERN GATE.
SO IT HAD TO GO WEST— WHERE THERE IS NO GATE!
QUITE ASTUTE.
CLAP CLAP CLAP
IT'S AN HONOR TO MEET YOU.

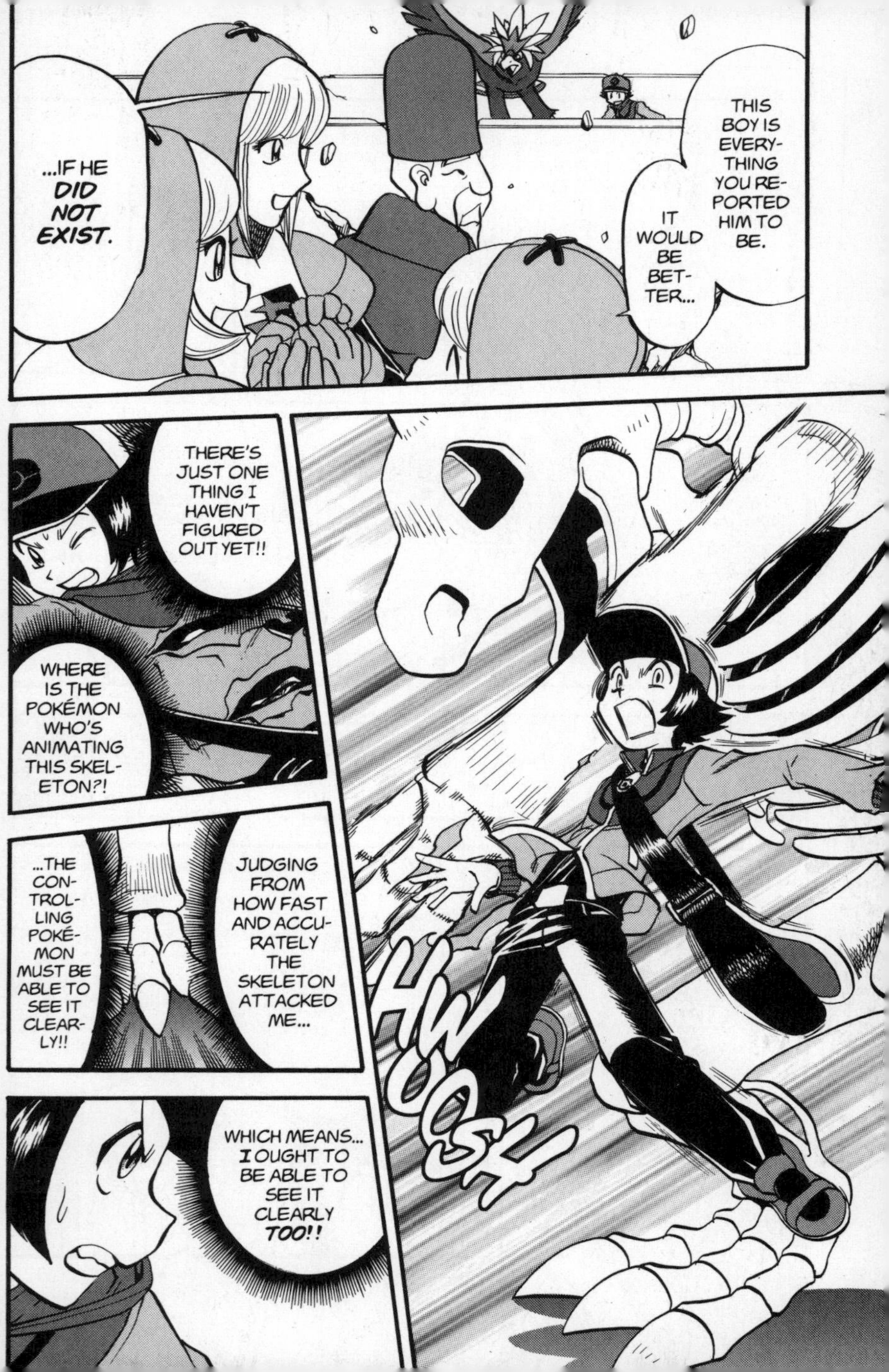
THIS BOY IS EVERYTHING YOU REPORTED HIM TO BE.
IT WOULD BE BETTER...
...IF HE *DID NOT EXIST*.
WHOOSH!
THERE'S JUST ONE THING I HAVEN'T FIGURED OUT YET!!
WHERE IS THE POKÉMON WHO'S ANIMATING THIS SKELETON?!
JUDGING FROM HOW FAST AND ACCURATELY THE SKELETON ATTACKED ME...
...THE CONTROLLING POKÉMON MUST BE ABLE TO SEE IT CLEARLY!!
WHICH MEANS... *I* OUGHT TO BE ABLE TO SEE IT CLEARLY *TOO*!!

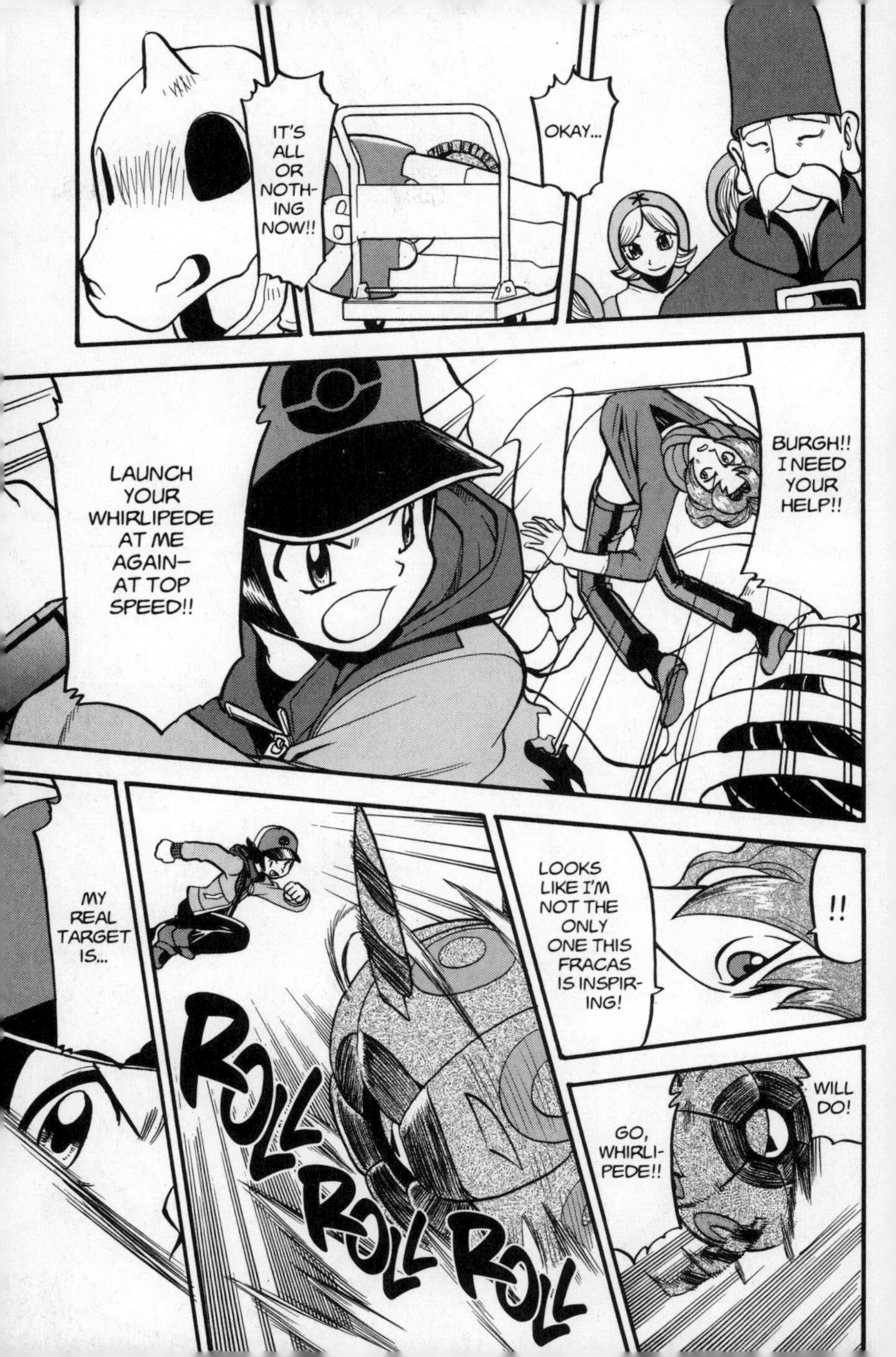

OKAY...
IT'S ALL OR NOTHING NOW!!
BURGH!! I NEED YOUR HELP!!
LAUNCH YOUR WHIRLIPEDE AT ME AGAIN—AT TOP SPEED!!
!!
LOOKS LIKE I'M NOT THE ONLY ONE THIS FRACAS IS INSPIRING!
WILL DO!
GO, WHIRLIPEDE!!
MY REAL TARGET IS...
ROLL ROLL ROLL

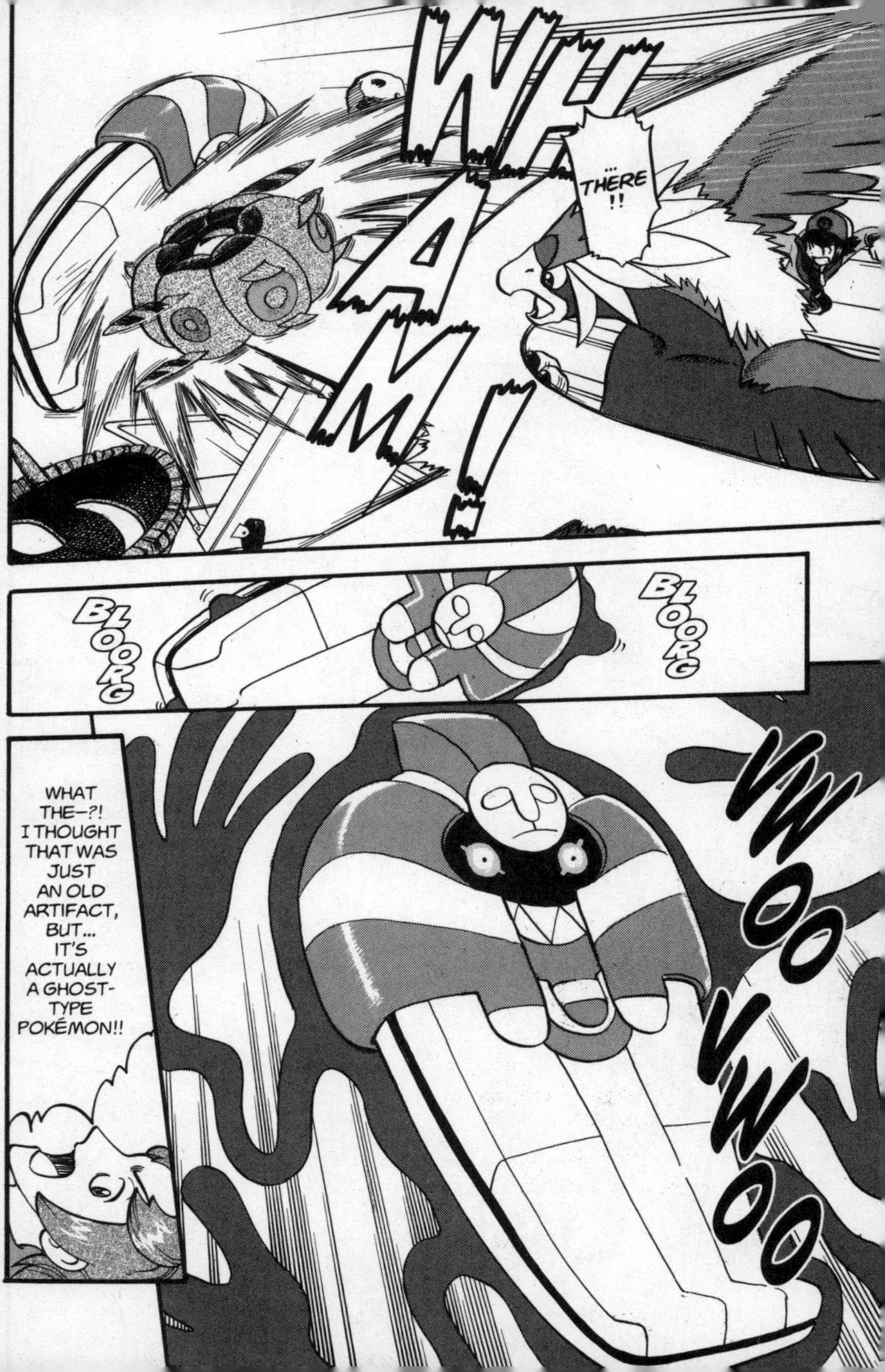
...THERE!!
WHAM!
BLOORG
BLOORG
VWOO VWOO
WHAT THE-?! I THOUGHT THAT WAS JUST AN OLD ARTIFACT, BUT... IT'S ACTUALLY A GHOST-TYPE POKÉMON!!

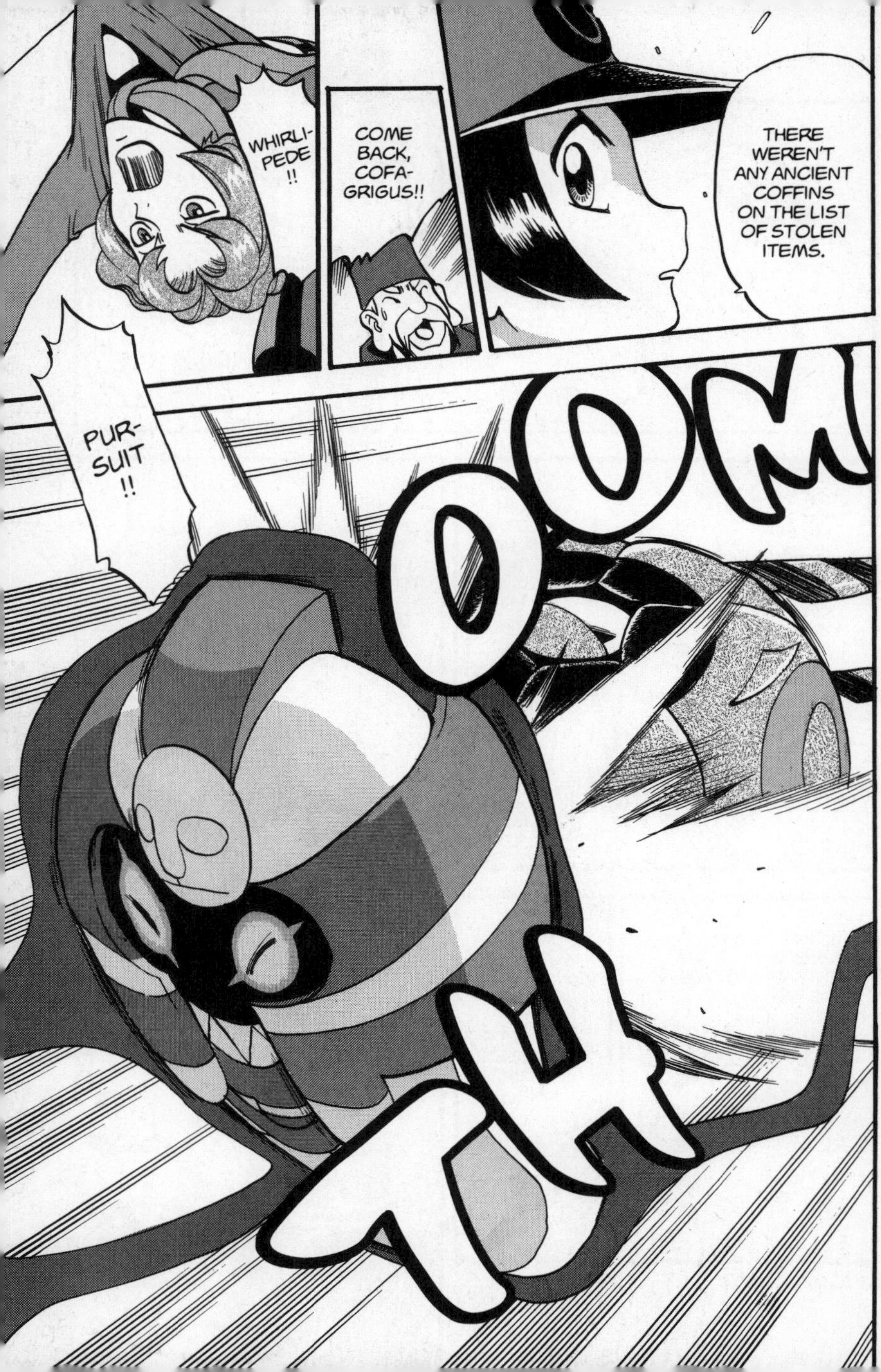
THERE WEREN'T ANY ANCIENT COFFINS ON THE LIST OF STOLEN ITEMS.
COME BACK, COFA-GRIGUS!!
WHIRLI-PEDE!!
PUR-SUIT!!
THOOOM

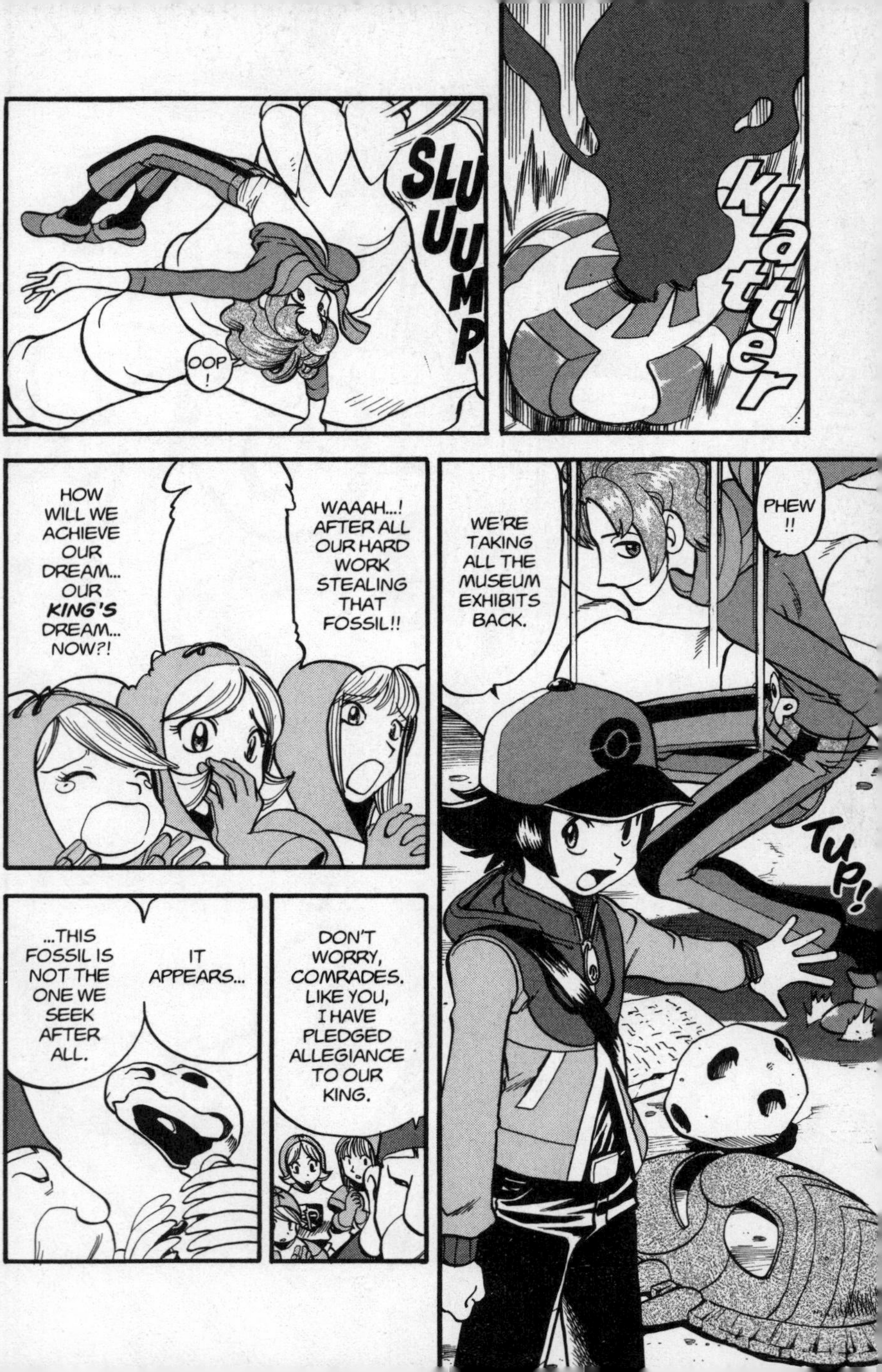
klatter
SLUUUMP
OOP!
PHEW!!
WE'RE TAKING ALL THE MUSEUM EXHIBITS BACK.
TUP!
WAAAH...! AFTER ALL OUR HARD WORK STEALING THAT FOSSIL!!
HOW WILL WE ACHIEVE OUR DREAM... OUR **KING'S** DREAM... NOW?!
DON'T WORRY, COMRADES. LIKE YOU, I HAVE PLEDGED ALLEGIANCE TO OUR KING.
IT APPEARS...
...THIS FOSSIL IS NOT THE ONE WE SEEK AFTER ALL.

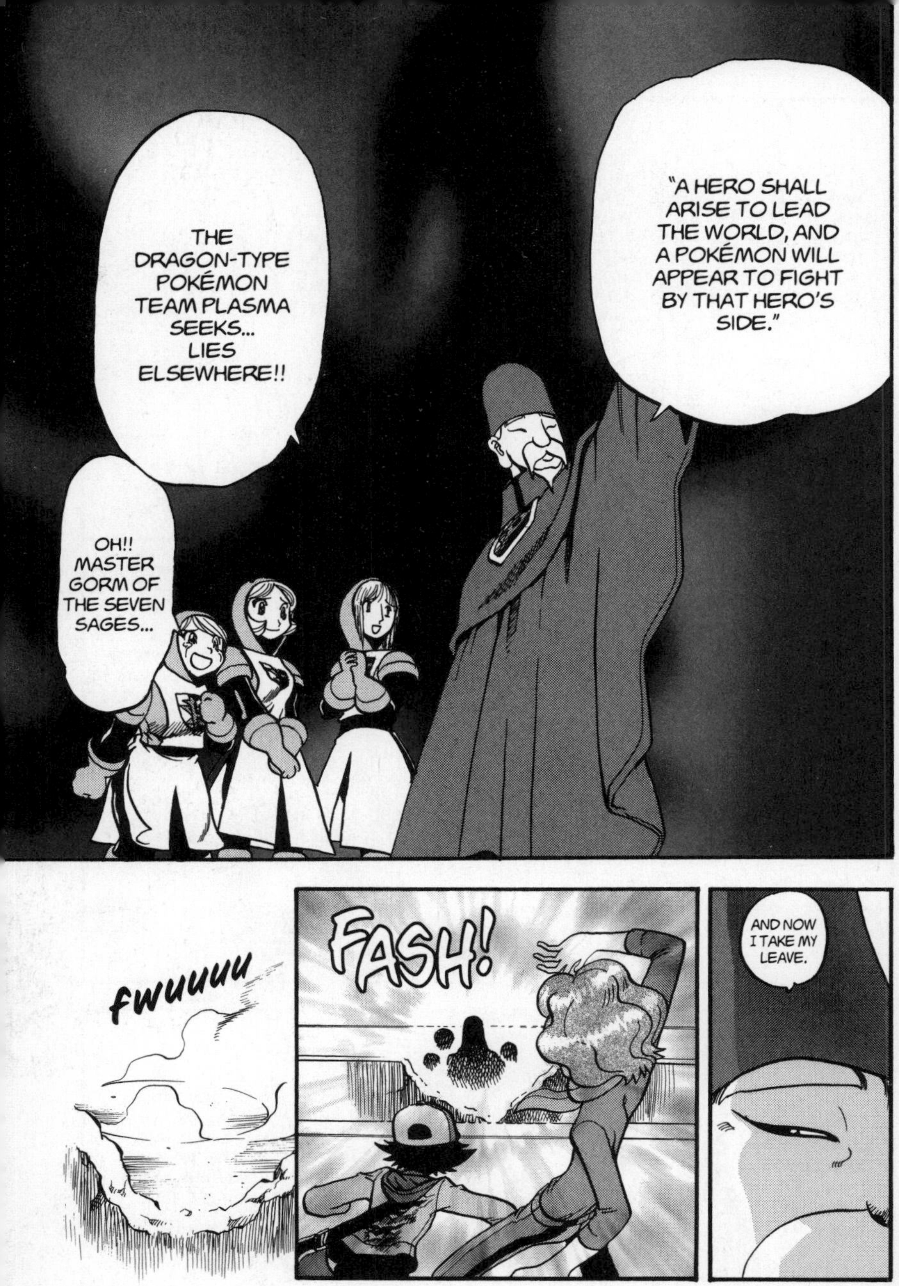
"A HERO SHALL ARISE TO LEAD THE WORLD, AND A POKÉMON WILL APPEAR TO FIGHT BY THAT HERO'S SIDE."
THE DRAGON-TYPE POKÉMON TEAM PLASMA SEEKS... LIES ELSEWHERE!!
OH!! MASTER GORM OF THE SEVEN SAGES...
AND NOW I TAKE MY LEAVE.
FASH!
FWUUUU

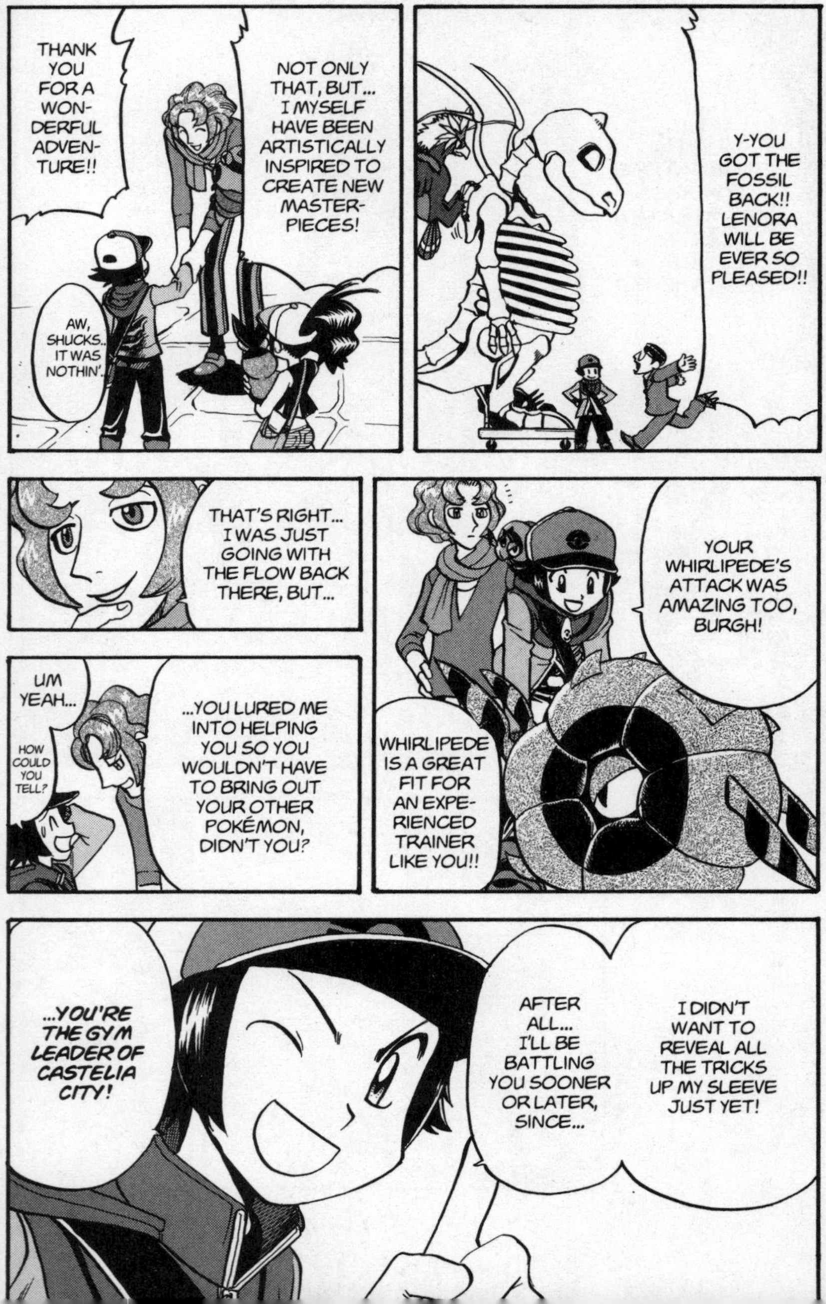
Y-YOU GOT THE FOSSIL BACK!! LENORA WILL BE EVER SO PLEASED!!
THANK YOU FOR A WONDERFUL ADVENTURE!!
NOT ONLY THAT, BUT... I MYSELF HAVE BEEN ARTISTICALLY INSPIRED TO CREATE NEW MASTERPIECES!
AW, SHUCKS.. IT WAS NOTHIN'.
YOUR WHIRLIPEDE'S ATTACK WAS AMAZING TOO, BURGH!
WHIRLIPEDE IS A GREAT FIT FOR AN EXPERIENCED TRAINER LIKE YOU!!
THAT'S RIGHT... I WAS JUST GOING WITH THE FLOW BACK THERE, BUT...
...YOU LURED ME INTO HELPING YOU SO YOU WOULDN'T HAVE TO BRING OUT YOUR OTHER POKÉMON, DIDN'T YOU?
UM YEAH...
HOW COULD YOU TELL?
I DIDN'T WANT TO REVEAL ALL THE TRICKS UP MY SLEEVE JUST YET!
AFTER ALL... I'LL BE BATTLING YOU SOONER OR LATER, SINCE...
...YOU'RE THE GYM LEADER OF CASTELIA CITY!

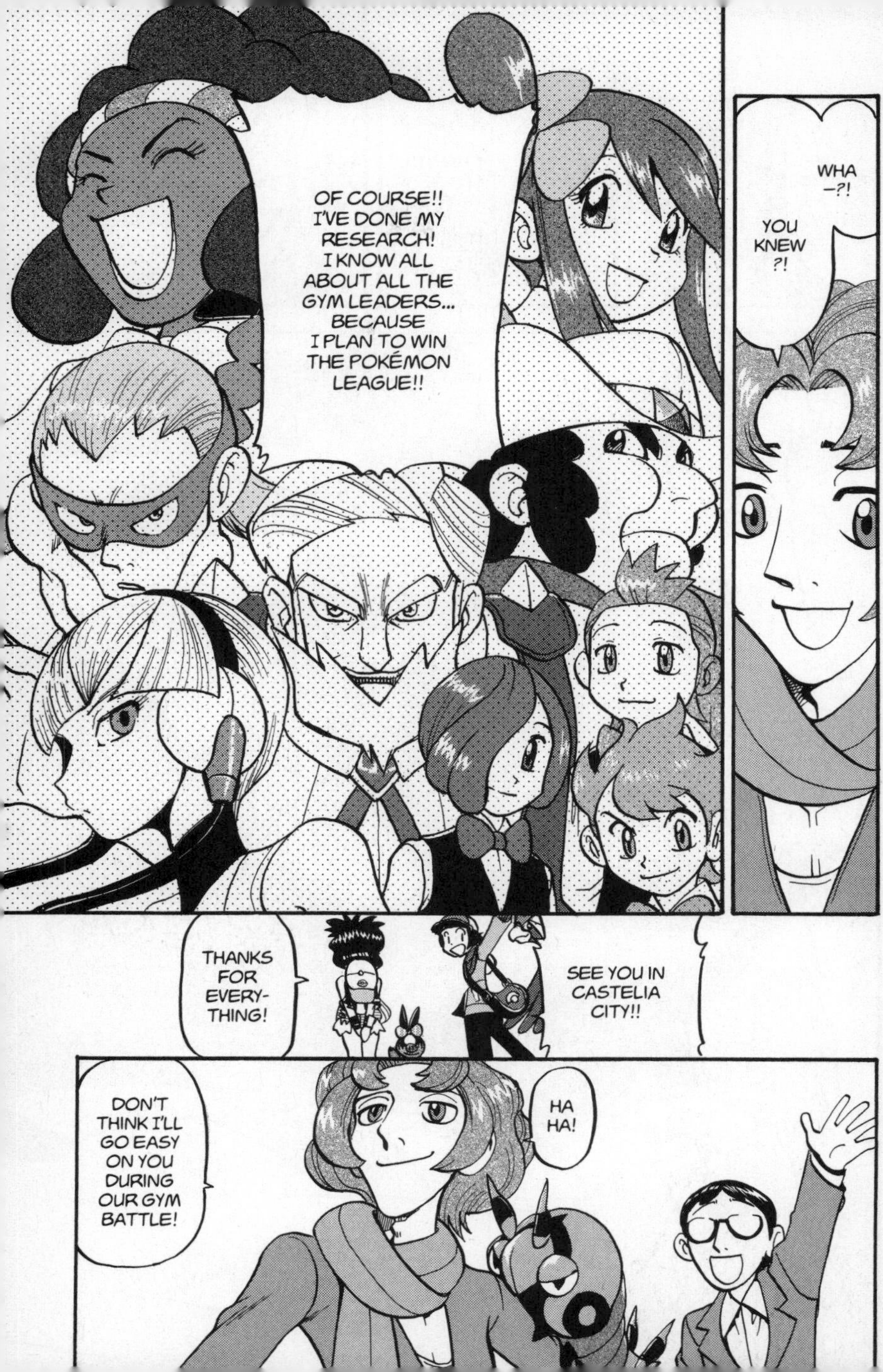
WHA —?!
YOU KNEW ?!
OF COURSE!! I'VE DONE MY RESEARCH! I KNOW ALL ABOUT ALL THE GYM LEADERS... BECAUSE I PLAN TO WIN THE POKÉMON LEAGUE!!
SEE YOU IN CASTELIA CITY!!
THANKS FOR EVERY-THING!
HA HA!
DON'T THINK I'LL GO EASY ON YOU DURING OUR GYM BATTLE!

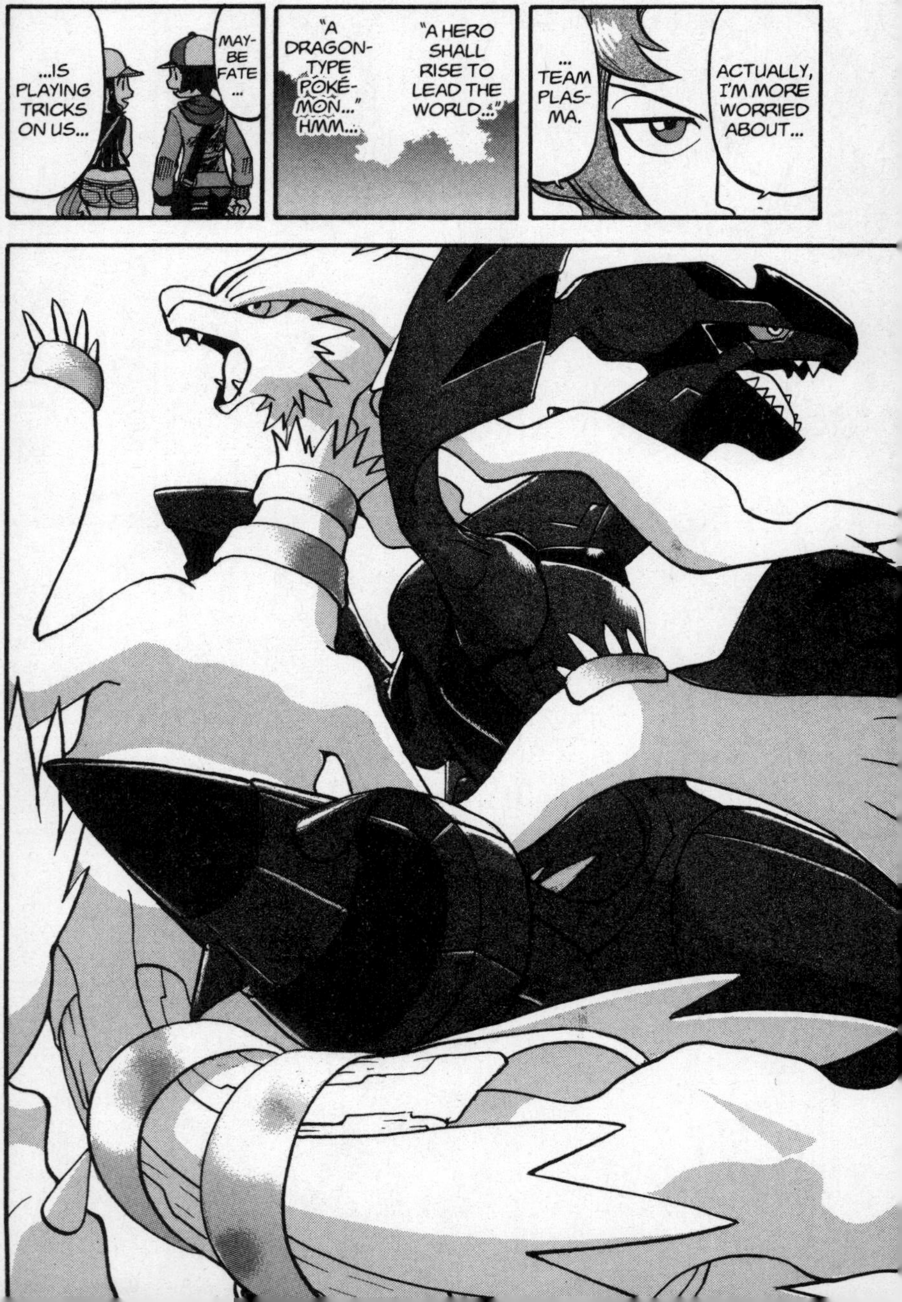
ACTUALLY, I'M MORE WORRIED ABOUT...
...TEAM PLASMA.
"A HERO SHALL RISE TO LEAD THE WORLD..."
"A DRAGON-TYPE POKÉMON..." HMM...
MAY-BE FATE...
...IS PLAYING TRICKS ON US...

ADVENTURE MAP

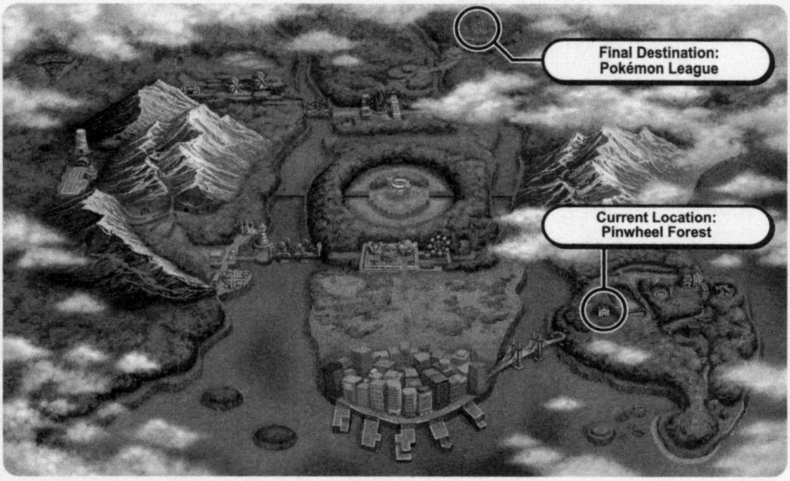

Final Destination:
Pokémon League
Current Location:
Pinwheel Forest

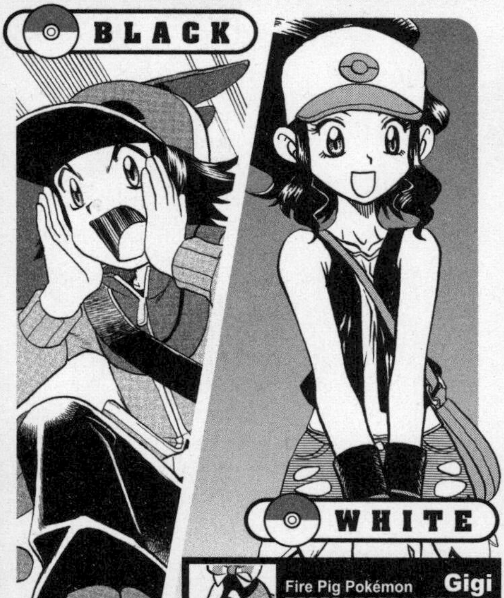

BLACK
WHITE

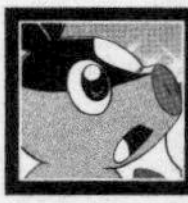
Fire Pig Pokémon **Tep**
Tepig♂ Fire
Lv.16 Ability: Blaze

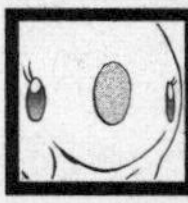
Dream Eater Pokémon **Musha**
Munna♂ Psychic
Lv.39 Ability: Forewarn

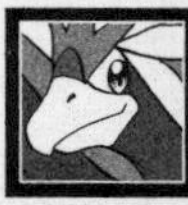
Valiant Pokémon **Brav**
Braviary♂ Normal Flying
Lv.54 Ability: Sheer Force

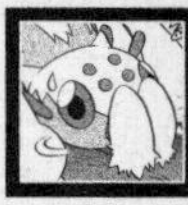
EleSpider Pokémon **Tula**
Galvantula♂ Bug Electric
Lv.38 Ability: Unnerve

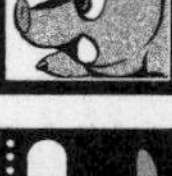
Fire Pig Pokémon **Gigi**
Tepig♀ Fire
Lv.05 Ability: Blaze

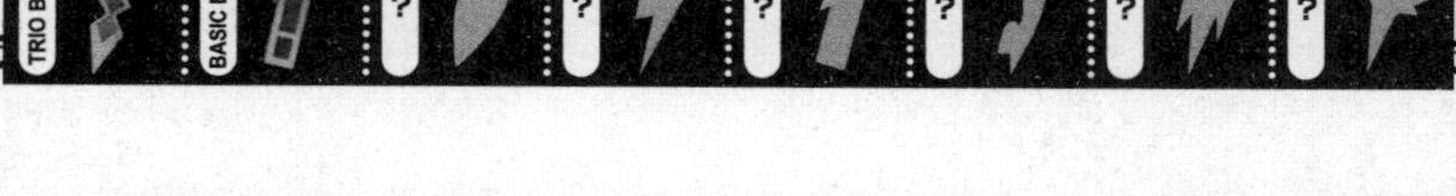

TRIO BADGE
BASIC BADGE
?
?
?
?
?
?

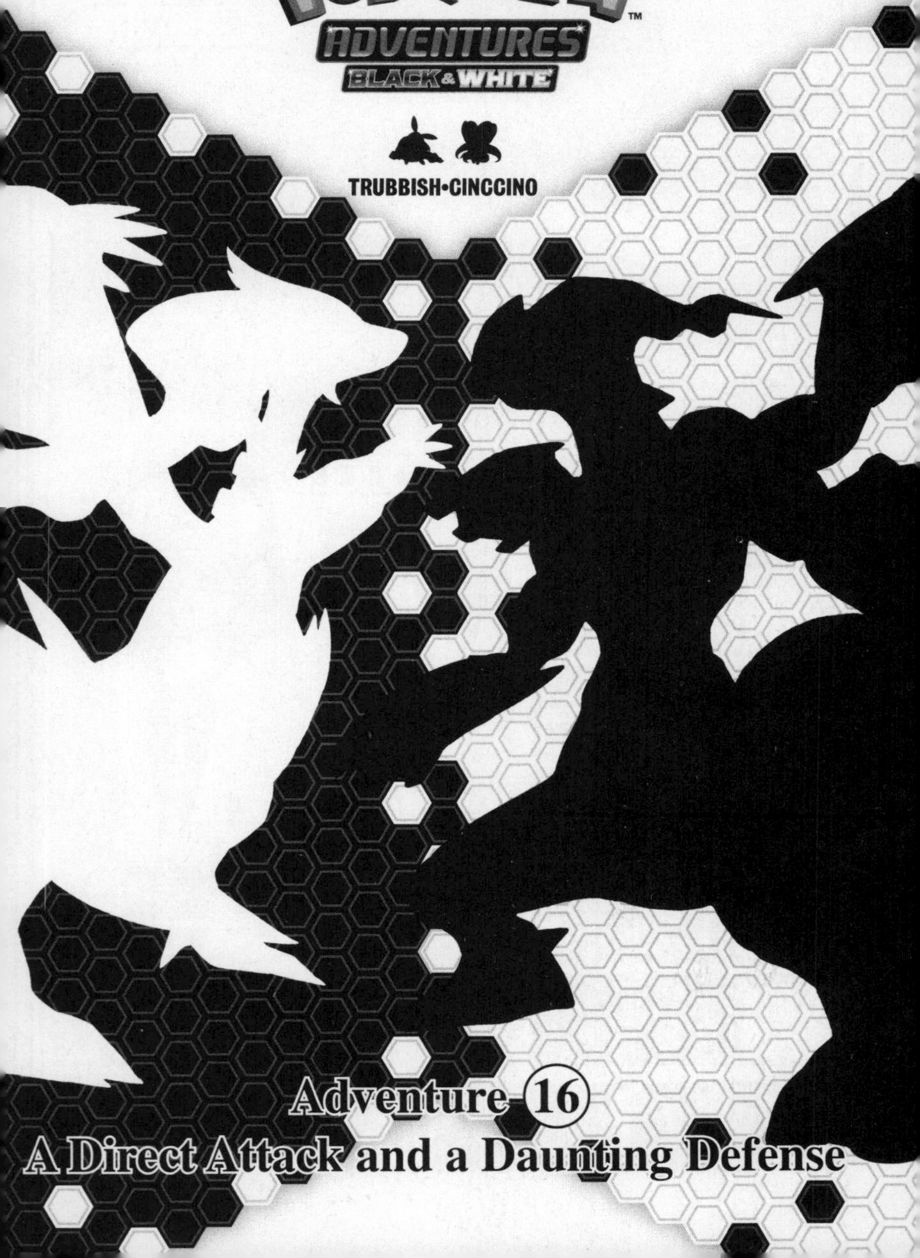

POKÉMON ADVENTURES BLACK & WHITE

TRUBBISH•CINCCINO

Adventure 16
A Direct Attack and a Daunting Defense

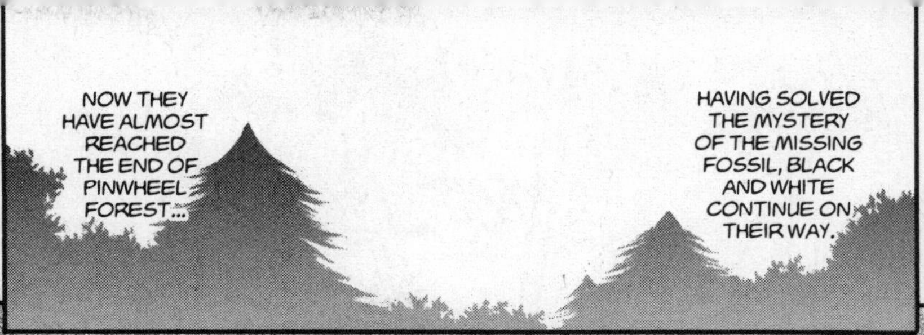
HAVING SOLVED THE MYSTERY OF THE MISSING FOSSIL, BLACK AND WHITE CONTINUE ON THEIR WAY.
NOW THEY HAVE ALMOST REACHED THE END OF PINWHEEL FOREST...
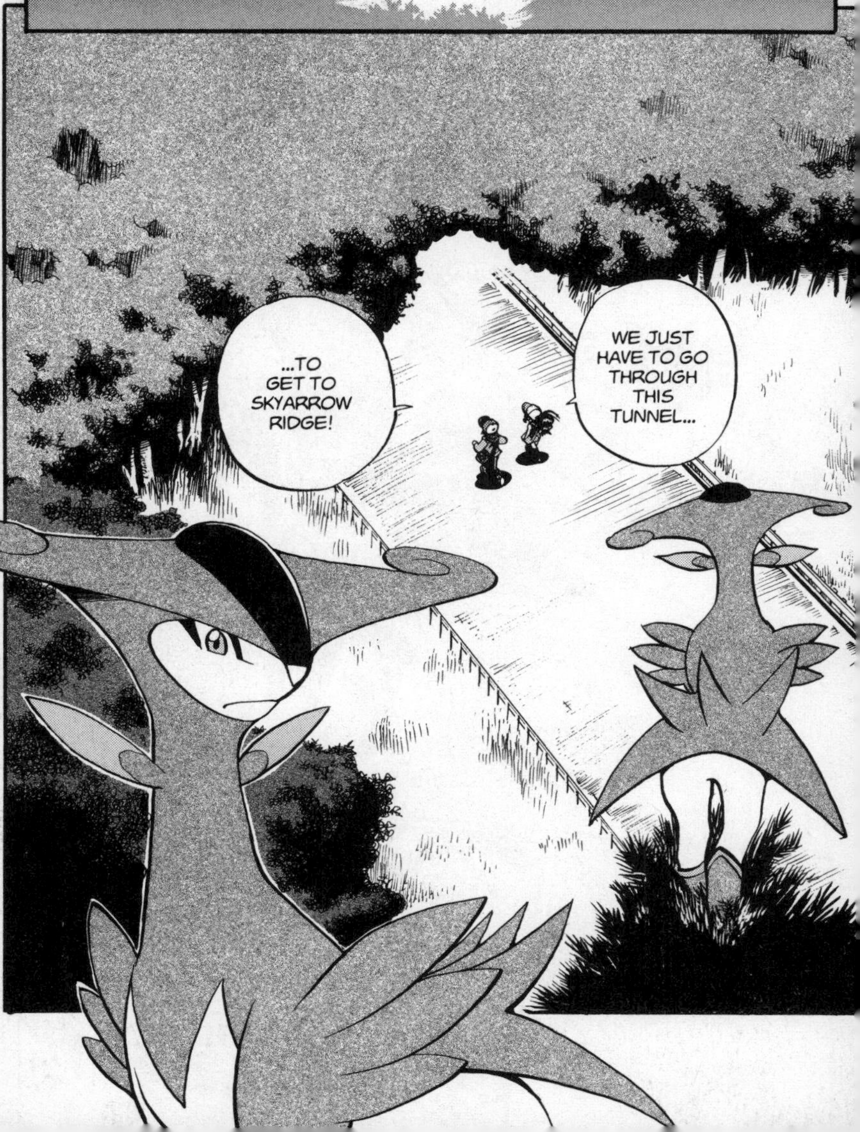
WE JUST HAVE TO GO THROUGH THIS TUNNEL...
...TO GET TO SKYARROW RIDGE!

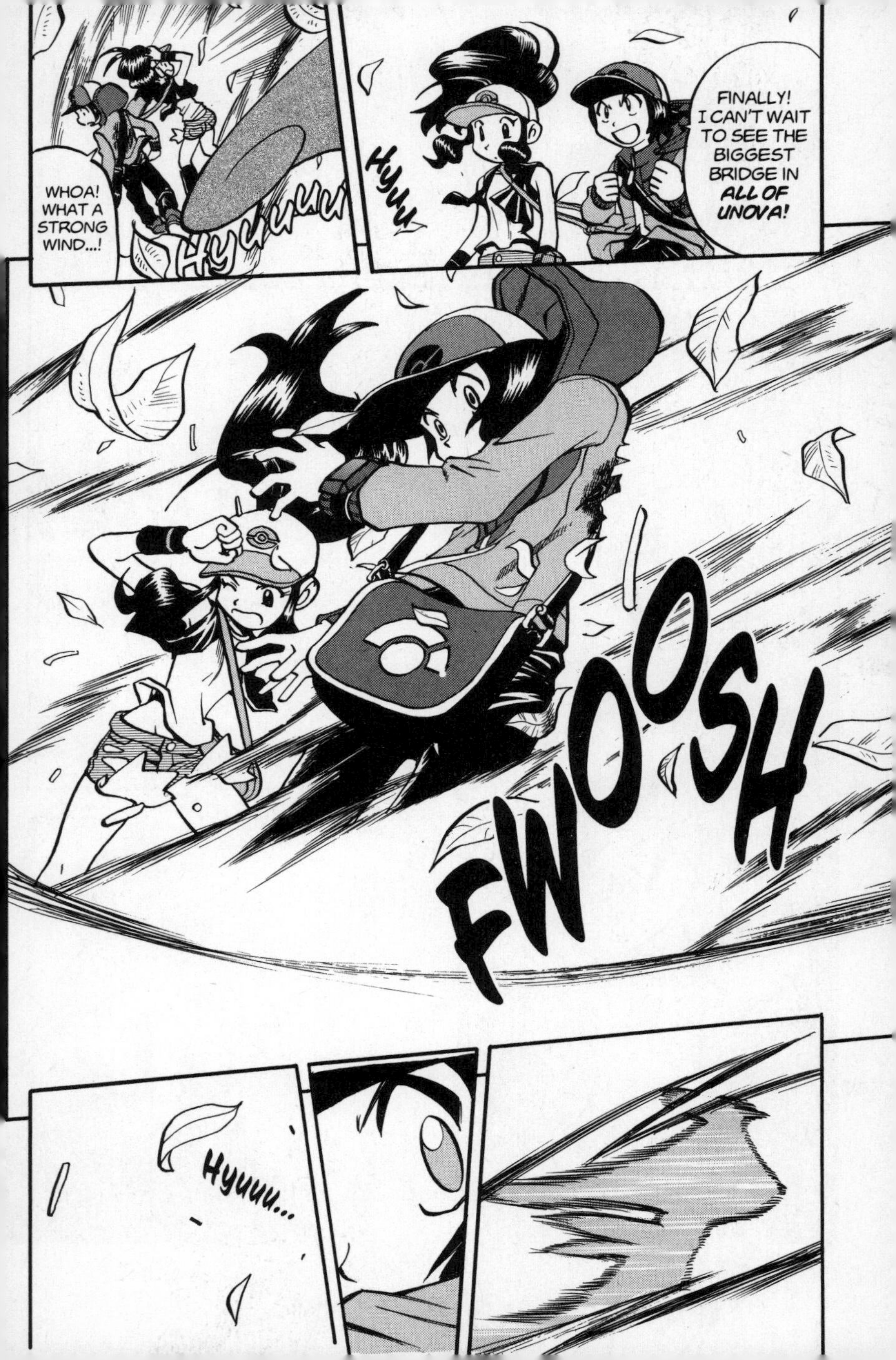
FINALLY! I CAN'T WAIT TO SEE THE BIGGEST BRIDGE IN ALL OF UNOVA!
HYUUU
WHOA! WHAT A STRONG WIND...!
Hyuuuu
FWOOOSH
Hyuuu...

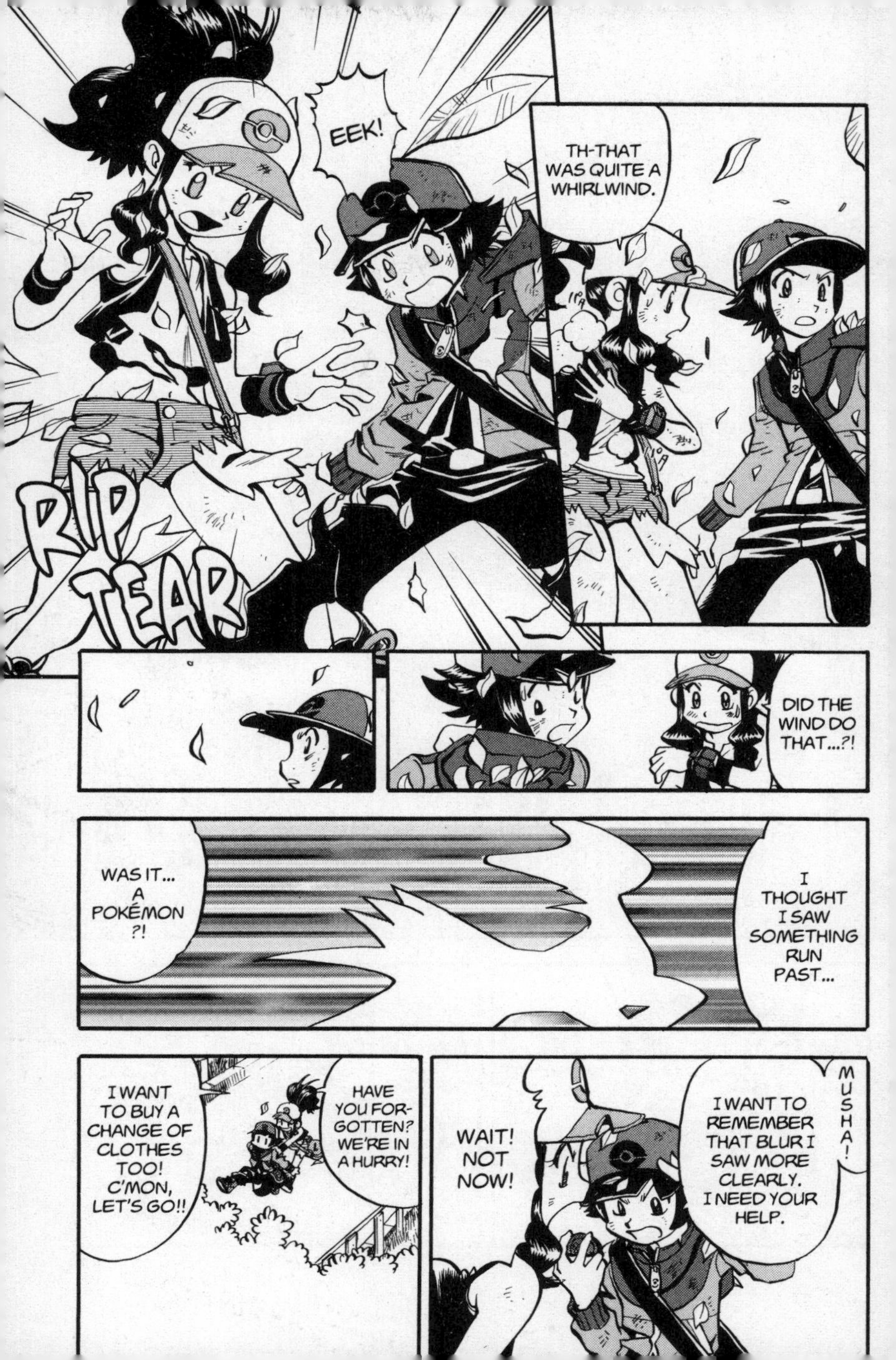
TH-THAT WAS QUITE A WHIRLWIND.
EEK!
RIP
TEAR
DID THE WIND DO THAT...?!
I THOUGHT I SAW SOMETHING RUN PAST...
WAS IT... A POKÉMON ?!
MUSHA!
I WANT TO REMEMBER THAT BLUR I SAW MORE CLEARLY. I NEED YOUR HELP.
WAIT! NOT NOW!
HAVE YOU FOR-GOTTEN? WE'RE IN A HURRY!
I WANT TO BUY A CHANGE OF CLOTHES TOO! C'MON, LET'S GO!!

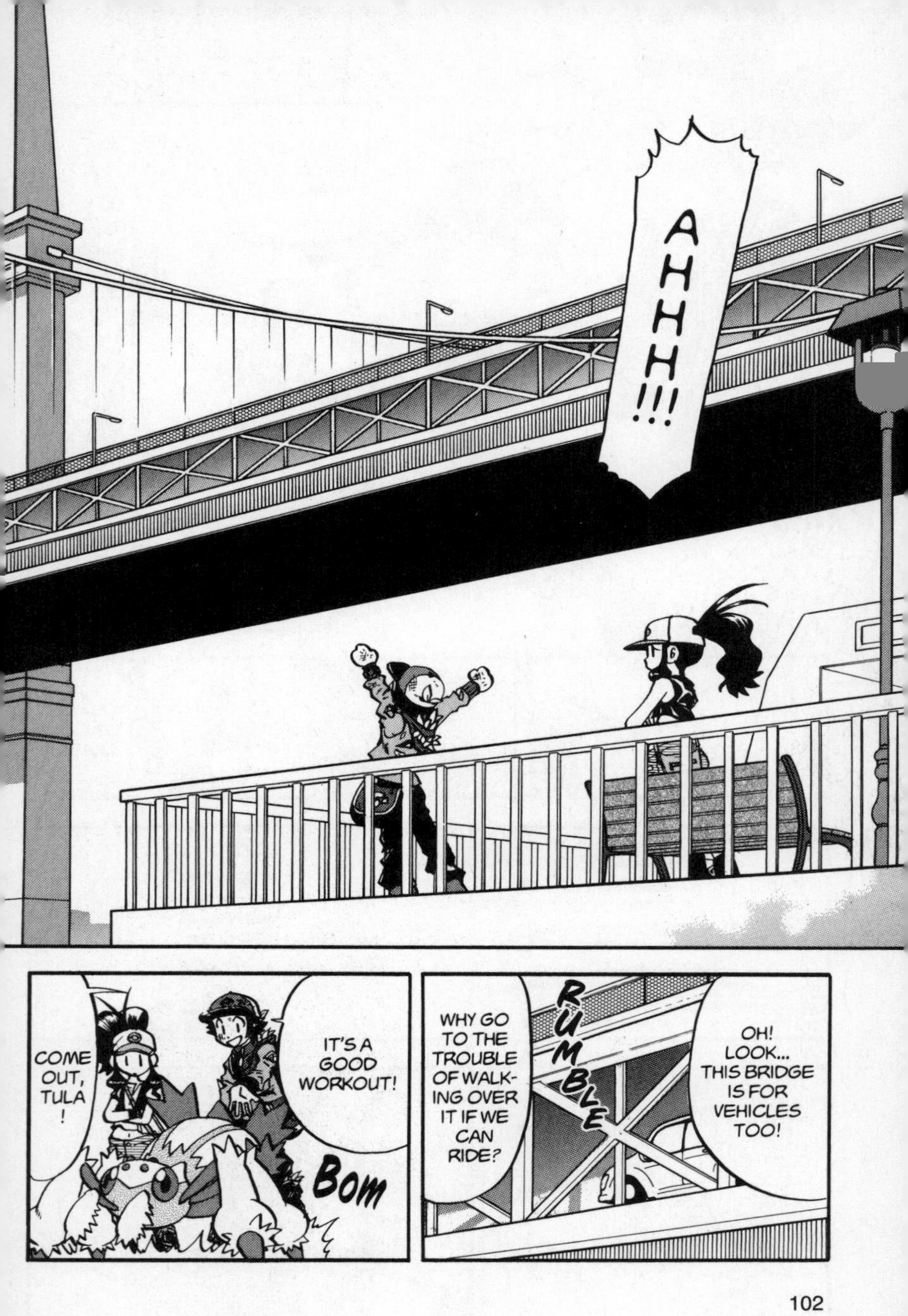
AHHH!!!
OH! LOOK... THIS BRIDGE IS FOR VEHICLES TOO!
RUMBLE
WHY GO TO THE TROUBLE OF WALK-ING OVER IT IF WE CAN RIDE?
IT'S A GOOD WORKOUT!
COME OUT, TULA!
Bom

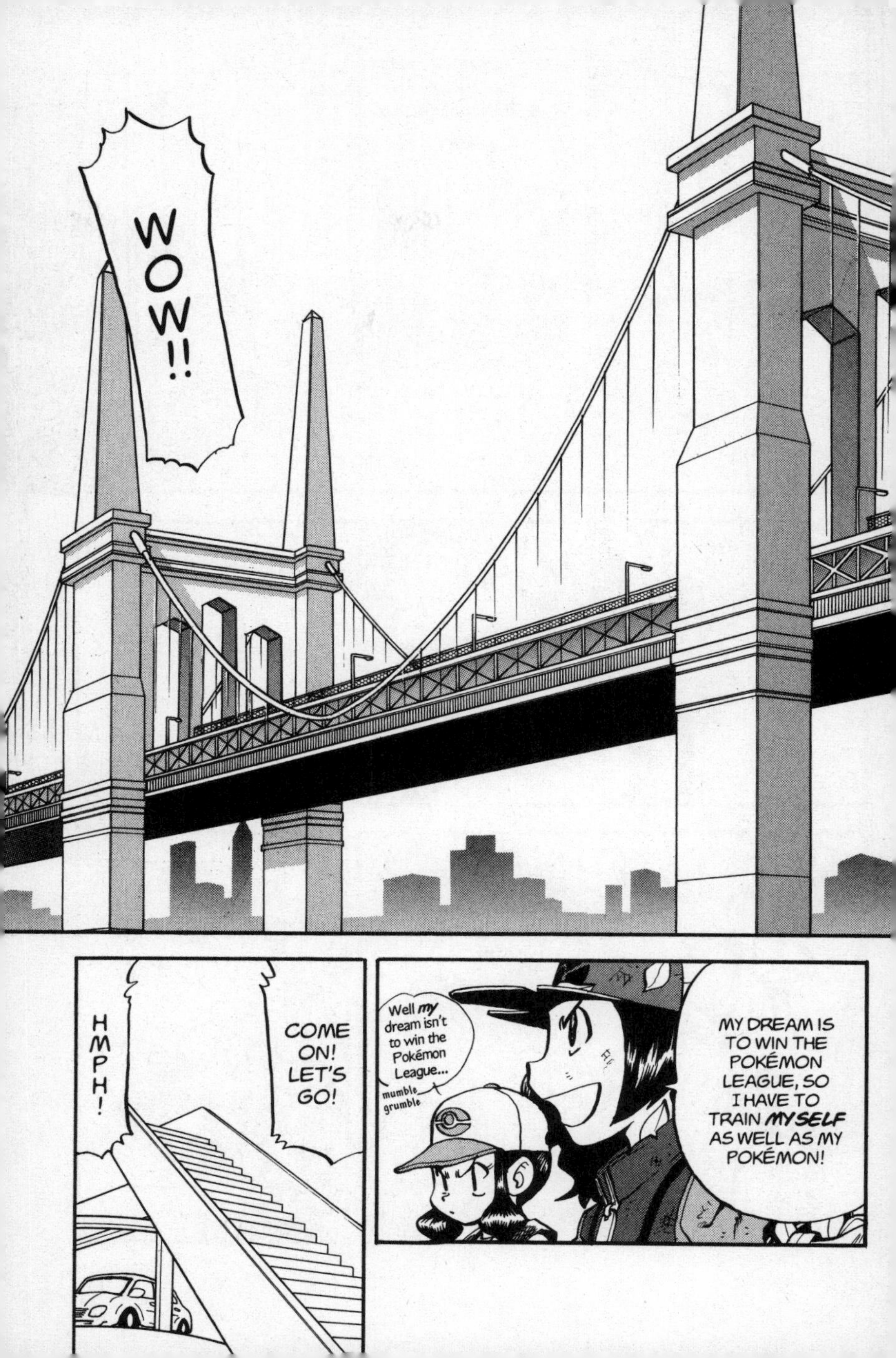
WOW!!
MY DREAM IS TO WIN THE POKÉMON LEAGUE, SO I HAVE TO TRAIN *MYSELF* AS WELL AS MY POKÉMON!
Well *my* dream isn't to win the Pokémon League...
mumble grumble
COME ON! LET'S GO!
HMPH!

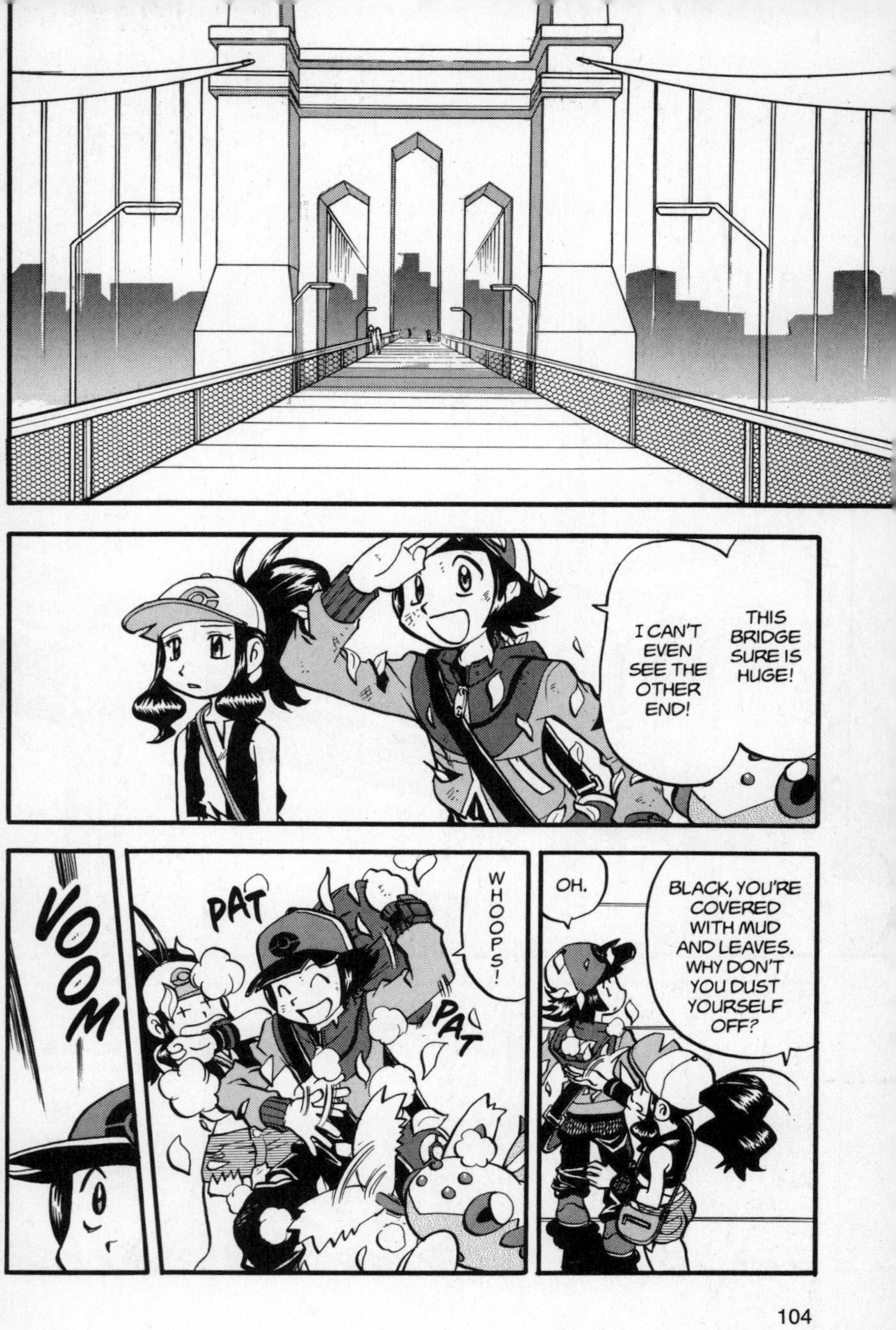
THIS BRIDGE SURE IS HUGE!
I CAN'T EVEN SEE THE OTHER END!
BLACK, YOU'RE COVERED WITH MUD AND LEAVES. WHY DON'T YOU DUST YOURSELF OFF?
OH.
WHOOPS!
PAT
PAT
VOOM

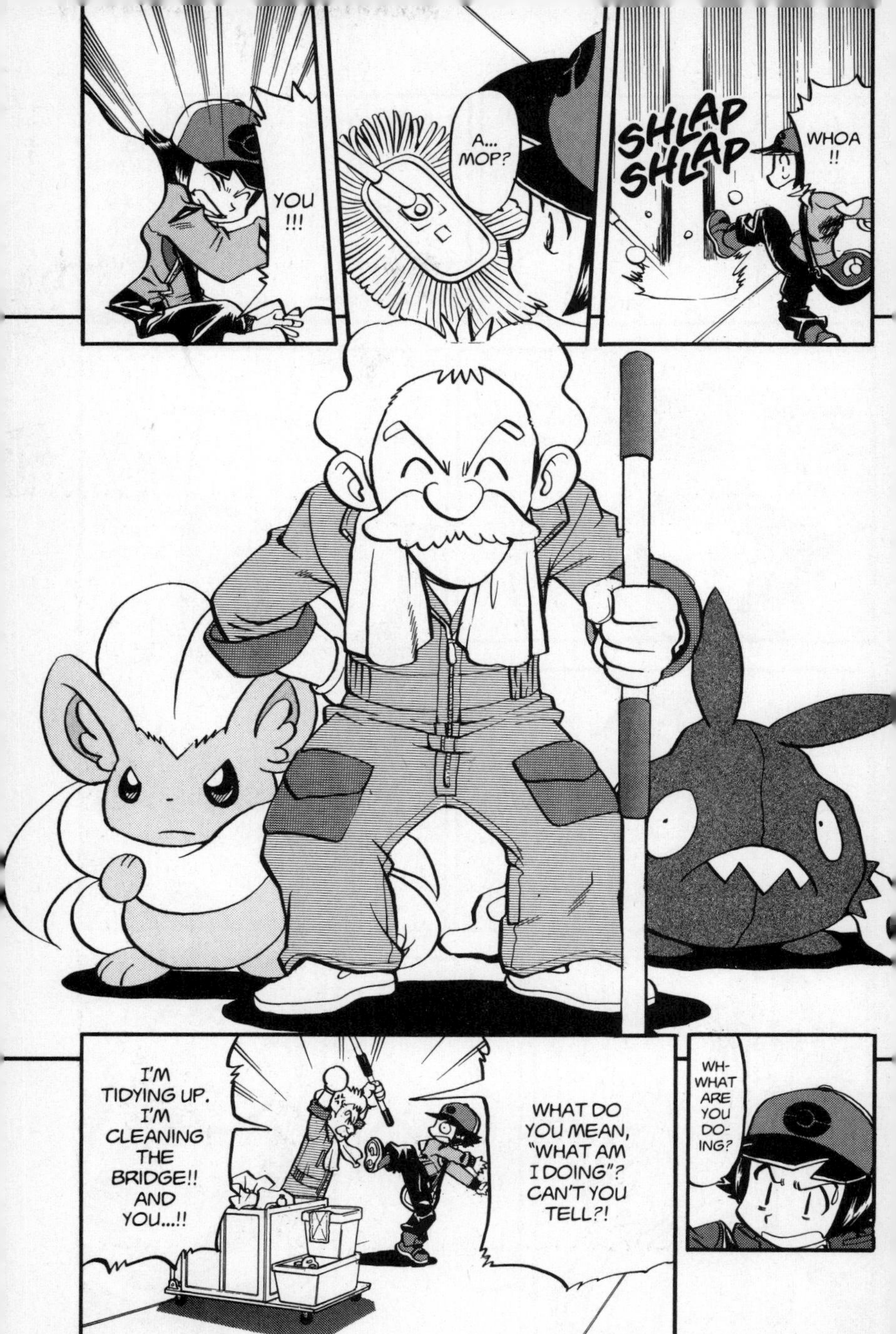
WHOA !!
SHLAP SHLAP
A... MOP?
YOU !!!
WH-WHAT ARE YOU DO-ING?
WHAT DO YOU MEAN, "WHAT AM I DOING"? CAN'T YOU TELL?!
I'M TIDYING UP. I'M CLEANING THE BRIDGE!! AND YOU...!!

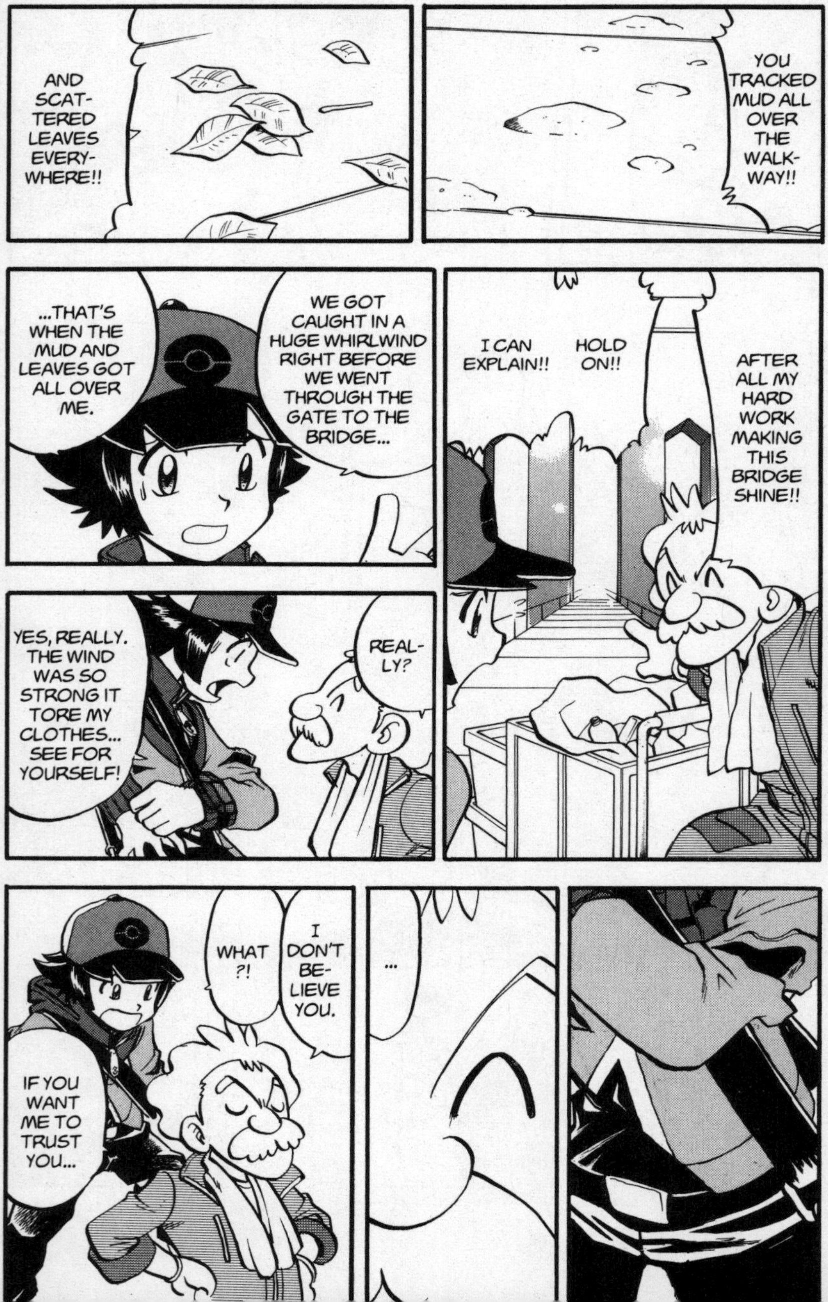
YOU TRACKED MUD ALL OVER THE WALKWAY!!
AND SCATTERED LEAVES EVERYWHERE!!
AFTER ALL MY HARD WORK MAKING THIS BRIDGE SHINE!!
HOLD ON!!
I CAN EXPLAIN!!
WE GOT CAUGHT IN A HUGE WHIRLWIND RIGHT BEFORE WE WENT THROUGH THE GATE TO THE BRIDGE...
...THAT'S WHEN THE MUD AND LEAVES GOT ALL OVER ME.
REALLY?
YES, REALLY. THE WIND WAS SO STRONG IT TORE MY CLOTHES... SEE FOR YOURSELF!
...
I DON'T BELIEVE YOU.
WHAT?!
IF YOU WANT ME TO TRUST YOU...

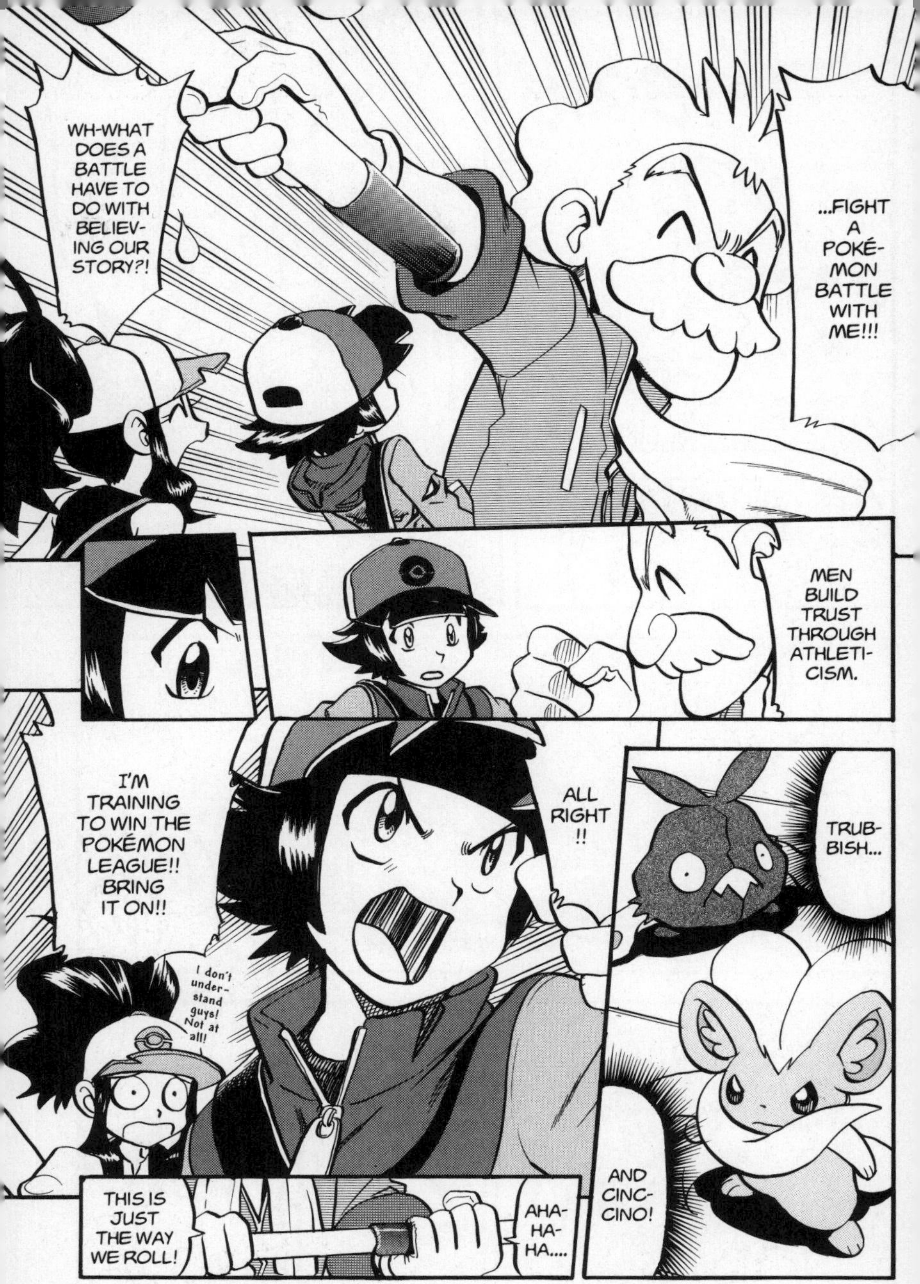
...FIGHT A POKÉMON BATTLE WITH ME!!!
WH-WHAT DOES A BATTLE HAVE TO DO WITH BELIEVING OUR STORY?!
MEN BUILD TRUST THROUGH ATHLETICISM.
TRUBBISH...
AND CINCCINO!
ALL RIGHT !!
I'M TRAINING TO WIN THE POKÉMON LEAGUE!! BRING IT ON!!
I don't understand guys! Not at all!
AHA-HA-HA....
THIS IS JUST THE WAY WE ROLL!

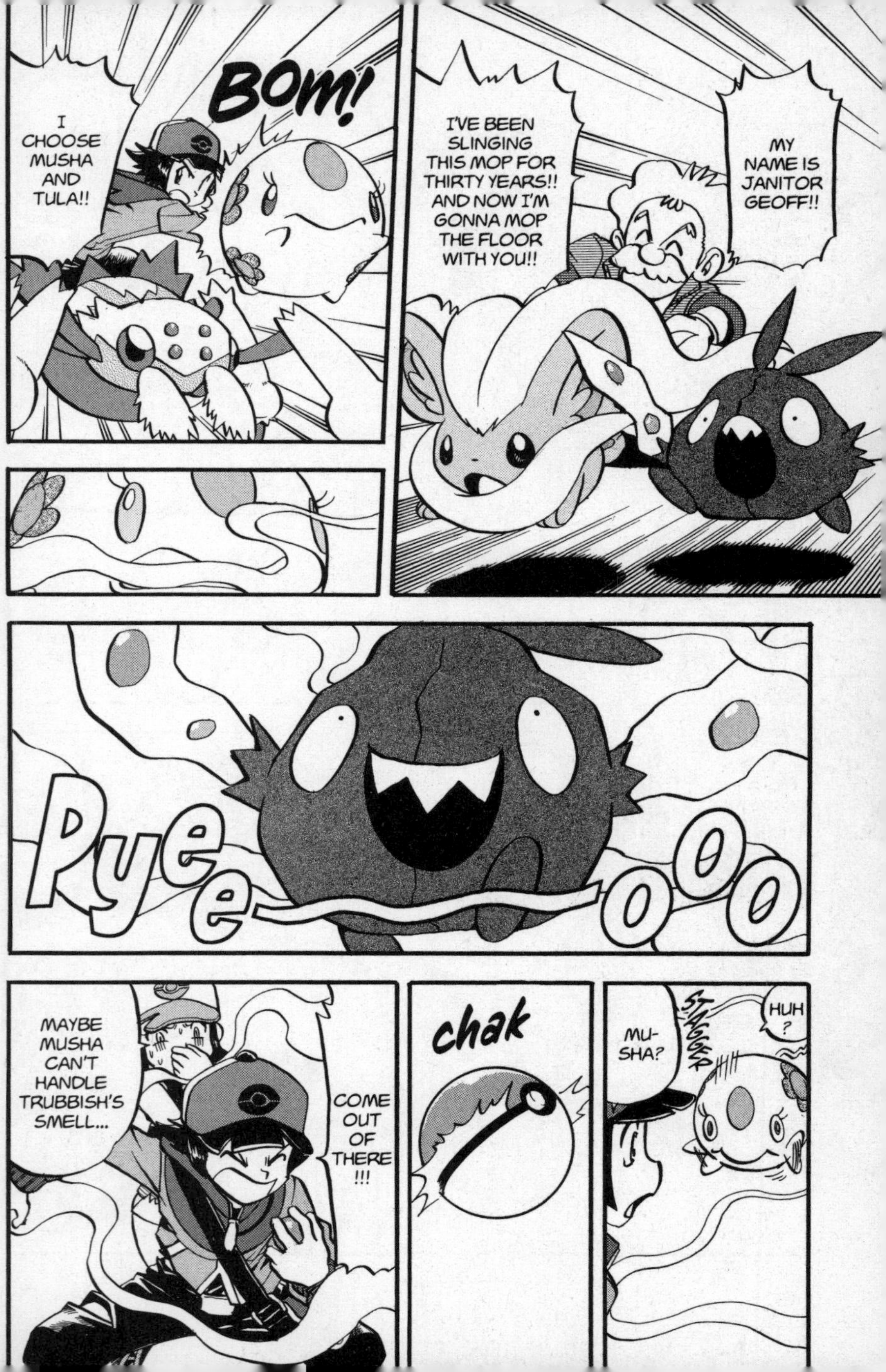
MY NAME IS JANITOR GEOFF!!
I'VE BEEN SLINGING THIS MOP FOR THIRTY YEARS!! AND NOW I'M GONNA MOP THE FLOOR WITH YOU!!
BOM!
I CHOOSE MUSHA AND TULA!!
Pyee—ooo
HUH?
STAGGER
MU-SHA?
chak
COME OUT OF THERE!!!
MAYBE MUSHA CAN'T HANDLE TRUBBISH'S SMELL...

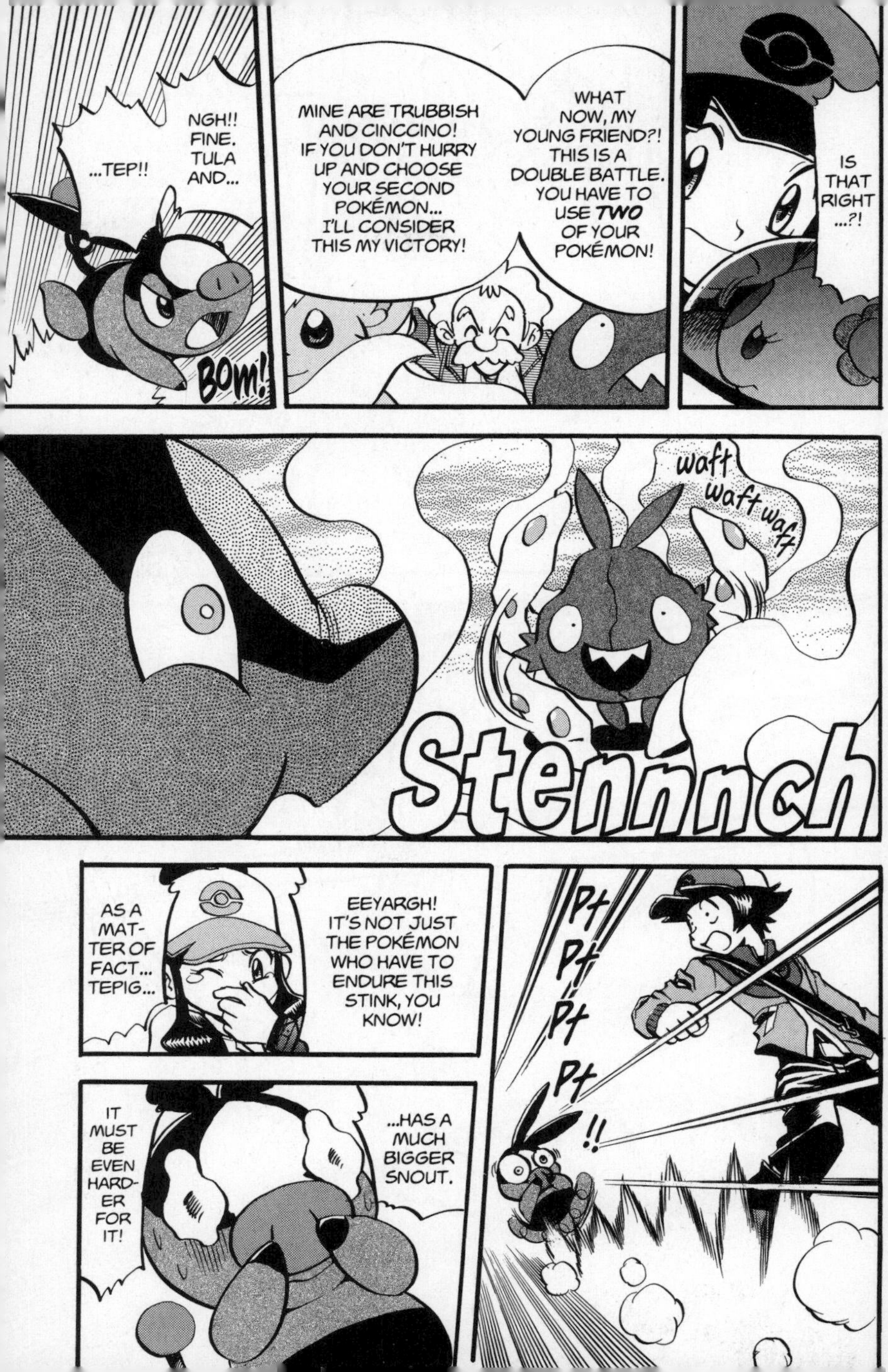
IS THAT RIGHT ...?!
WHAT NOW, MY YOUNG FRIEND?! THIS IS A DOUBLE BATTLE. YOU HAVE TO USE TWO OF YOUR POKÉMON!
MINE ARE TRUBBISH AND CINCCINO! IF YOU DON'T HURRY UP AND CHOOSE YOUR SECOND POKÉMON... I'LL CONSIDER THIS MY VICTORY!
NGH!! FINE. TULA AND...
...TEP!!
BOM!
waft waft waft
Stennnch
Pt Pt Pt Pt
!!
EEYARGH! IT'S NOT JUST THE POKÉMON WHO HAVE TO ENDURE THIS STINK, YOU KNOW!
AS A MAT-TER OF FACT... TEPIG...
...HAS A MUCH BIGGER SNOUT.
IT MUST BE EVEN HARD-ER FOR IT!

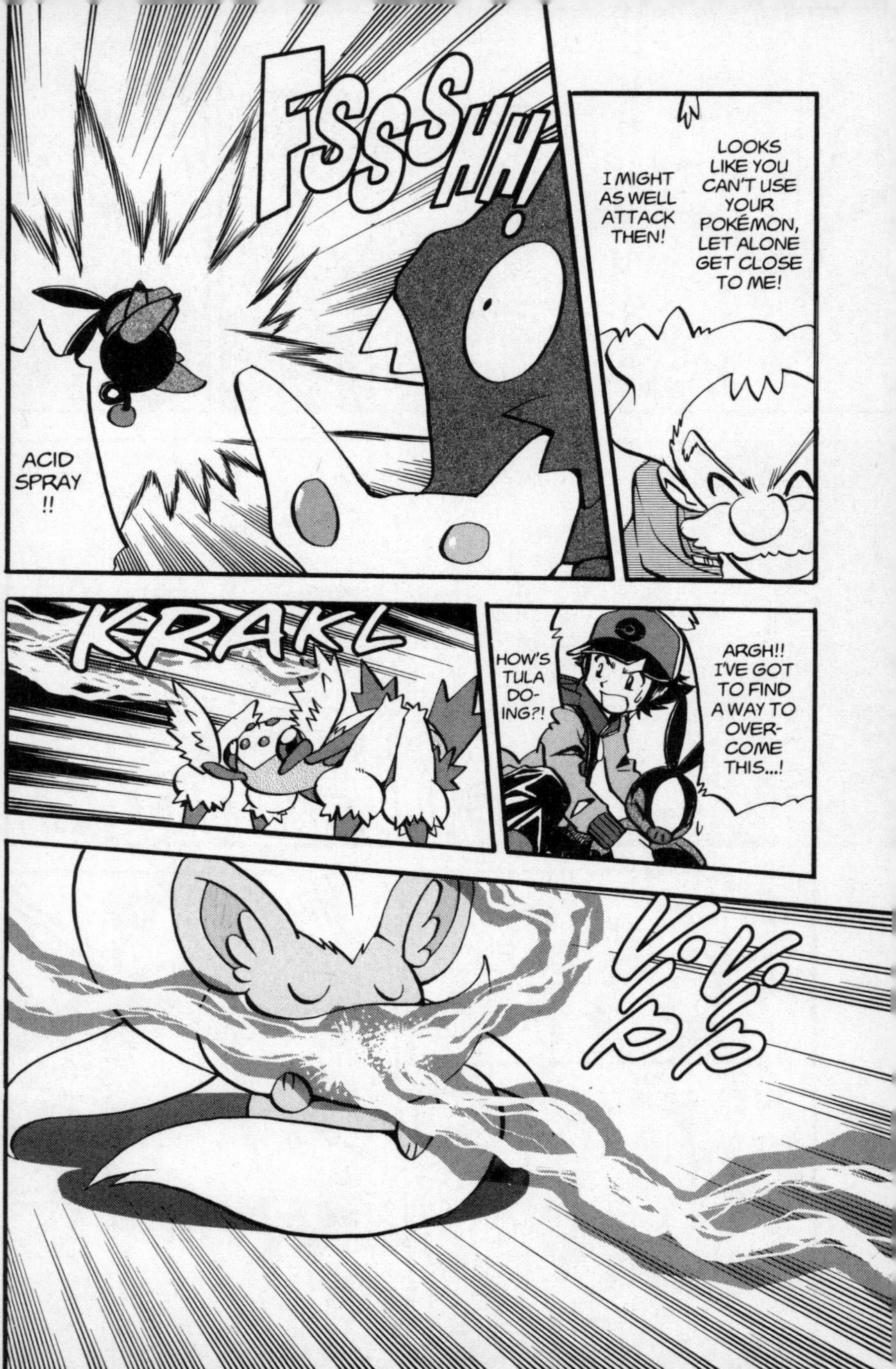
LOOKS LIKE YOU CAN'T USE YOUR POKÉMON, LET ALONE GET CLOSE TO ME!
I MIGHT AS WELL ATTACK THEN!
FSSSHH!
ACID SPRAY !!
ARGH!! I'VE GOT TO FIND A WAY TO OVER-COME THIS...!
HOW'S TULA DO-ING?!
KRAKL
VVIPP

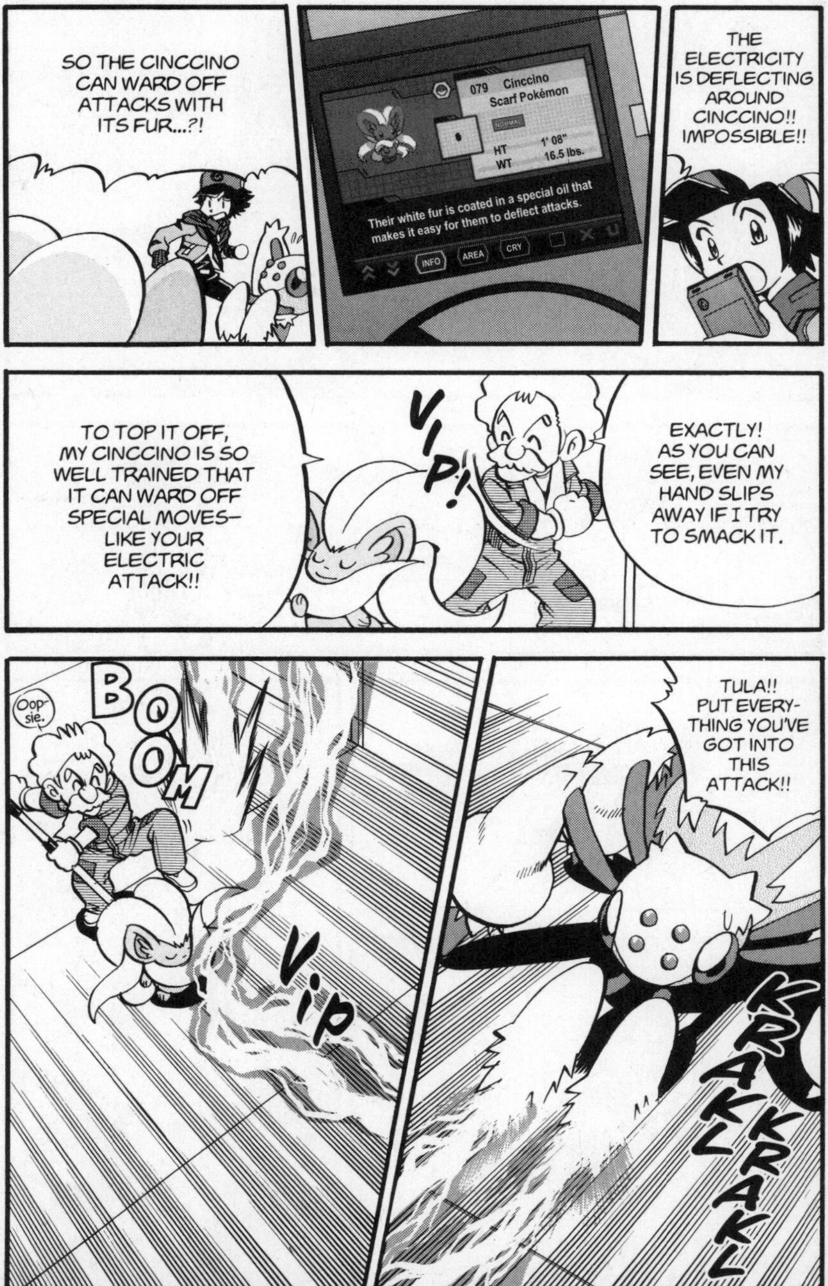
THE ELECTRICITY IS DEFLECTING AROUND CINCCINO!! IMPOSSIBLE!!
079 Cinccino
Scarf Pokémon
NORMAL
HT 1' 08"
WT 16.5 lbs.
Their white fur is coated in a special oil that makes it easy for them to deflect attacks.
INFO
AREA
CRY
SO THE CINCCINO CAN WARD OFF ATTACKS WITH ITS FUR...?!
EXACTLY! AS YOU CAN SEE, EVEN MY HAND SLIPS AWAY IF I TRY TO SMACK IT.
VIP!
TO TOP IT OFF, MY CINCCINO IS SO WELL TRAINED THAT IT CAN WARD OFF SPECIAL MOVES—LIKE YOUR ELECTRIC ATTACK!!
TULA!! PUT EVERYTHING YOU'VE GOT INTO THIS ATTACK!!
KRAKL
KRAKL
BOOM
Oop-sie.
Vip

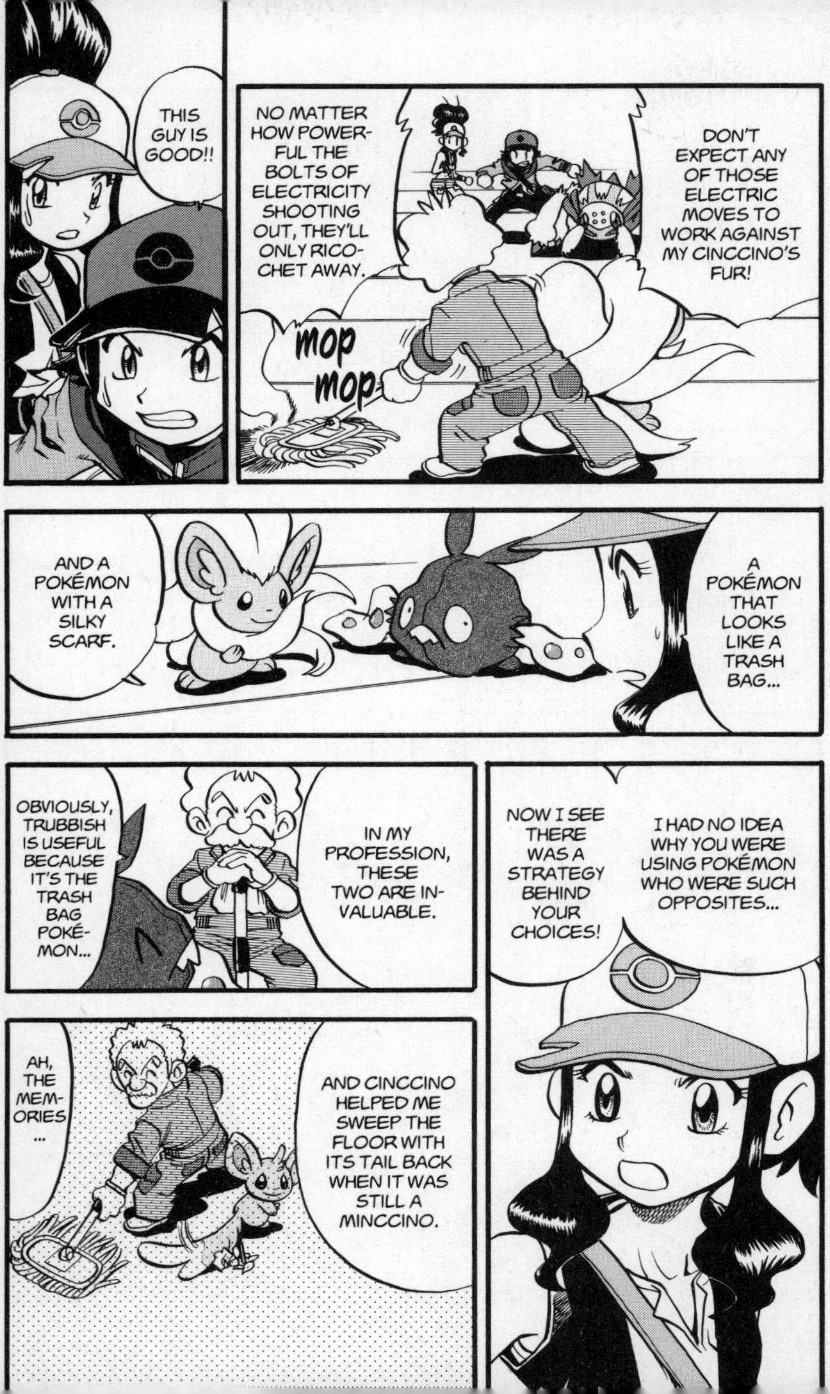
DON'T EXPECT ANY OF THOSE ELECTRIC MOVES TO WORK AGAINST MY CINCCINO'S FUR!
NO MATTER HOW POWERFUL THE BOLTS OF ELECTRICITY SHOOTING OUT, THEY'LL ONLY RICOCHET AWAY.
mop mop
THIS GUY IS GOOD!!
A POKÉMON THAT LOOKS LIKE A TRASH BAG...
AND A POKÉMON WITH A SILKY SCARF.
I HAD NO IDEA WHY YOU WERE USING POKÉMON WHO WERE SUCH OPPOSITES...
NOW I SEE THERE WAS A STRATEGY BEHIND YOUR CHOICES!
IN MY PROFESSION, THESE TWO ARE INVALUABLE.
OBVIOUSLY, TRUBBISH IS USEFUL BECAUSE IT'S THE TRASH BAG POKÉMON...
AND CINCCINO HELPED ME SWEEP THE FLOOR WITH ITS TAIL BACK WHEN IT WAS STILL A MINCCINO.
AH, THE MEMORIES...

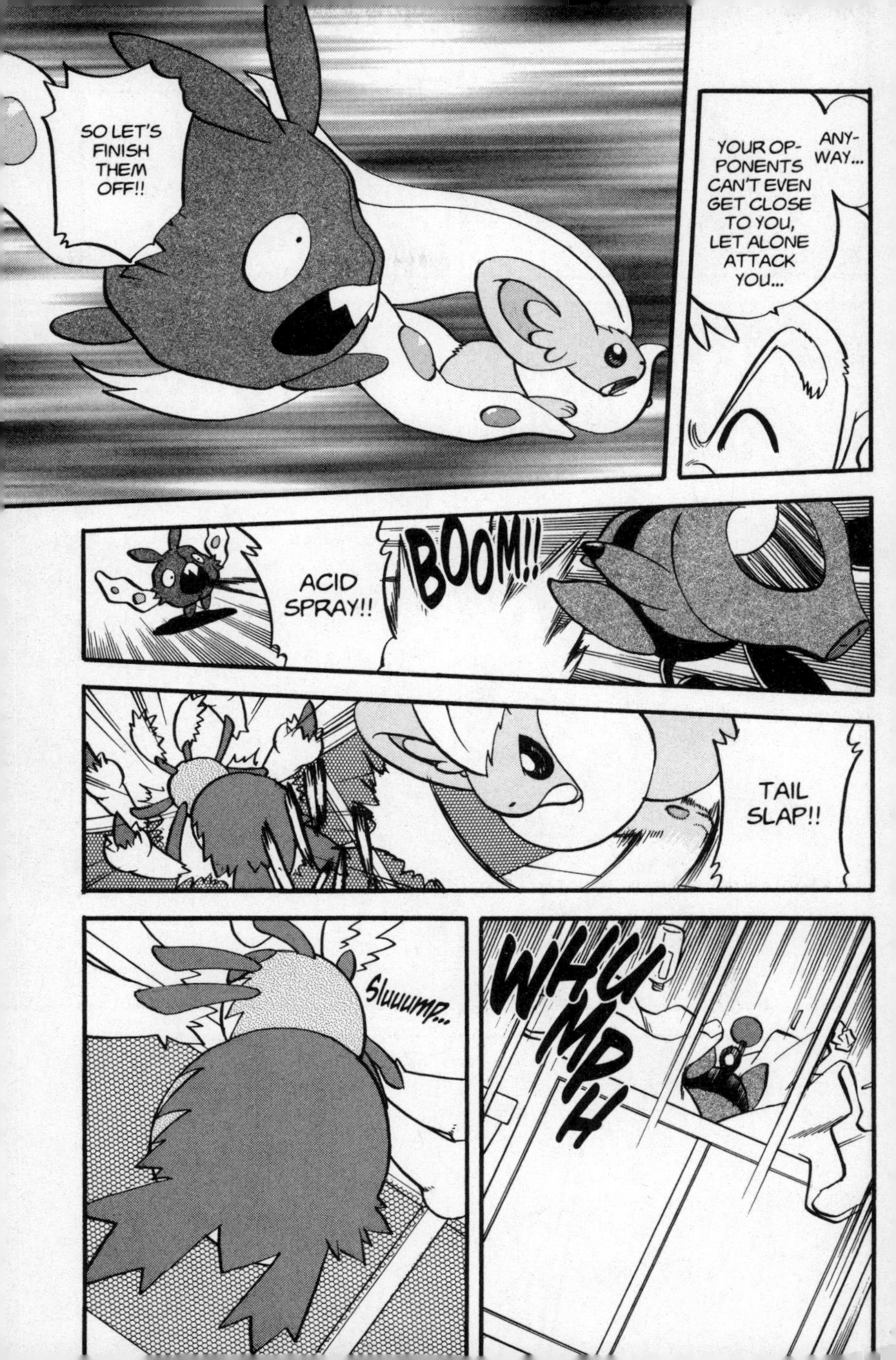
ANYWAY...
YOUR OPPONENTS CAN'T EVEN GET CLOSE TO YOU, LET ALONE ATTACK YOU...
SO LET'S FINISH THEM OFF!!
BOOM!!
ACID SPRAY!!
TAIL SLAP!!
WHUMPH
Sluuump...

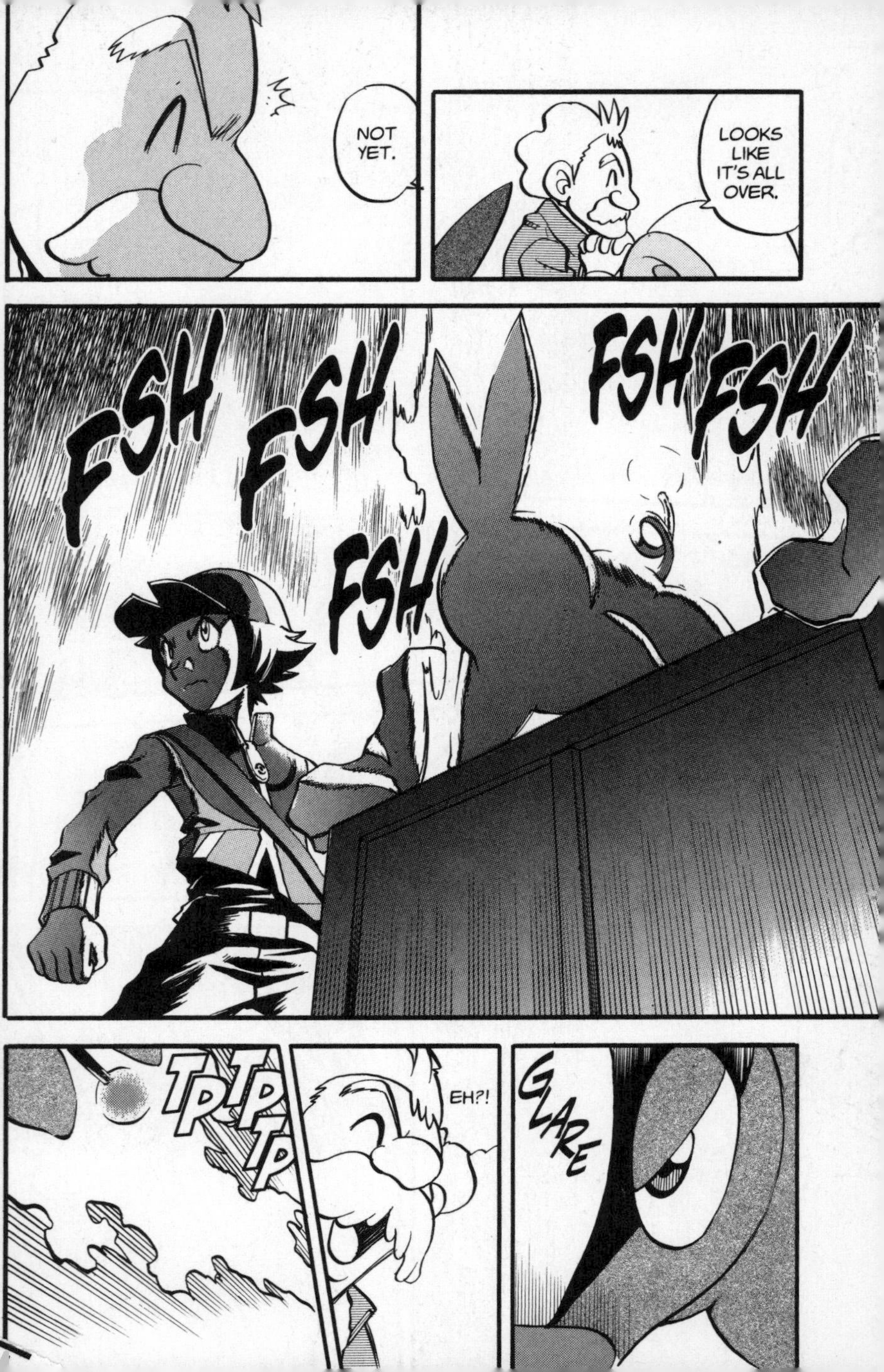
LOOKS LIKE IT'S ALL OVER.
NOT YET.
FSH
FSH
FSH
FSH
FSH
GLARE
EH?!
TP TP TP

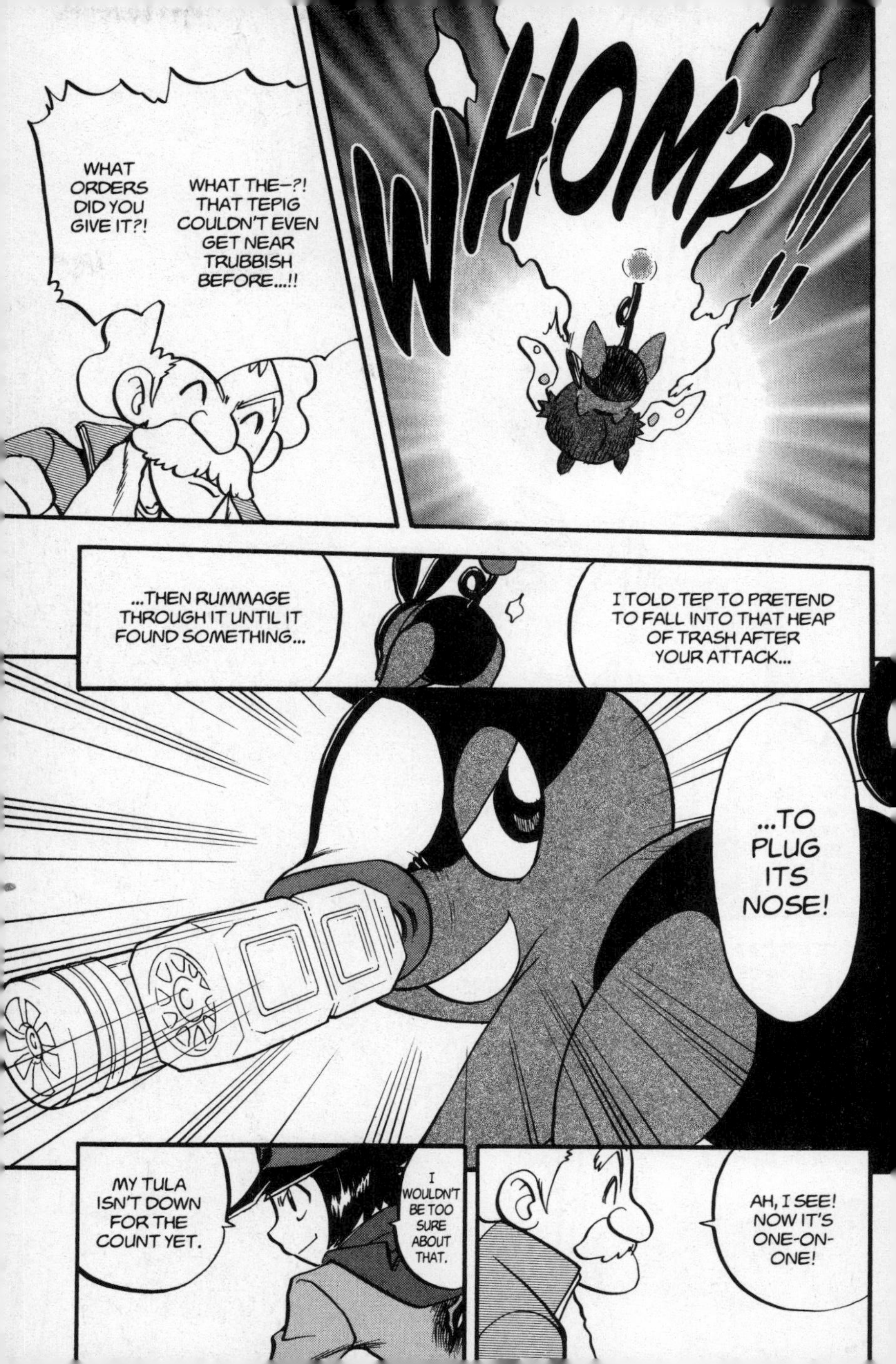
WHOMP!!
WHAT THE—?! THAT TEPIG COULDN'T EVEN GET NEAR TRUBBISH BEFORE...!!
WHAT ORDERS DID YOU GIVE IT?!
I TOLD TEP TO PRETEND TO FALL INTO THAT HEAP OF TRASH AFTER YOUR ATTACK...
...THEN RUMMAGE THROUGH IT UNTIL IT FOUND SOMETHING...
...TO PLUG ITS NOSE!
AH, I SEE! NOW IT'S ONE-ON-ONE!
I WOULDN'T BE TOO SURE ABOUT THAT.
MY TULA ISN'T DOWN FOR THE COUNT YET.

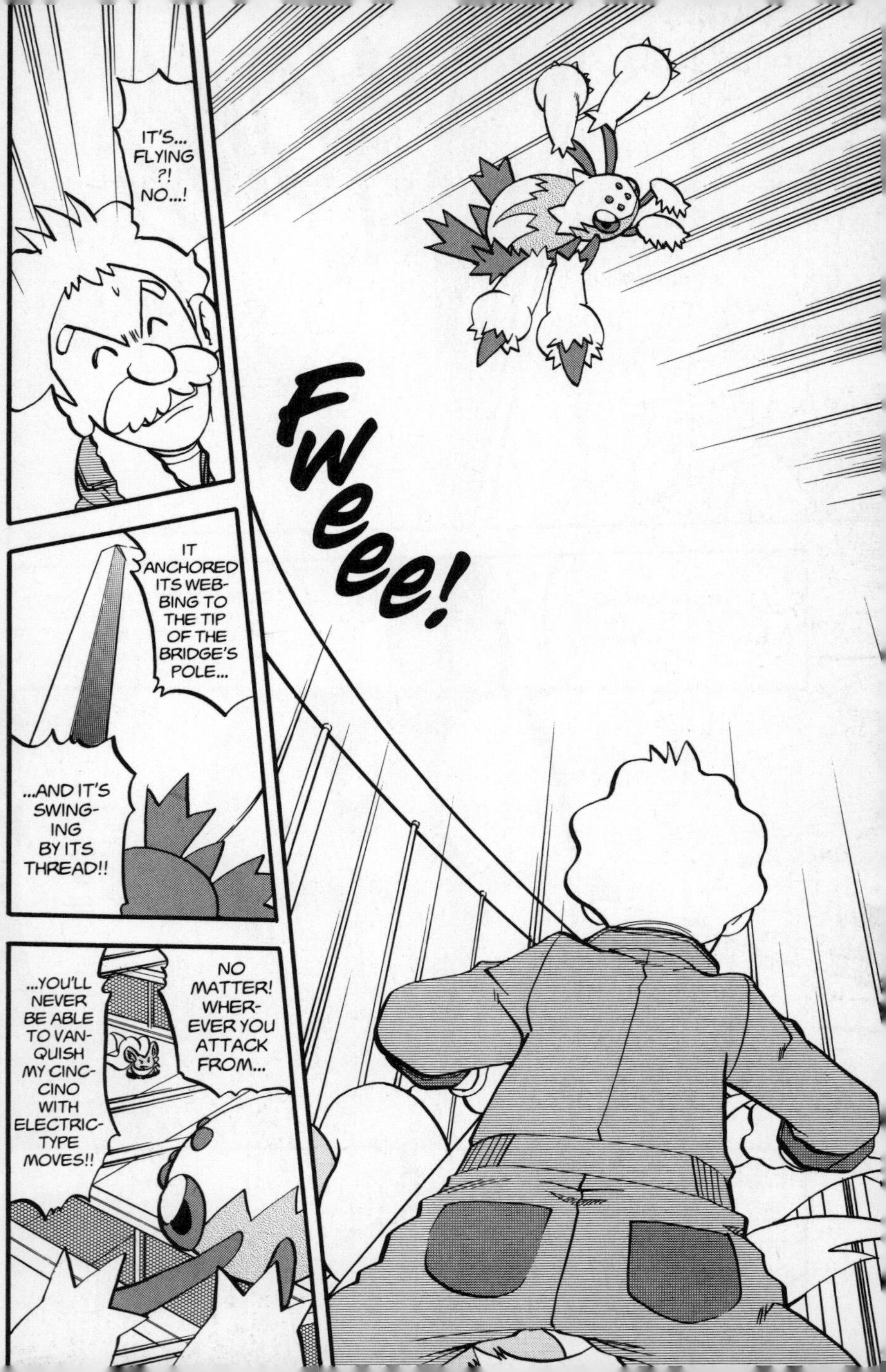
Fweee!
IT'S... FLYING?! NO...!
IT ANCHORED ITS WEBBING TO THE TIP OF THE BRIDGE'S POLE...
...AND IT'S SWINGING BY ITS THREAD!!
NO MATTER! WHEREVER YOU ATTACK FROM...
...YOU'LL NEVER BE ABLE TO VANQUISH MY CINCCINO WITH ELECTRIC-TYPE MOVES!!

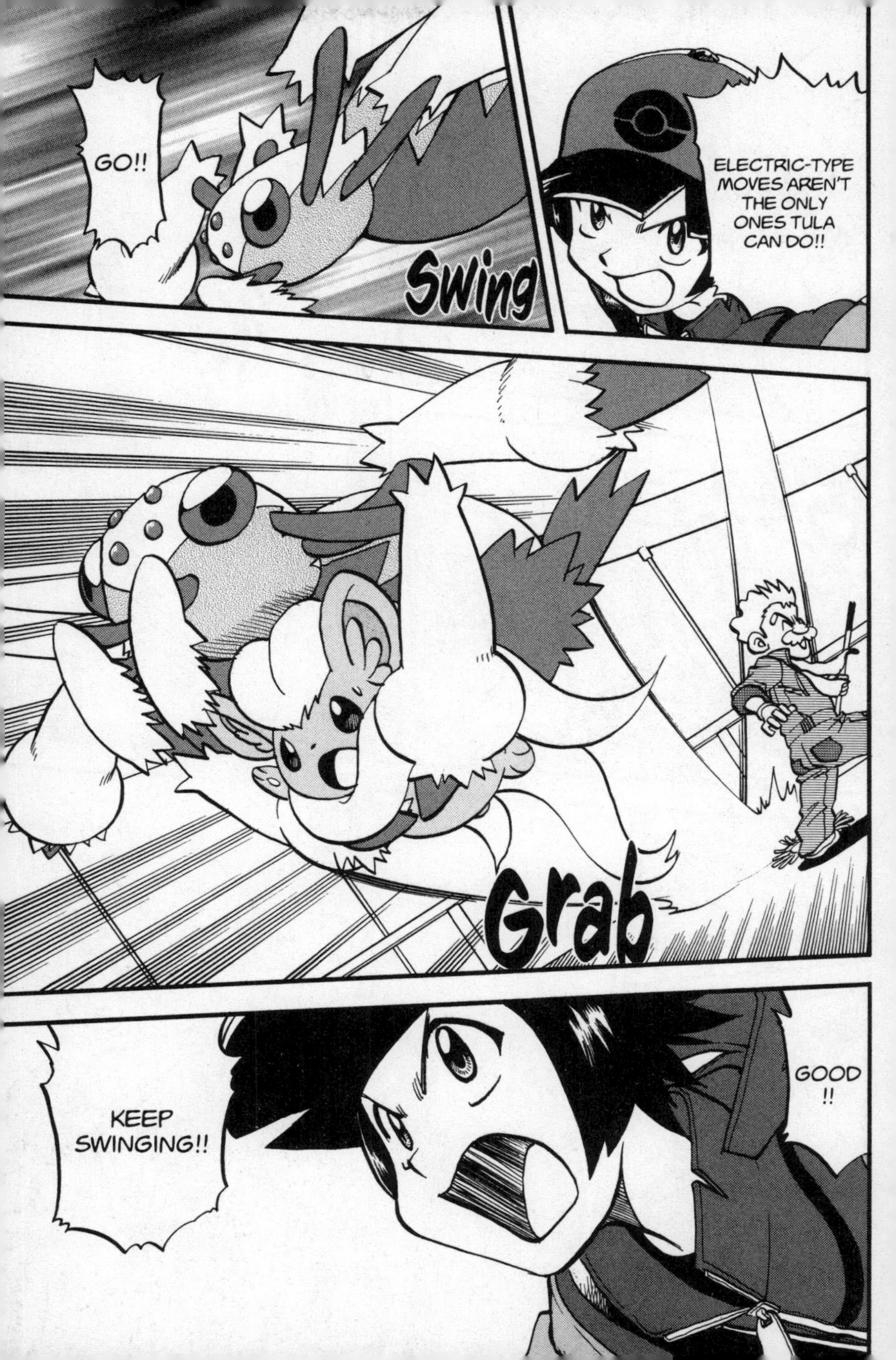
ELECTRIC-TYPE MOVES AREN'T THE ONLY ONES TULA CAN DO!!
Swing
GO!!
Grab
GOOD!!
KEEP SWINGING!!

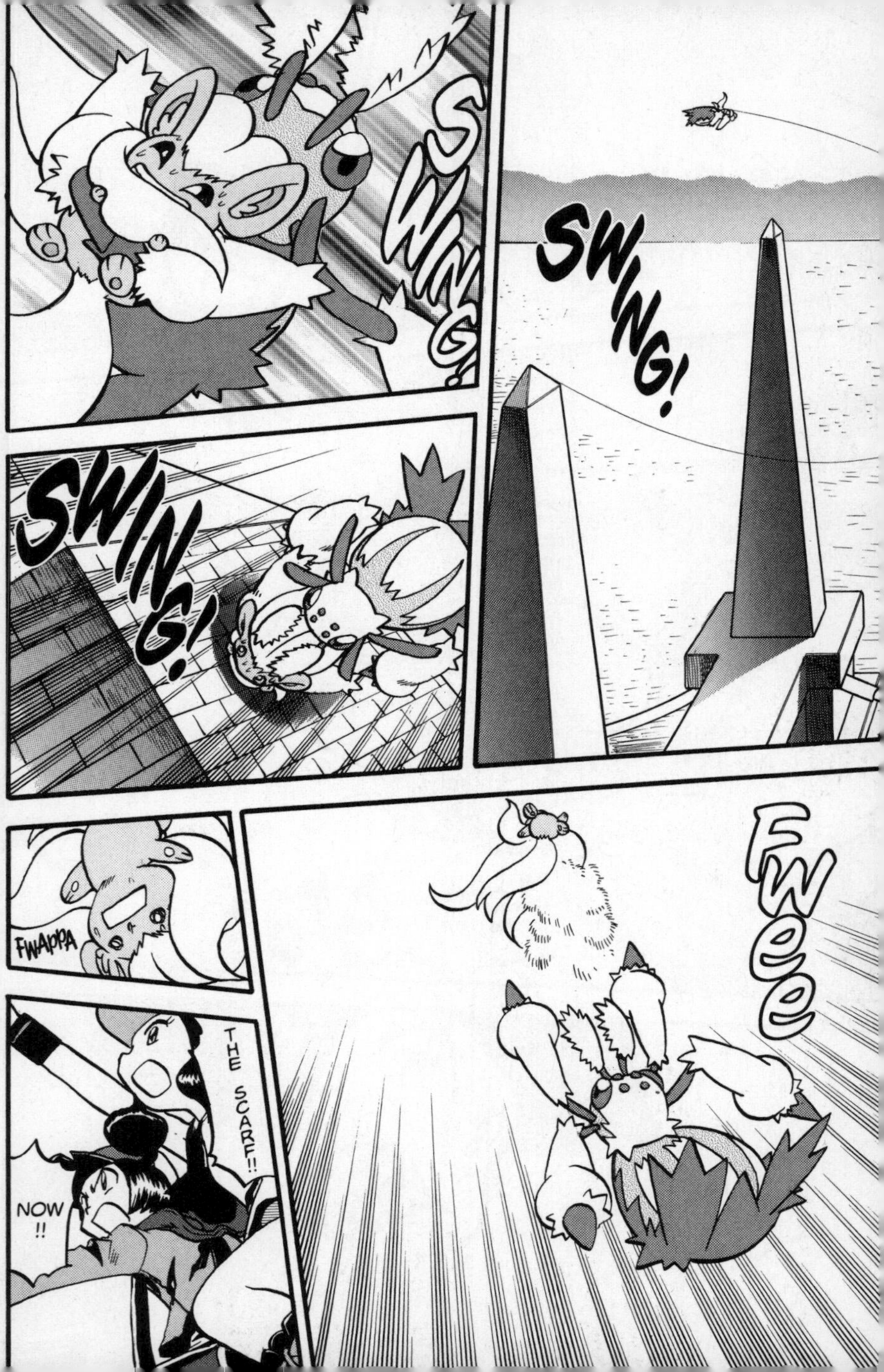
SWING!
SWING!
SWING!
Fwee
FWAPPA
THE SCARF!!
NOW!!

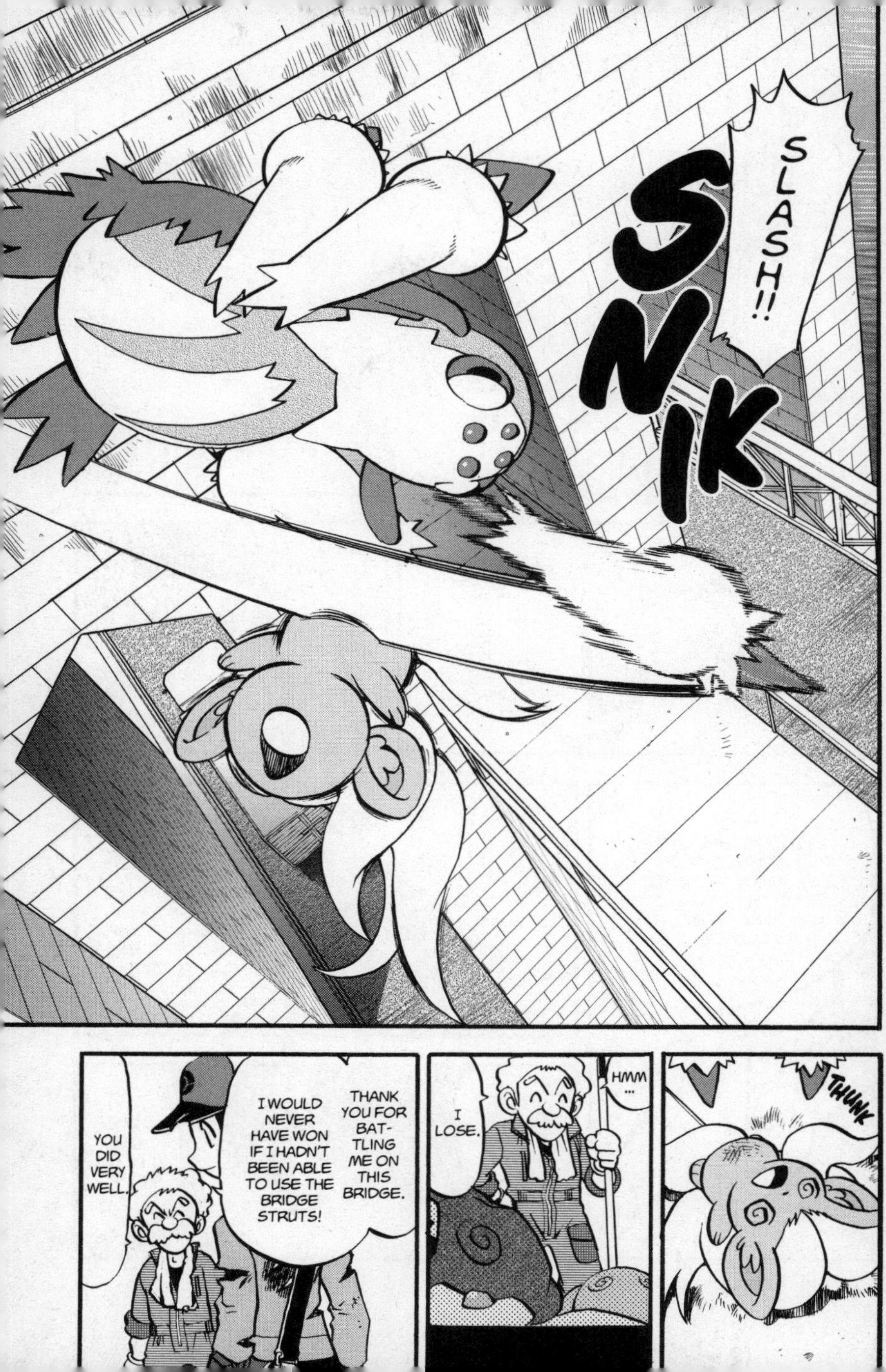
SLASH!!
SNIK
THUNK
HMM ...
I LOSE.
THANK YOU FOR BATTLING ME ON THIS BRIDGE.
I WOULD NEVER HAVE WON IF I HADN'T BEEN ABLE TO USE THE BRIDGE STRUTS!
YOU DID VERY WELL.

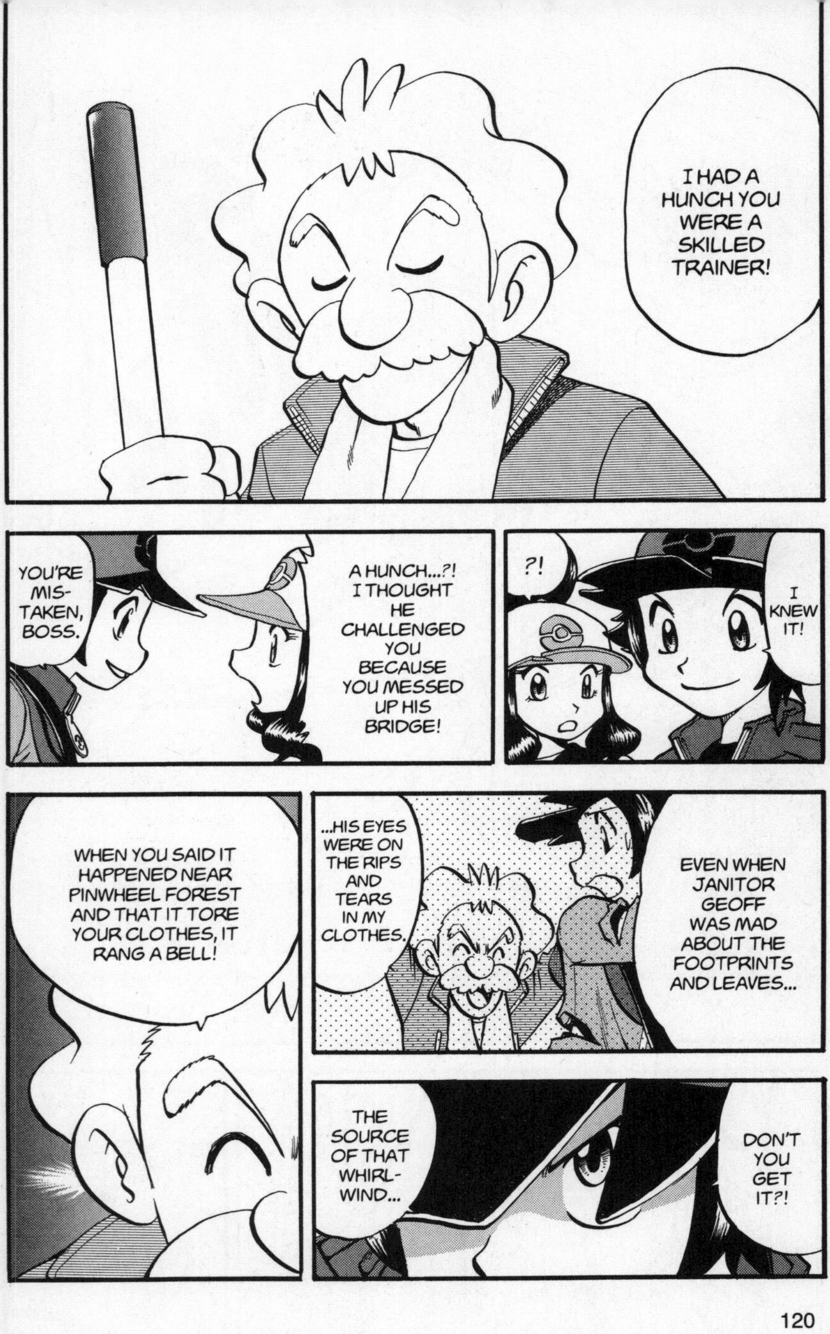
I HAD A HUNCH YOU WERE A SKILLED TRAINER!
I KNEW IT!
?!
A HUNCH...?! I THOUGHT HE CHALLENGED YOU BECAUSE YOU MESSED UP HIS BRIDGE!
YOU'RE MIS-TAKEN, BOSS.
EVEN WHEN JANITOR GEOFF WAS MAD ABOUT THE FOOTPRINTS AND LEAVES...
...HIS EYES WERE ON THE RIPS AND TEARS IN MY CLOTHES.
DON'T YOU GET IT?!
THE SOURCE OF THAT WHIRL-WIND...
WHEN YOU SAID IT HAPPENED NEAR PINWHEEL FOREST AND THAT IT TORE YOUR CLOTHES, IT RANG A BELL!

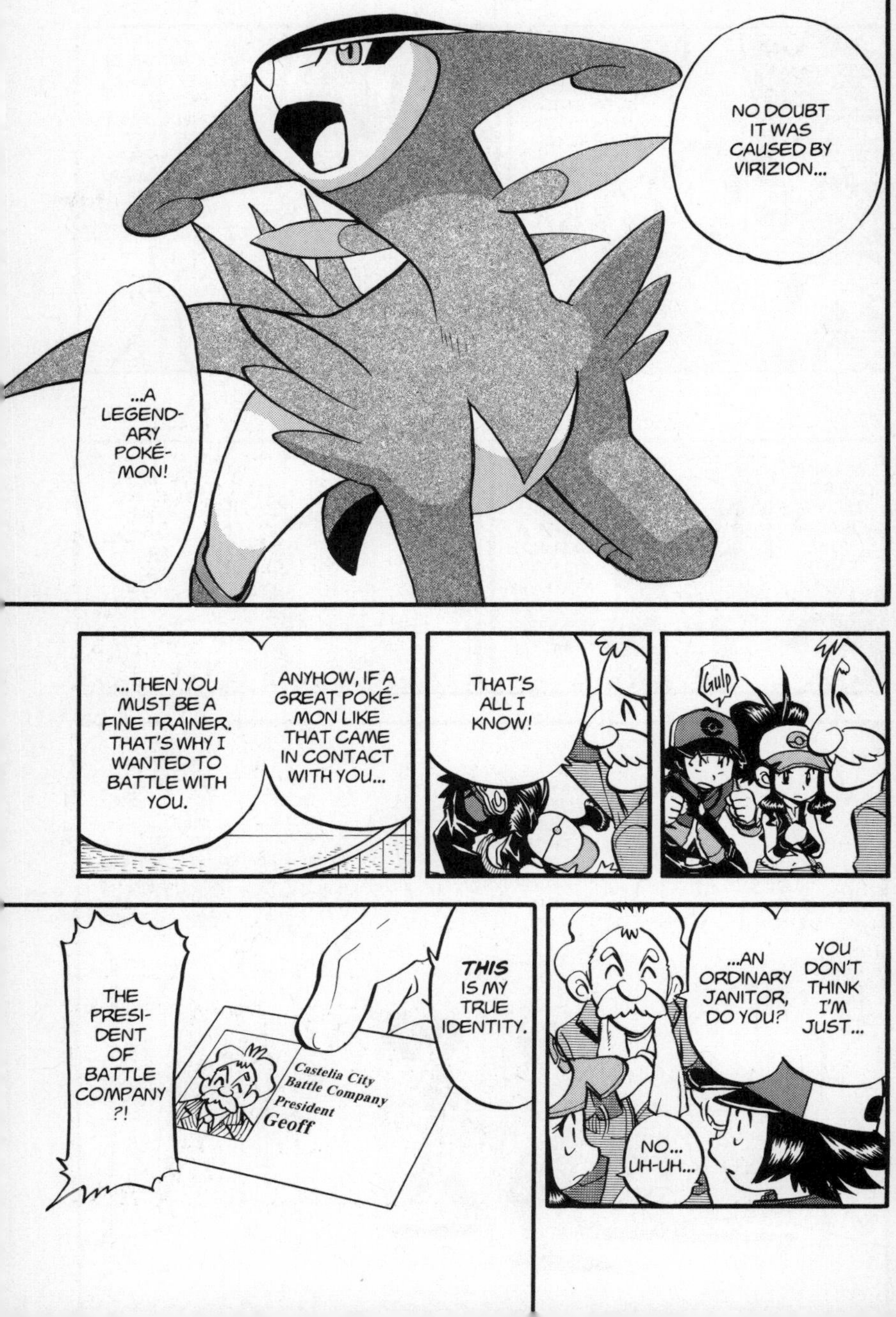
NO DOUBT IT WAS CAUSED BY VIRIZION...
...A LEGENDARY POKÉMON!
Gulp
THAT'S ALL I KNOW!
ANYHOW, IF A GREAT POKÉMON LIKE THAT CAME IN CONTACT WITH YOU...
...THEN YOU MUST BE A FINE TRAINER. THAT'S WHY I WANTED TO BATTLE WITH YOU.
YOU DON'T THINK I'M JUST...
...AN ORDINARY JANITOR, DO YOU?
NO... UH-UH...
THIS IS MY TRUE IDENTITY.
Castelia City Battle Company
President
Geoff
THE PRESIDENT OF BATTLE COMPANY?!

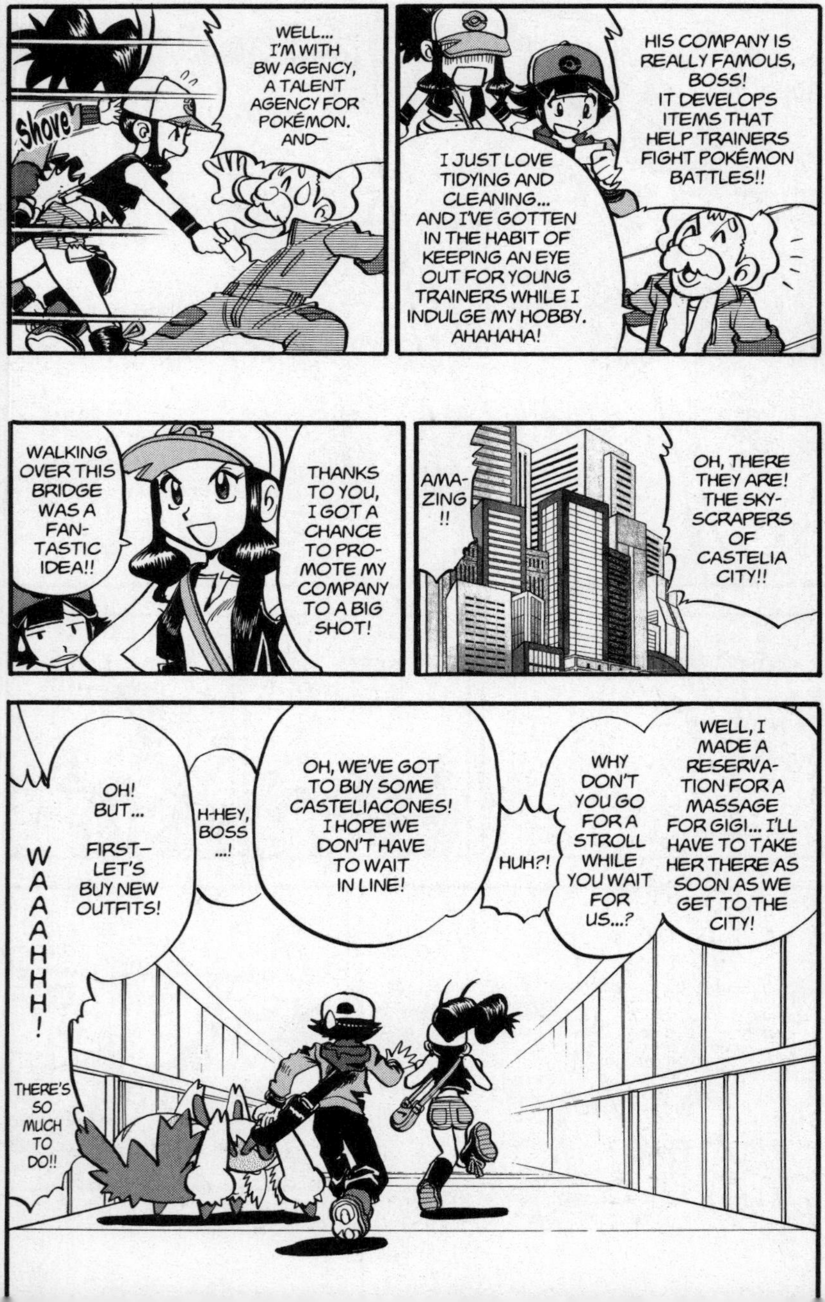
HIS COMPANY IS REALLY FAMOUS, BOSS! IT DEVELOPS ITEMS THAT HELP TRAINERS FIGHT POKÉMON BATTLES!!
I JUST LOVE TIDYING AND CLEANING... AND I'VE GOTTEN IN THE HABIT OF KEEPING AN EYE OUT FOR YOUNG TRAINERS WHILE I INDULGE MY HOBBY. AHAHAHA!
WELL... I'M WITH BW AGENCY, A TALENT AGENCY FOR POKÉMON. AND—
Shove
OH, THERE THEY ARE! THE SKY-SCRAPERS OF CASTELIA CITY!!
AMA-ZING!!
THANKS TO YOU, I GOT A CHANCE TO PRO-MOTE MY COMPANY TO A BIG SHOT!
WALKING OVER THIS BRIDGE WAS A FAN-TASTIC IDEA!!
WELL, I MADE A RESERVA-TION FOR A MASSAGE FOR GIGI... I'LL HAVE TO TAKE HER THERE AS SOON AS WE GET TO THE CITY!
WHY DON'T YOU GO FOR A STROLL WHILE YOU WAIT FOR US...?
HUH?!
OH, WE'VE GOT TO BUY SOME CASTELIACONES! I HOPE WE DON'T HAVE TO WAIT IN LINE!
H-HEY, BOSS ...!
OH! BUT... FIRST— LET'S BUY NEW OUTFITS!
WAAAAHHHH!
THERE'S SO MUCH TO DO!!

ADVENTURE MAP

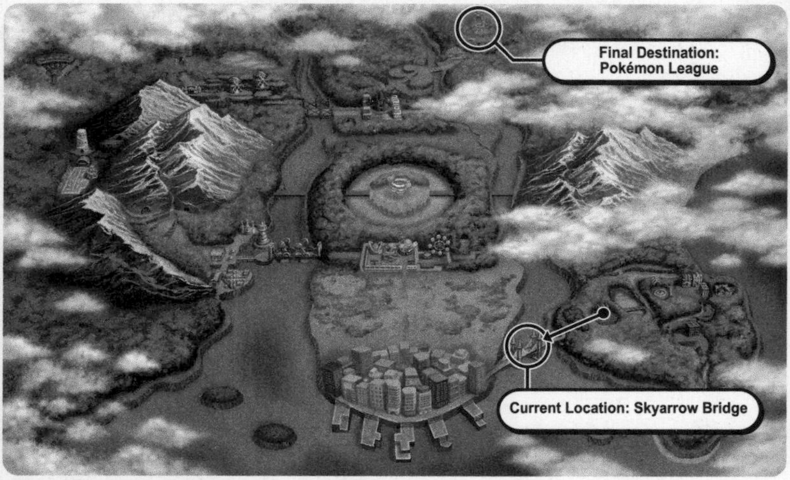
Final Destination: Pokémon League
Current Location: Skyarrow Bridge

Fire Pig Pokémon **Tep**
Tepig ♂ Fire
Lv.16 Ability: Blaze

Dream Eater Pokémon **Musha**
Munna ♂ Psychic
Lv.39 Ability: Forewarn

Valiant Pokémon **Brav**
Braviary ♂ Normal Flying
Lv.54 Ability: Sheer Force

EleSpider Pokémon **Tula**
Galvantula ♂ Bug Electric
Lv.40 Ability: Unnerve

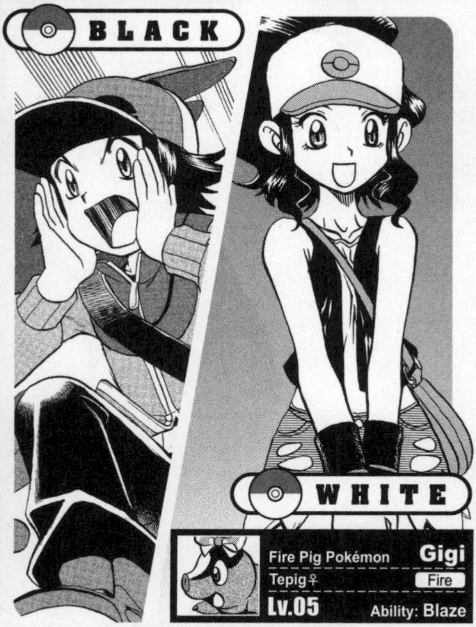
BLACK
WHITE

Fire Pig Pokémon **Gigi**
Tepig ♀ Fire
Lv.05 Ability: Blaze

TRIO BADGE | BASIC BADGE | ? | ? | ? | ? | ? | ?

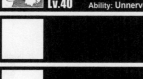

Pokémon™
Adventures
Black & White

ZORUA

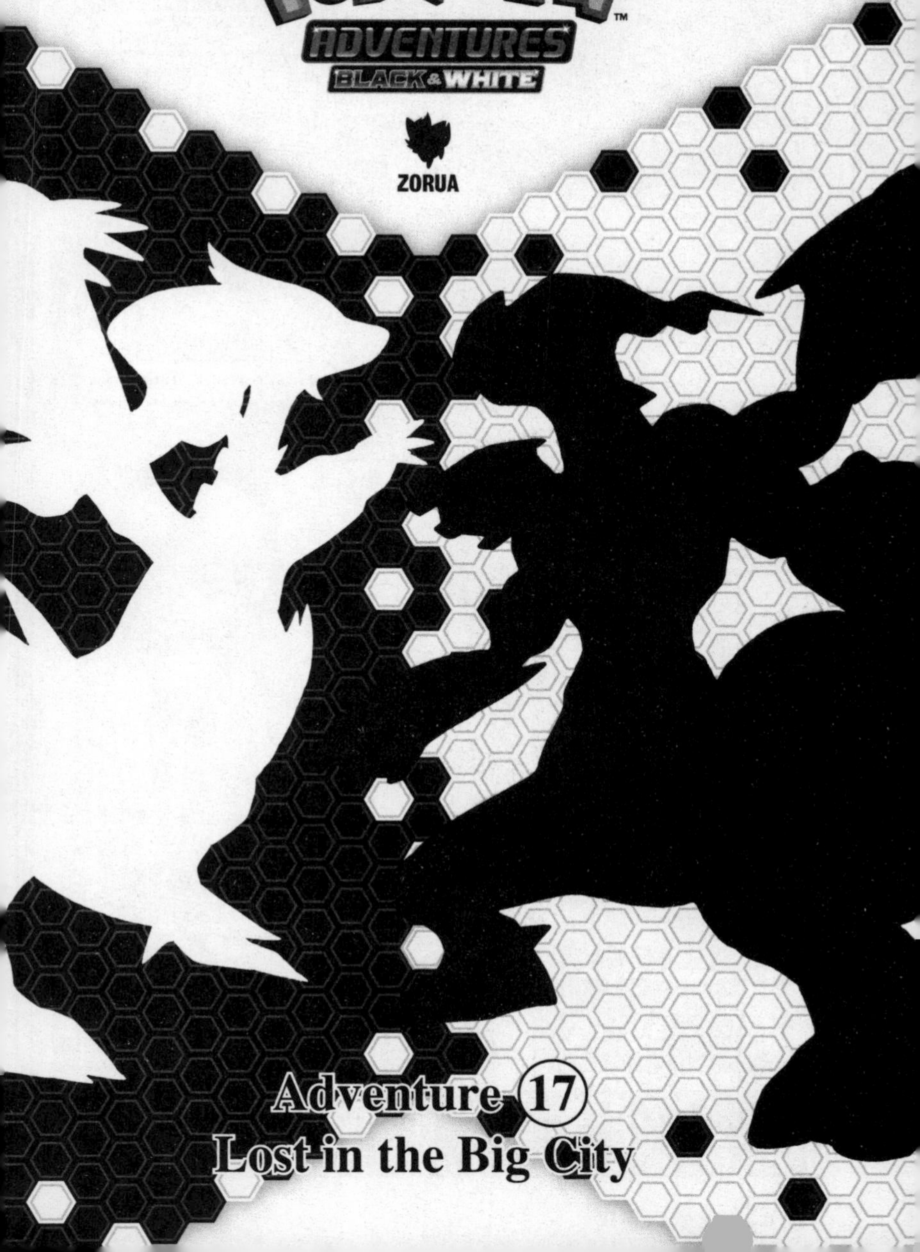

Adventure 17
Lost in the Big City

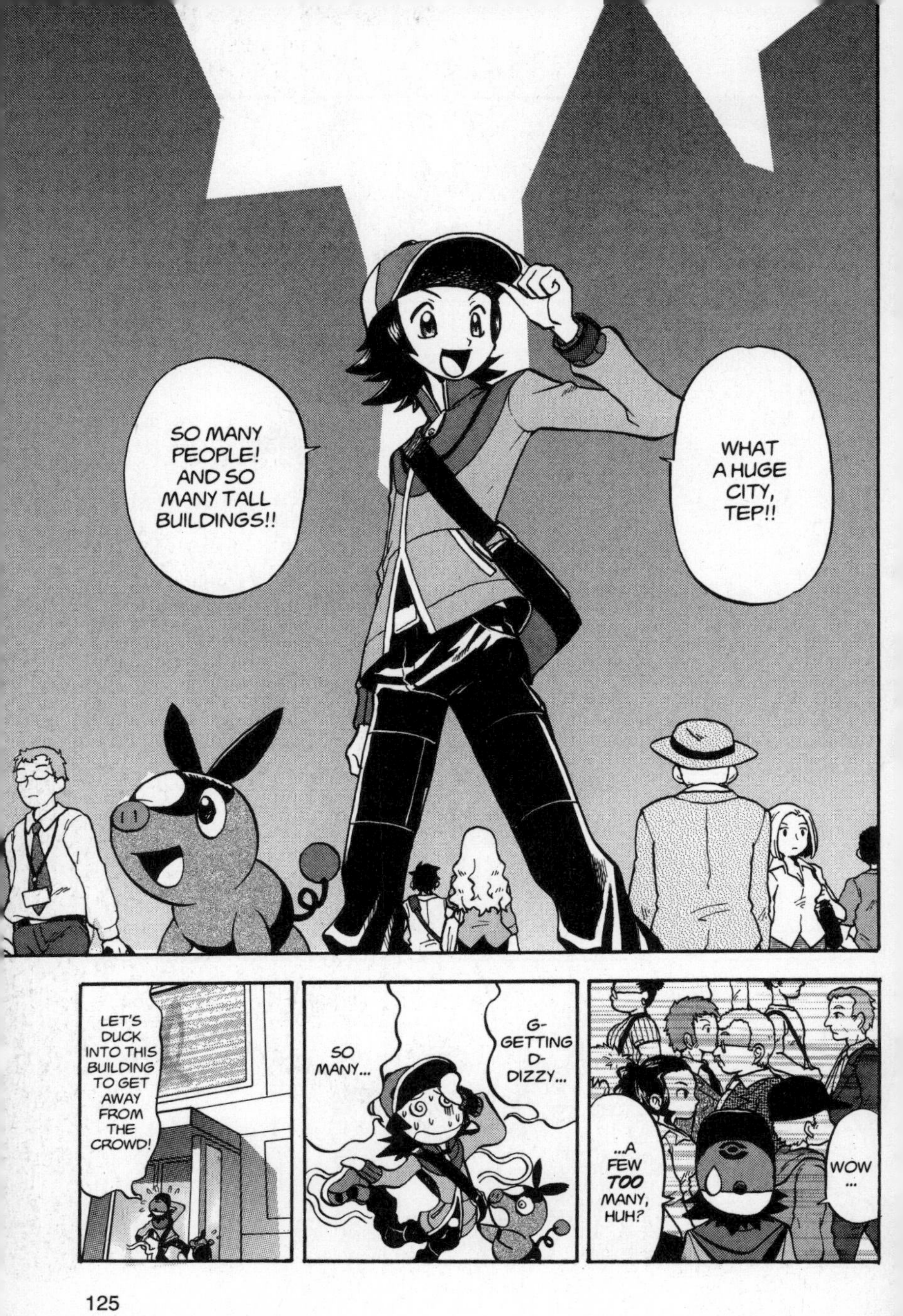
WHAT A HUGE CITY, TEP!!
SO MANY PEOPLE! AND SO MANY TALL BUILDINGS!!
WOW ...
...A FEW *TOO* MANY, HUH?
G-GETTING D-DIZZY...
SO MANY...
LET'S DUCK INTO THIS BUILDING TO GET AWAY FROM THE CROWD!

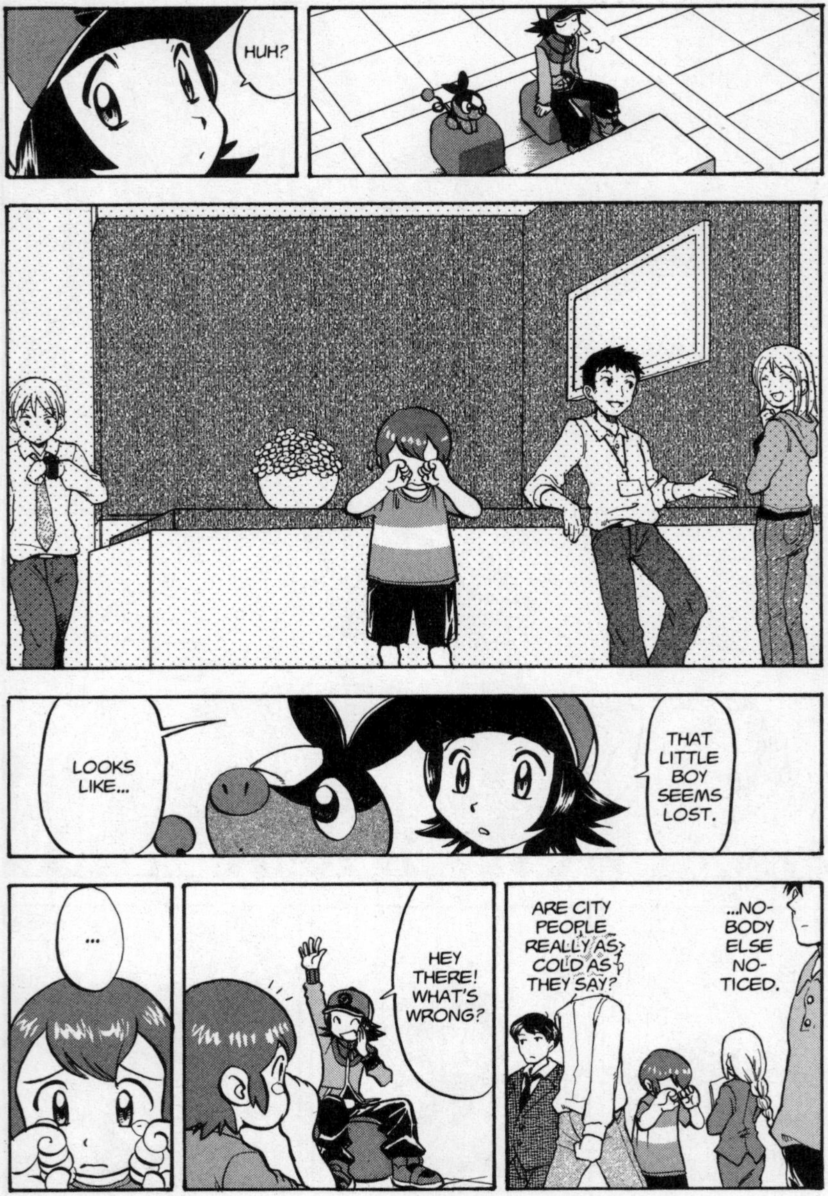
HUH?
THAT LITTLE BOY SEEMS LOST.
LOOKS LIKE...
...NOBODY ELSE NOTICED.
ARE CITY PEOPLE REALLY AS COLD AS THEY SAY?
HEY THERE! WHAT'S WRONG?
...

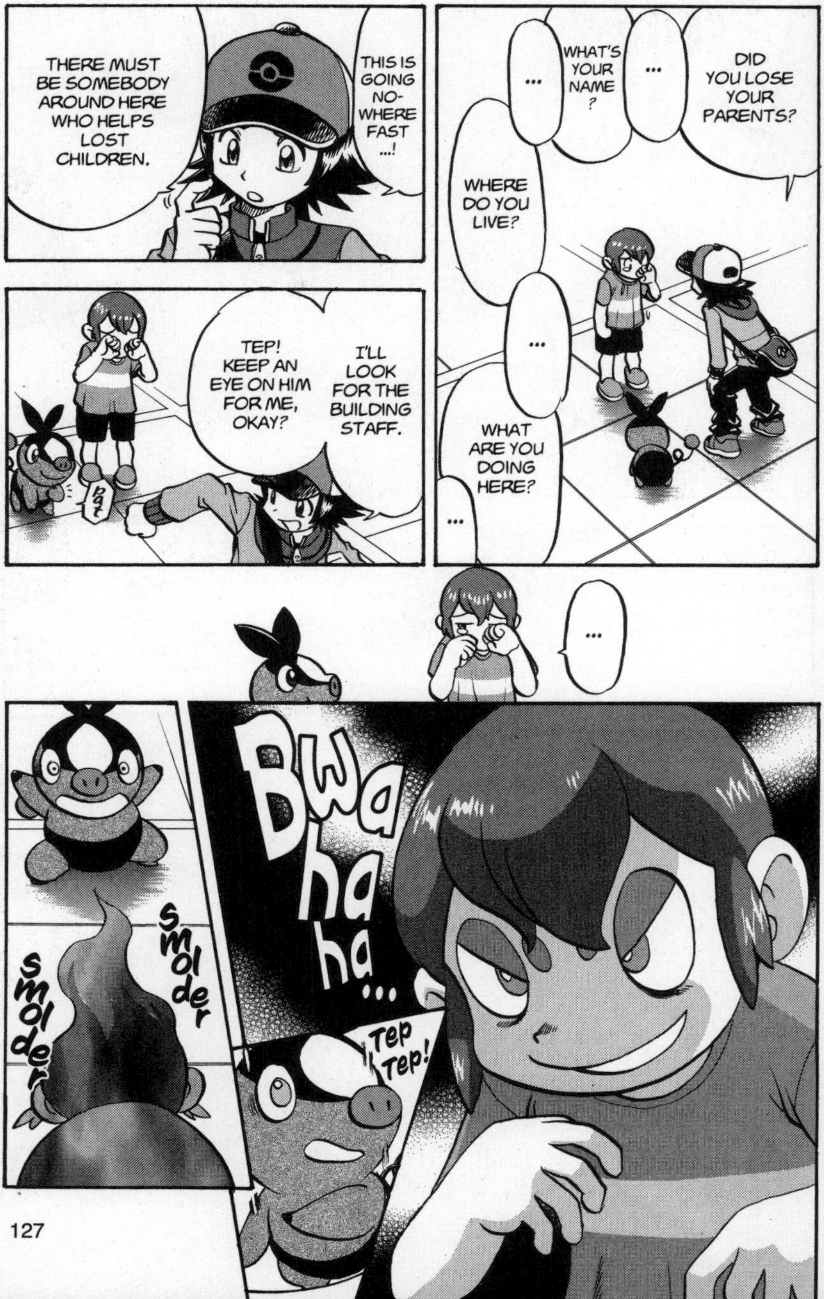
DID YOU LOSE YOUR PARENTS?
...
WHAT'S YOUR NAME?
...
WHERE DO YOU LIVE?
...
WHAT ARE YOU DOING HERE?
...
THIS IS GOING NO-WHERE FAST ...!
THERE MUST BE SOMEBODY AROUND HERE WHO HELPS LOST CHILDREN.
TEP! KEEP AN EYE ON HIM FOR ME, OKAY? I'LL LOOK FOR THE BUILDING STAFF.
pat
...
Bwahaha...
Tep Tep!
smolder
smolder

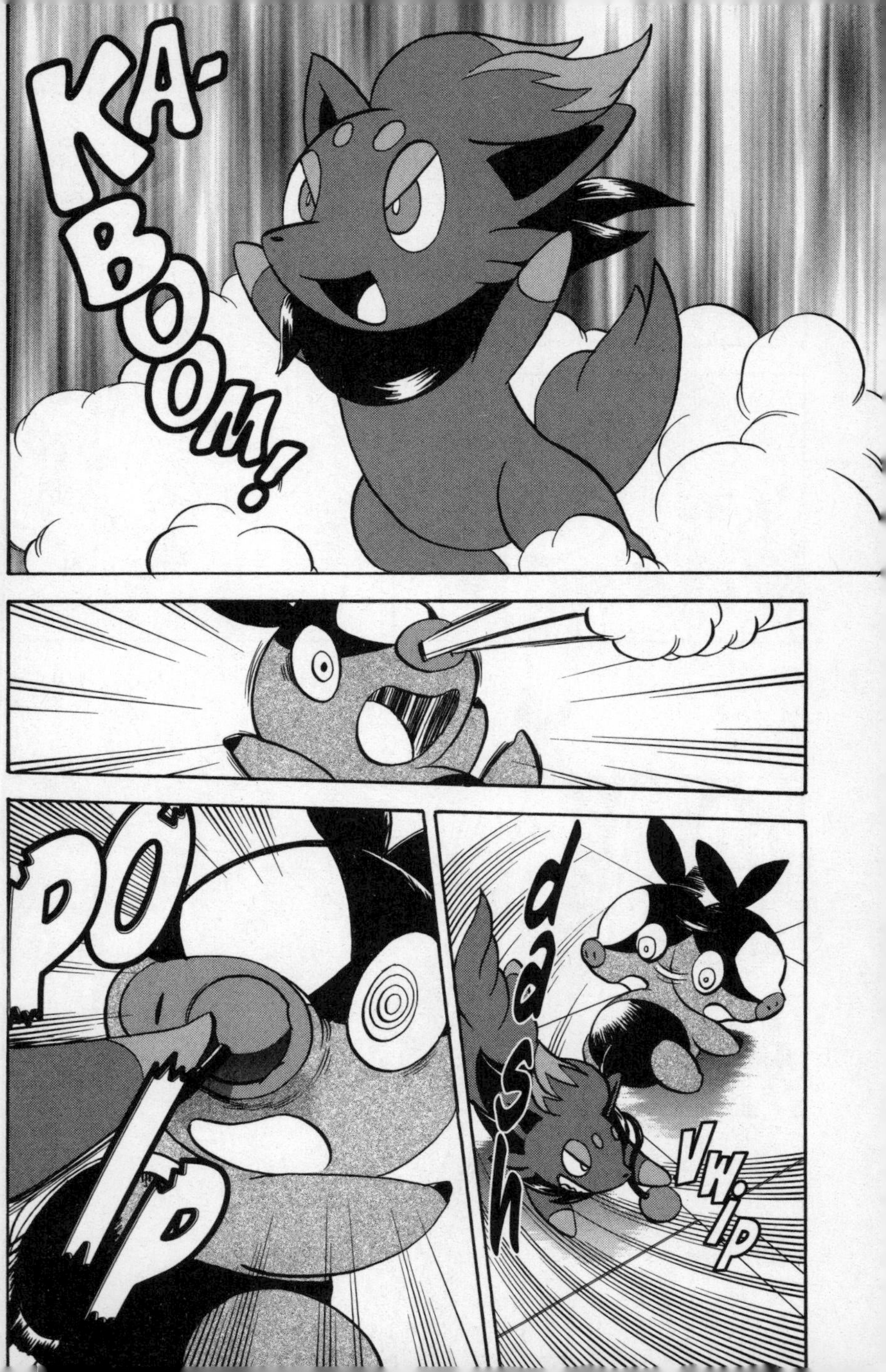
KA-BOOM!
dash
VWIP
POP

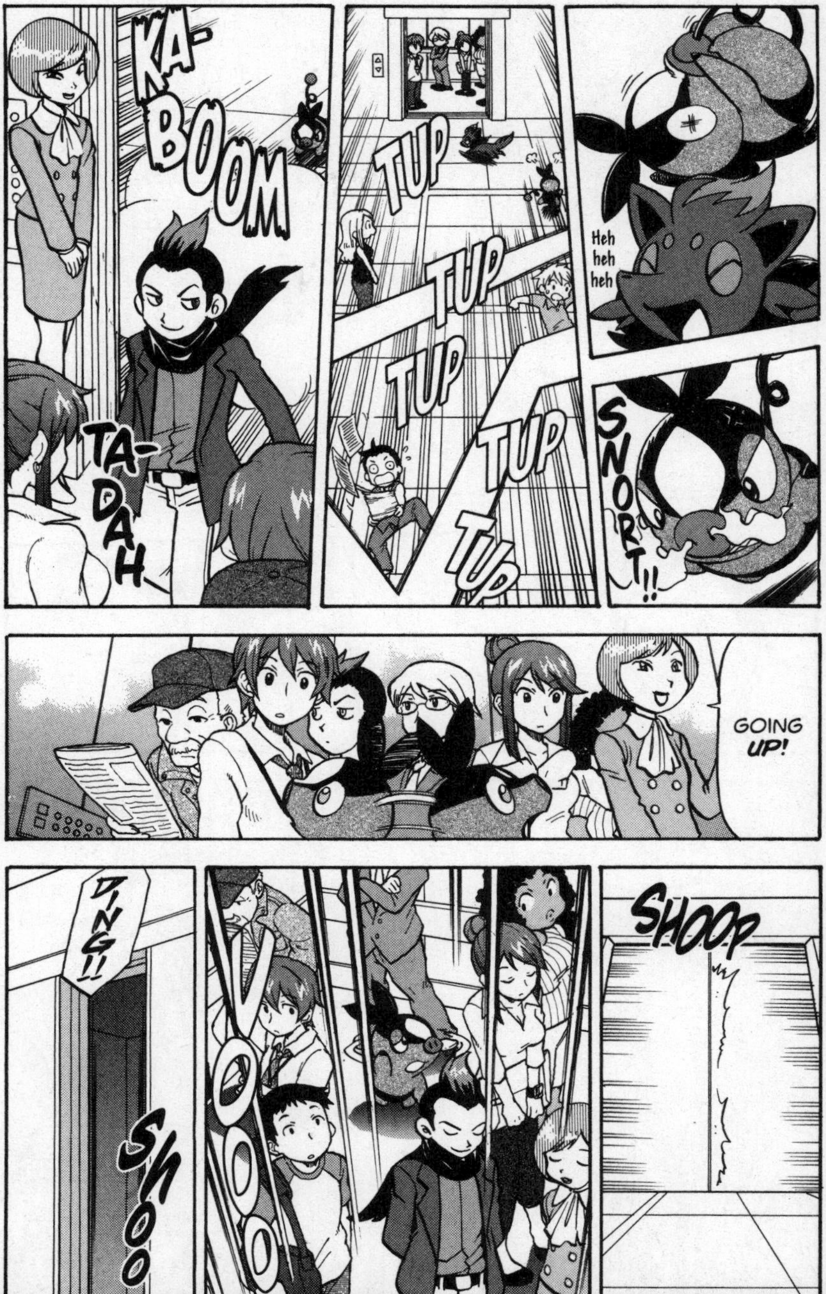
Heh heh heh
SNORT!!
TUP
TUP
TUP
TUP
TUP
KA-BOOM
TA-DAH
GOING UP!
SHOOP
VOOOO
DING!!
SHOO

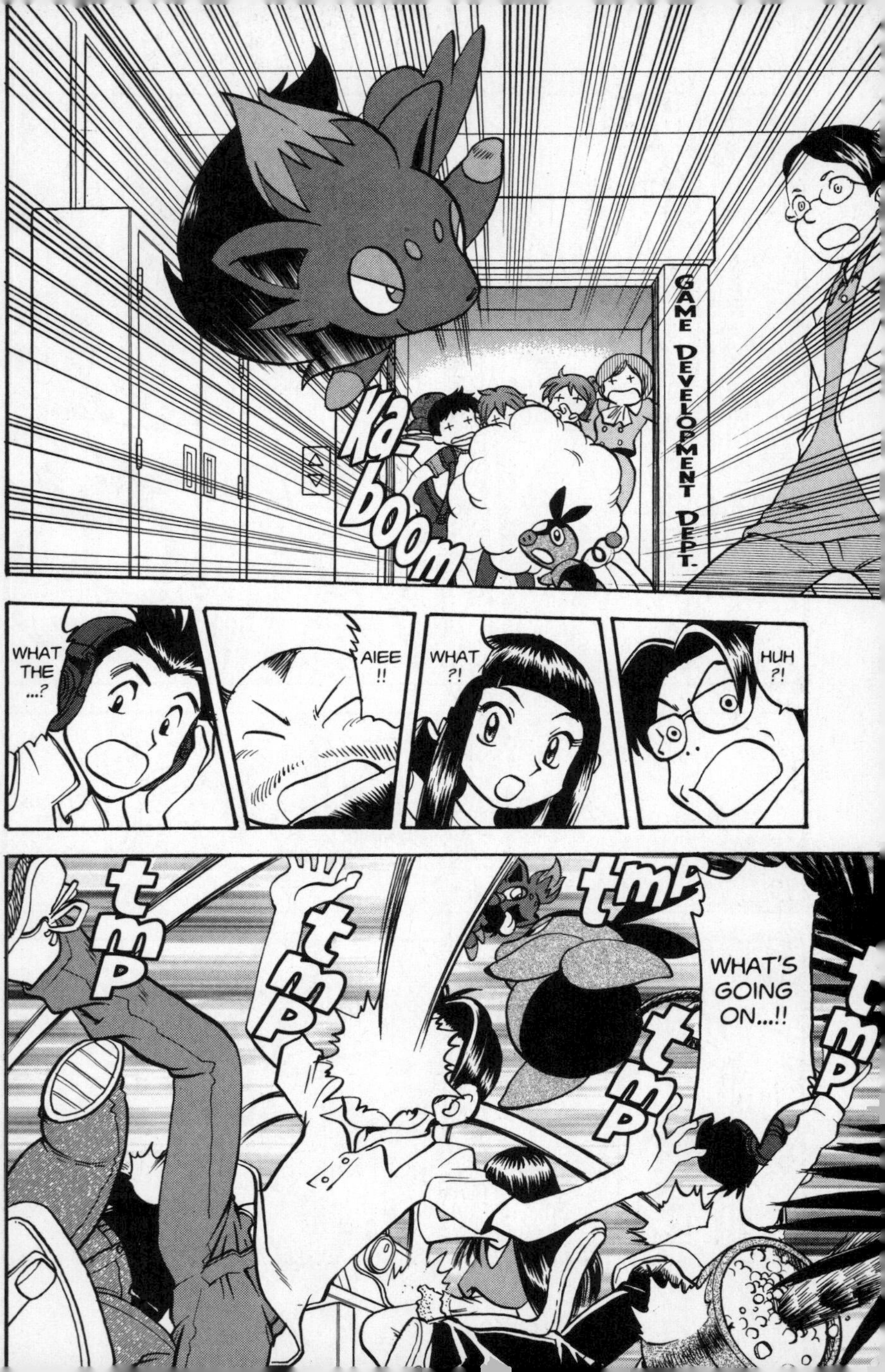
GAME DEVELOPMENT DEPT.
ka-boom
HUH ?!
WHAT ?!
AIEE !!
WHAT THE ...?
tmp
tmp
WHAT'S GOING ON...!!
tmp
tmp
tmp

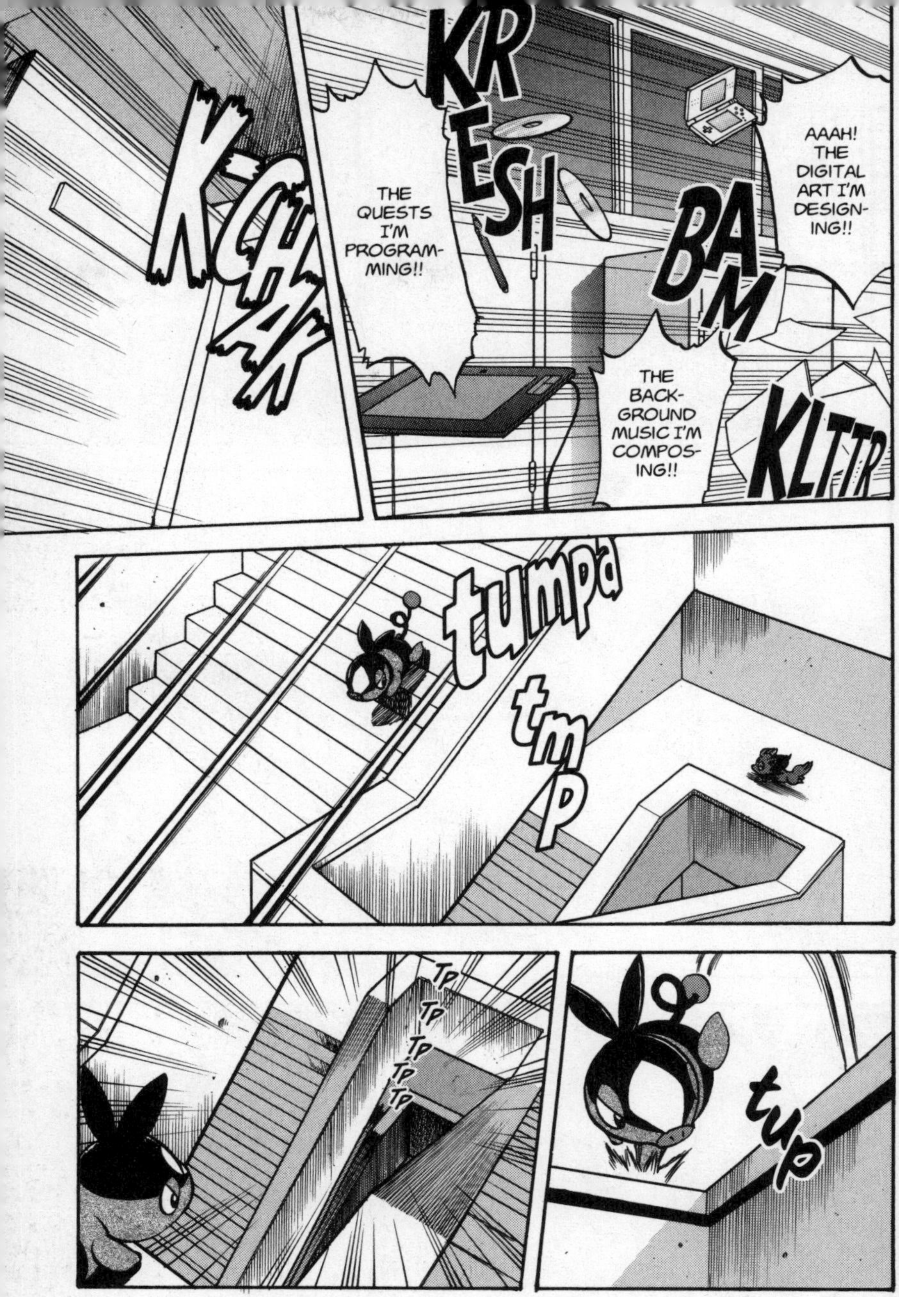
AAAH! THE DIGITAL ART I'M DESIGNING!!
KRESH
BAM
THE QUESTS I'M PROGRAMMING!!
THE BACKGROUND MUSIC I'M COMPOSING!!
KLTTR
K-CHAK
tumpa
tmp
tup
Tp Tp Tp Tp Tp

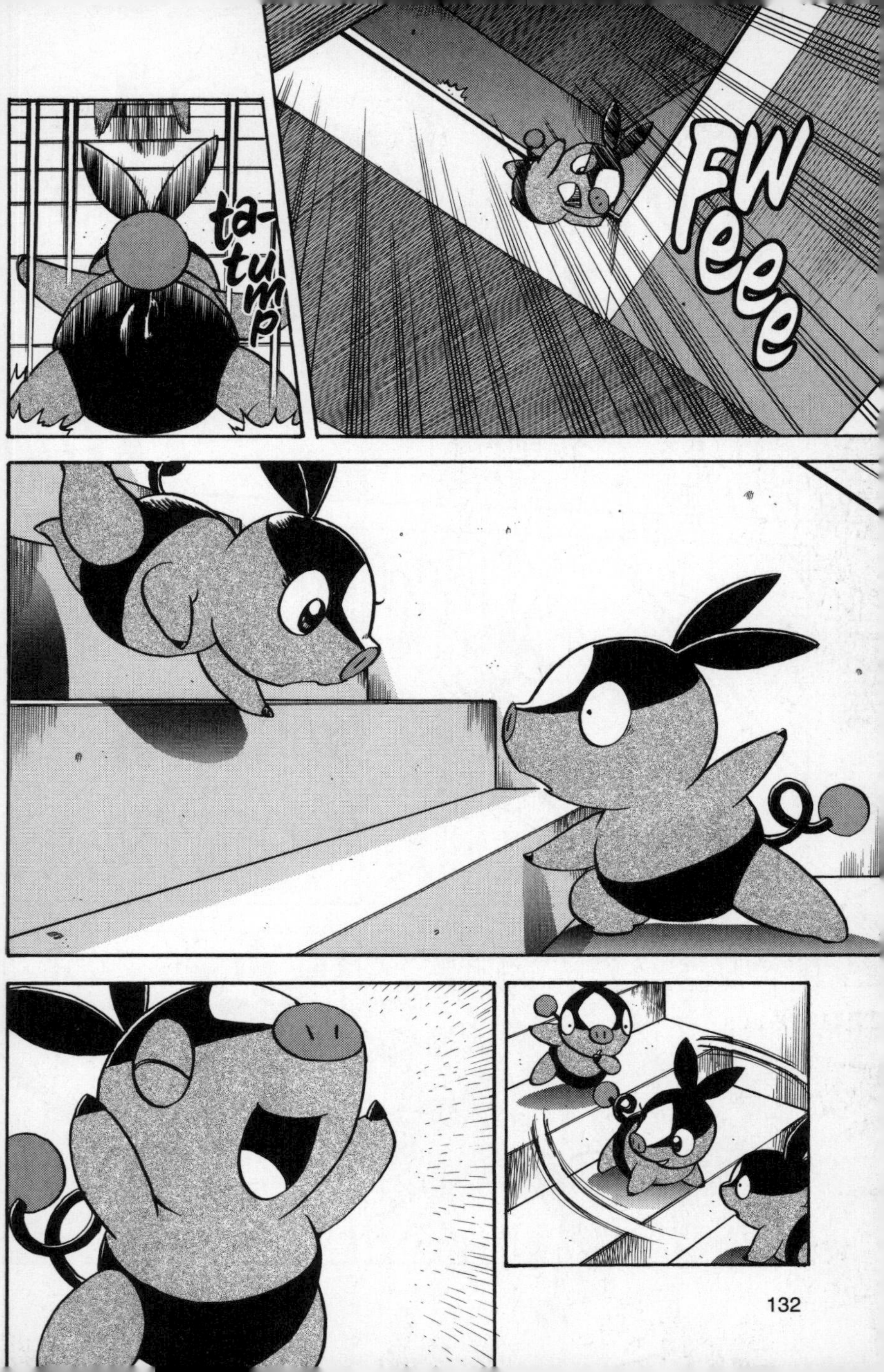
FWeeee
ta-tump

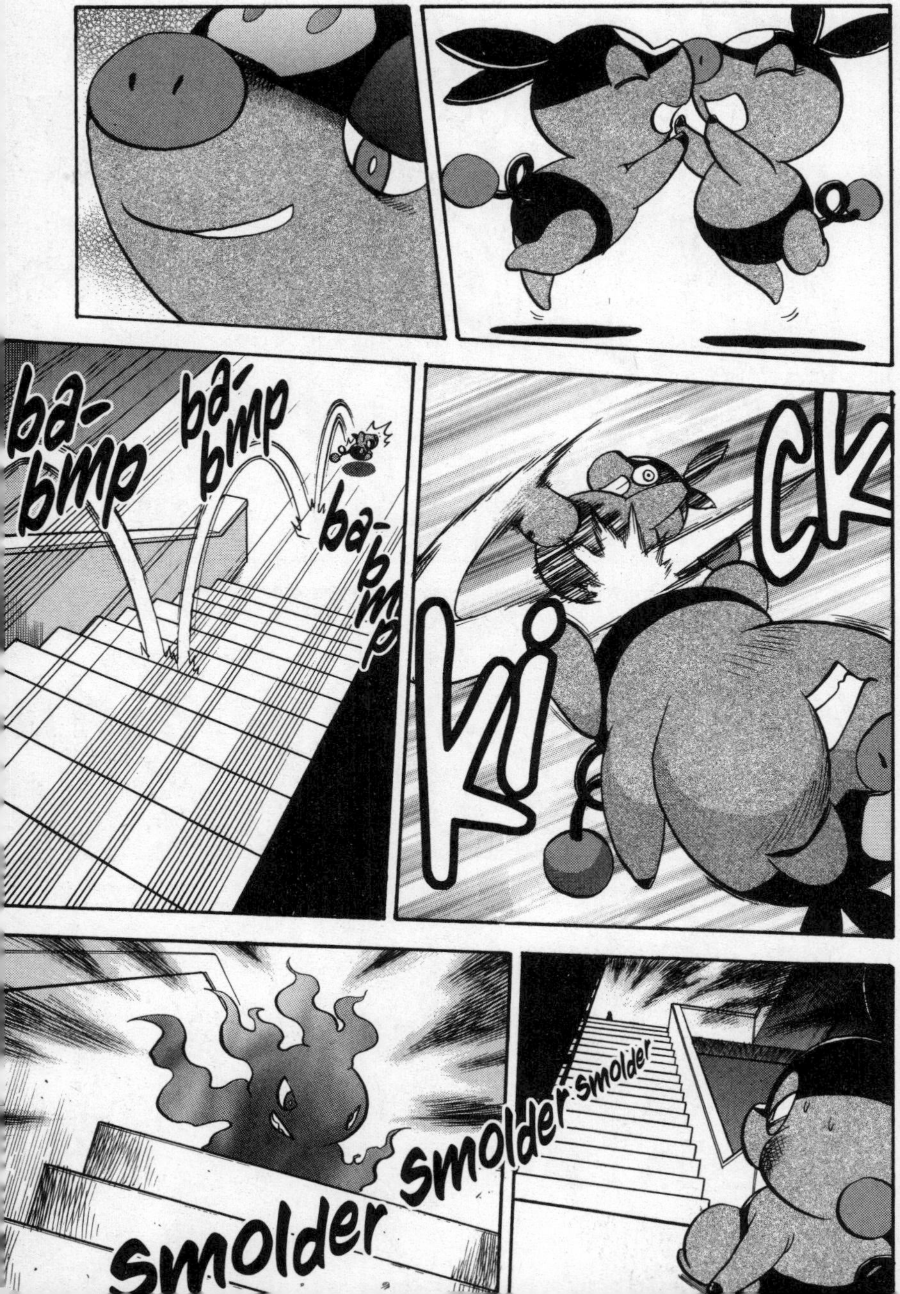
KiCK
ba-bmp
ba-bmp
ba-bmp
smolder smolder
smolder
smolder

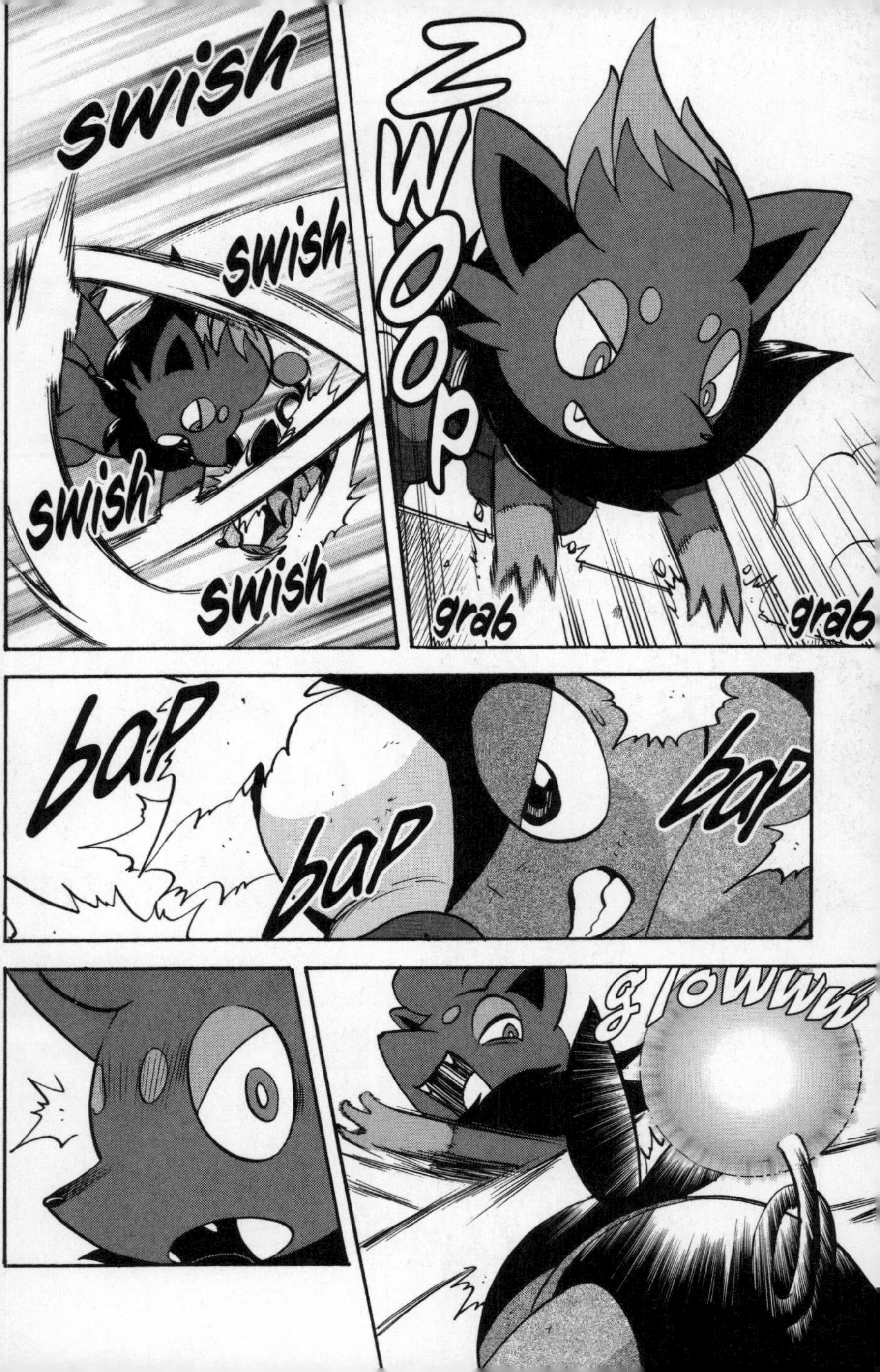
ZWOOP
grab
grab
swish
swish
swish
swish
bap
bap
bap
glowww

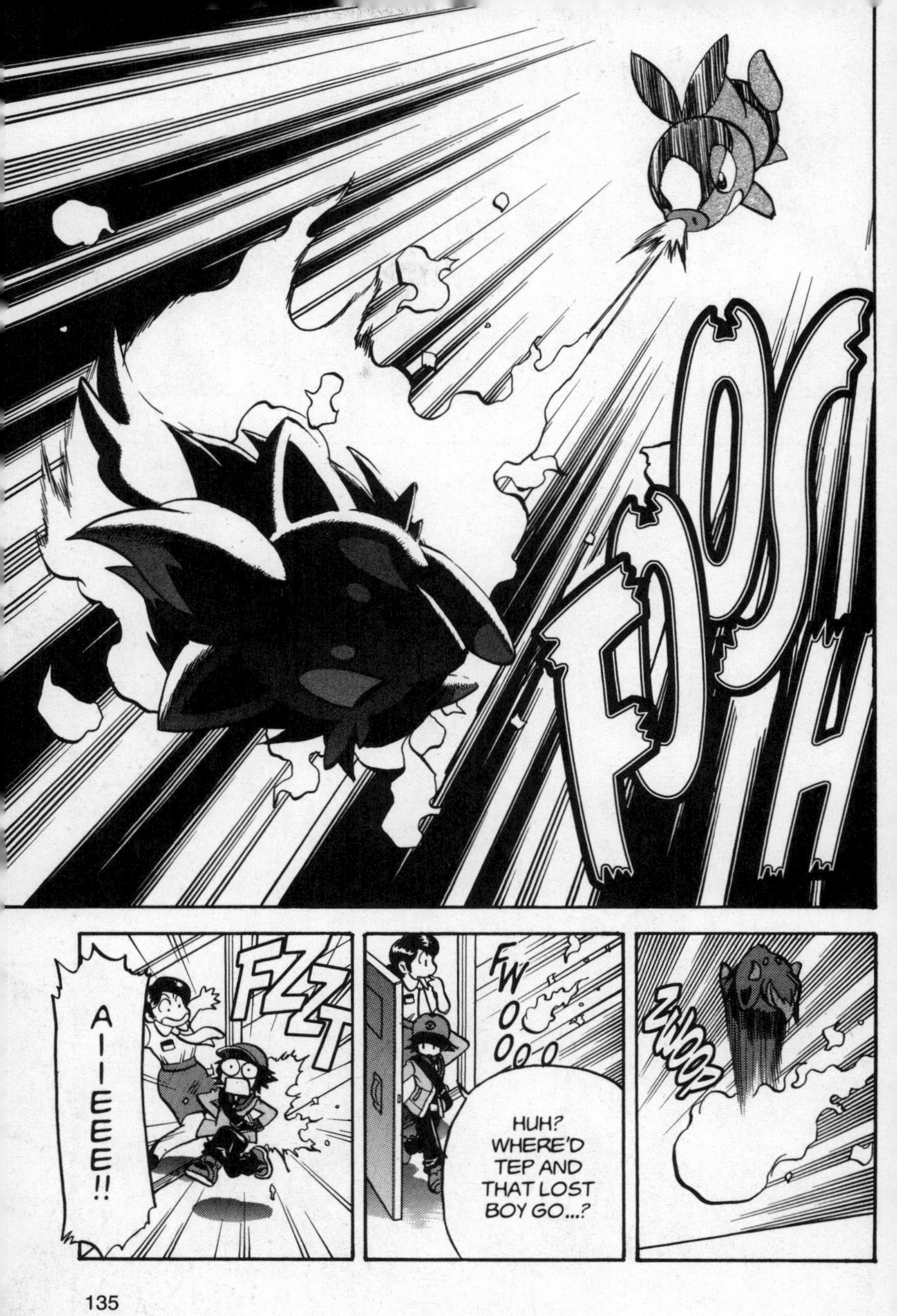
FOOSH
ZWOOP
FWOOOOO
HUH? WHERE'D TEP AND THAT LOST BOY GO...?
FZZT
AIIEEE!!

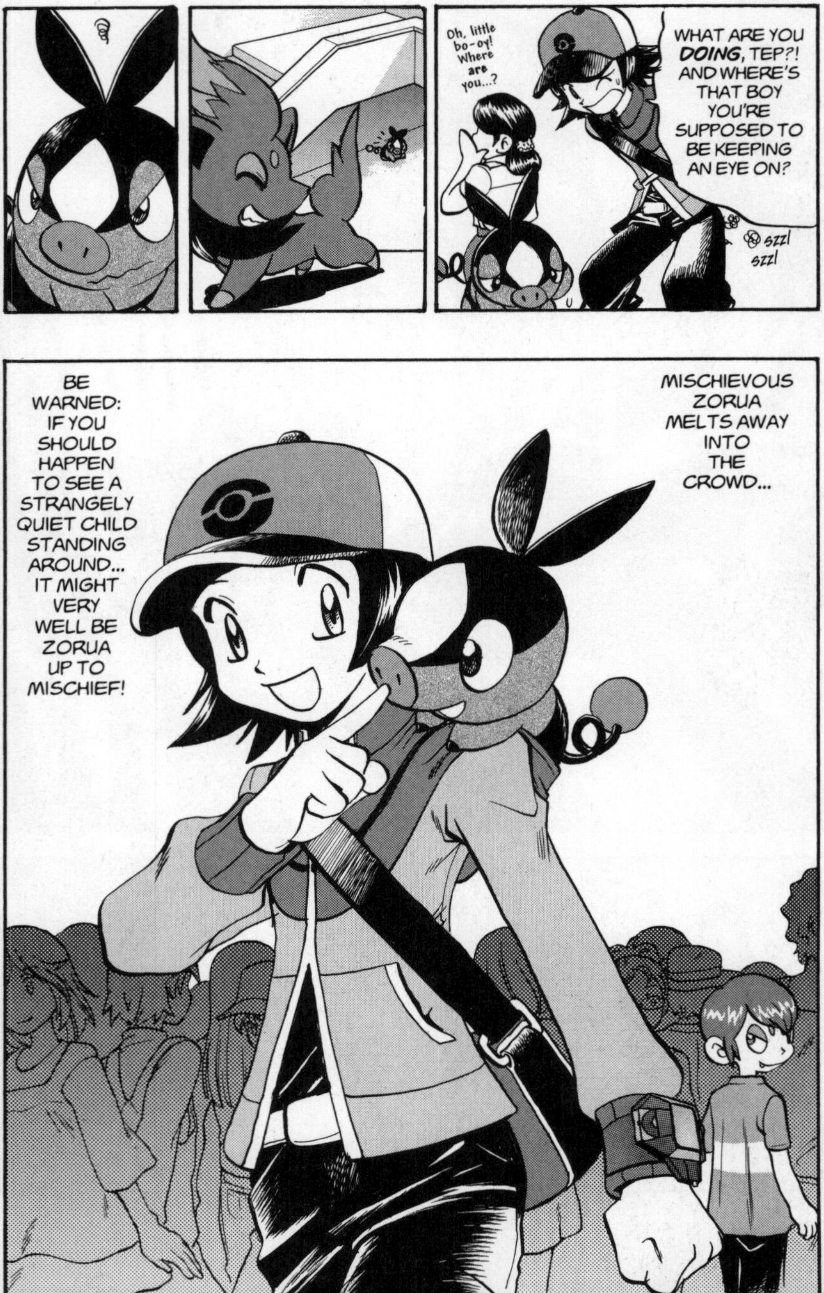
WHAT ARE YOU DOING, TEP?! AND WHERE'S THAT BOY YOU'RE SUPPOSED TO BE KEEPING AN EYE ON?
Oh, little bo-oy! Where are you...?
szzl szzl
MISCHIEVOUS ZORUA MELTS AWAY INTO THE CROWD...
BE WARNED: IF YOU SHOULD HAPPEN TO SEE A STRANGELY QUIET CHILD STANDING AROUND... IT MIGHT VERY WELL BE ZORUA UP TO MISCHIEF!

POKÉMON ADVENTURES BLACK & WHITE™

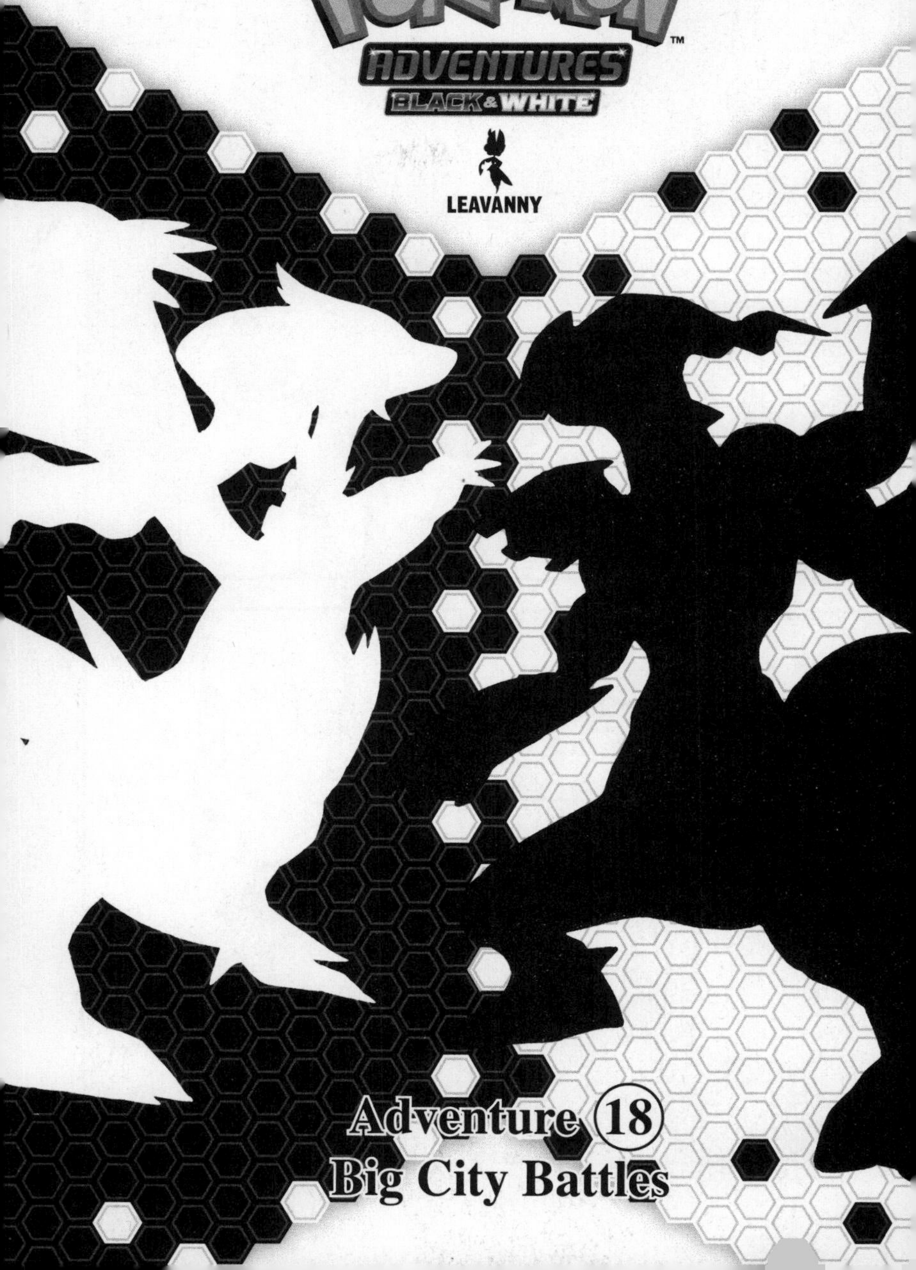
LEAVANNY

Adventure 18
Big City Battles

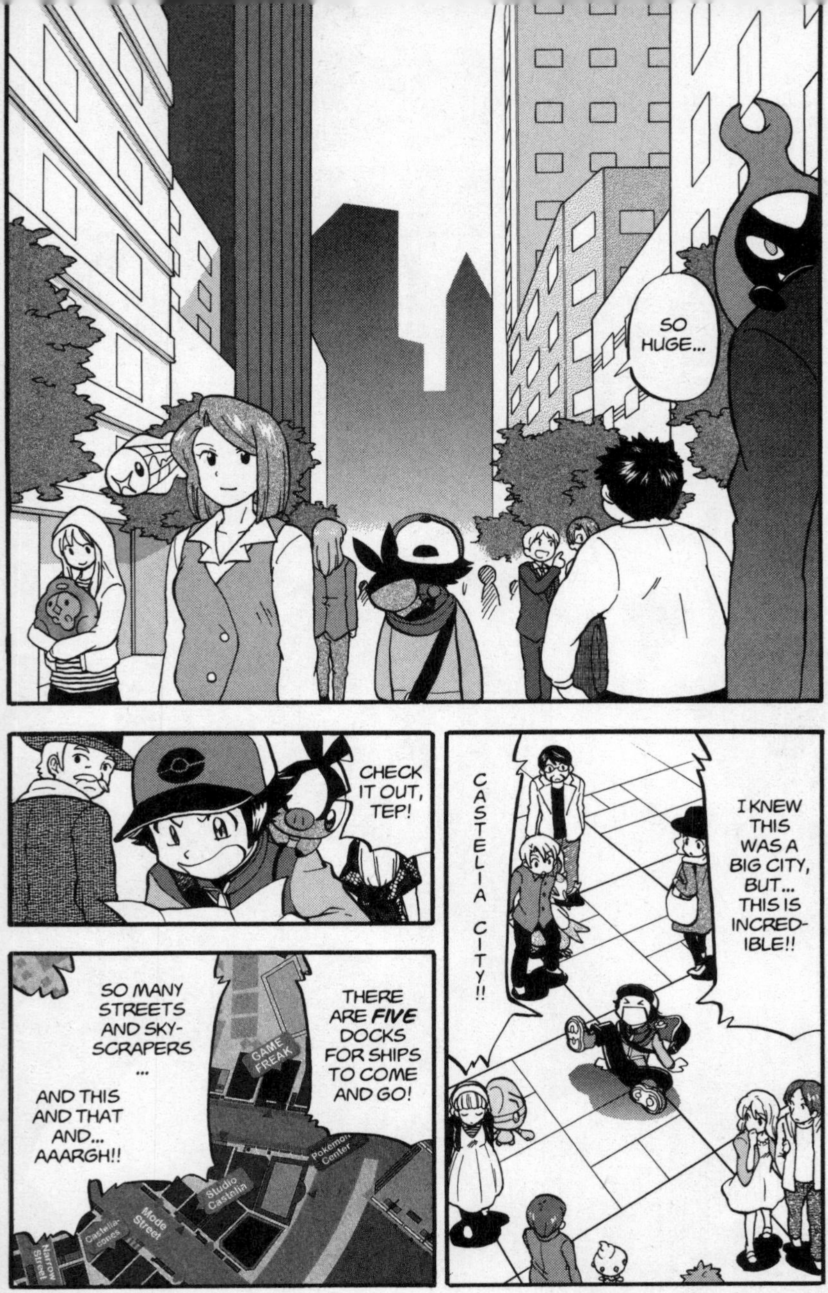
SO HUGE...
I KNEW THIS WAS A BIG CITY, BUT... THIS IS INCREDIBLE!!
CASTELIA CITY!!
CHECK IT OUT, TEP!
THERE ARE *FIVE* DOCKS FOR SHIPS TO COME AND GO!
SO MANY STREETS AND SKY-SCRAPERS...
AND THIS AND THAT AND... AAARGH!!
GAME FREAK
Pokémon Center
Studio Castelia
Mode Street
Castelia-cones
Narrow Street

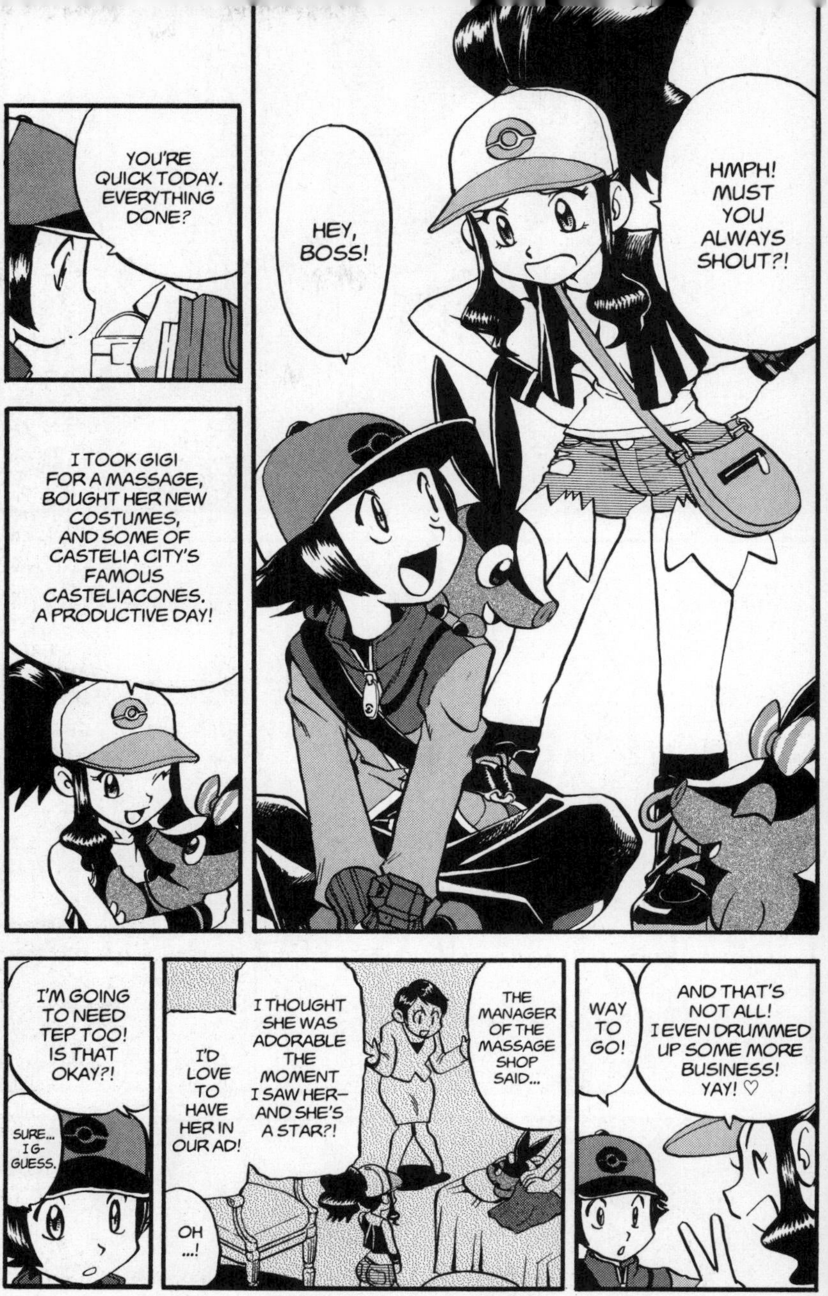
HEY, BOSS!
HMPH! MUST YOU ALWAYS SHOUT?!
YOU'RE QUICK TODAY. EVERYTHING DONE?
I TOOK GIGI FOR A MASSAGE, BOUGHT HER NEW COSTUMES, AND SOME OF CASTELIA CITY'S FAMOUS CASTELIACONES. A PRODUCTIVE DAY!
AND THAT'S NOT ALL! I EVEN DRUMMED UP SOME MORE BUSINESS! YAY! ♡
WAY TO GO!
THE MANAGER OF THE MASSAGE SHOP SAID...
I THOUGHT SHE WAS ADORABLE THE MOMENT I SAW HER— AND SHE'S A STAR?!
I'D LOVE TO HAVE HER IN OUR AD!
OH ...!
I'M GOING TO NEED TEP TOO! IS THAT OKAY?!
SURE... I G-GUESS.

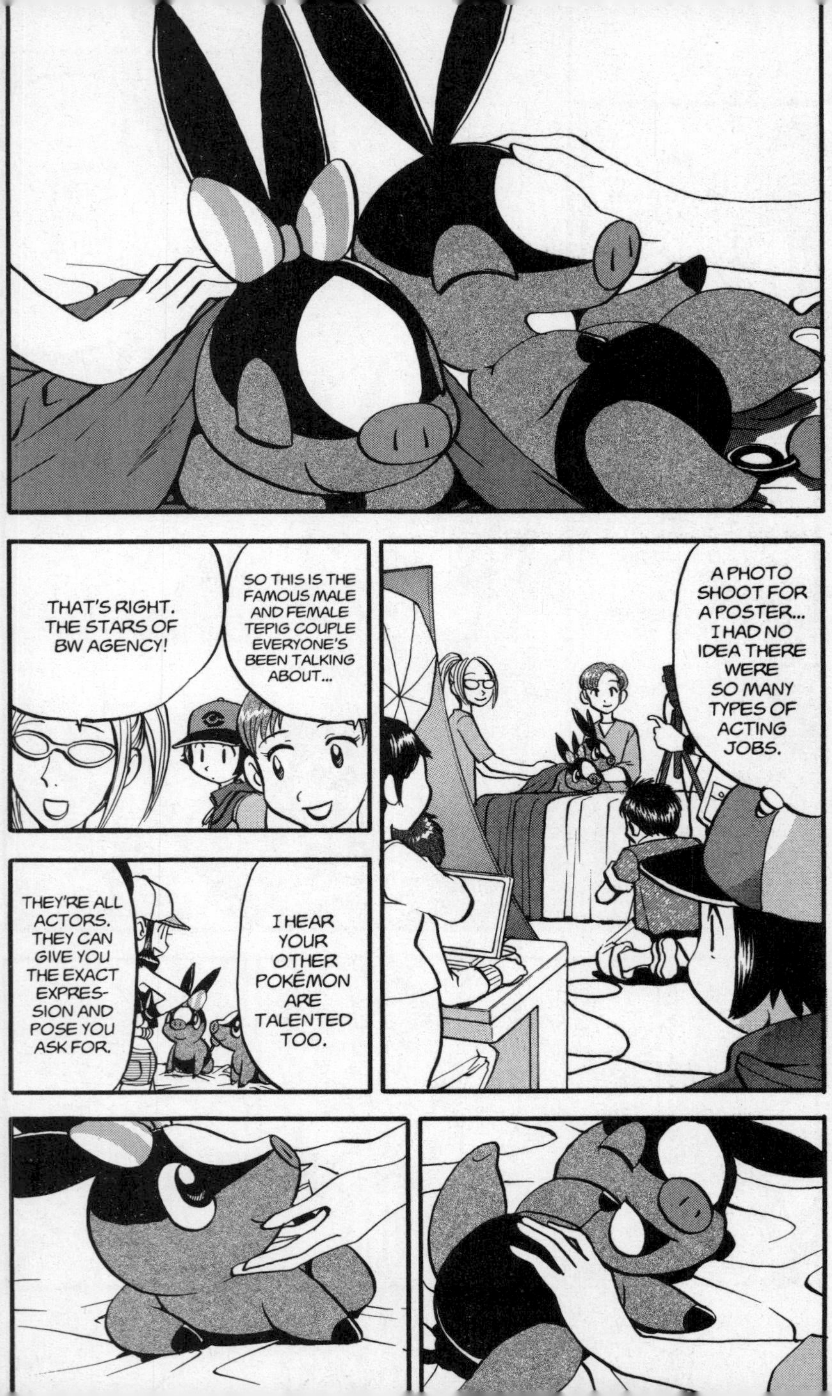
A PHOTO SHOOT FOR A POSTER... I HAD NO IDEA THERE WERE SO MANY TYPES OF ACTING JOBS.
SO THIS IS THE FAMOUS MALE AND FEMALE TEPIG COUPLE EVERYONE'S BEEN TALKING ABOUT...
THAT'S RIGHT. THE STARS OF BW AGENCY!
I HEAR YOUR OTHER POKÉMON ARE TALENTED TOO.
THEY'RE ALL ACTORS. THEY CAN GIVE YOU THE EXACT EXPRES-SION AND POSE YOU ASK FOR.

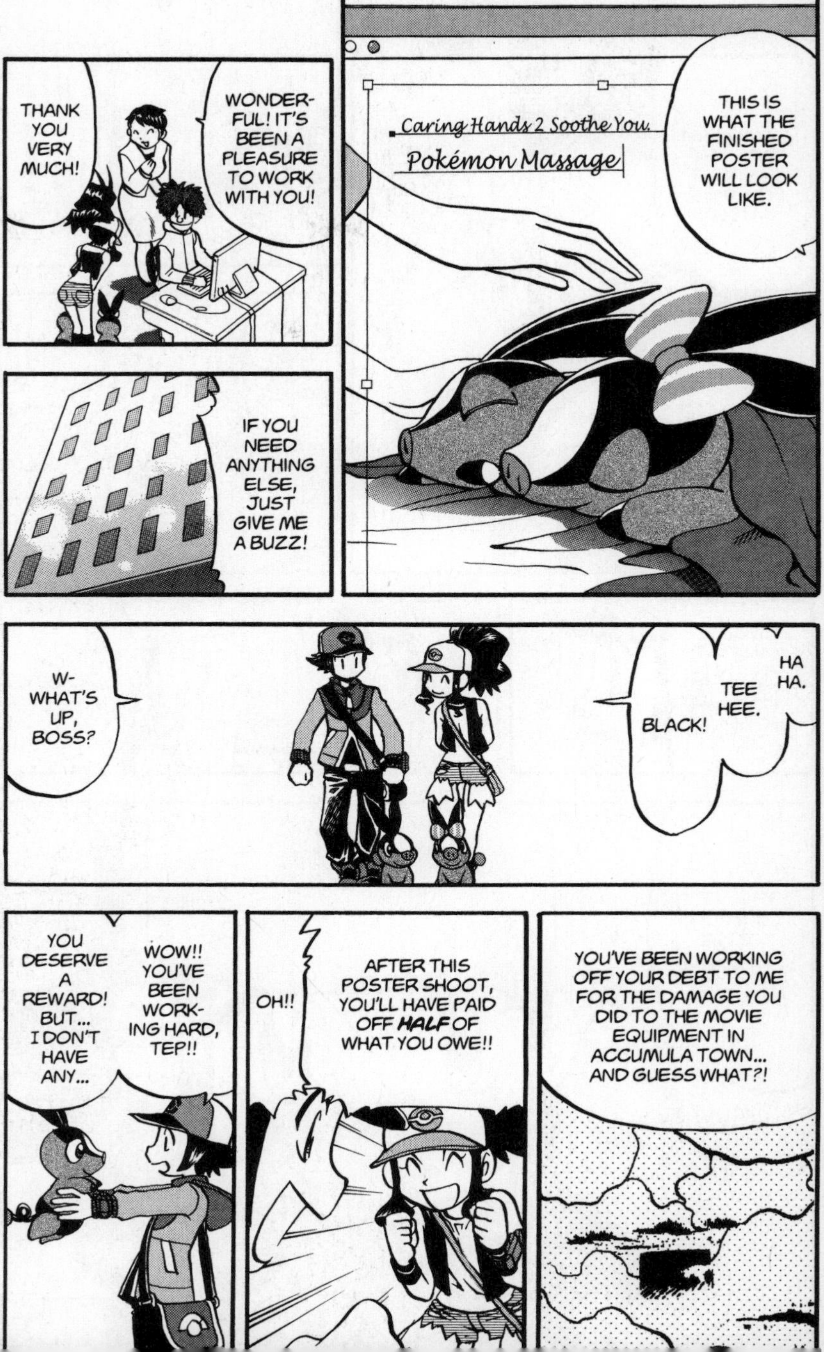
Caring Hands 2 Soothe You.
Pokémon Massage
THIS IS WHAT THE FINISHED POSTER WILL LOOK LIKE.
WONDERFUL! IT'S BEEN A PLEASURE TO WORK WITH YOU!
THANK YOU VERY MUCH!
IF YOU NEED ANYTHING ELSE, JUST GIVE ME A BUZZ!
HA HA. TEE HEE. BLACK!
W-WHAT'S UP, BOSS?
YOU'VE BEEN WORKING OFF YOUR DEBT TO ME FOR THE DAMAGE YOU DID TO THE MOVIE EQUIPMENT IN ACCUMULA TOWN... AND GUESS WHAT?!
AFTER THIS POSTER SHOOT, YOU'LL HAVE PAID OFF ***HALF*** OF WHAT YOU OWE!!
OH!!
WOW!! YOU'VE BEEN WORKING HARD, TEP!!
YOU DESERVE A REWARD! BUT... I DON'T HAVE ANY...

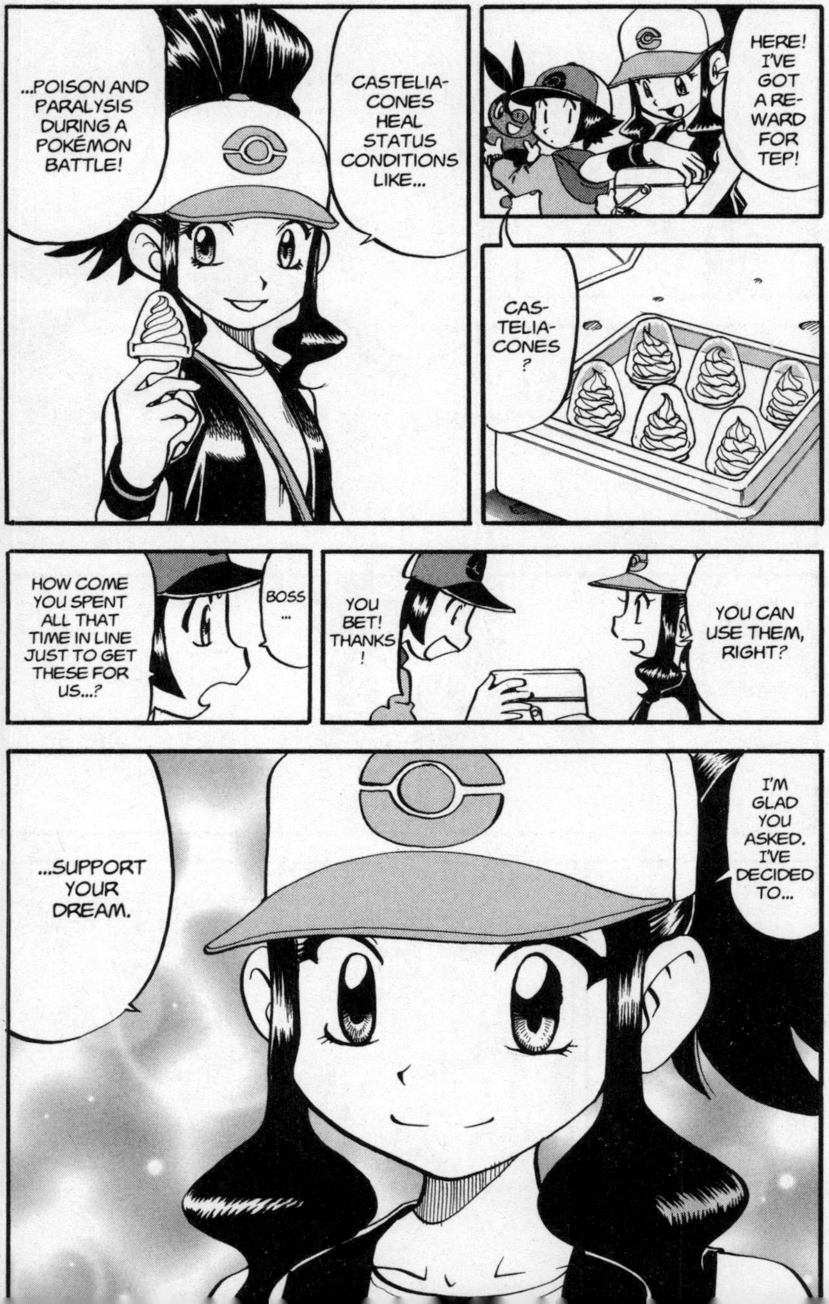
HERE! I'VE GOT A RE-WARD FOR TEP!
CAS-TELIA-CONES?
CASTELIA-CONES HEAL STATUS CONDITIONS LIKE...
...POISON AND PARALYSIS DURING A POKÉMON BATTLE!
YOU CAN USE THEM, RIGHT?
YOU BET! THANKS!
BOSS...
HOW COME YOU SPENT ALL THAT TIME IN LINE JUST TO GET THESE FOR US...?
I'M GLAD YOU ASKED. I'VE DECIDED TO...
...SUPPORT YOUR DREAM.

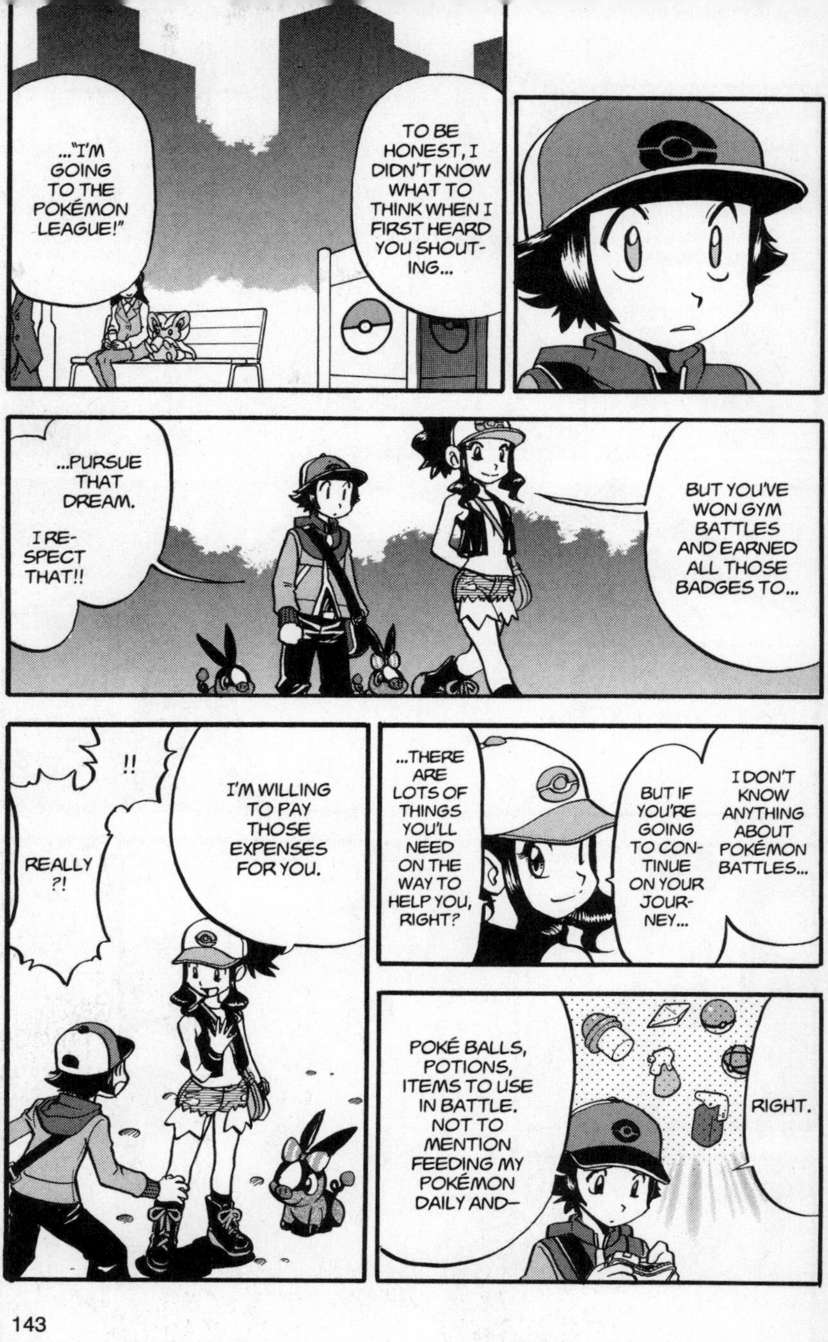
TO BE HONEST, I DIDN'T KNOW WHAT TO THINK WHEN I FIRST HEARD YOU SHOUTING...
..."I'M GOING TO THE POKÉMON LEAGUE!"
BUT YOU'VE WON GYM BATTLES AND EARNED ALL THOSE BADGES TO...
...PURSUE THAT DREAM.
I RESPECT THAT!!
I DON'T KNOW ANYTHING ABOUT POKÉMON BATTLES...
BUT IF YOU'RE GOING TO CONTINUE ON YOUR JOURNEY...
...THERE ARE LOTS OF THINGS YOU'LL NEED ON THE WAY TO HELP YOU, RIGHT?
RIGHT.
POKÉ BALLS, POTIONS, ITEMS TO USE IN BATTLE. NOT TO MENTION FEEDING MY POKÉMON DAILY AND—
I'M WILLING TO PAY THOSE EXPENSES FOR YOU.
!!
REALLY?!

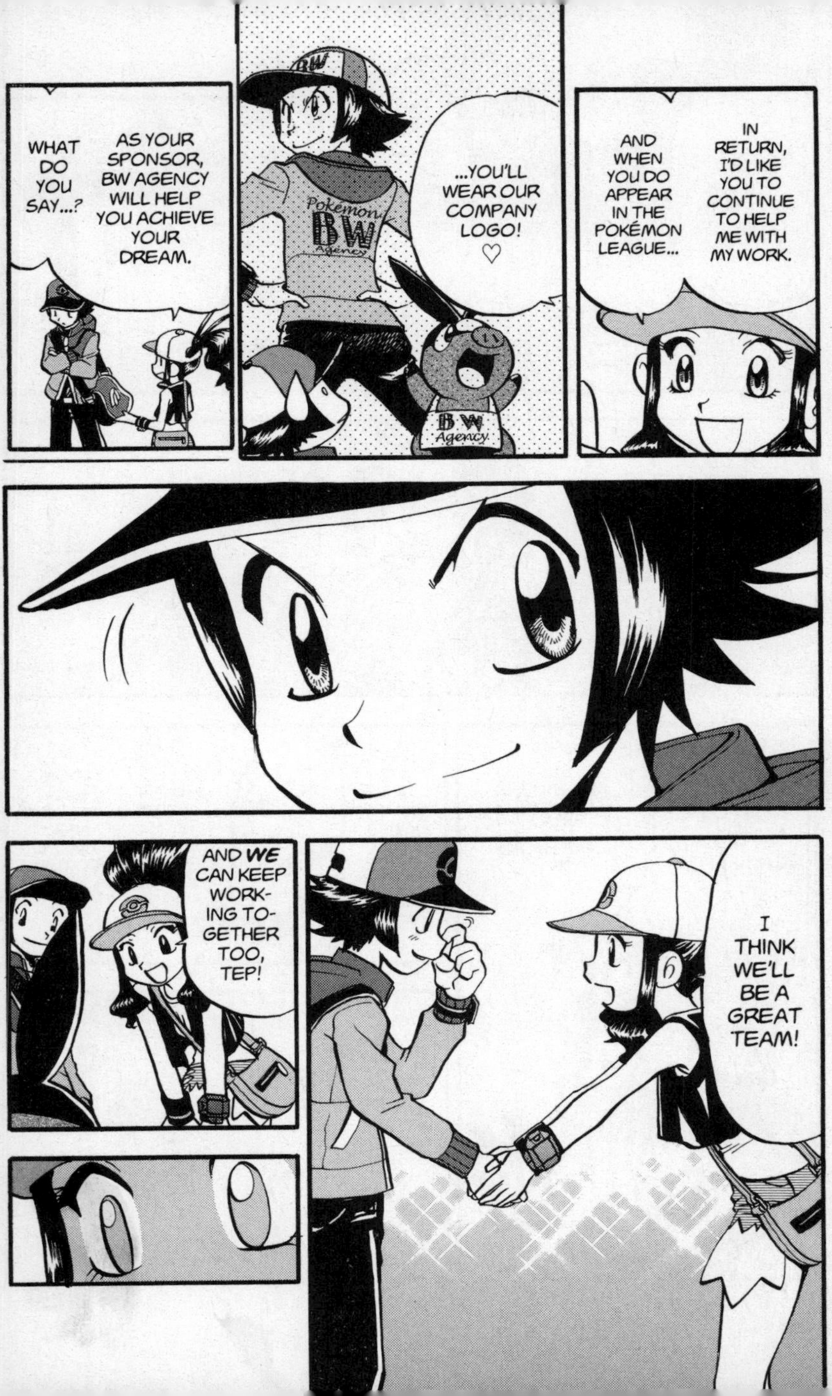
IN RETURN, I'D LIKE YOU TO CONTINUE TO HELP ME WITH MY WORK.
AND WHEN YOU DO APPEAR IN THE POKÉMON LEAGUE...
...YOU'LL WEAR OUR COMPANY LOGO! ♡
AS YOUR SPONSOR, BW AGENCY WILL HELP YOU ACHIEVE YOUR DREAM.
WHAT DO YOU SAY...?
I THINK WE'LL BE A GREAT TEAM!
AND **WE** CAN KEEP WORKING TOGETHER TOO, TEP!

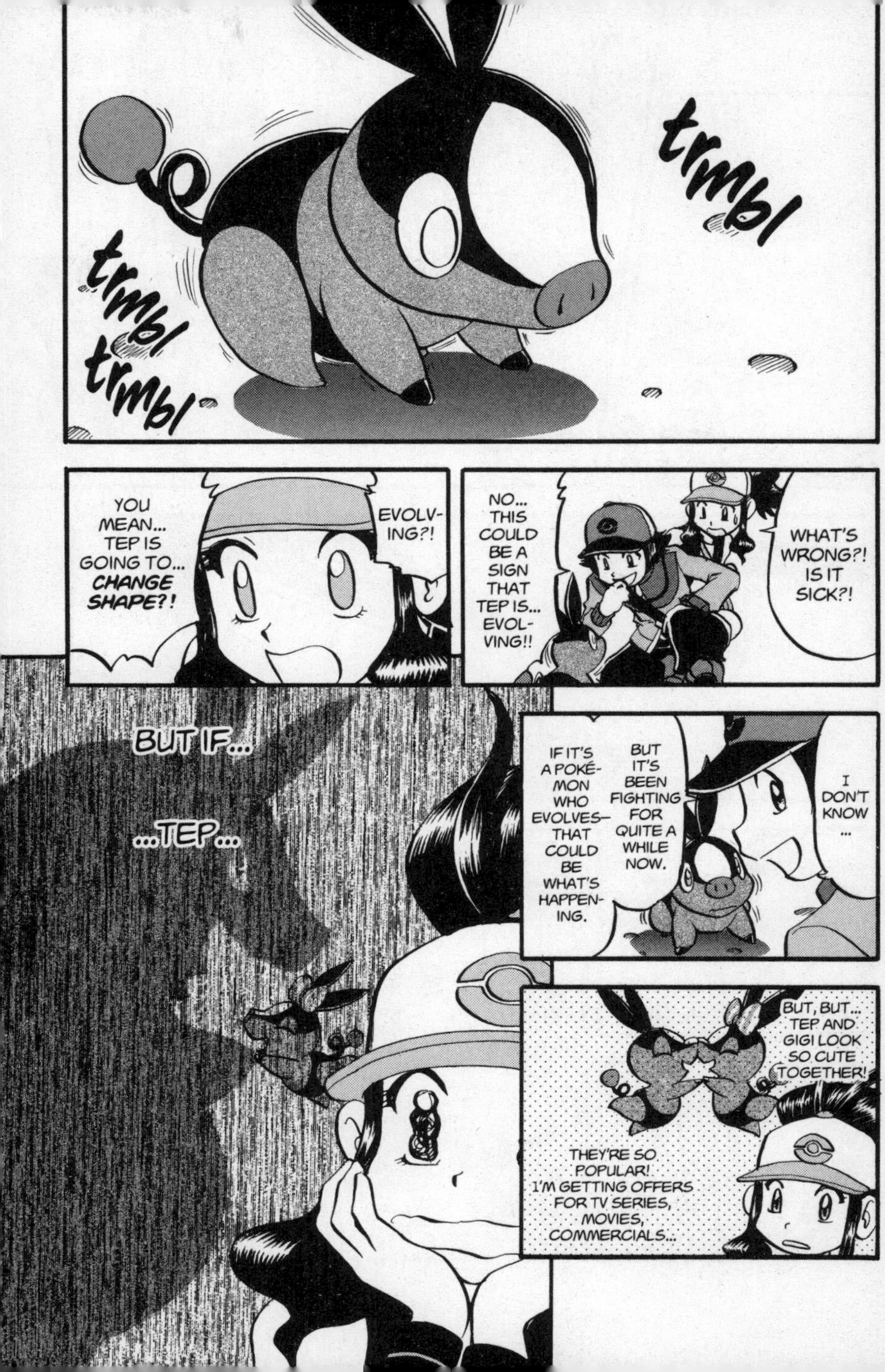
trmbl
trmbl
trmbl
WHAT'S WRONG?! IS IT SICK?!
NO... THIS COULD BE A SIGN THAT TEP IS... EVOLVING!!
EVOLVING?!
YOU MEAN... TEP IS GOING TO... ***CHANGE SHAPE?!***
I DON'T KNOW...
BUT IT'S BEEN FIGHTING FOR QUITE A WHILE NOW.
IF IT'S A POKÉMON WHO EVOLVES—THAT COULD BE WHAT'S HAPPENING.
BUT, BUT... TEP AND GIGI LOOK SO CUTE TOGETHER!
THEY'RE SO POPULAR! I'M GETTING OFFERS FOR TV SERIES, MOVIES, COMMERCIALS...
BUT IF...
...TEP...

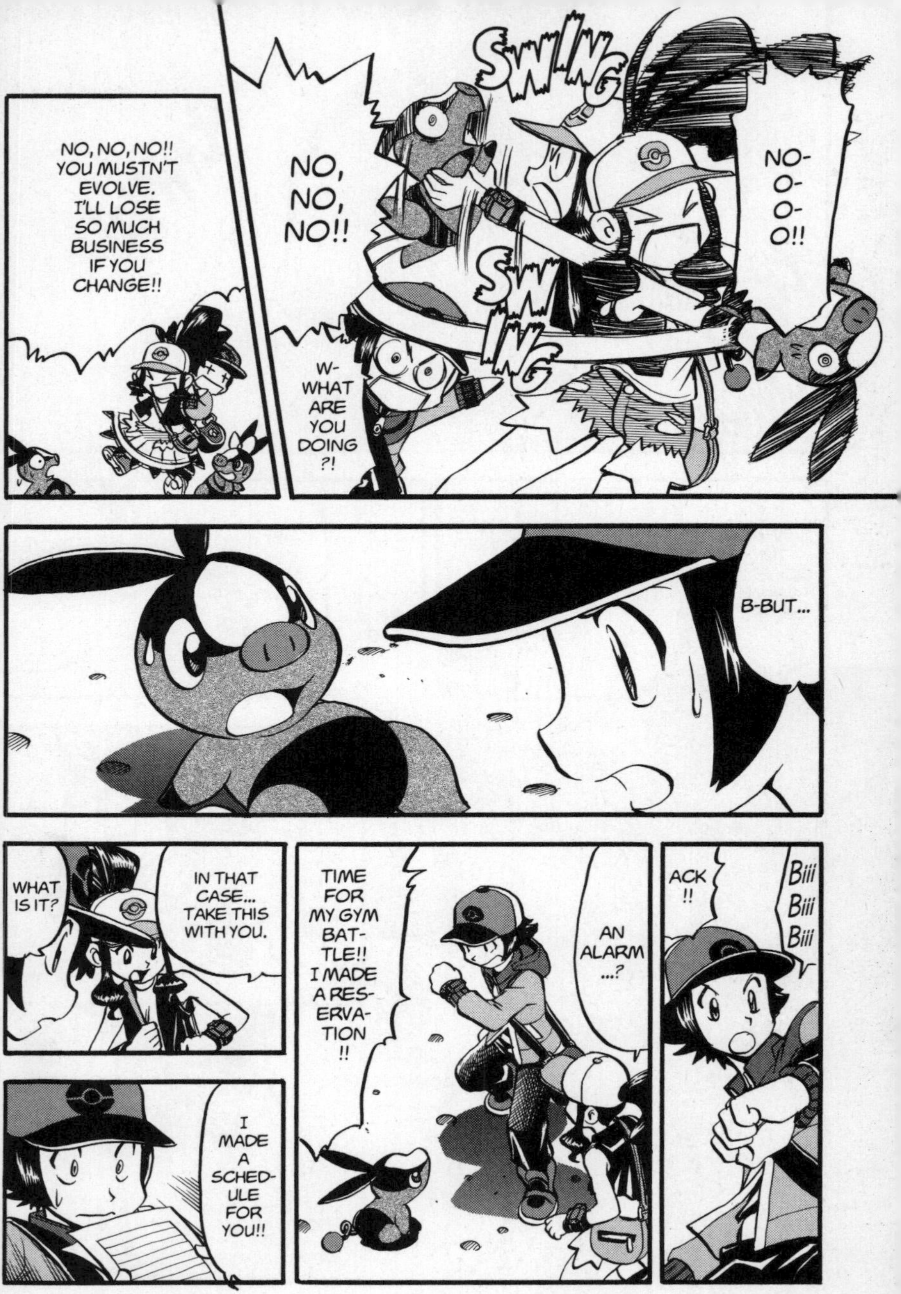
SWING
NO-O-O-O!!
NO, NO, NO!!
SWING
W-WHAT ARE YOU DOING?!
NO, NO, NO!! YOU MUSTN'T EVOLVE. I'LL LOSE SO MUCH BUSINESS IF YOU CHANGE!!
B-BUT...
Biii Biii Biii
ACK!!
AN ALARM...?
TIME FOR MY GYM BAT-TLE!! I MADE A RES-ERVA-TION!!
IN THAT CASE... TAKE THIS WITH YOU.
WHAT IS IT?
I MADE A SCHED-ULE FOR YOU!!

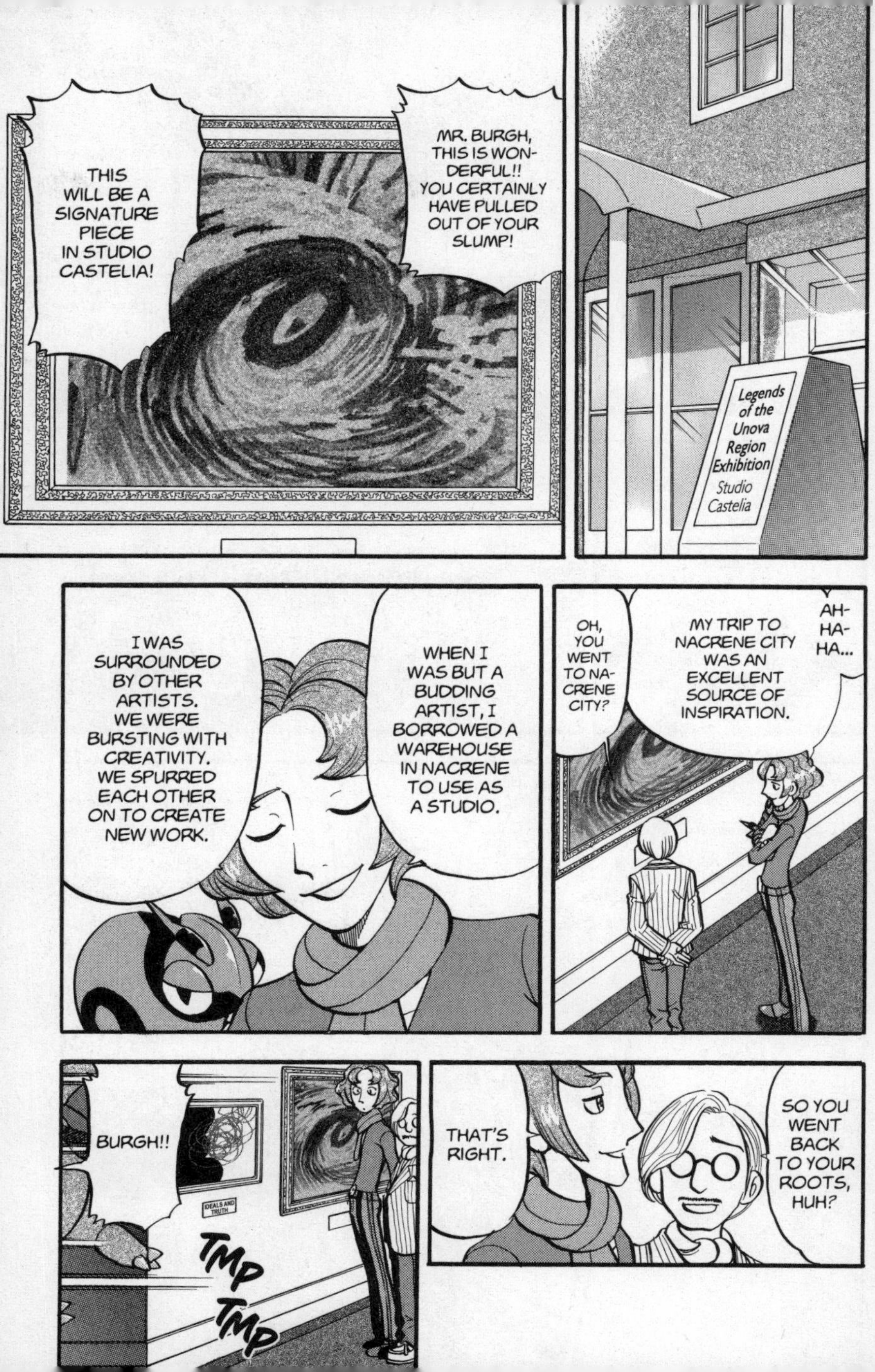
Legends of the Unova Region Exhibition
Studio Castelia
MR. BURGH, THIS IS WONDERFUL!! YOU CERTAINLY HAVE PULLED OUT OF YOUR SLUMP!
THIS WILL BE A SIGNATURE PIECE IN STUDIO CASTELIA!
AH-HA-HA...
MY TRIP TO NACRENE CITY WAS AN EXCELLENT SOURCE OF INSPIRATION.
OH, YOU WENT TO NACRENE CITY?
WHEN I WAS BUT A BUDDING ARTIST, I BORROWED A WAREHOUSE IN NACRENE TO USE AS A STUDIO.
I WAS SURROUNDED BY OTHER ARTISTS. WE WERE BURSTING WITH CREATIVITY. WE SPURRED EACH OTHER ON TO CREATE NEW WORK.
SO YOU WENT BACK TO YOUR ROOTS, HUH?
THAT'S RIGHT.
BURGH!!
IDEALS AND TRUTH
TMP TMP

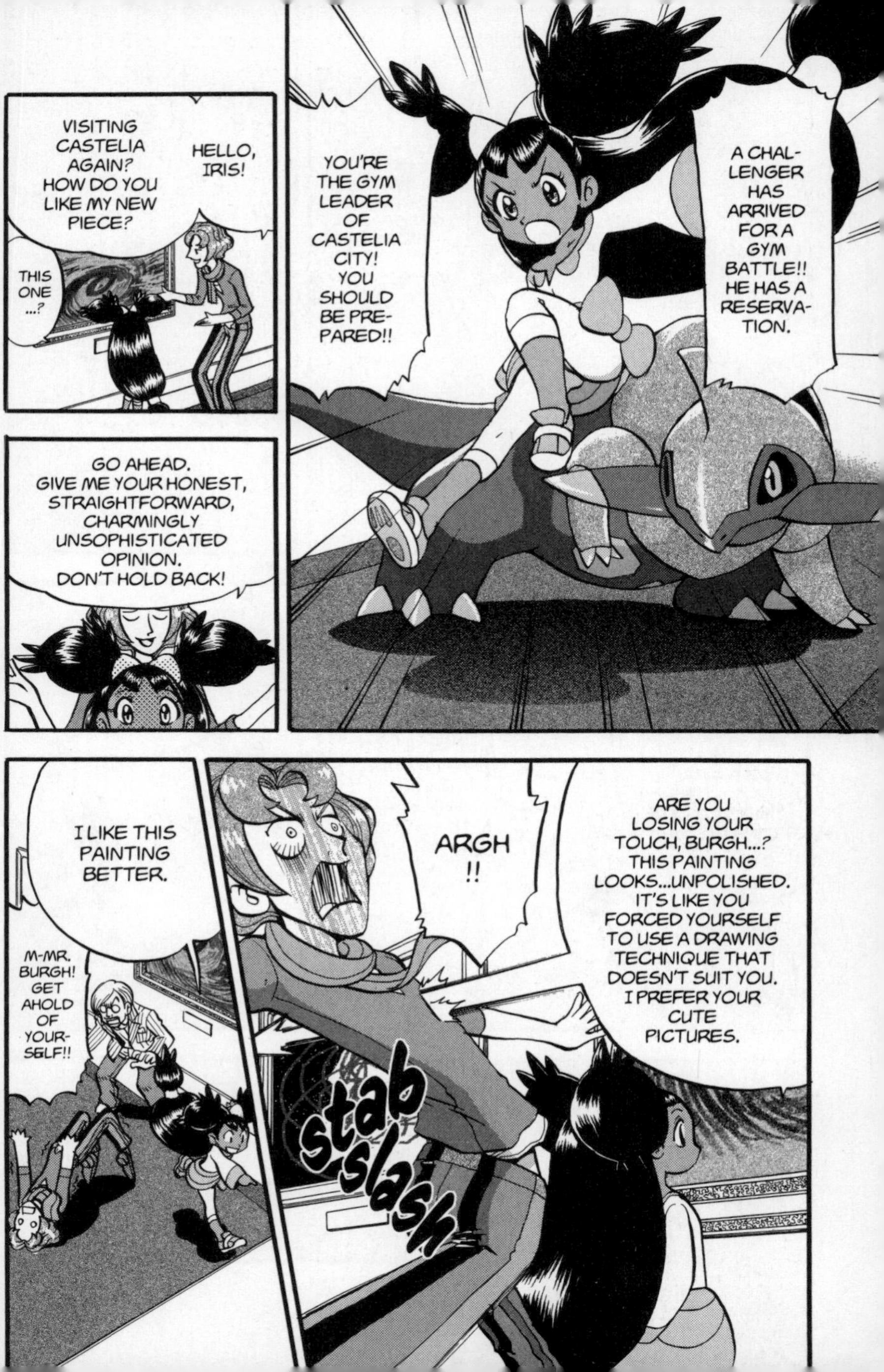
A CHAL-LENGER HAS ARRIVED FOR A GYM BATTLE!! HE HAS A RESERVA-TION.
YOU'RE THE GYM LEADER OF CASTELIA CITY! YOU SHOULD BE PRE-PARED!!
HELLO, IRIS!
VISITING CASTELIA AGAIN? HOW DO YOU LIKE MY NEW PIECE?
THIS ONE ...?
GO AHEAD. GIVE ME YOUR HONEST, STRAIGHTFORWARD, CHARMINGLY UNSOPHISTICATED OPINION. DON'T HOLD BACK!
ARE YOU LOSING YOUR TOUCH, BURGH...? THIS PAINTING LOOKS...UNPOLISHED. IT'S LIKE YOU FORCED YOURSELF TO USE A DRAWING TECHNIQUE THAT DOESN'T SUIT YOU. I PREFER YOUR CUTE PICTURES.
ARGH !!
stab
slash
I LIKE THIS PAINTING BETTER.
M-MR. BURGH! GET AHOLD OF YOUR-SELF!!

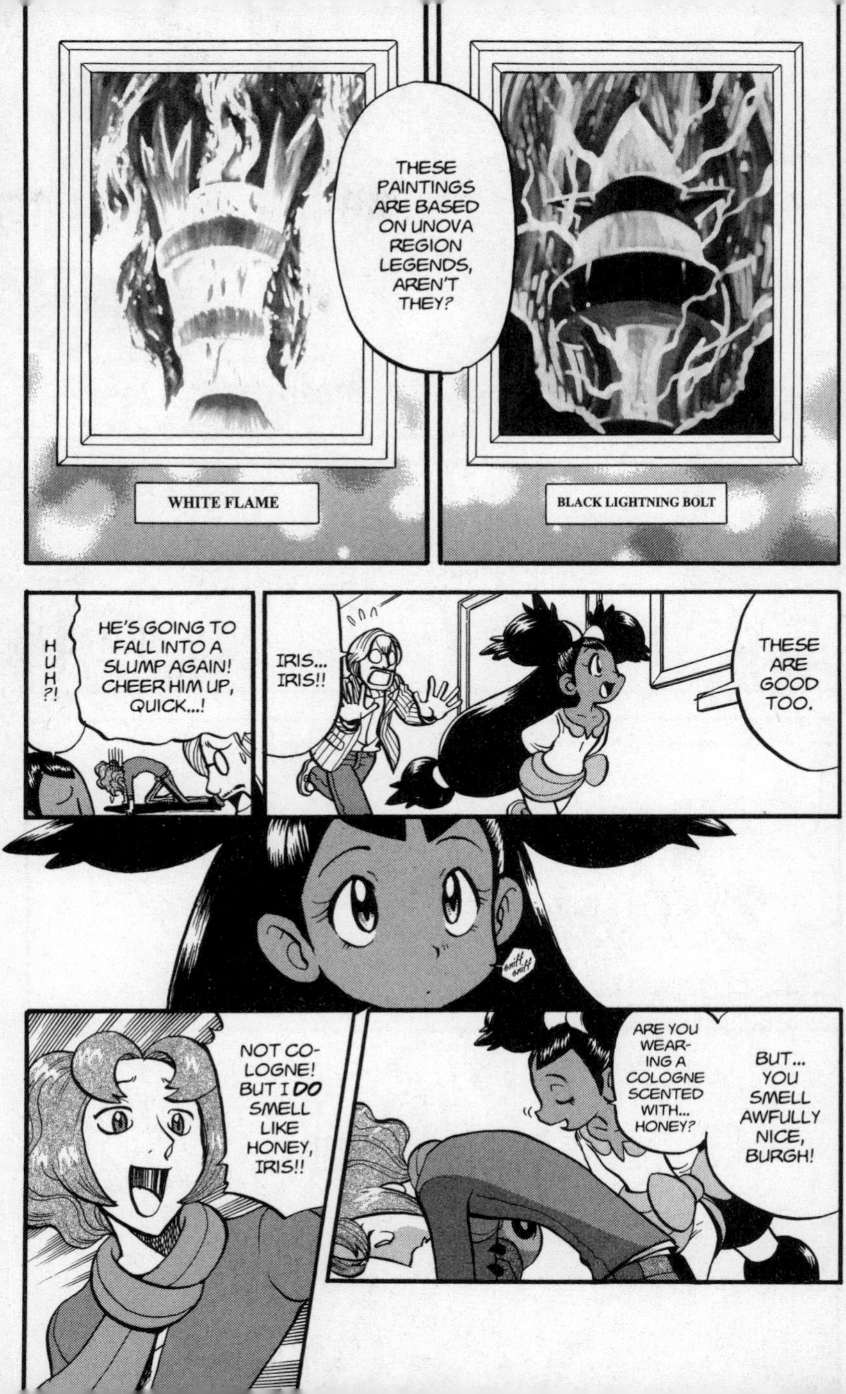
THESE PAINTINGS ARE BASED ON UNOVA REGION LEGENDS, AREN'T THEY?
BLACK LIGHTNING BOLT
WHITE FLAME
THESE ARE GOOD TOO.
IRIS... IRIS!!
HE'S GOING TO FALL INTO A SLUMP AGAIN! CHEER HIM UP, QUICK...!
HUH?!
sniff sniff
BUT... YOU SMELL AWFULLY NICE, BURGH!
ARE YOU WEARING A COLOGNE SCENTED WITH... HONEY?
NOT COLOGNE! BUT I ***DO*** SMELL LIKE HONEY, IRIS!!

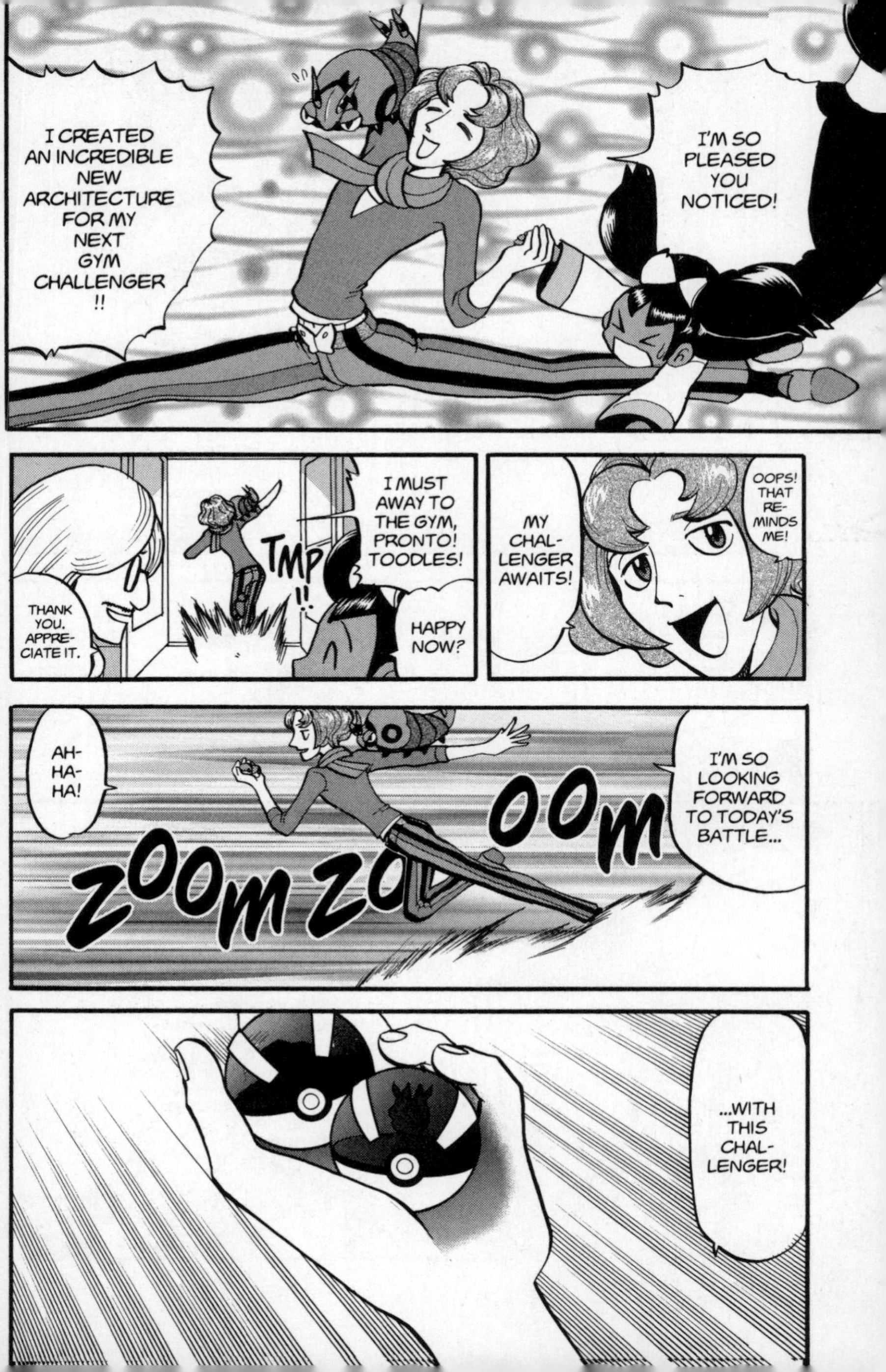
I'M SO PLEASED YOU NOTICED!
I CREATED AN INCREDIBLE NEW ARCHITECTURE FOR MY NEXT GYM CHALLENGER !!
OOPS! THAT RE-MINDS ME!
MY CHAL-LENGER AWAITS!
I MUST AWAY TO THE GYM, PRONTO! TOODLES!
TMP !!
HAPPY NOW?
THANK YOU. APPRE-CIATE IT.
I'M SO LOOKING FORWARD TO TODAY'S BATTLE...
AH-HA-HA!
ZOOM ZOOOM
...WITH THIS CHAL-LENGER!

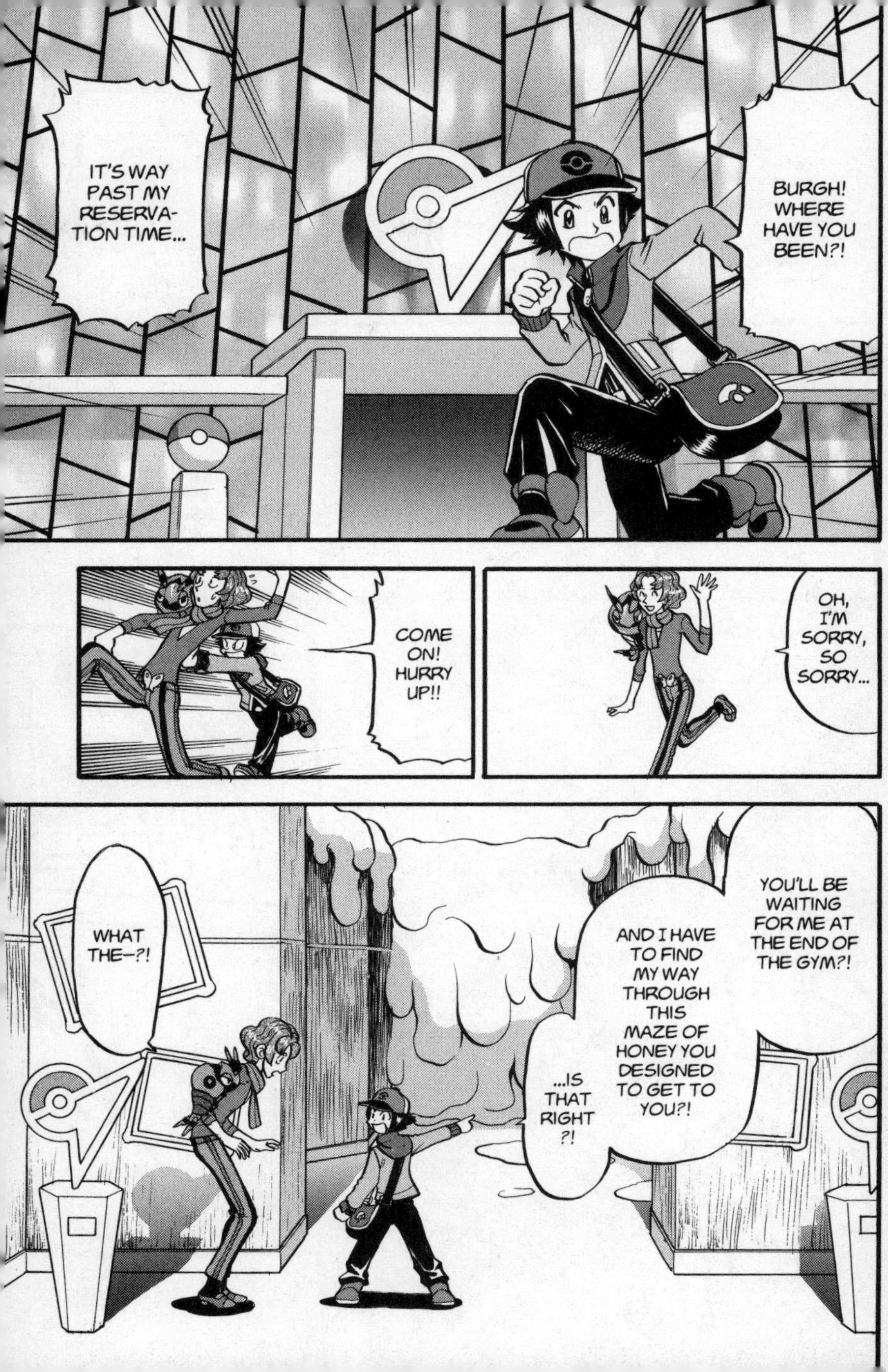
BURGH! WHERE HAVE YOU BEEN?!
IT'S WAY PAST MY RESERVATION TIME...
OH, I'M SORRY, SO SORRY...
COME ON! HURRY UP!!
YOU'LL BE WAITING FOR ME AT THE END OF THE GYM?!
AND I HAVE TO FIND MY WAY THROUGH THIS MAZE OF HONEY YOU DESIGNED TO GET TO YOU?!
...IS THAT RIGHT?!
WHAT THE—?!

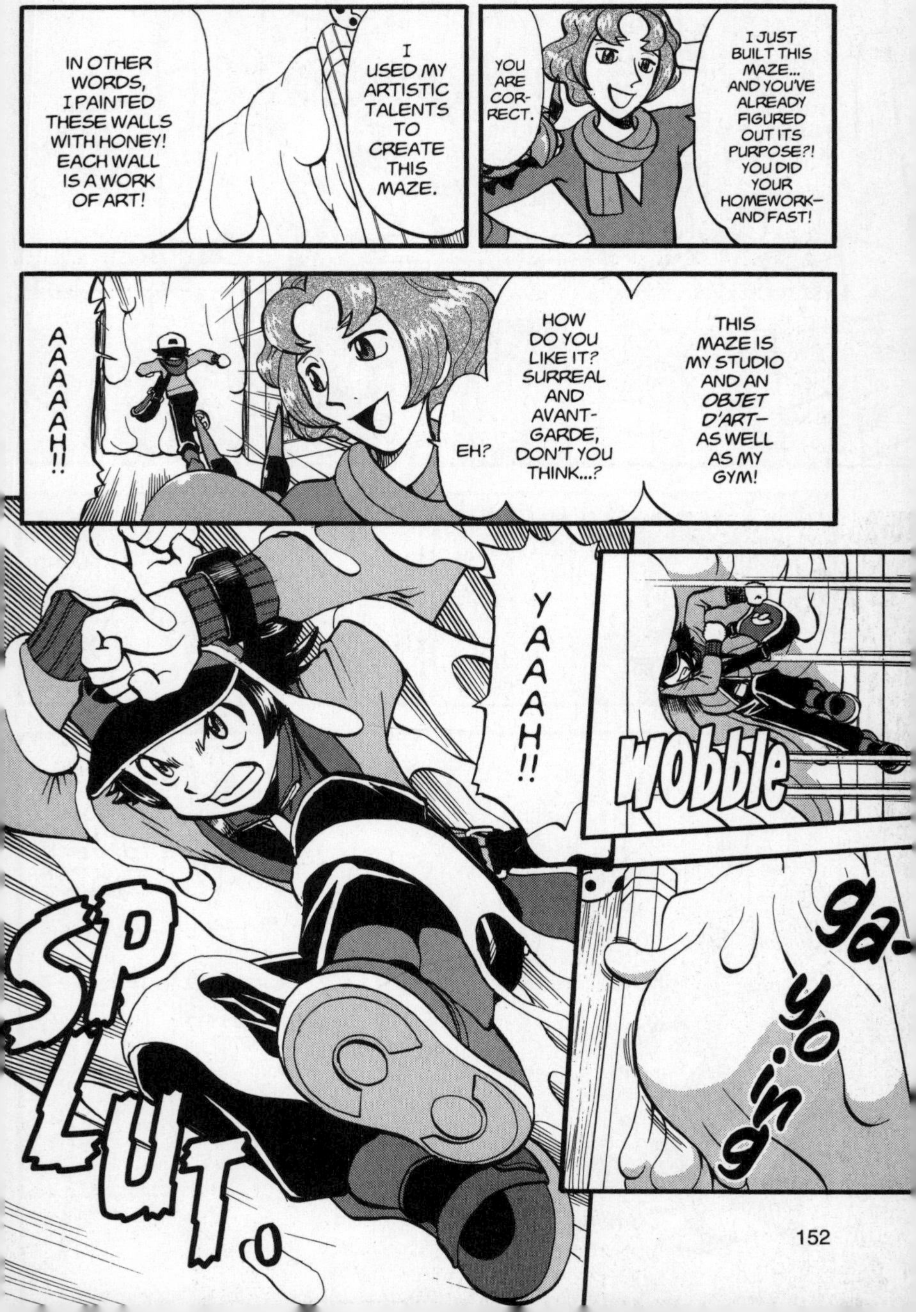
I JUST BUILT THIS MAZE... AND YOU'VE ALREADY FIGURED OUT ITS PURPOSE?! YOU DID YOUR HOMEWORK—AND FAST!
YOU ARE COR-RECT.
I USED MY ARTISTIC TALENTS TO CREATE THIS MAZE.
IN OTHER WORDS, I PAINTED THESE WALLS WITH HONEY! EACH WALL IS A WORK OF ART!
THIS MAZE IS MY STUDIO AND AN OBJET D'ART—AS WELL AS MY GYM!
HOW DO YOU LIKE IT? SURREAL AND AVANT-GARDE, DON'T YOU THINK...?
EH?
AAAAAAH!!
wobble
ga-yo-ing
YAAAAH!!
SPLUT

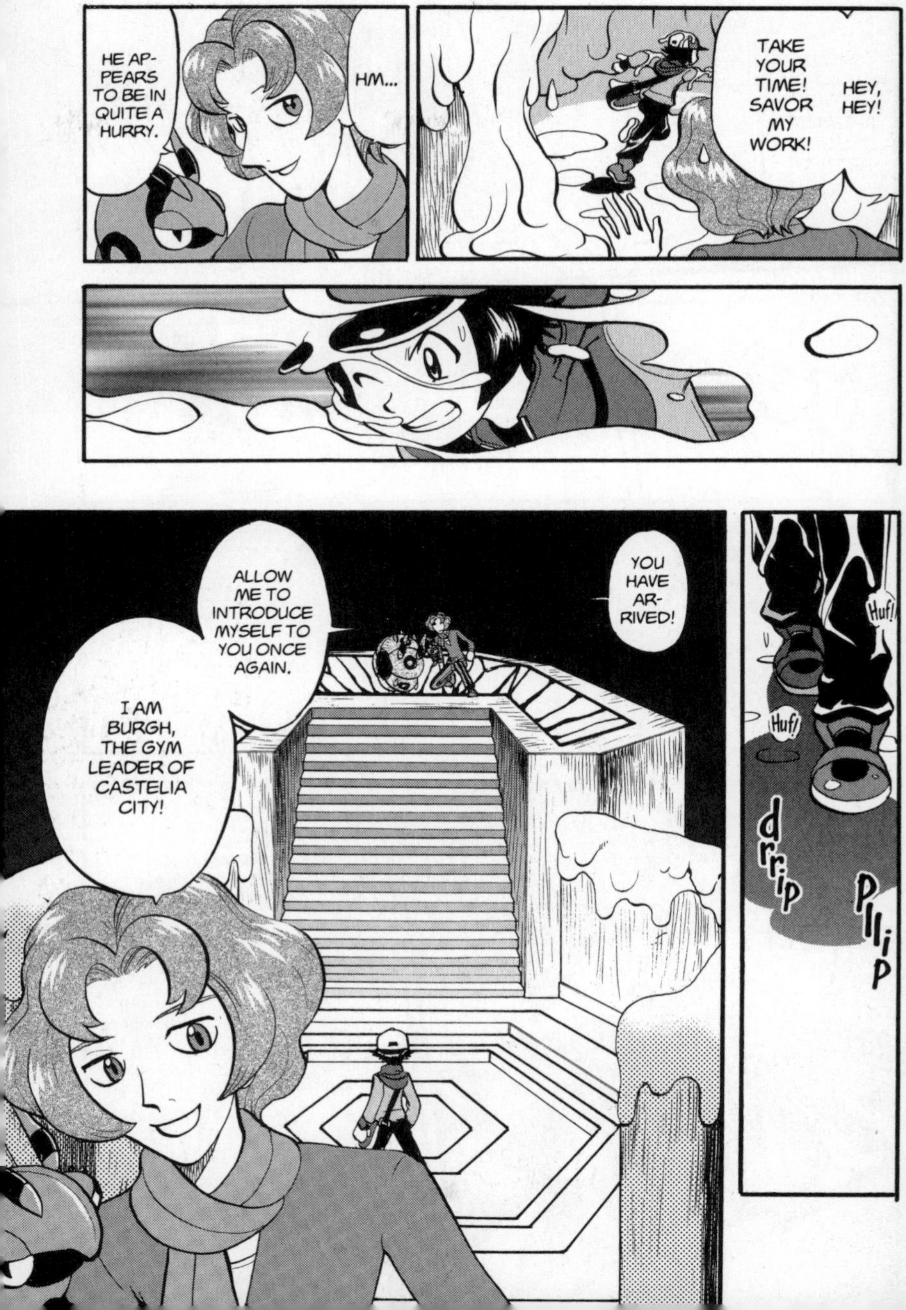
HEY, HEY!
TAKE YOUR TIME! SAVOR MY WORK!
HM...
HE AP-PEARS TO BE IN QUITE A HURRY.
Huf!
Huf!
drrip
Pllip
YOU HAVE AR-RIVED!
ALLOW ME TO INTRODUCE MYSELF TO YOU ONCE AGAIN.
I AM BURGH, THE GYM LEADER OF CASTELIA CITY!

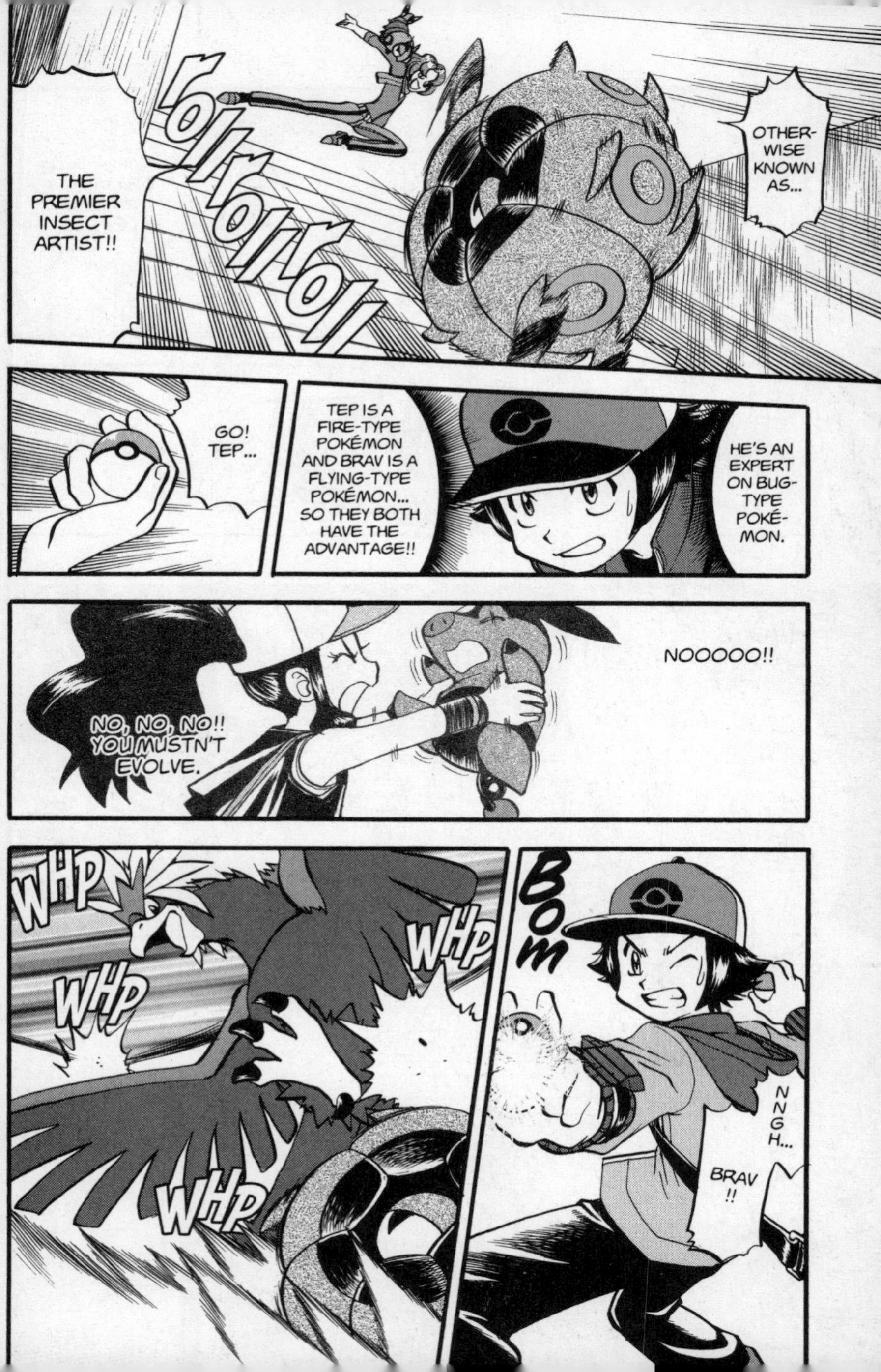
OTHER-WISE KNOWN AS...
THE PREMIER INSECT ARTIST!!
HE'S AN EXPERT ON BUG-TYPE POKÉ-MON.
TEP IS A FIRE-TYPE POKÉMON AND BRAV IS A FLYING-TYPE POKÉMON... SO THEY BOTH HAVE THE ADVANTAGE!!
GO! TEP...
NOOOOO!!
NO, NO, NO!! YOU MUSTN'T EVOLVE.
Boom
NNGH...
BRAV!!
WHP
WHP
WHP
WHP

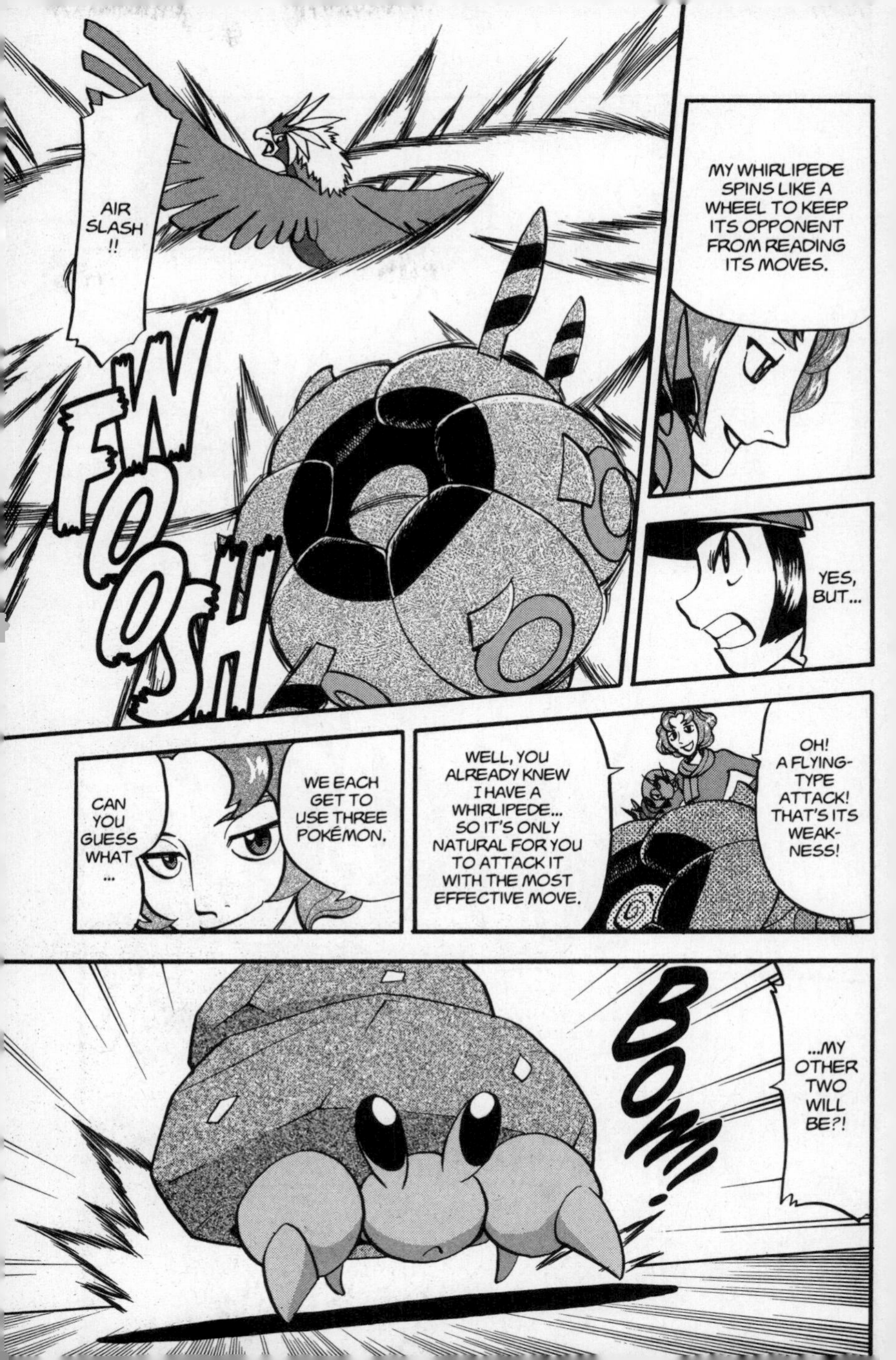
MY WHIRLIPEDE SPINS LIKE A WHEEL TO KEEP ITS OPPONENT FROM READING ITS MOVES.
YES, BUT...
AIR SLASH !!
FWOOSH
OH! A FLYING-TYPE ATTACK! THAT'S ITS WEAK-NESS!
WELL, YOU ALREADY KNEW I HAVE A WHIRLIPEDE... SO IT'S ONLY NATURAL FOR YOU TO ATTACK IT WITH THE MOST EFFECTIVE MOVE.
WE EACH GET TO USE THREE POKÉMON.
CAN YOU GUESS WHAT ...
BOOM!
...MY OTHER TWO WILL BE?!

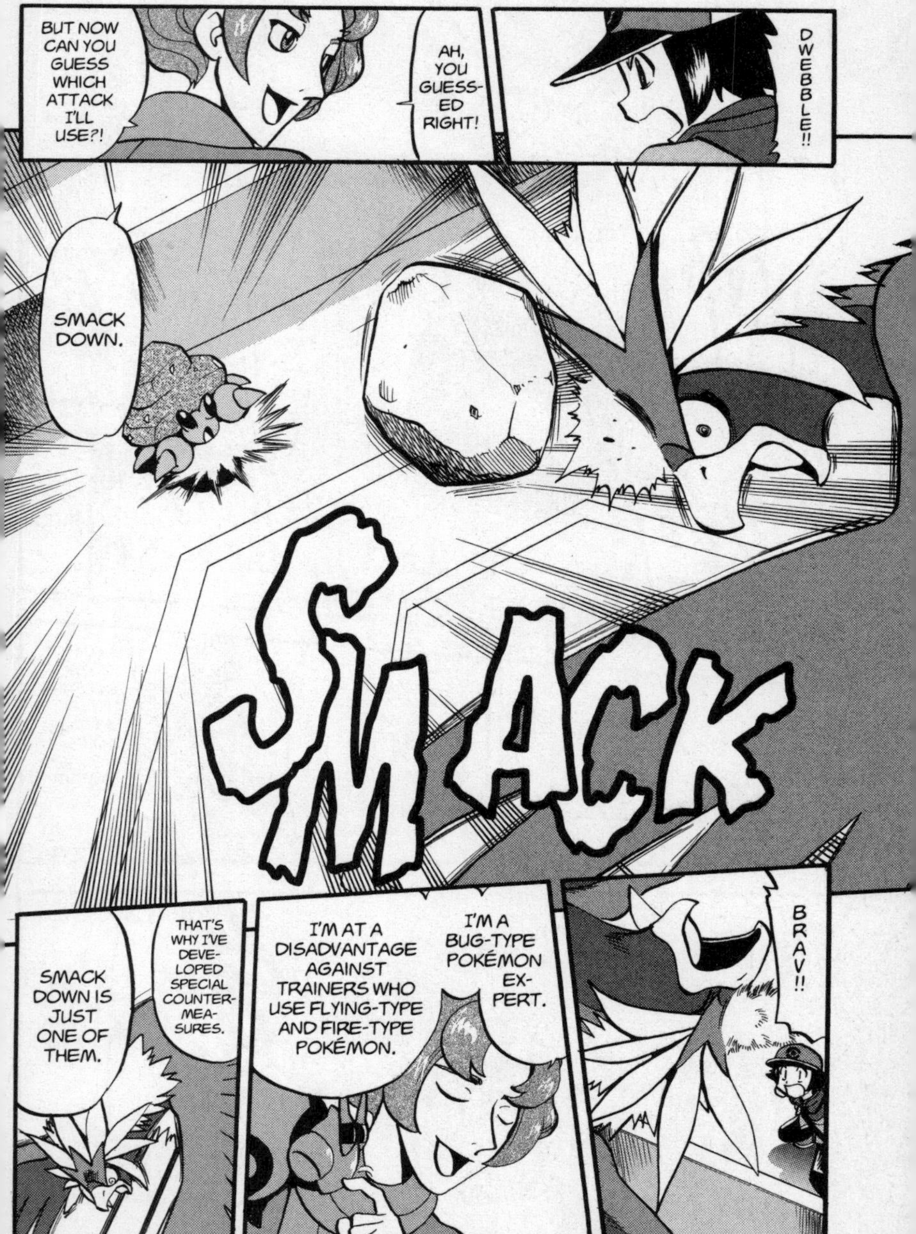
DWEBBLE!!
AH, YOU GUESSED RIGHT!
BUT NOW CAN YOU GUESS WHICH ATTACK I'LL USE?!
SMACK DOWN.
SMACK
BRAV!!
I'M A BUG-TYPE POKÉMON EXPERT.
I'M AT A DISADVANTAGE AGAINST TRAINERS WHO USE FLYING-TYPE AND FIRE-TYPE POKÉMON.
THAT'S WHY I'VE DEVELOPED SPECIAL COUNTERMEASURES.
SMACK DOWN IS JUST ONE OF THEM.

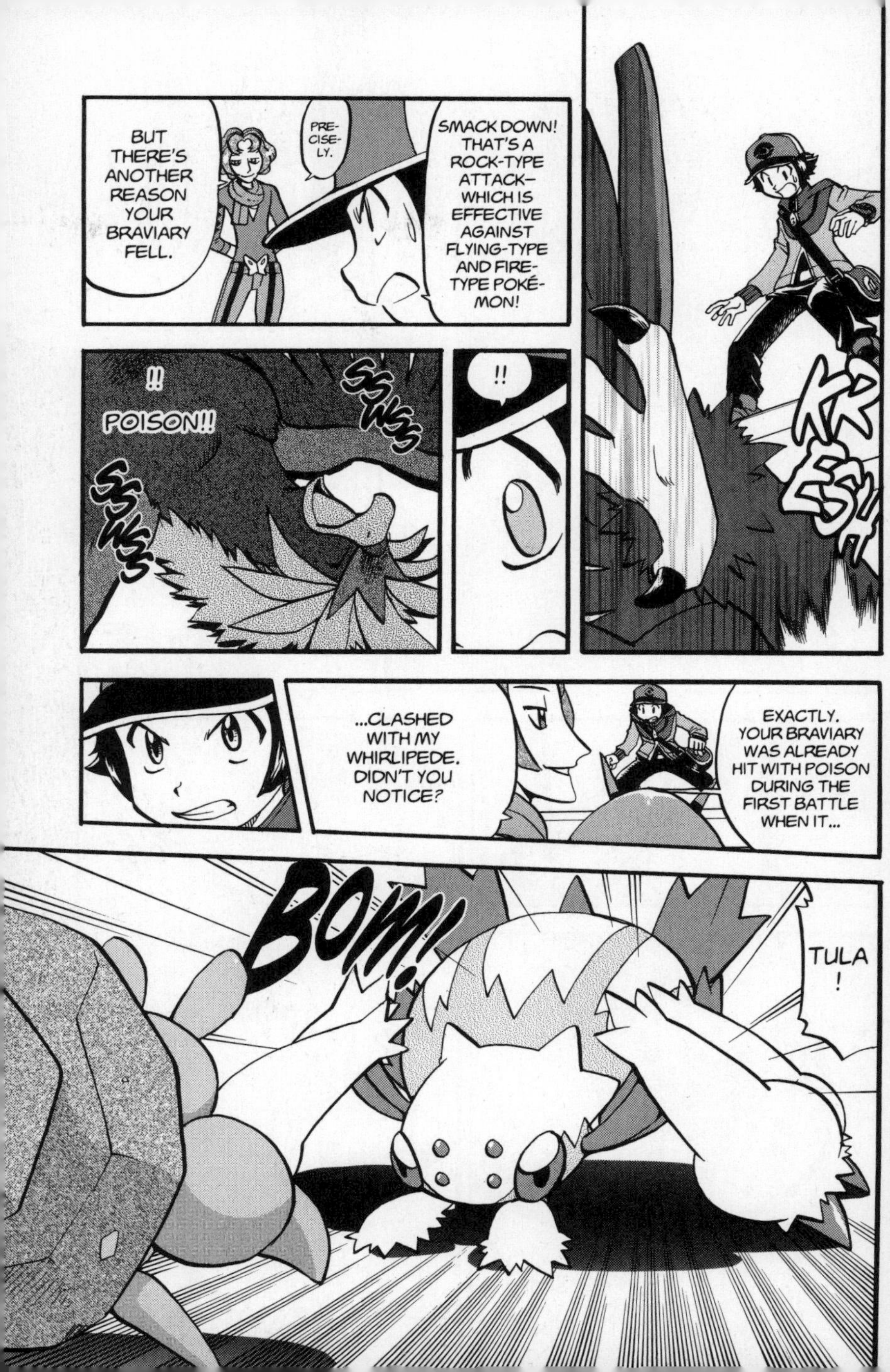
KRESH!!
SMACK DOWN! THAT'S A ROCK-TYPE ATTACK—WHICH IS EFFECTIVE AGAINST FLYING-TYPE AND FIRE-TYPE POKÉMON!
PRE-CISE-LY.
BUT THERE'S ANOTHER REASON YOUR BRAVIARY FELL.
!!
SSWSS
!!
POISON!!
SSWSS
EXACTLY. YOUR BRAVIARY WAS ALREADY HIT WITH POISON DURING THE FIRST BATTLE WHEN IT...
...CLASHED WITH MY WHIRLIPEDE. DIDN'T YOU NOTICE?
TULA!
BOM!

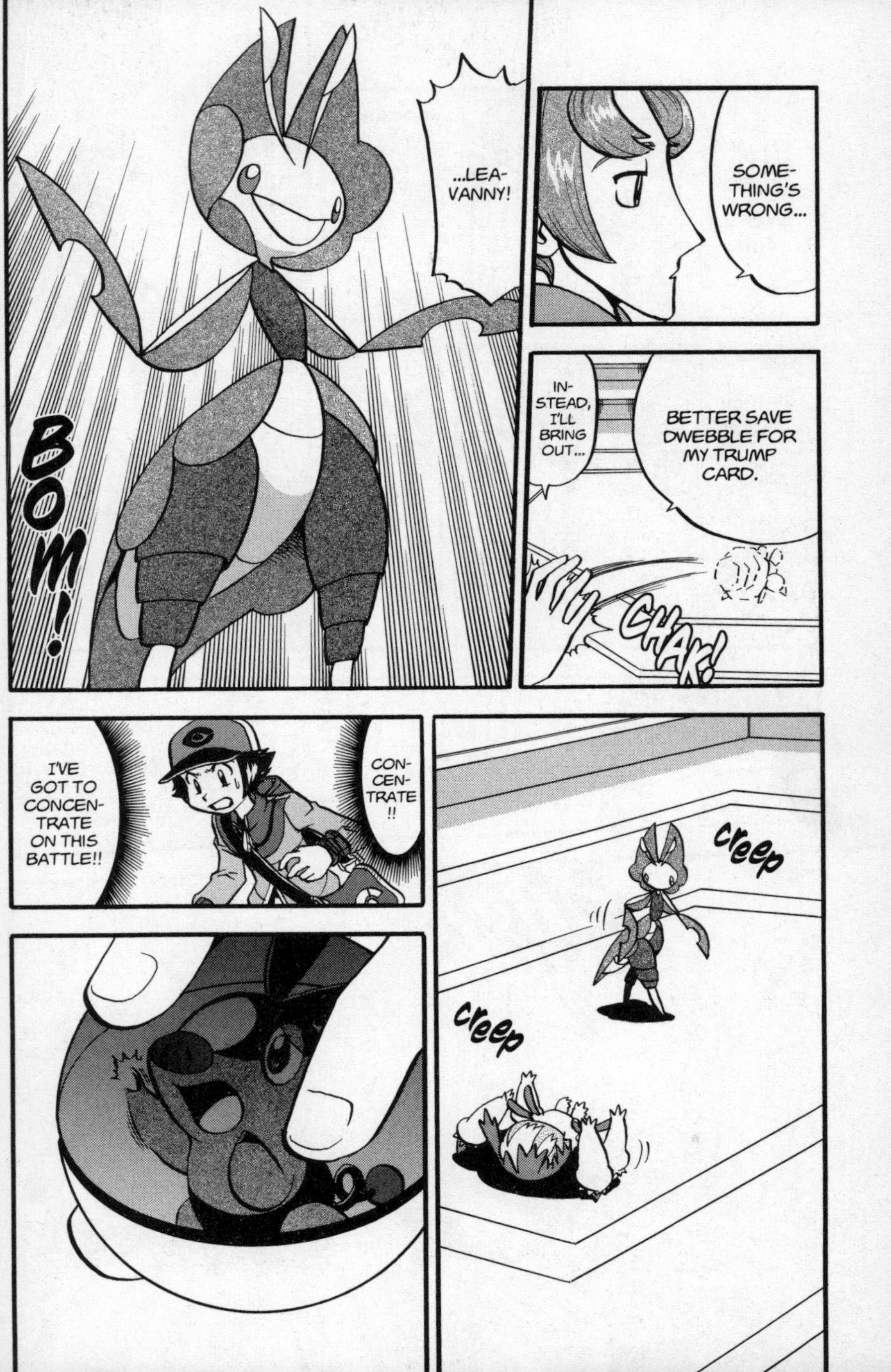
SOME-THING'S WRONG...
BETTER SAVE DWEBBLE FOR MY TRUMP CARD.
IN-STEAD, I'LL BRING OUT...
CHAK!
...LEA-VANNY!
BOM!
creep
creep
CONCEN-TRATE!!
I'VE GOT TO CONCEN-TRATE ON THIS BATTLE!!

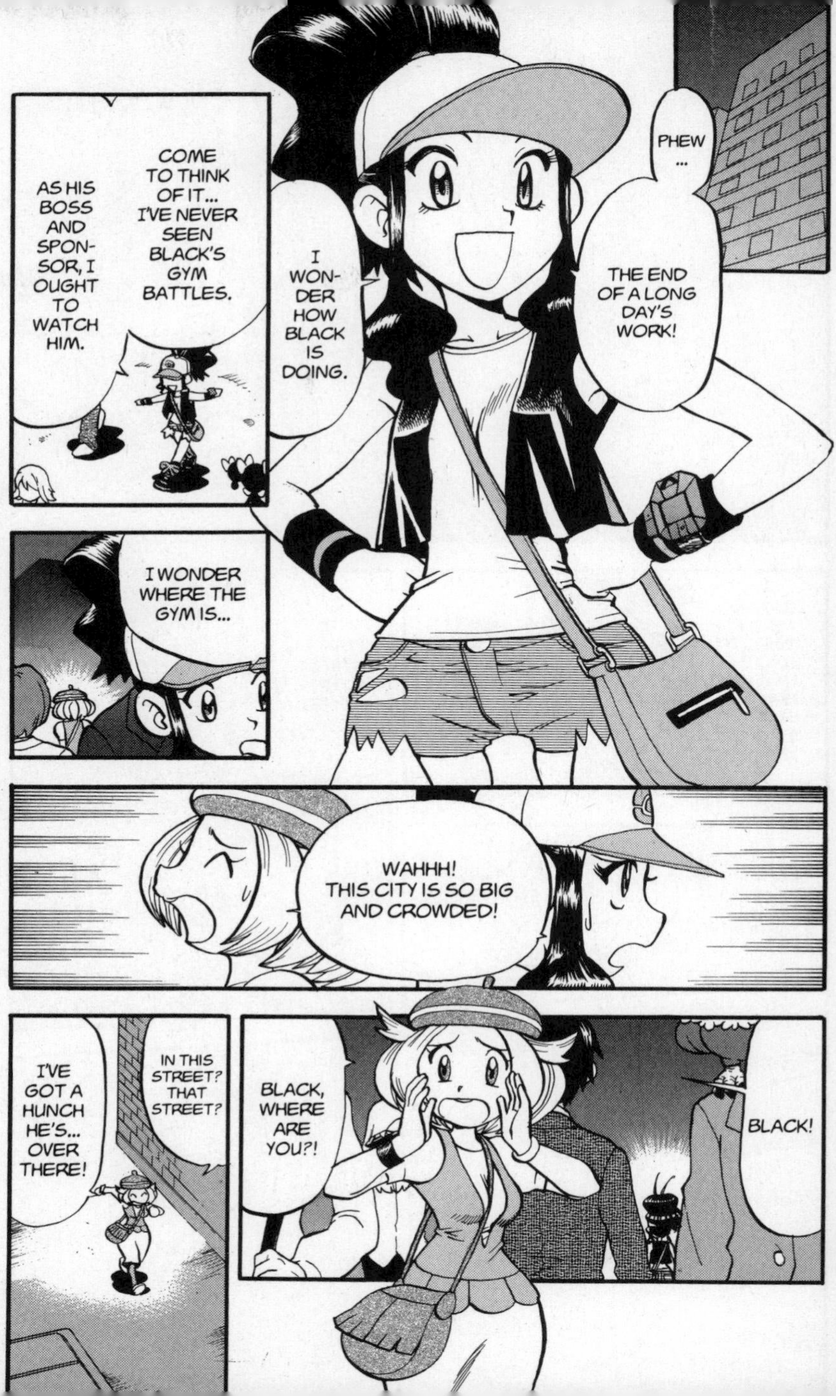
PHEW...
THE END OF A LONG DAY'S WORK!
I WONDER HOW BLACK IS DOING.
COME TO THINK OF IT... I'VE NEVER SEEN BLACK'S GYM BATTLES.
AS HIS BOSS AND SPONSOR, I OUGHT TO WATCH HIM.
I WONDER WHERE THE GYM IS...
WAHHH! THIS CITY IS SO BIG AND CROWDED!
BLACK!
BLACK, WHERE ARE YOU?!
IN THIS STREET? THAT STREET?
I'VE GOT A HUNCH HE'S... OVER THERE!

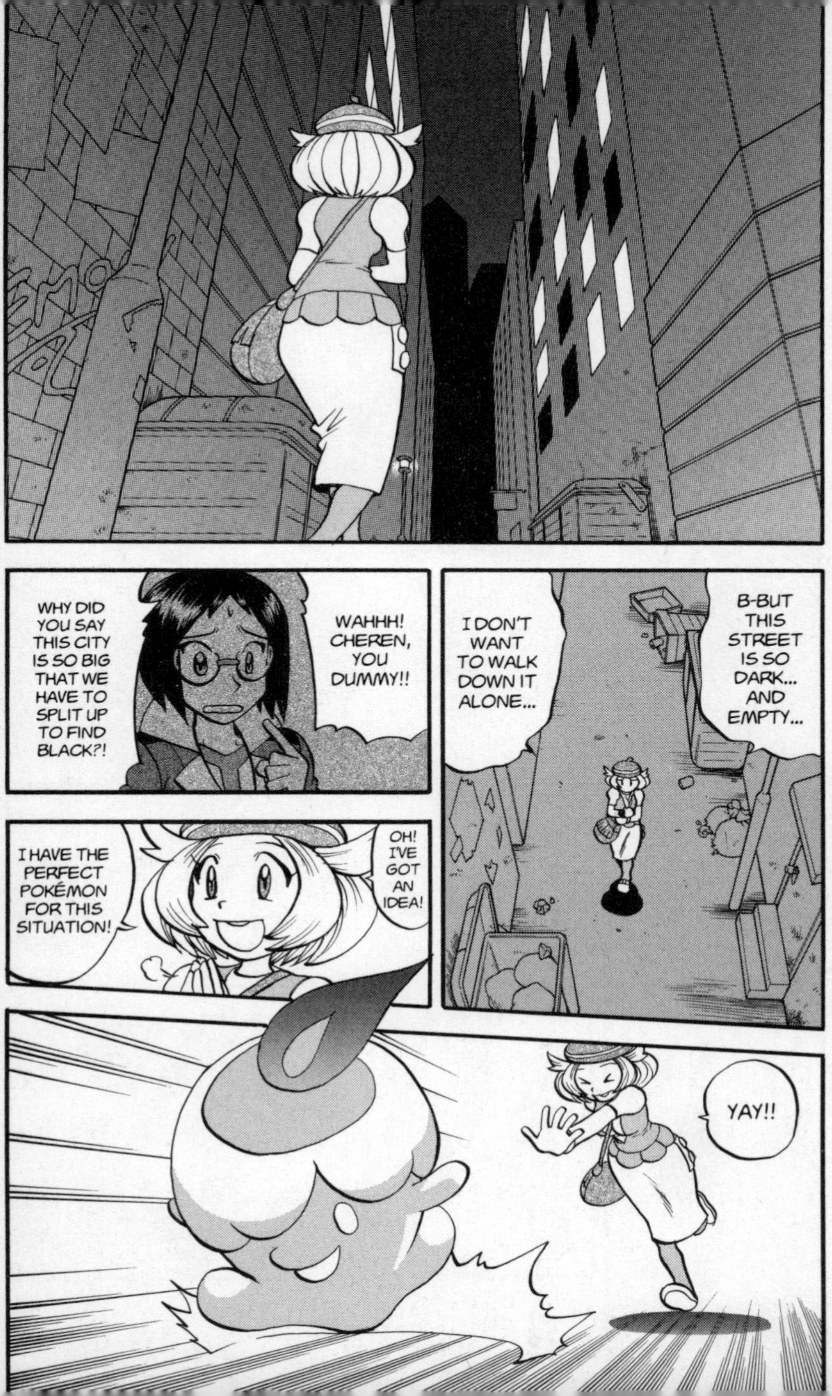
B-BUT THIS STREET IS SO DARK... AND EMPTY...
I DON'T WANT TO WALK DOWN IT ALONE...
WAHHH! CHEREN, YOU DUMMY!!
WHY DID YOU SAY THIS CITY IS SO BIG THAT WE HAVE TO SPLIT UP TO FIND BLACK?!
OH! I'VE GOT AN IDEA!
I HAVE THE PERFECT POKÉMON FOR THIS SITUATION!
YAY!!

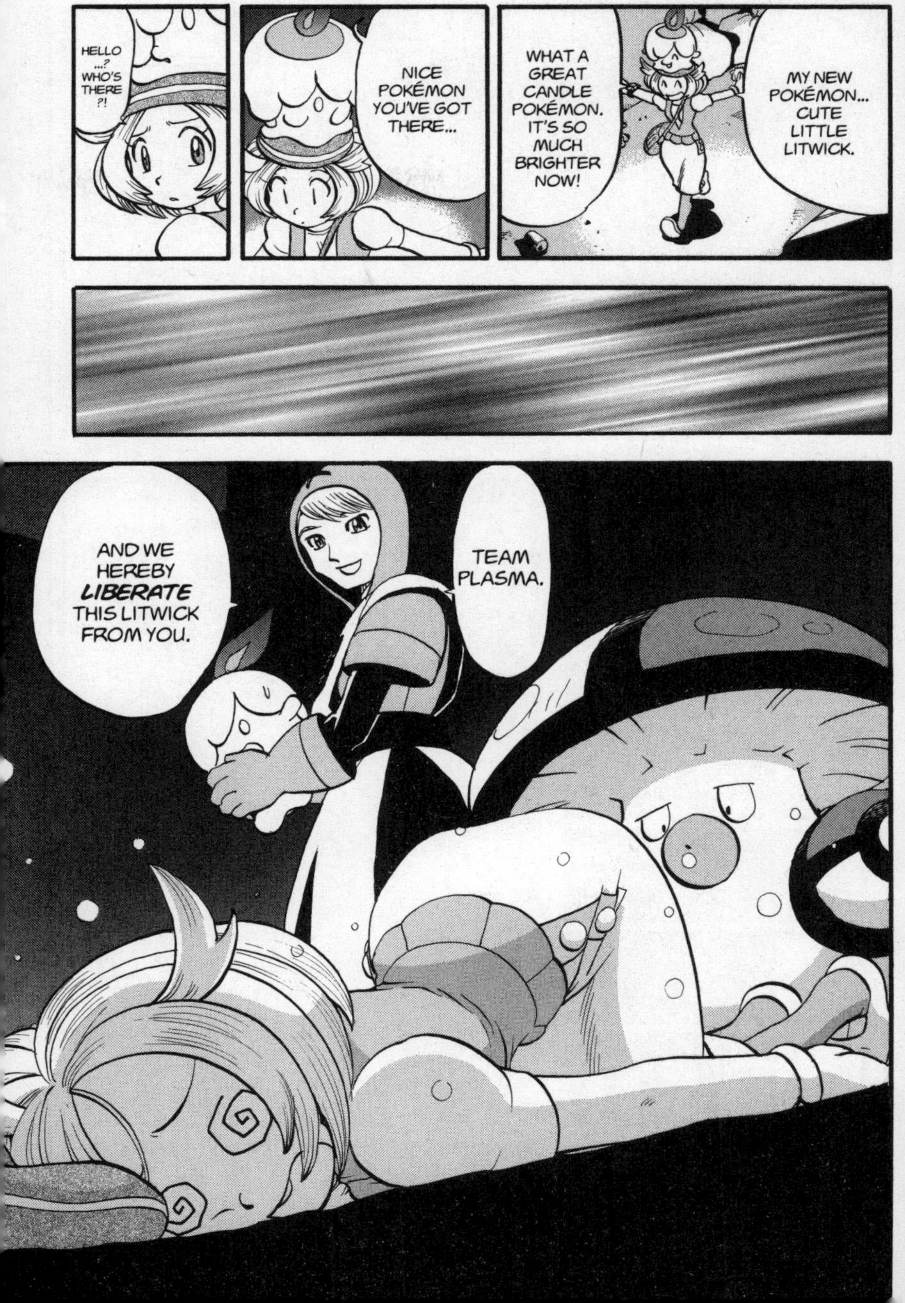
MY NEW POKÉMON... CUTE LITTLE LITWICK.
WHAT A GREAT CANDLE POKÉMON. IT'S SO MUCH BRIGHTER NOW!
NICE POKÉMON YOU'VE GOT THERE...
HELLO ...? WHO'S THERE ?!
TEAM PLASMA.
AND WE HEREBY ***LIBERATE*** THIS LITWICK FROM YOU.

ADVENTURE MAP

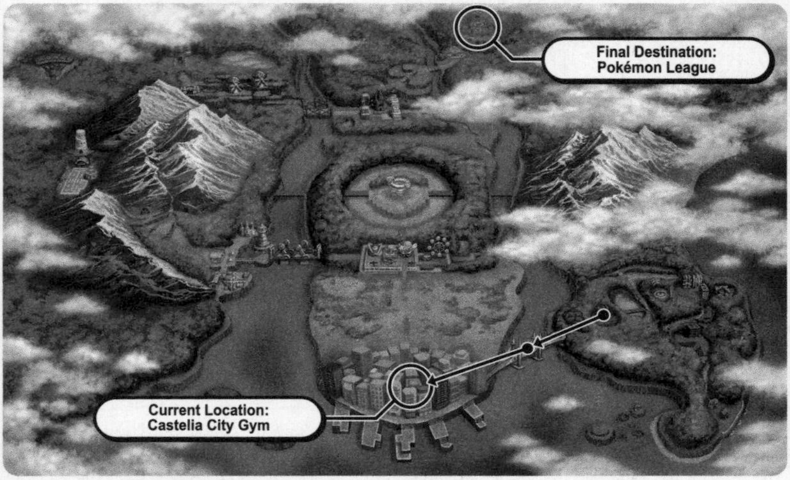

Final Destination:
Pokémon League
Current Location:
Castelia City Gym

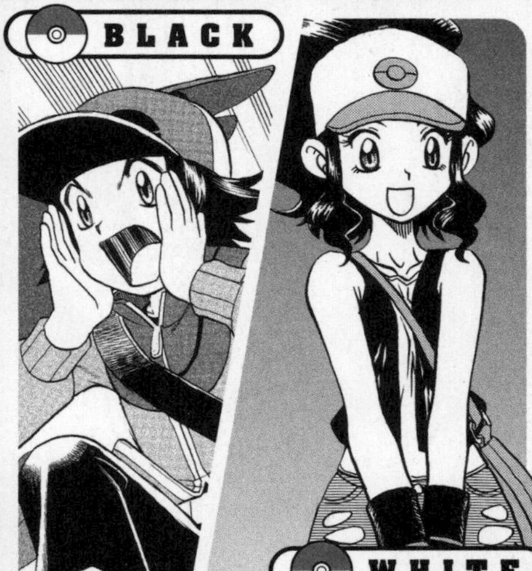

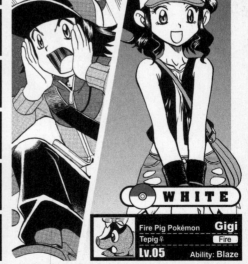

BLACK
WHITE

Fire Pig Pokémon **Tep**
Tepig♂ Fire
Lv.16 Ability: Blaze

Dream Eater Pokémon **Musha**
Munna♂ Psychic
Lv.39 Ability: Forewarn

Valiant Pokémon **Brav**
Braviary♂ Normal Flying
Lv.54 Ability: Sheer Force

EleSpider Pokémon **Tula**
Galvantula♂ Bug Electric
Lv.41 Ability: Unnerve

Fire Pig Pokémon **Gigi**
Tepig♀ Fire
Lv.05 Ability: Blaze

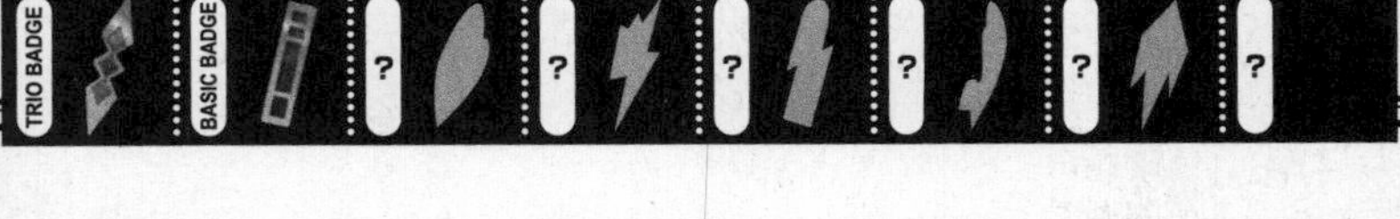

TRIO BADGE
BASIC BADGE
?
?
?
?
?
?

Pokémon™ Adventures Black & White

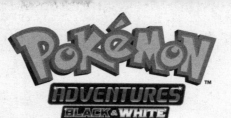

AMOONGUSS

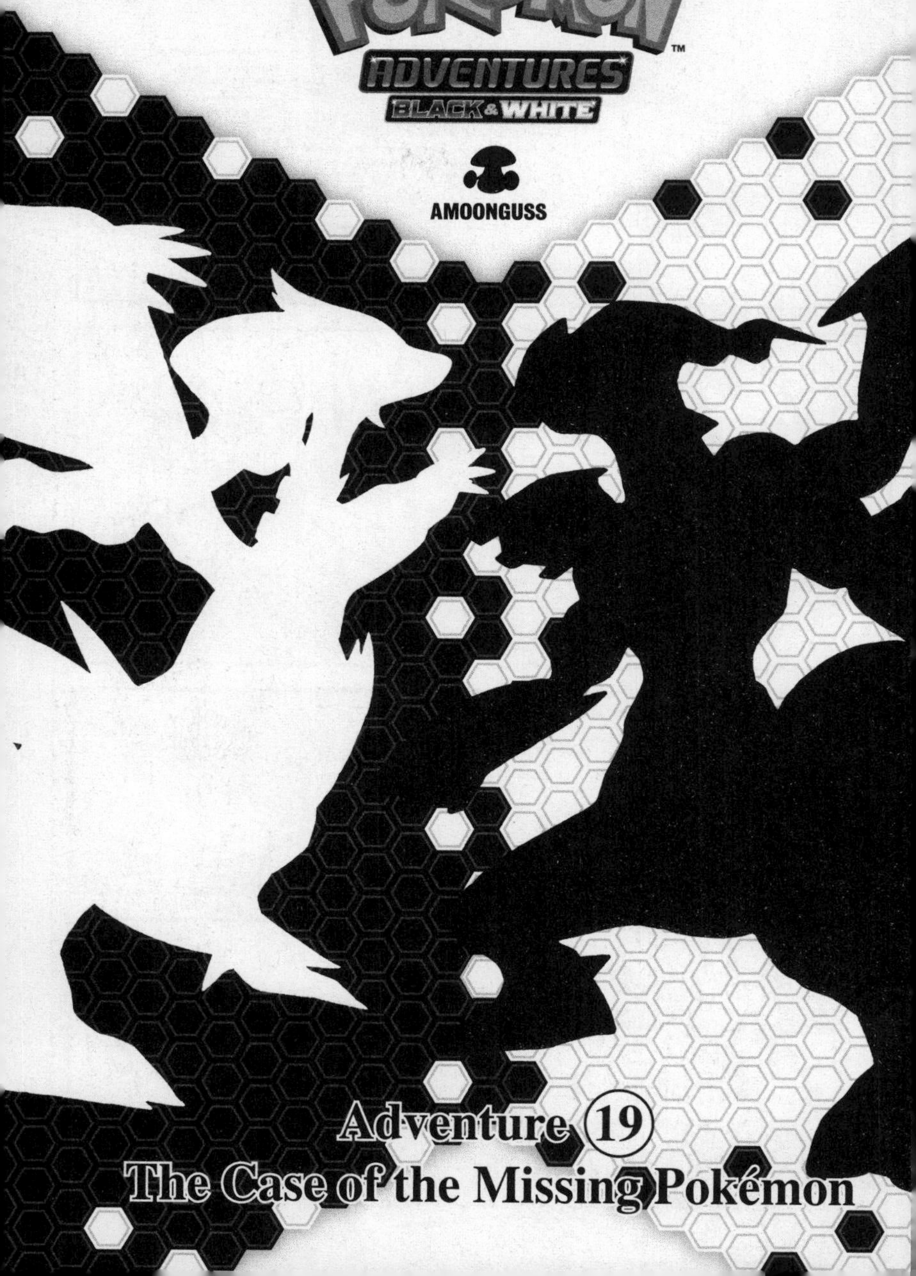

Adventure 19
The Case of the Missing Pokémon

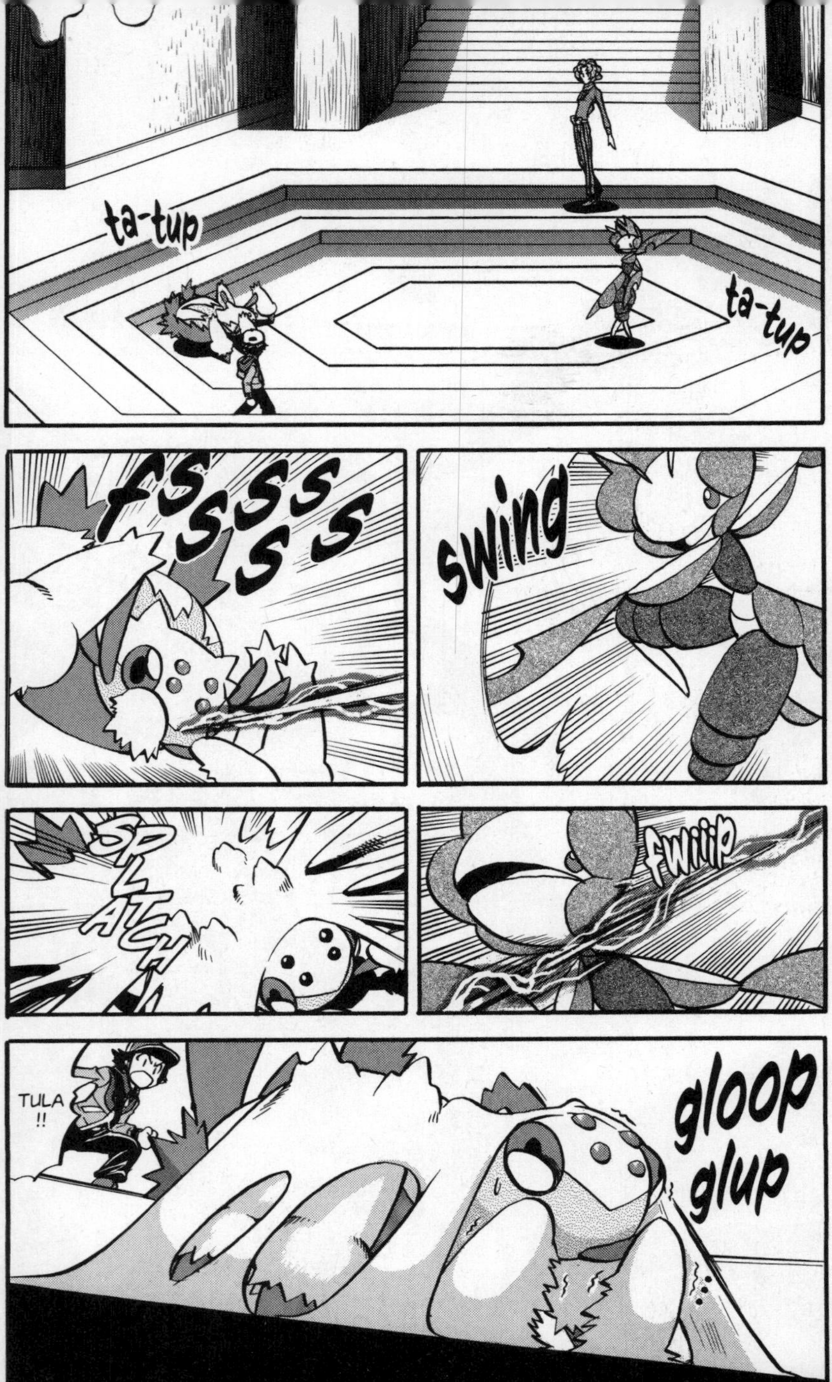
ta-tup
ta-tup
swing
fsssssss
fwiiip
SPLATCH
gloop
glup
TULA !!

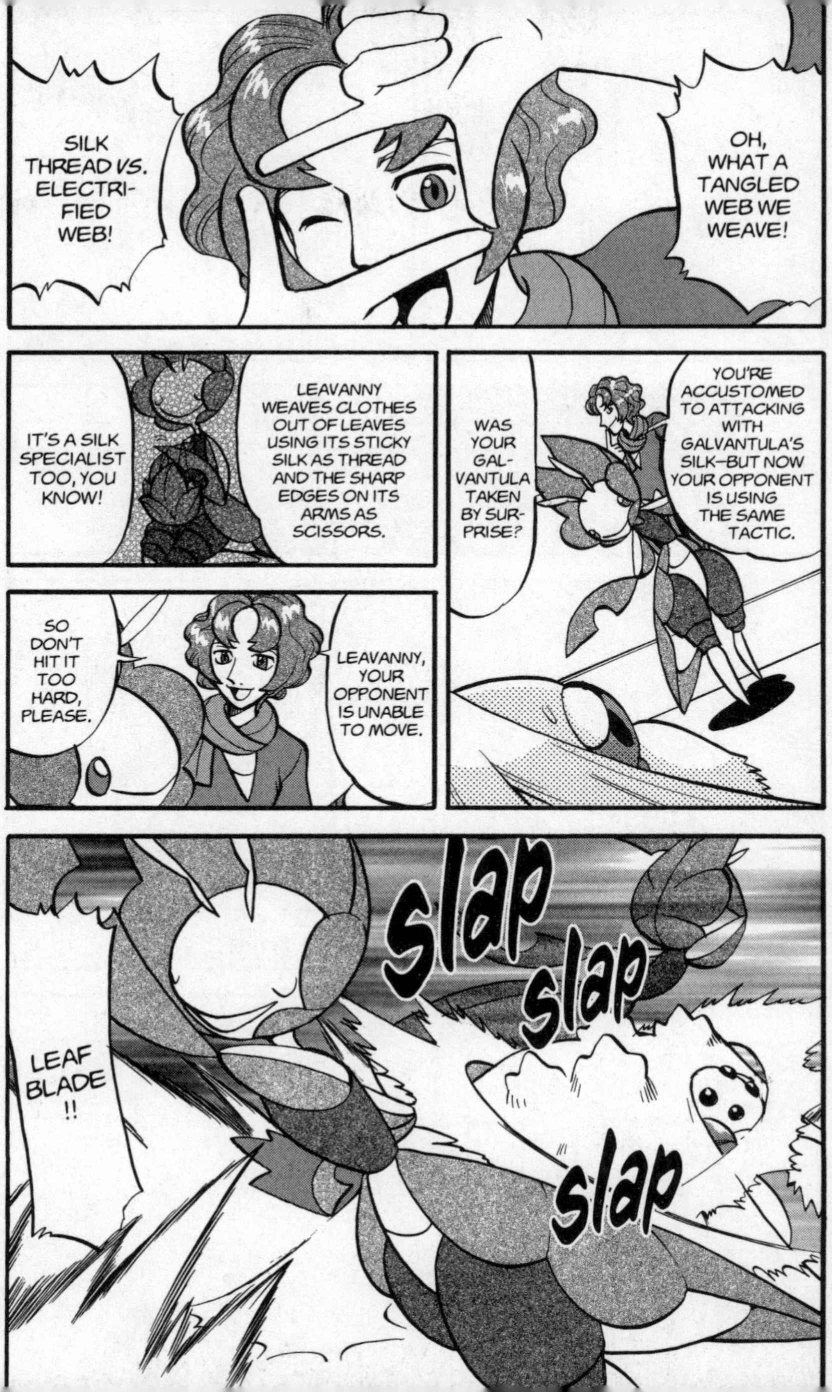
OH, WHAT A TANGLED WEB WE WEAVE!
SILK THREAD VS. ELECTRIFIED WEB!
YOU'RE ACCUSTOMED TO ATTACKING WITH GALVANTULA'S SILK—BUT NOW YOUR OPPONENT IS USING THE SAME TACTIC.
WAS YOUR GALVANTULA TAKEN BY SURPRISE?
LEAVANNY WEAVES CLOTHES OUT OF LEAVES USING ITS STICKY SILK AS THREAD AND THE SHARP EDGES ON ITS ARMS AS SCISSORS.
IT'S A SILK SPECIALIST TOO, YOU KNOW!
LEAVANNY, YOUR OPPONENT IS UNABLE TO MOVE.
SO DON'T HIT IT TOO HARD, PLEASE.
slap
slap
slap
LEAF BLADE !!

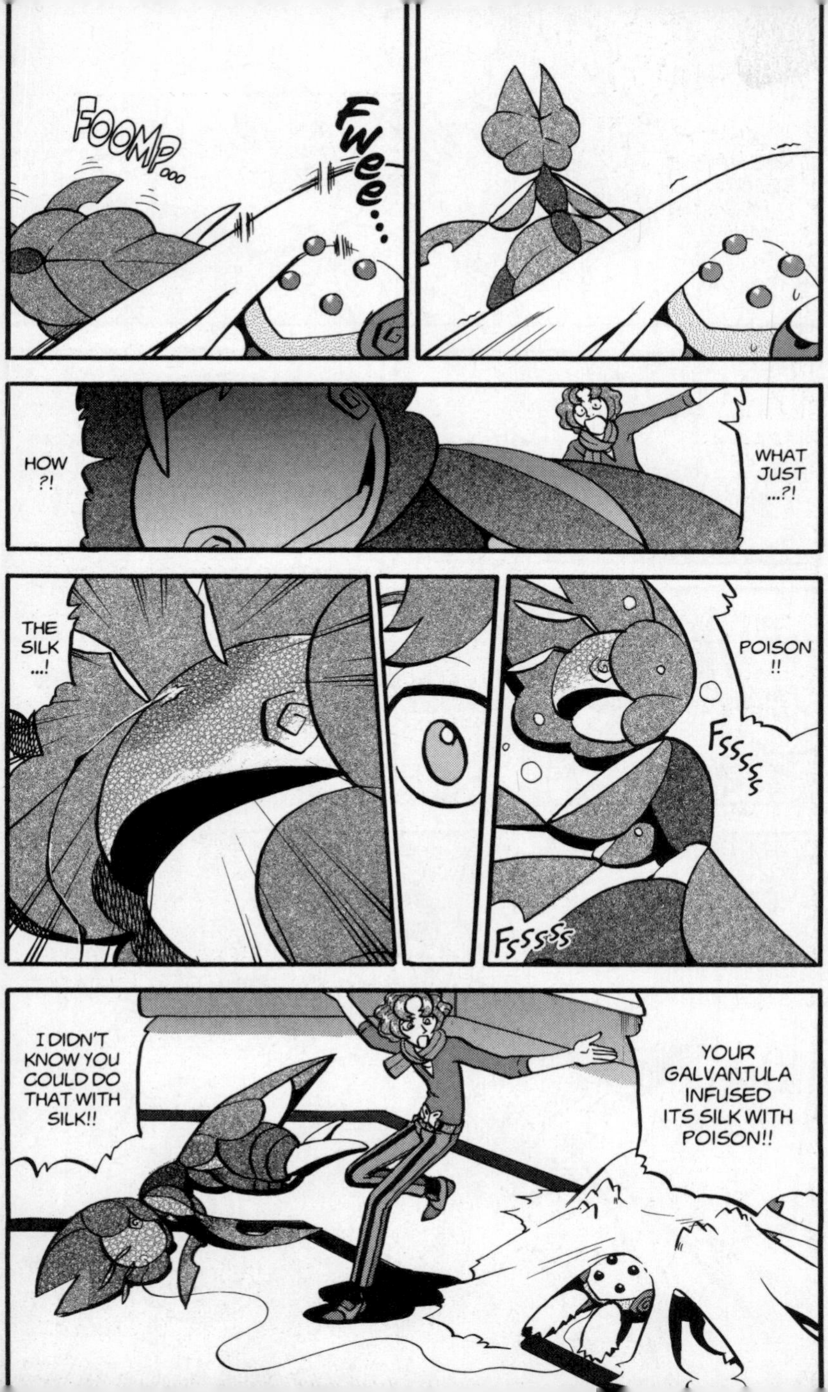
Fwee...
FOOMP...
WHAT JUST ...?!
HOW ?!
POISON !!
Fsssss
Fsssss
THE SILK ...!
YOUR GALVANTULA INFUSED ITS SILK WITH POISON!!
I DIDN'T KNOW YOU COULD DO THAT WITH SILK!!

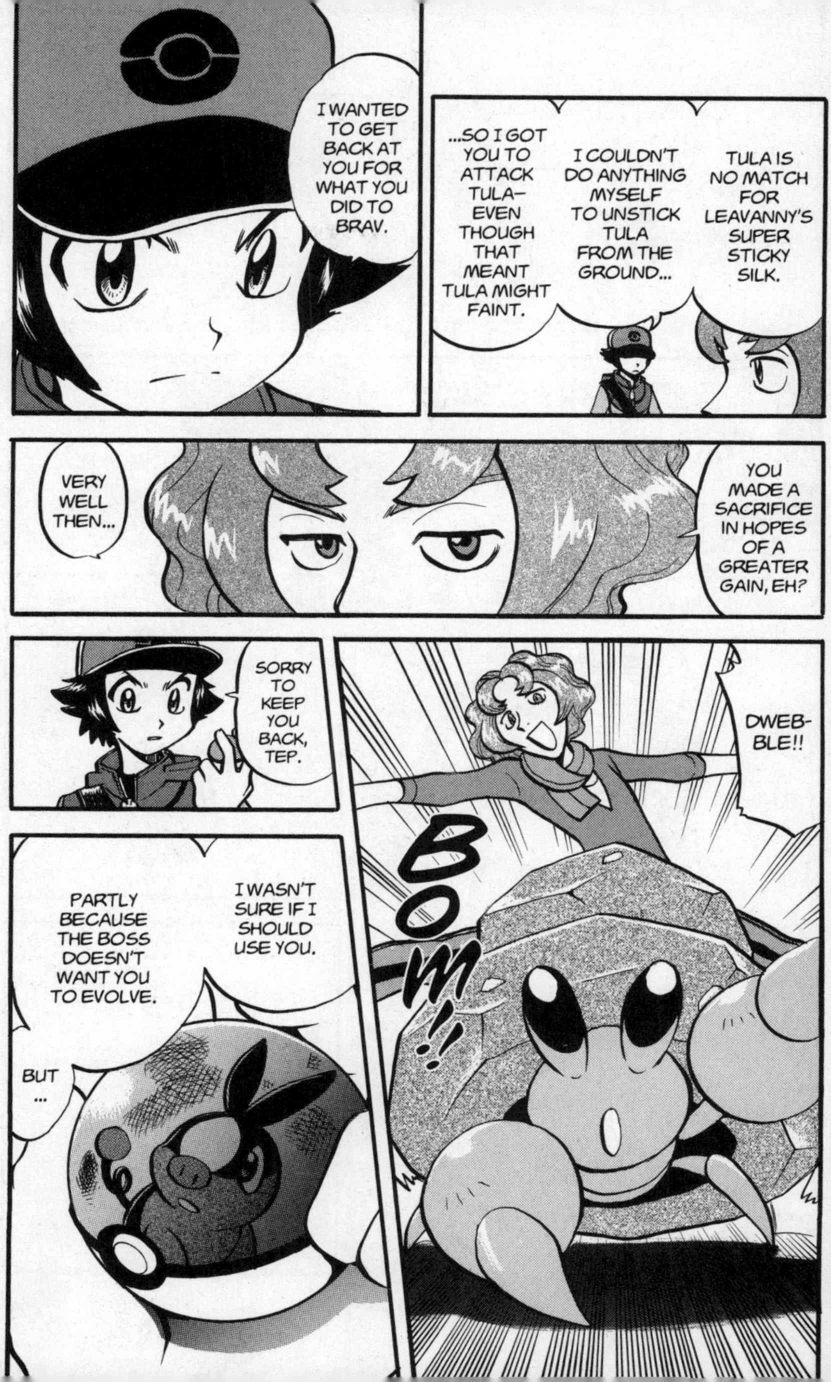
TULA IS NO MATCH FOR LEAVANNY'S SUPER STICKY SILK.
I COULDN'T DO ANYTHING MYSELF TO UNSTICK TULA FROM THE GROUND...
...SO I GOT YOU TO ATTACK TULA—EVEN THOUGH THAT MEANT TULA MIGHT FAINT.
I WANTED TO GET BACK AT YOU FOR WHAT YOU DID TO BRAV.
YOU MADE A SACRIFICE IN HOPES OF A GREATER GAIN, EH?
VERY WELL THEN...
DWEB-BLE!!
BOM!!
SORRY TO KEEP YOU BACK, TEP.
I WASN'T SURE IF I SHOULD USE YOU.
PARTLY BECAUSE THE BOSS DOESN'T WANT YOU TO EVOLVE.
BUT ...

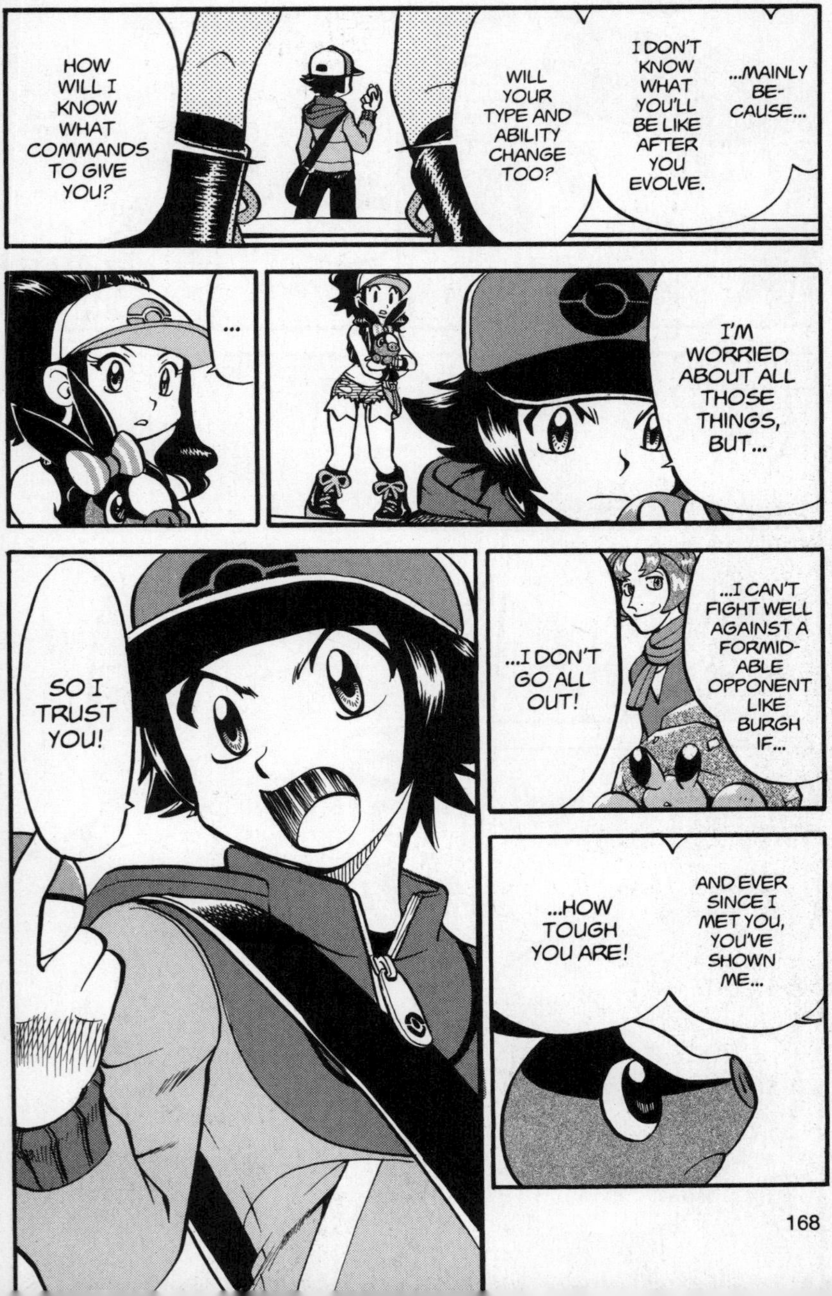
...MAINLY BE-CAUSE...
I DON'T KNOW WHAT YOU'LL BE LIKE AFTER YOU EVOLVE.
WILL YOUR TYPE AND ABILITY CHANGE TOO?
HOW WILL I KNOW WHAT COMMANDS TO GIVE YOU?
I'M WORRIED ABOUT ALL THOSE THINGS, BUT...
...
...I CAN'T FIGHT WELL AGAINST A FORMID-ABLE OPPONENT LIKE BURGH IF...
...I DON'T GO ALL OUT!
AND EVER SINCE I MET YOU, YOU'VE SHOWN ME...
...HOW TOUGH YOU ARE!
SO I TRUST YOU!

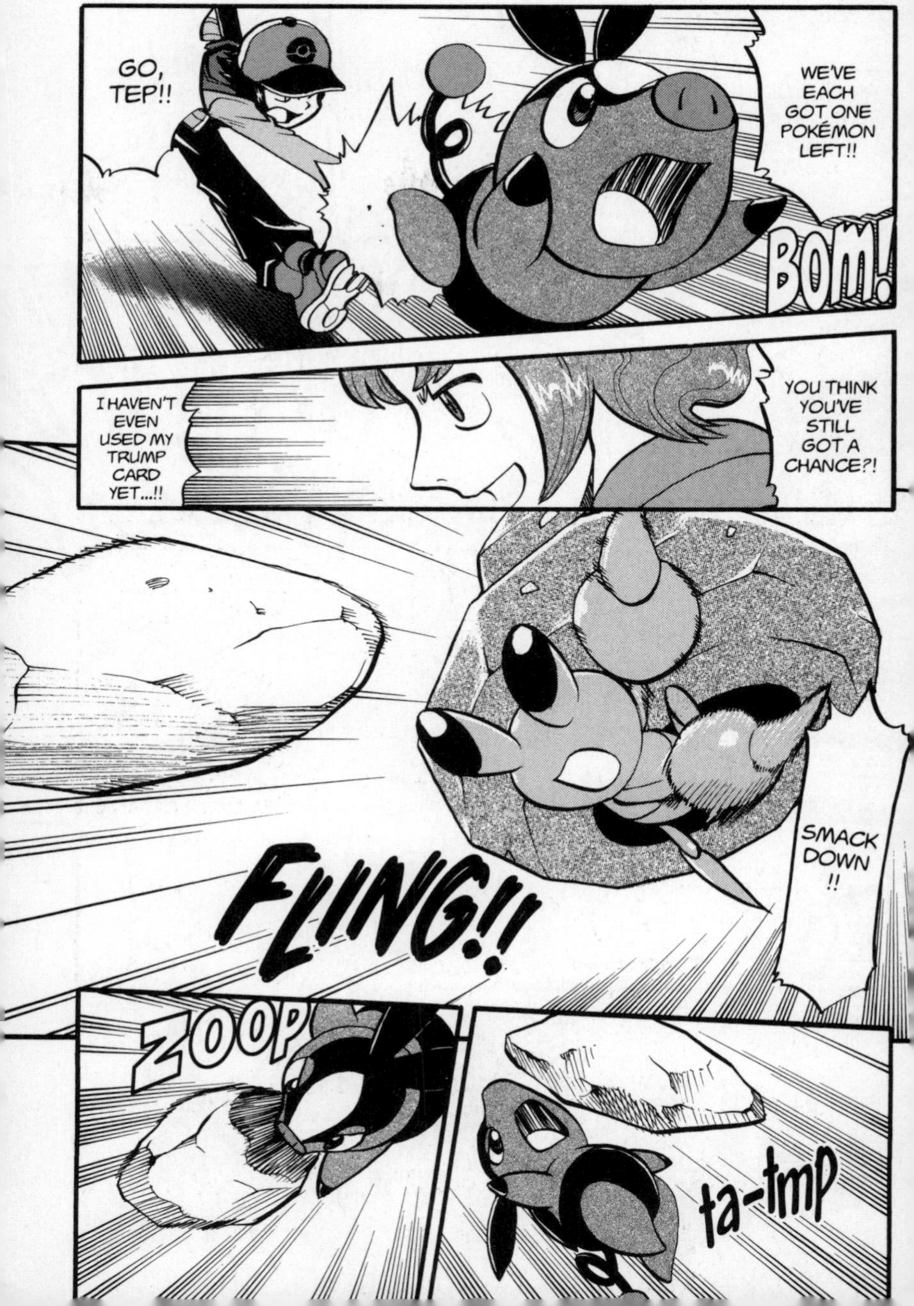
WE'VE EACH GOT ONE POKÉMON LEFT!!
GO, TEP!!
BOM!
YOU THINK YOU'VE STILL GOT A CHANCE?!
I HAVEN'T EVEN USED MY TRUMP CARD YET...!!
SMACK DOWN!!
FLING!!
ta-tmp
ZOOP

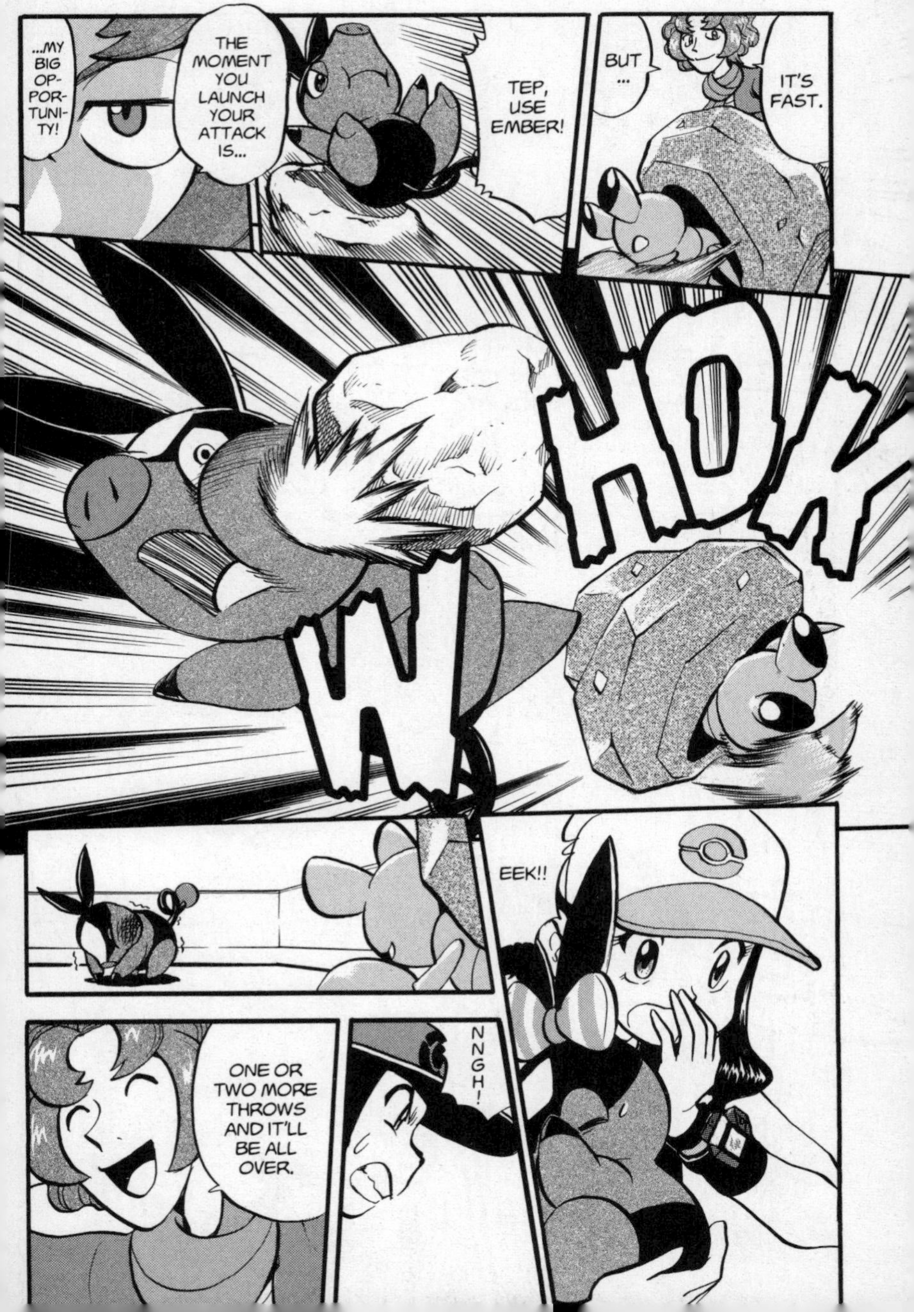
IT'S FAST.
BUT ...
TEP, USE EMBER!
THE MOMENT YOU LAUNCH YOUR ATTACK IS...
...MY BIG OPPORTUNITY!
WHOK
EEK!!
NNGH!
ONE OR TWO MORE THROWS AND IT'LL BE ALL OVER.

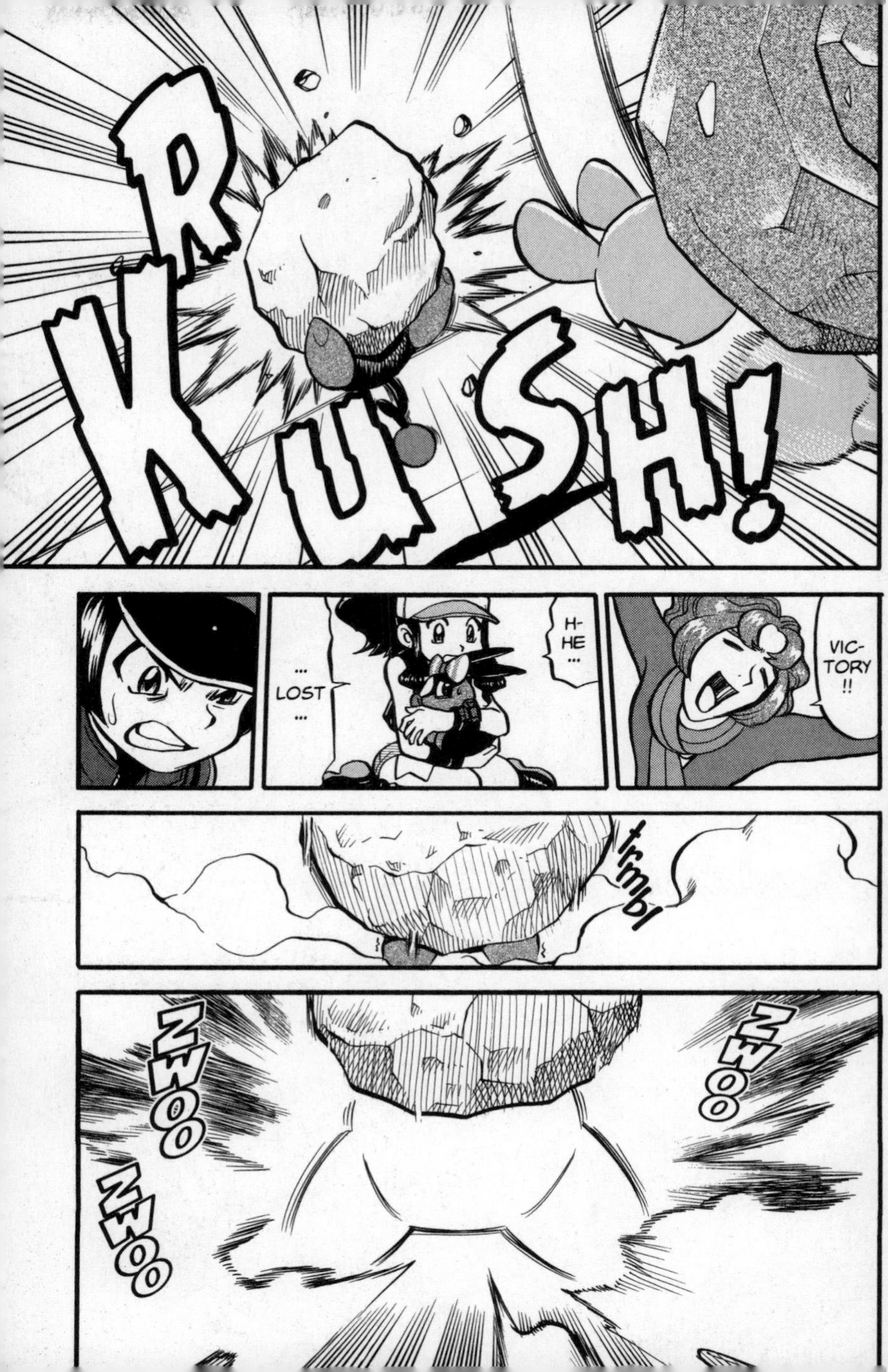
KRUSH!
VICTORY!!
H-HE...
...LOST...
trmbl
ZWOO
ZWOO
ZWOO

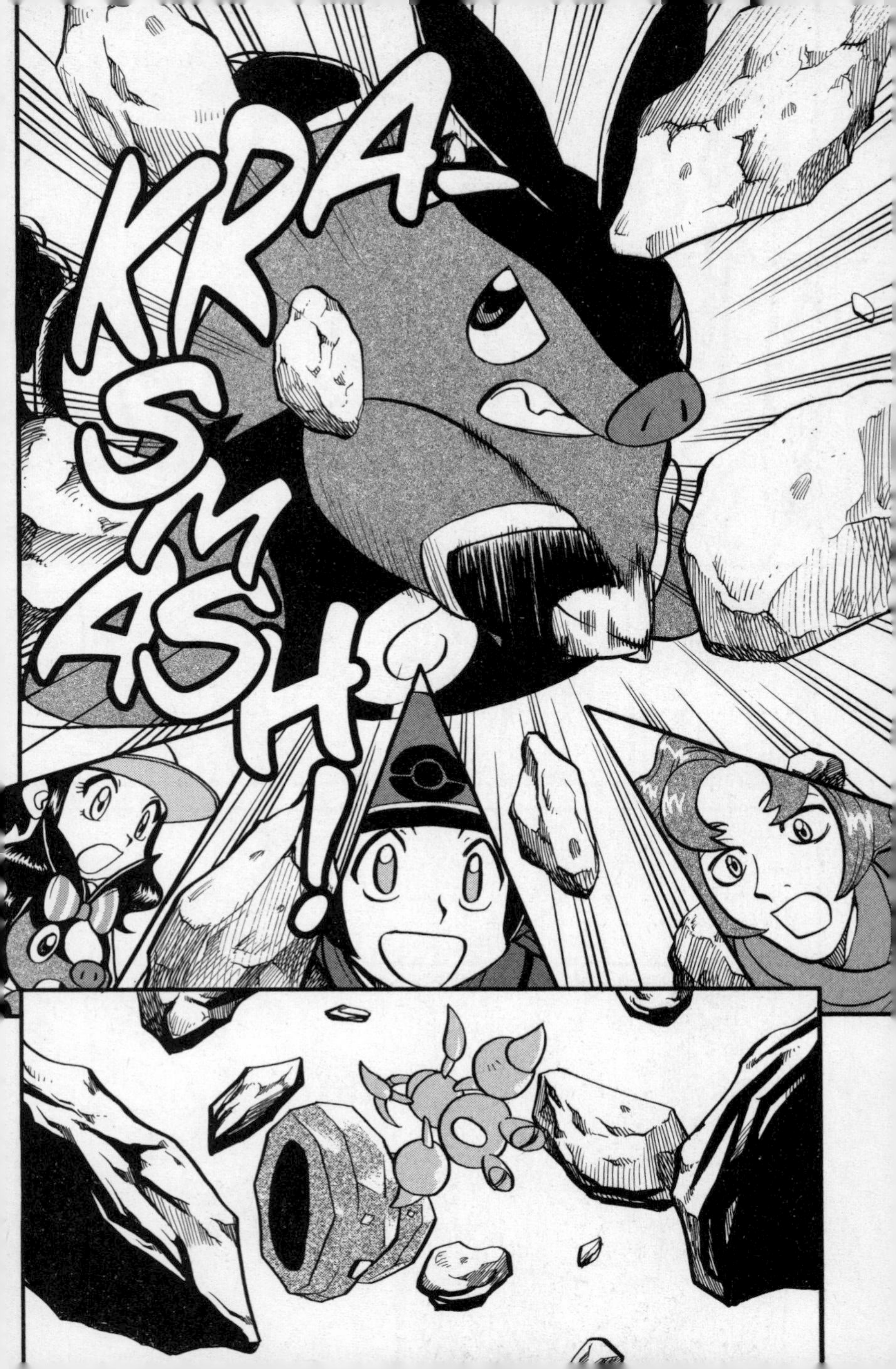
KRASMASH!

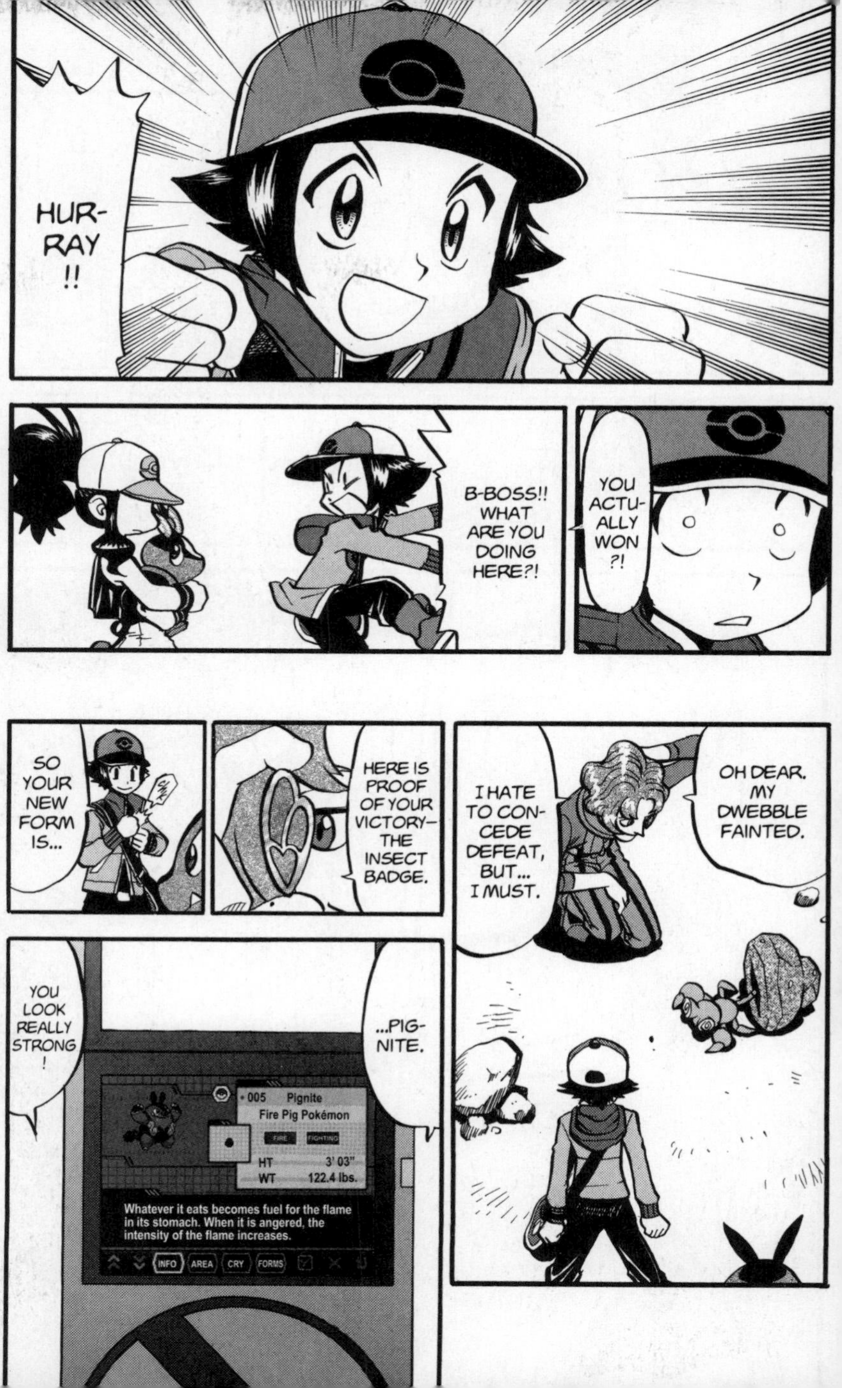
HUR-RAY!!
YOU ACTU-ALLY WON?!
B-BOSS!! WHAT ARE YOU DOING HERE?!
OH DEAR. MY DWEBBLE FAINTED.
I HATE TO CON-CEDE DEFEAT, BUT... I MUST.
HERE IS PROOF OF YOUR VICTORY—THE INSECT BADGE.
SO YOUR NEW FORM IS...
...PIG-NITE.
YOU LOOK REALLY STRONG!
005 Pignite
Fire Pig Pokémon
FIRE
FIGHTING
HT 3' 03"
WT 122.4 lbs.
Whatever it eats becomes fuel for the flame in its stomach. When it is angered, the intensity of the flame increases.
INFO
AREA
CRY
FORMS

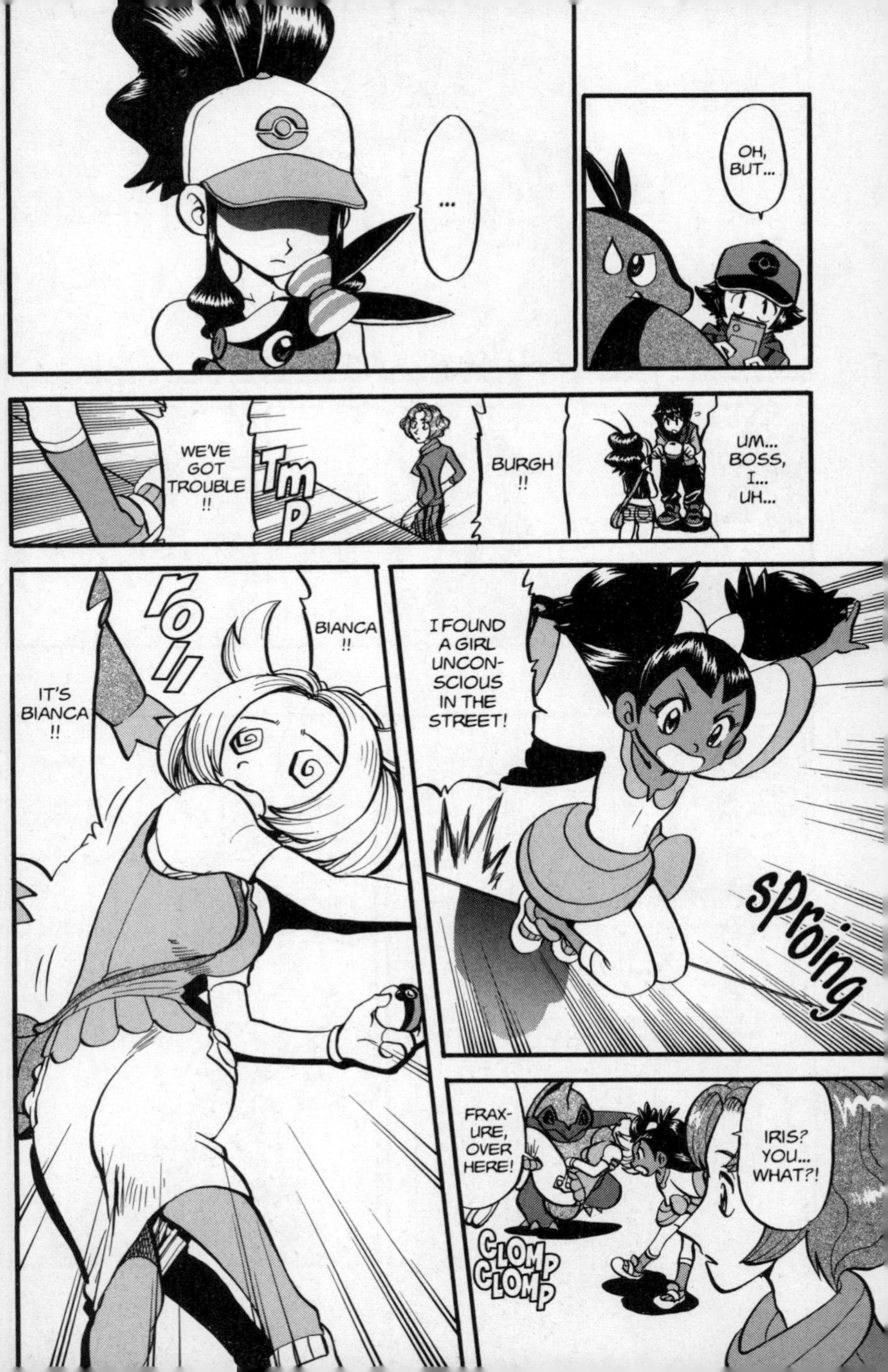
OH, BUT...
...
UM... BOSS, I... UH...
BURGH !!
Tmp
WE'VE GOT TROUBLE !!
I FOUND A GIRL UNCONSCIOUS IN THE STREET!
sproing
IRIS? YOU... WHAT?!
FRAXURE, OVER HERE!
CLOMP CLOMP
BIANCA !!
roll
IT'S BIANCA !!

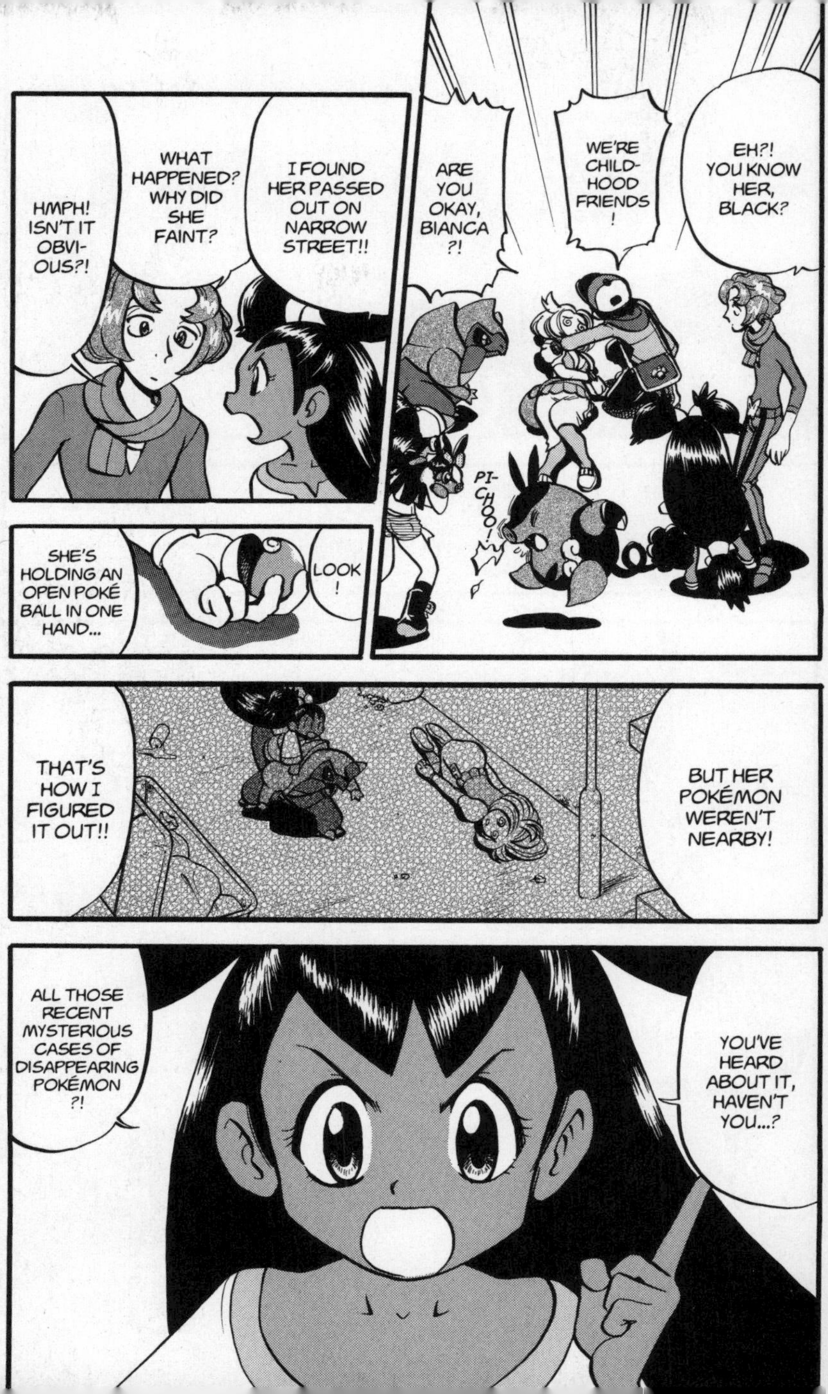
EH?! YOU KNOW HER, BLACK?
WE'RE CHILD-HOOD FRIENDS!
ARE YOU OKAY, BIANCA?!
PI-CHOO!
I FOUND HER PASSED OUT ON NARROW STREET!!
WHAT HAPPENED? WHY DID SHE FAINT?
HMPH! ISN'T IT OBVI-OUS?!
LOOK!
SHE'S HOLDING AN OPEN POKÉ BALL IN ONE HAND...
BUT HER POKÉMON WEREN'T NEARBY!
THAT'S HOW I FIGURED IT OUT!!
YOU'VE HEARD ABOUT IT, HAVEN'T YOU...?
ALL THOSE RECENT MYSTERIOUS CASES OF DISAPPEARING POKÉMON?!

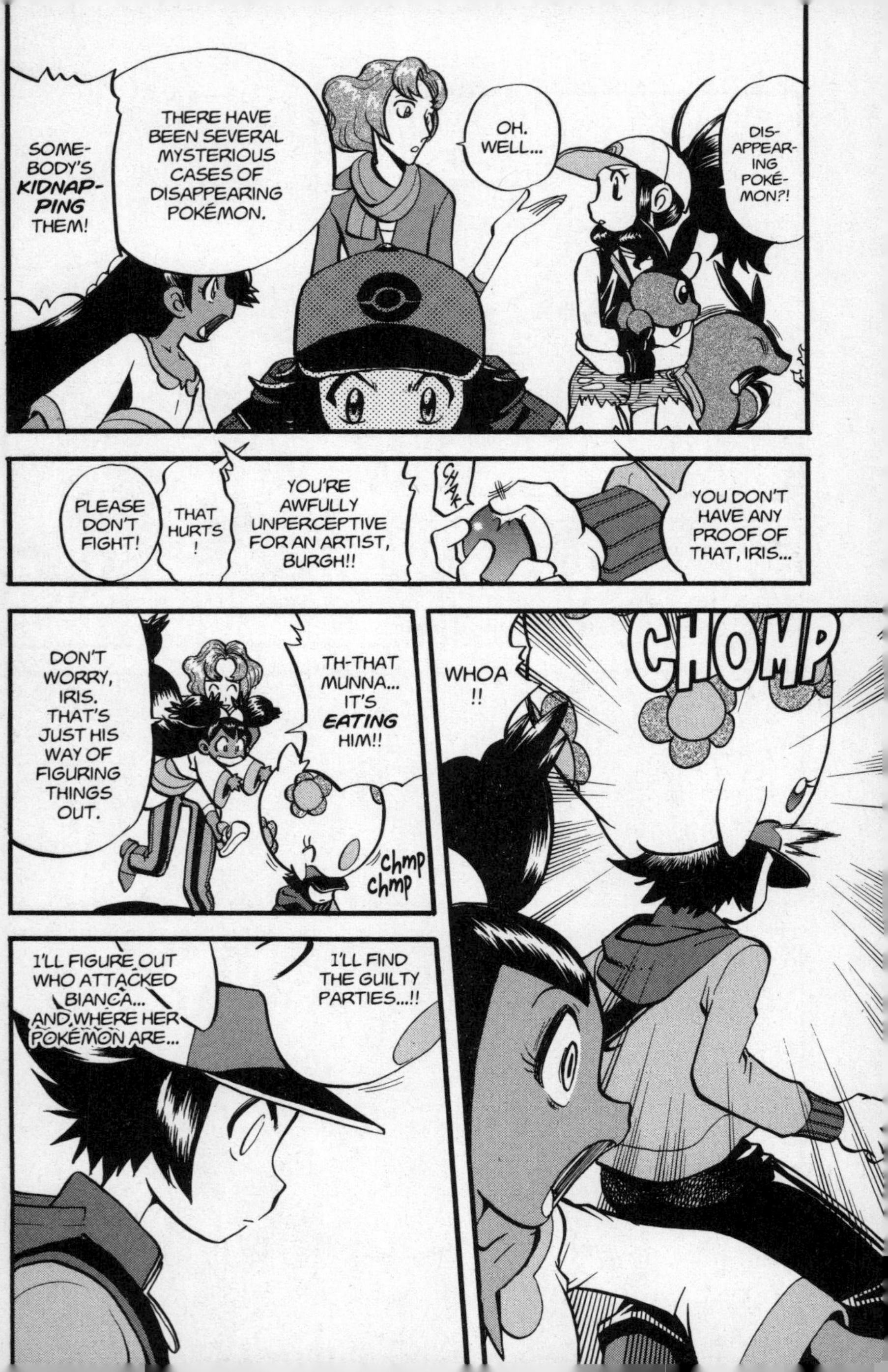
DIS-APPEARING POKÉMON?!
OH. WELL...
THERE HAVE BEEN SEVERAL MYSTERIOUS CASES OF DISAPPEARING POKÉMON.
SOMEBODY'S KIDNAPPING THEM!
YOU DON'T HAVE ANY PROOF OF THAT, IRIS...
CHAK
YOU'RE AWFULLY UNPERCEPTIVE FOR AN ARTIST, BURGH!!
THAT HURTS!
PLEASE DON'T FIGHT!
CHOMP
WHOA!!
TH-THAT MUNNA... IT'S EATING HIM!!
DON'T WORRY, IRIS. THAT'S JUST HIS WAY OF FIGURING THINGS OUT.
Chmp Chmp
I'LL FIND THE GUILTY PARTIES...!!
I'LL FIGURE OUT WHO ATTACKED BIANCA... AND WHERE HER POKÉMON ARE...

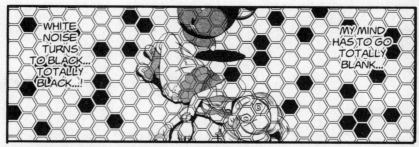

MY MIND HAS TO GO TOTALLY BLANK...
WHITE NOISE TURNS TO BLACK... TOTALLY BLACK...!
BURGH, THIS GYM SMELLS REALLY STRONGLY OF HONEY, RIGHT?
CORRECT! YOU DETECT THE SCENT OF MY ART INSTALLA-TION!
UN-CHOMP!
BUT...
OUR NOSES CAN'T DISTINGUISH ANY LESS OBVIOUS SCENTS BECAUSE THE HONEY SMELL OVERWHELMS THEM...
...PIGNITE HAS A BETTER SENSE OF SMELL.
PII...
PII...

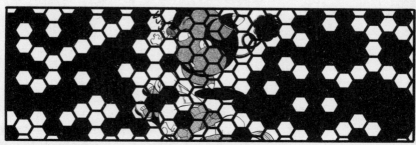

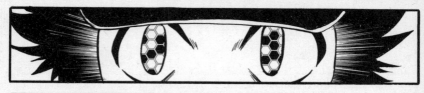

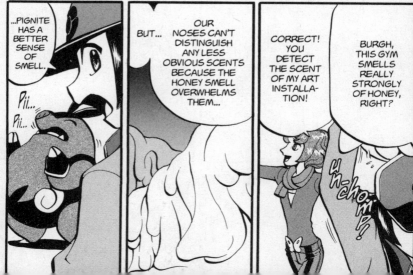

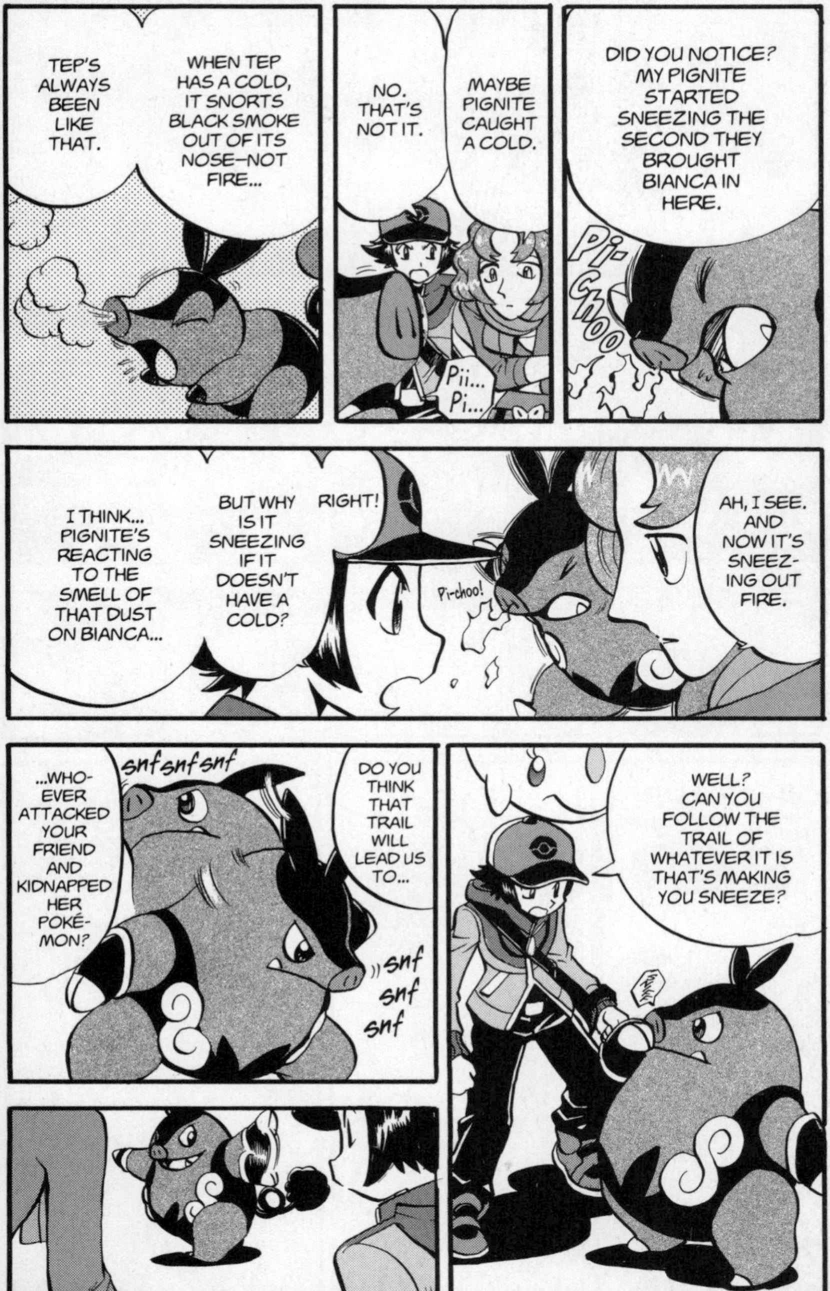
DID YOU NOTICE? MY PIGNITE STARTED SNEEZING THE SECOND THEY BROUGHT BIANCA IN HERE.
Pi-choo
MAYBE PIGNITE CAUGHT A COLD.
NO. THAT'S NOT IT.
Pii... Pi...
WHEN TEP HAS A COLD, IT SNORTS BLACK SMOKE OUT OF ITS NOSE—NOT FIRE...
TEP'S ALWAYS BEEN LIKE THAT.
AH, I SEE. AND NOW IT'S SNEEZ-ING OUT FIRE.
Pi-choo!
RIGHT!
BUT WHY IS IT SNEEZING IF IT DOESN'T HAVE A COLD?
I THINK... PIGNITE'S REACTING TO THE SMELL OF THAT DUST ON BIANCA...
WELL? CAN YOU FOLLOW THE TRAIL OF WHATEVER IT IS THAT'S MAKING YOU SNEEZE?
DO YOU THINK THAT TRAIL WILL LEAD US TO...
...WHO-EVER ATTACKED YOUR FRIEND AND KIDNAPPED HER POKÉ-MON?
snf snf snf
snf snf snf

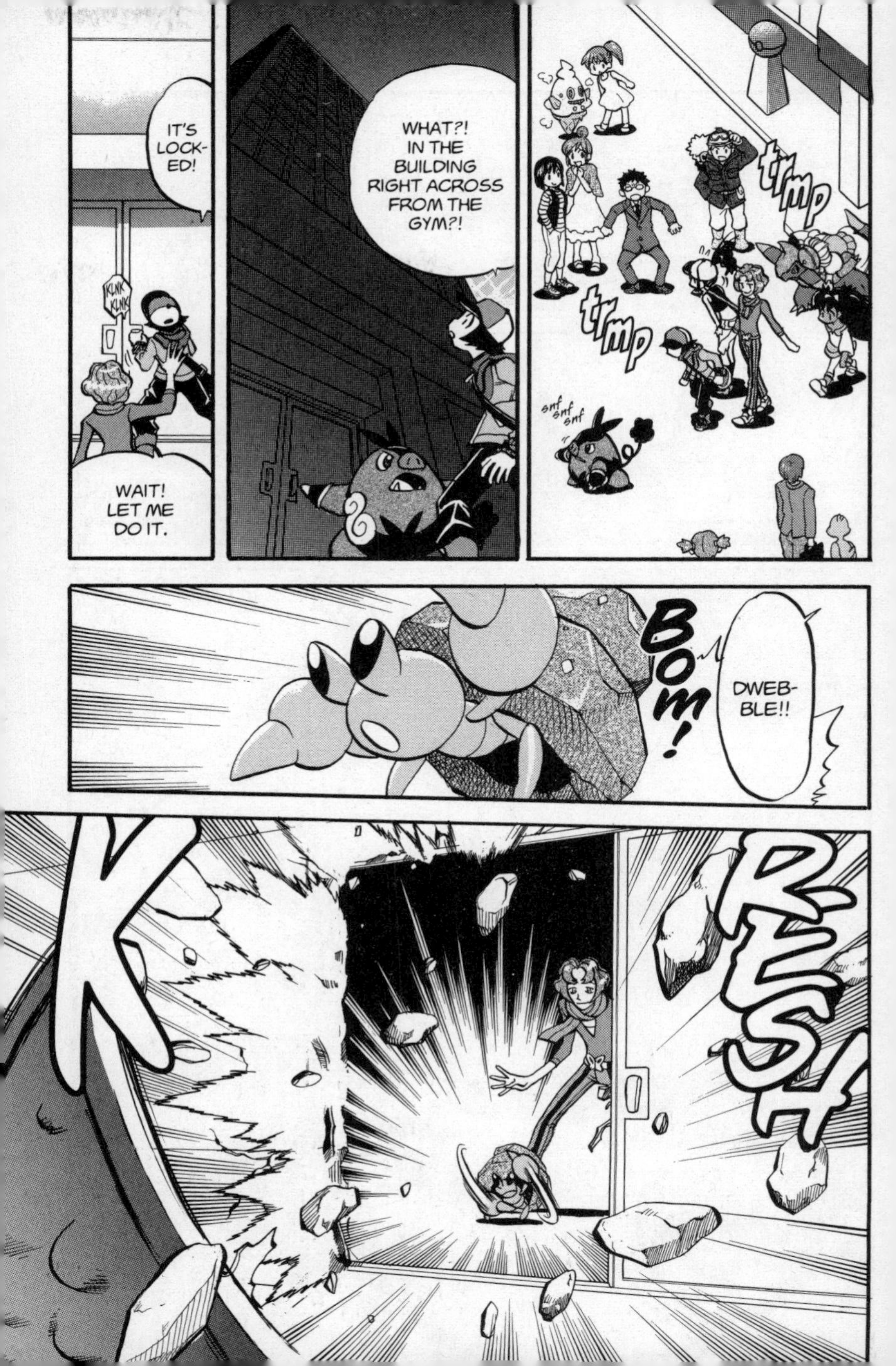
trmp
trmp
snf snf snf
WHAT?! IN THE BUILDING RIGHT ACROSS FROM THE GYM?!
IT'S LOCK-ED!
KLNK KLNK
WAIT! LET ME DO IT.
DWEB-BLE!!
BOM!
KRSH

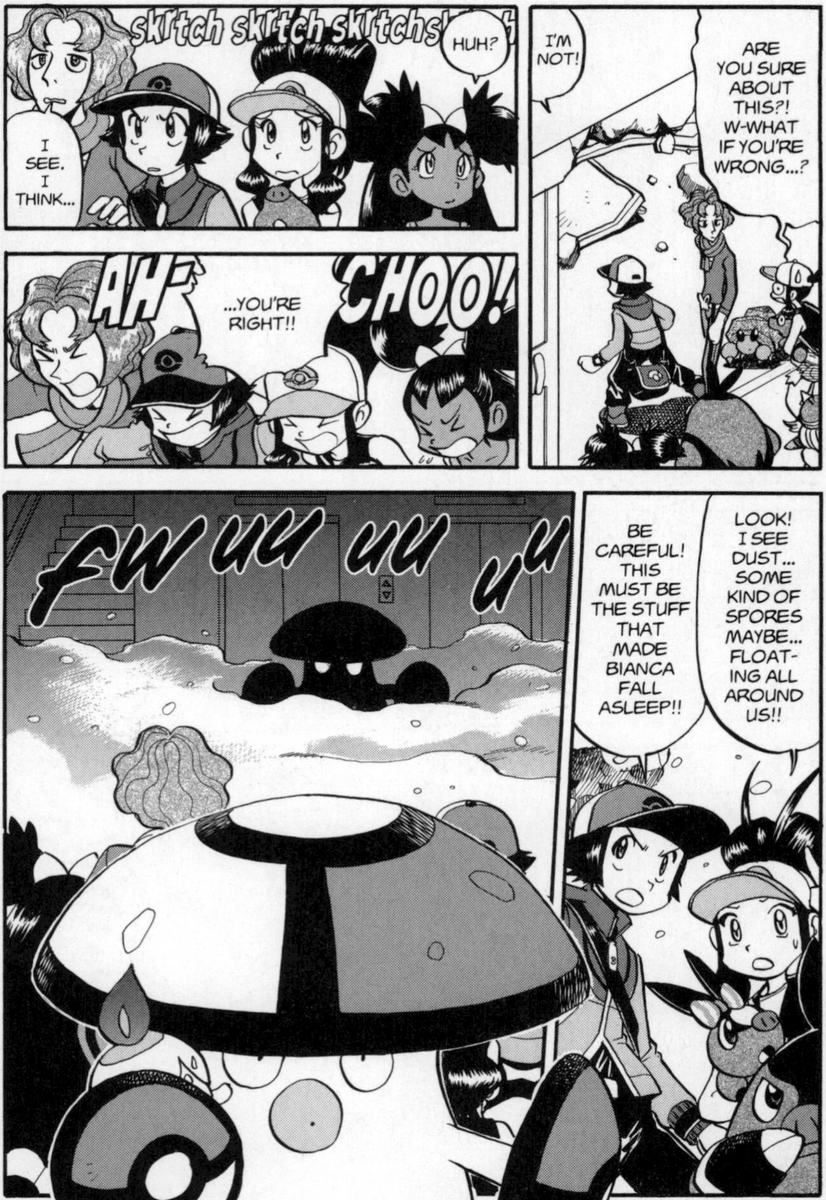
ARE YOU SURE ABOUT THIS?! W-WHAT IF YOU'RE WRONG...?
I'M NOT!
skrtch skrtch skrtch
HUH?
I SEE. I THINK...
AH-CHOO!
...YOU'RE RIGHT!!
LOOK! I SEE DUST... SOME KIND OF SPORES MAYBE... FLOATING ALL AROUND US!!
BE CAREFUL! THIS MUST BE THE STUFF THAT MADE BIANCA FALL ASLEEP!!
fwuuuuuuu

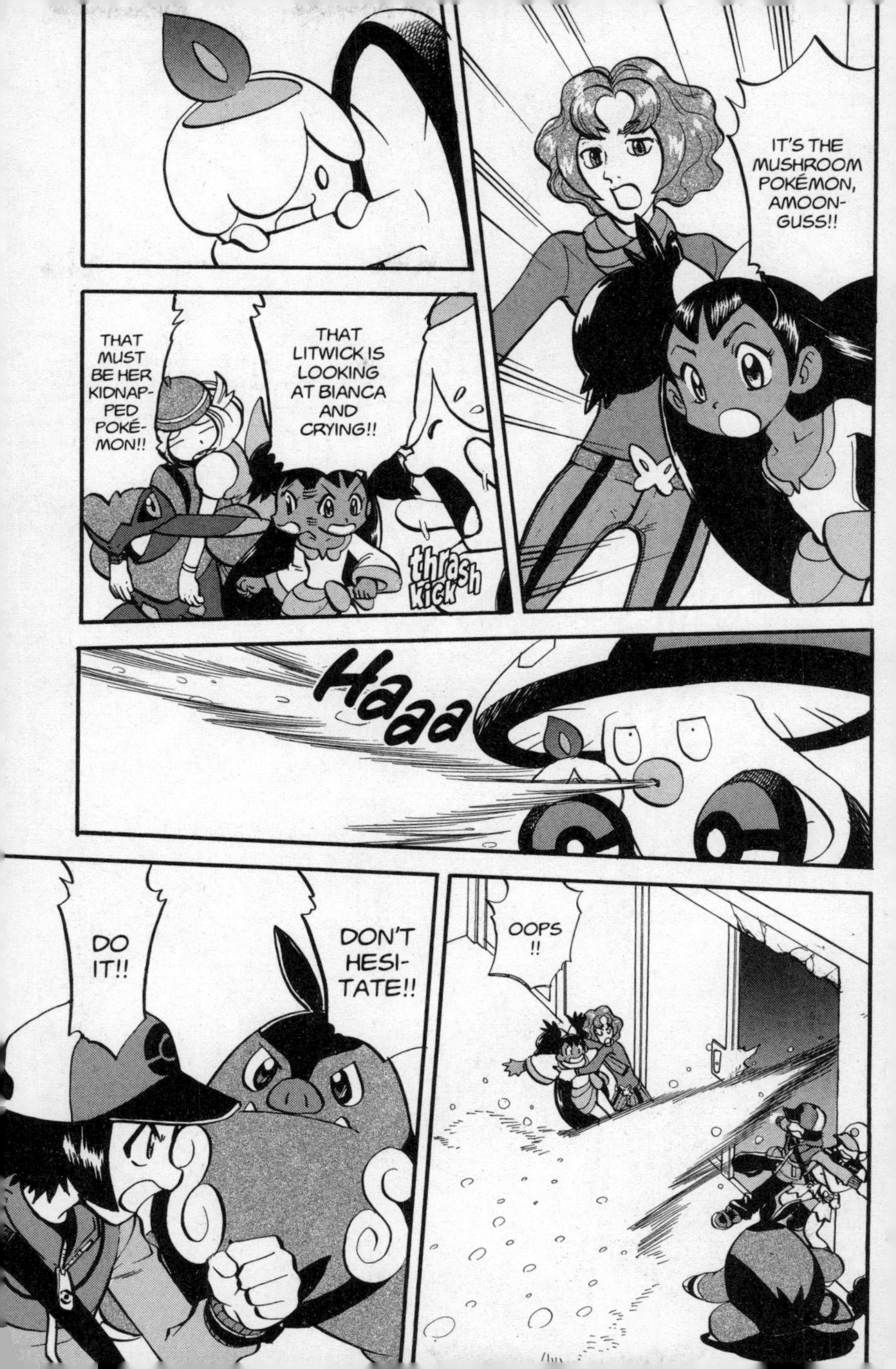
IT'S THE MUSHROOM POKÉMON, AMOONGUSS!!
THAT LITWICK IS LOOKING AT BIANCA AND CRYING!!
THAT MUST BE HER KIDNAPPED POKÉMON!!
thrash kick
Haaa
OOPS !!
DON'T HESITATE!!
DO IT!!

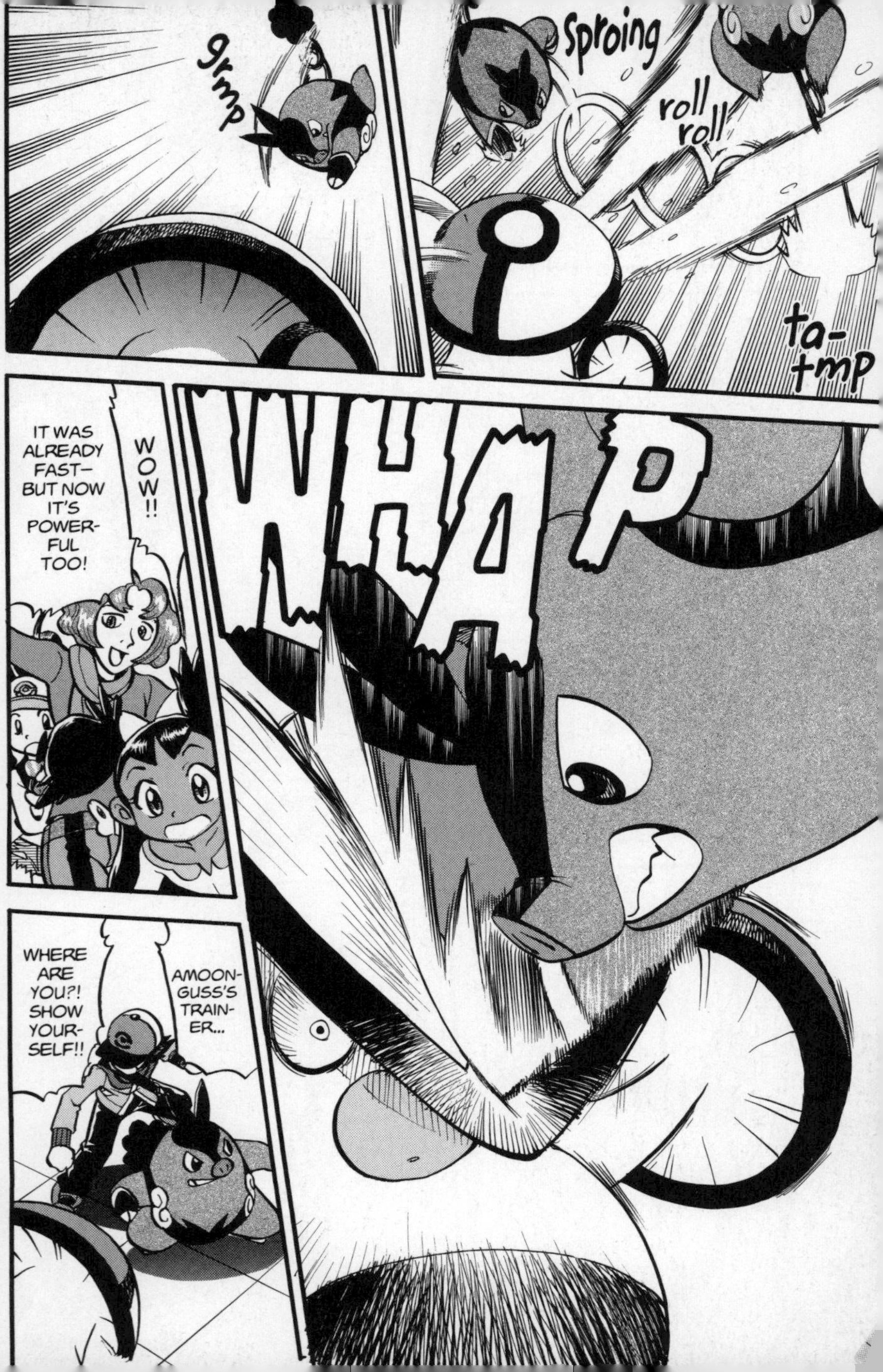
Sproing
roll roll
ta-tmp
grmp
WHAP
WOW!!
IT WAS ALREADY FAST—BUT NOW IT'S POWERFUL TOO!
AMOONGUSS'S TRAINER...
WHERE ARE YOU?! SHOW YOURSELF!!

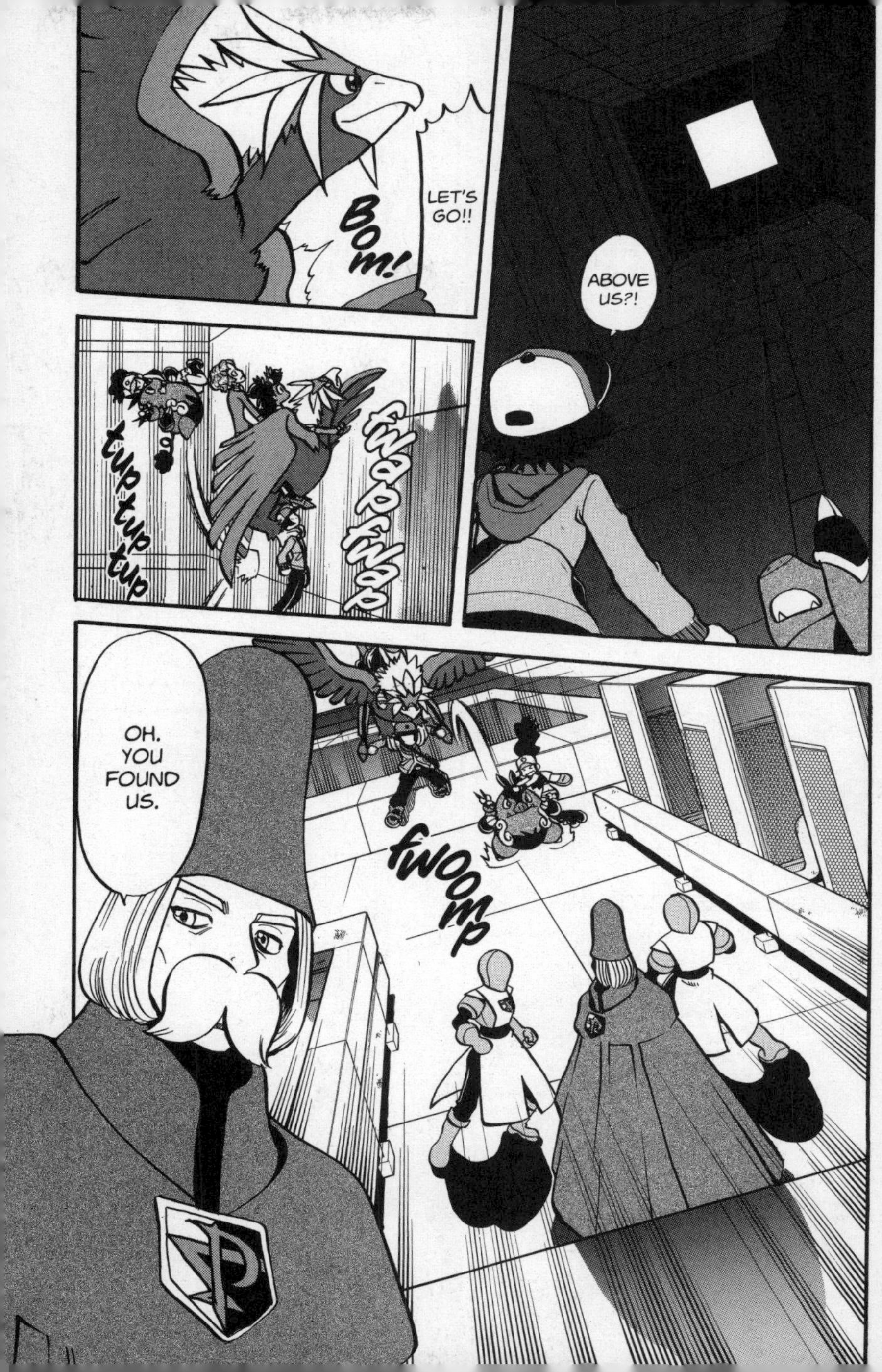
ABOVE US?!
LET'S GO!!
BOOM!
FWAP FWAP
TUP TUP TUP
OH. YOU FOUND US.
FWOOMP

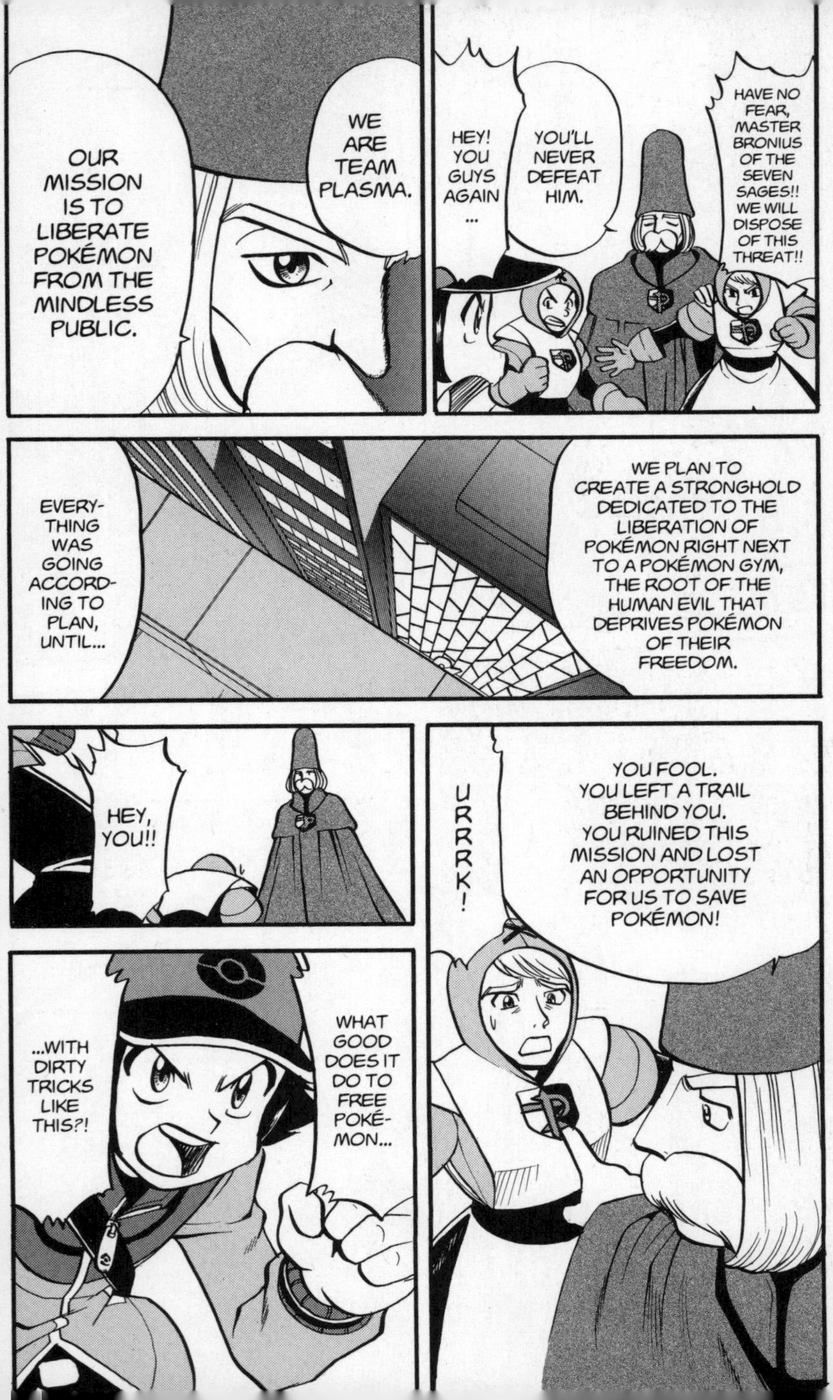
HAVE NO FEAR, MASTER BRONIUS OF THE SEVEN SAGES!! WE WILL DISPOSE OF THIS THREAT!!
YOU'LL NEVER DEFEAT HIM.
HEY! YOU GUYS AGAIN ...
WE ARE TEAM PLASMA.
OUR MISSION IS TO LIBERATE POKÉMON FROM THE MINDLESS PUBLIC.
WE PLAN TO CREATE A STRONGHOLD DEDICATED TO THE LIBERATION OF POKÉMON RIGHT NEXT TO A POKÉMON GYM, THE ROOT OF THE HUMAN EVIL THAT DEPRIVES POKÉMON OF THEIR FREEDOM.
EVERY-THING WAS GOING ACCORD-ING TO PLAN, UNTIL...
YOU FOOL. YOU LEFT A TRAIL BEHIND YOU. YOU RUINED THIS MISSION AND LOST AN OPPORTUNITY FOR US TO SAVE POKÉMON!
URRRK!
HEY, YOU!!
WHAT GOOD DOES IT DO TO FREE POKÉ-MON...
...WITH DIRTY TRICKS LIKE THIS?!

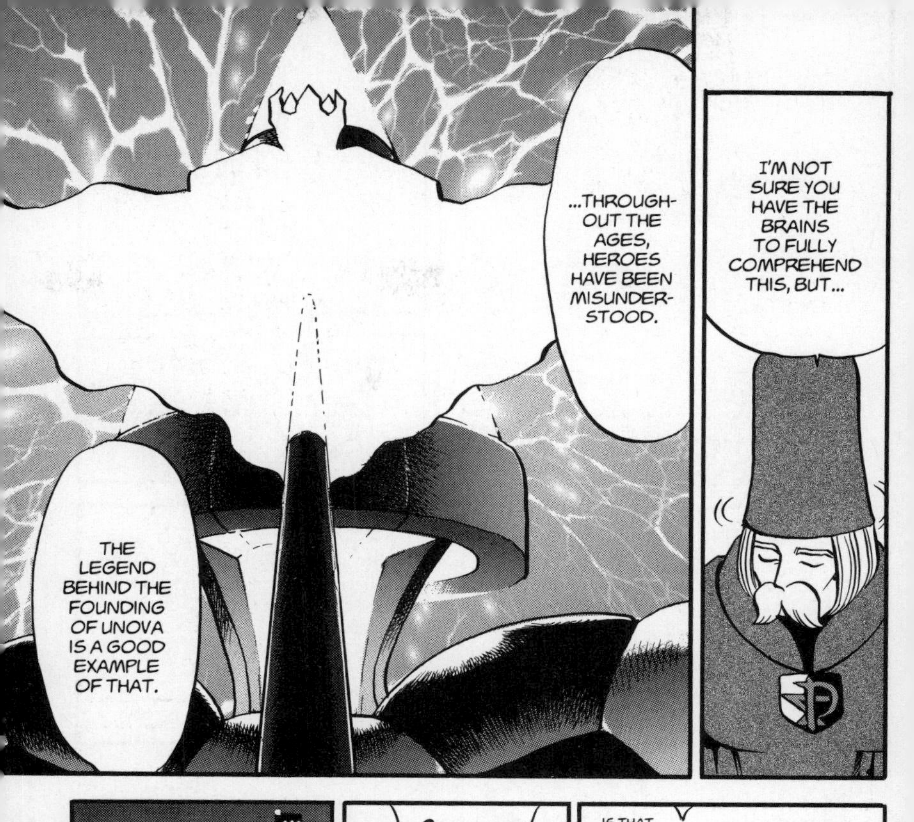

I'M NOT SURE YOU HAVE THE BRAINS TO FULLY COMPREHEND THIS, BUT...
...THROUGH-OUT THE AGES, HEROES HAVE BEEN MISUNDER-STOOD.
THE LEGEND BEHIND THE FOUNDING OF UNOVA IS A GOOD EXAMPLE OF THAT.
WE SHALL BRING BACK THE ***HERO*** AND THE ***BLACK LIGHTNING BOLT*** TO UNITE THE MINDS OF THE PEOPLE OF UNOVA AS ONE.
IS THAT SOME-THING YOUR FEEBLE MIND CAN GRASP?!
AND NOW ...
foooo
...FARE-WELL.
AFTER THE DEPARTURE OF TEAM PLASMA, ALL THE MISSING POKÉMON WERE FOUND IN THEIR STRONGHOLD...
...AND RETURNED TO THEIR TRAINERS—THANKS TO THE EFFORTS OF BLACK AND THE OTHERS.

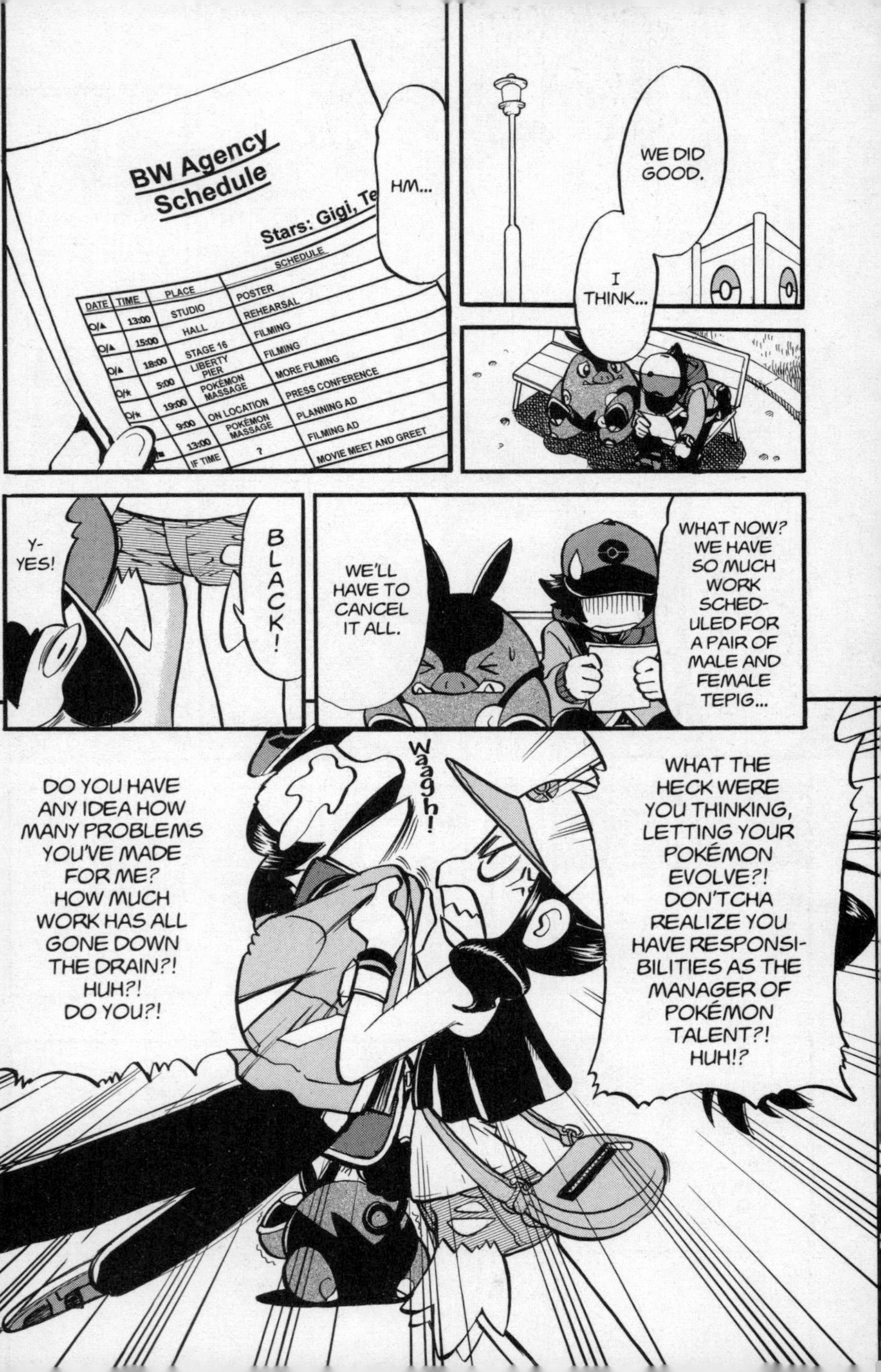
WE DID GOOD.
I THINK...
HM...
BW Agency Schedule
Stars: Gigi, Te
SCHEDULE
DATE TIME PLACE POSTER
O/▲ 13:00 STUDIO REHEARSAL
O/▲ 15:00 HALL FILMING
O/▲ 18:00 STAGE 16 FILMING
O/★ 5:00 LIBERTY PIER MORE FILMING
O/★ 19:00 POKÉMON MASSAGE PRESS CONFERENCE
9:00 ON LOCATION PLANNING AD
13:00 POKÉMON MASSAGE FILMING AD
IF TIME ? MOVIE MEET AND GREET
WHAT NOW? WE HAVE SO MUCH WORK SCHED-ULED FOR A PAIR OF MALE AND FEMALE TEPIG...
WE'LL HAVE TO CANCEL IT ALL.
BLACK!
Y-YES!
WHAT THE HECK WERE YOU THINKING, LETTING YOUR POKÉMON EVOLVE?! DON'TCHA REALIZE YOU HAVE RESPONSI-BILITIES AS THE MANAGER OF POKÉMON TALENT?! HUH!?
Waagh!
DO YOU HAVE ANY IDEA HOW MANY PROBLEMS YOU'VE MADE FOR ME? HOW MUCH WORK HAS ALL GONE DOWN THE DRAIN?! HUH?! DO YOU?!

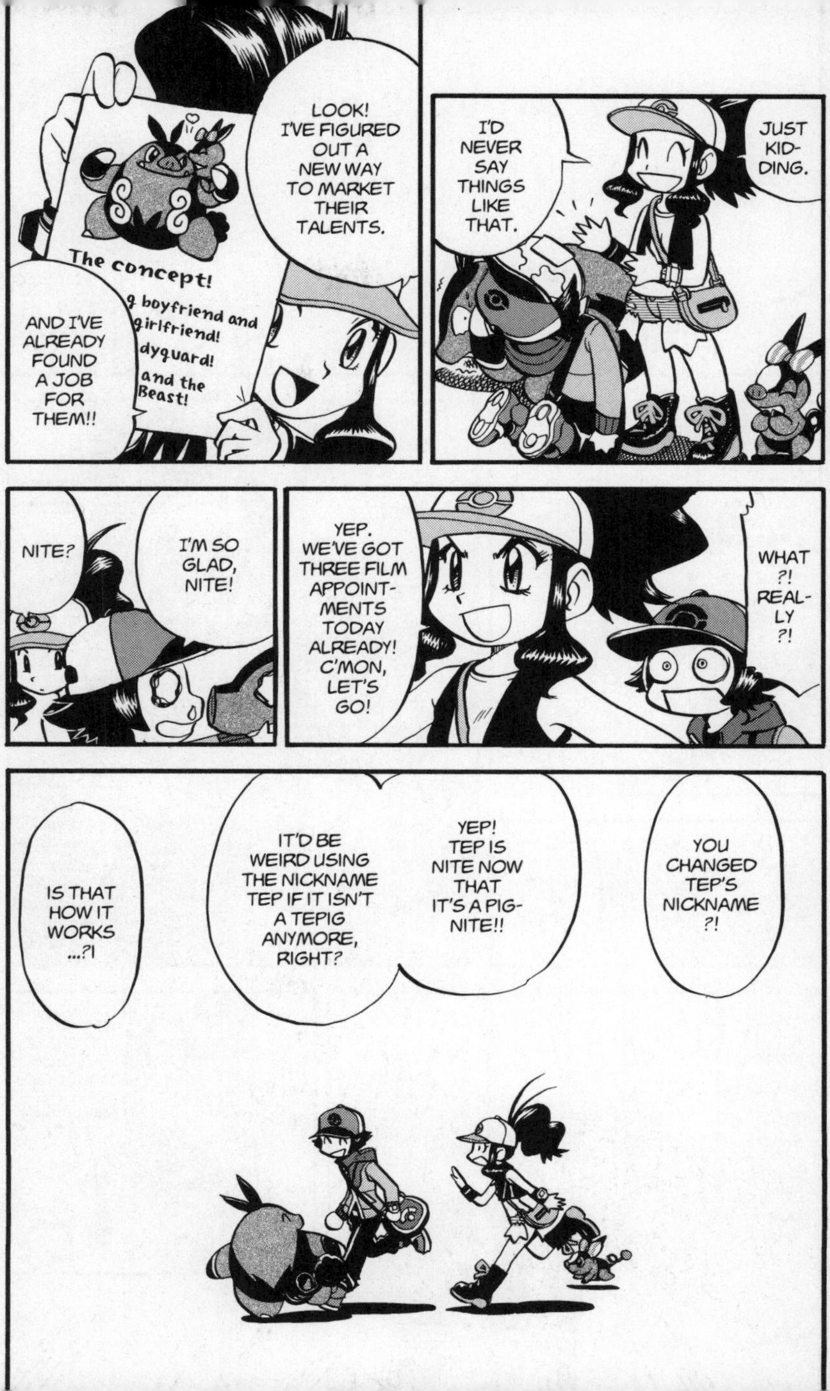
JUST KID-DING.
I'D NEVER SAY THINGS LIKE THAT.
LOOK! I'VE FIGURED OUT A NEW WAY TO MARKET THEIR TALENTS.
The concept!
a boyfriend and girlfriend!
dyguard!
and the Beast!
AND I'VE ALREADY FOUND A JOB FOR THEM!!
WHAT?! REAL-LY?!
YEP. WE'VE GOT THREE FILM APPOINT-MENTS TODAY ALREADY! C'MON, LET'S GO!
I'M SO GLAD, NITE!
NITE?
YOU CHANGED TEP'S NICKNAME?!
YEP! TEP IS NITE NOW THAT IT'S A PIG-NITE!!
IT'D BE WEIRD USING THE NICKNAME TEP IF IT ISN'T A TEPIG ANYMORE, RIGHT?
IS THAT HOW IT WORKS...?!

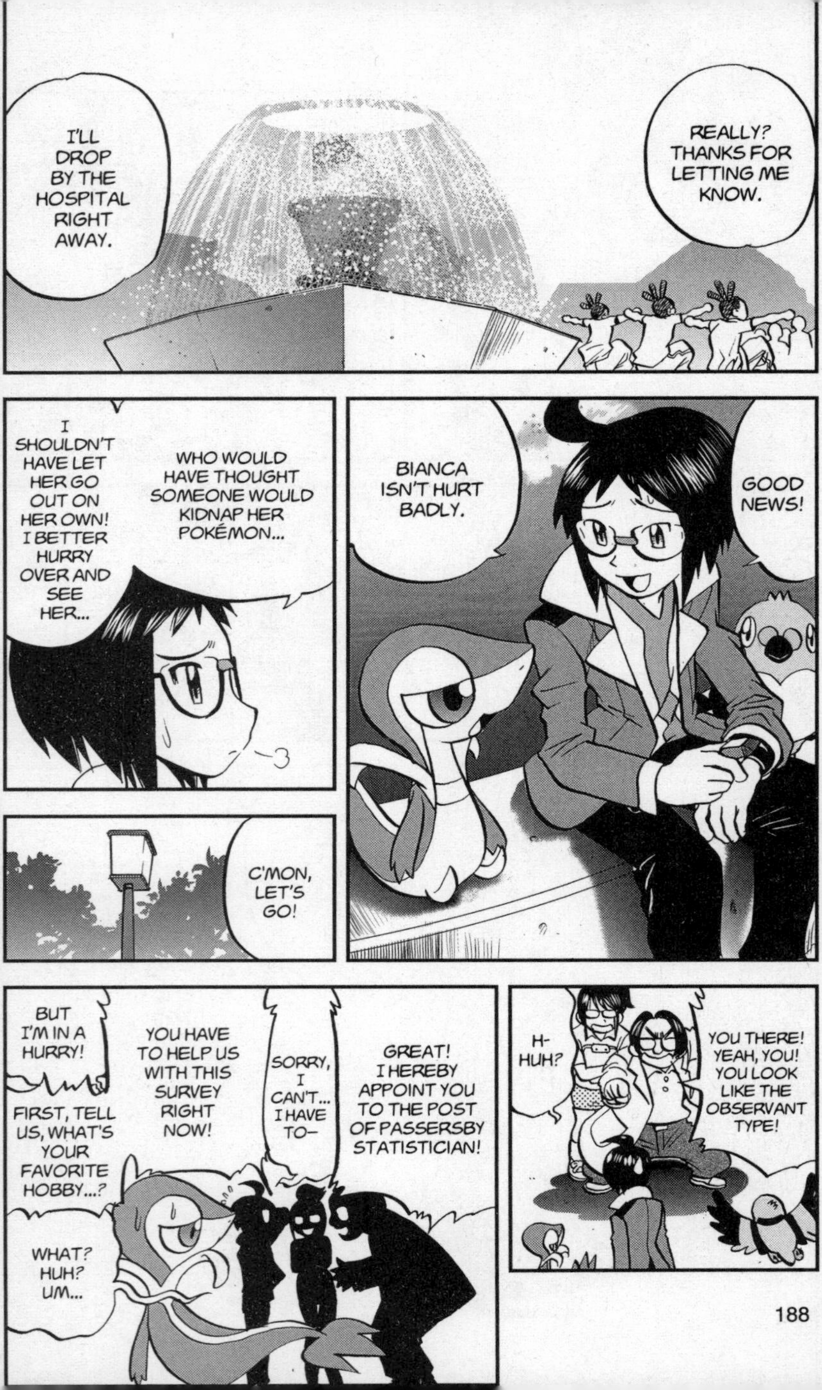
REALLY? THANKS FOR LETTING ME KNOW.
I'LL DROP BY THE HOSPITAL RIGHT AWAY.
GOOD NEWS!
BIANCA ISN'T HURT BADLY.
WHO WOULD HAVE THOUGHT SOMEONE WOULD KIDNAP HER POKÉMON...
I SHOULDN'T HAVE LET HER GO OUT ON HER OWN! I BETTER HURRY OVER AND SEE HER...
C'MON, LET'S GO!
YOU THERE! YEAH, YOU! YOU LOOK LIKE THE OBSERVANT TYPE!
H-HUH?
GREAT! I HEREBY APPOINT YOU TO THE POST OF PASSERSBY STATISTICIAN!
SORRY, I CAN'T... I HAVE TO—
YOU HAVE TO HELP US WITH THIS SURVEY RIGHT NOW!
BUT I'M IN A HURRY!
FIRST, TELL US, WHAT'S YOUR FAVORITE HOBBY...?
WHAT? HUH? UM...

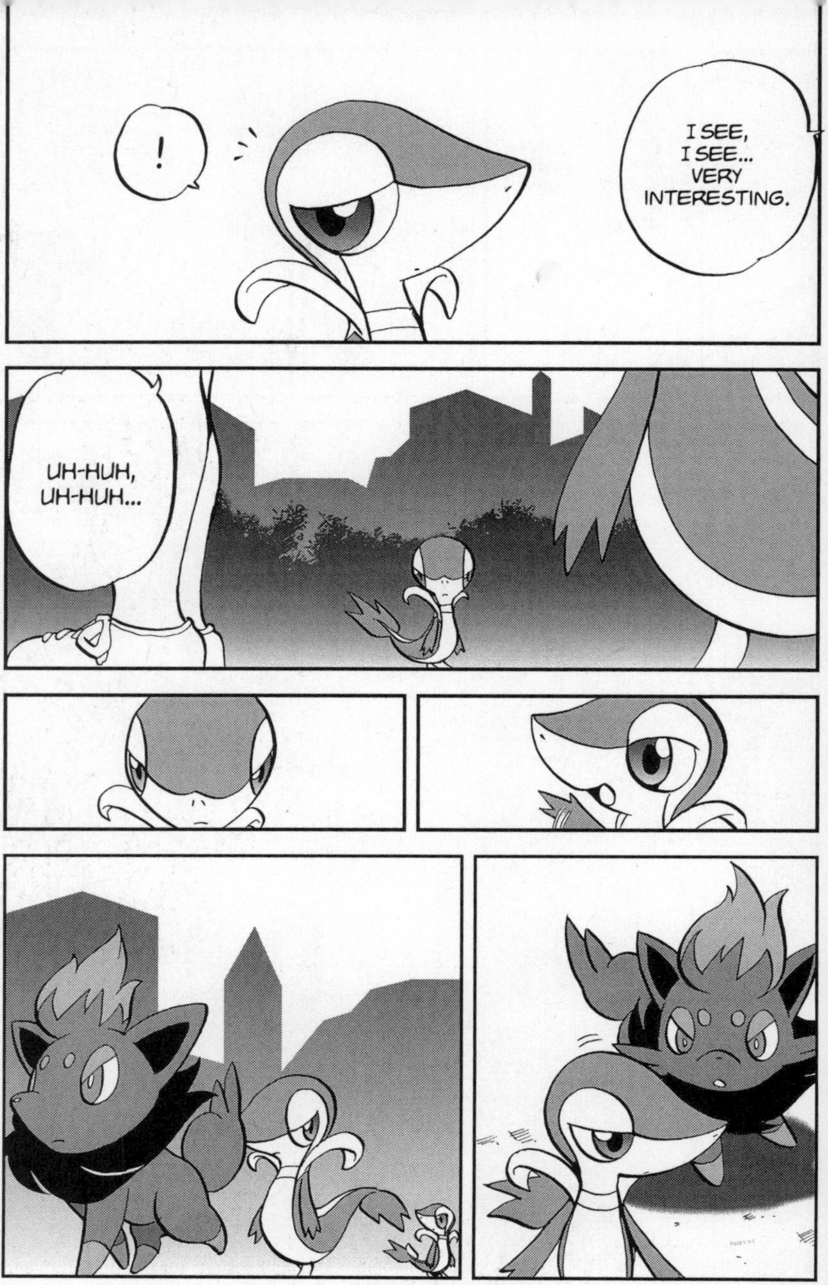
I SEE, I SEE... VERY INTERESTING.
!
UH-HUH, UH-HUH...

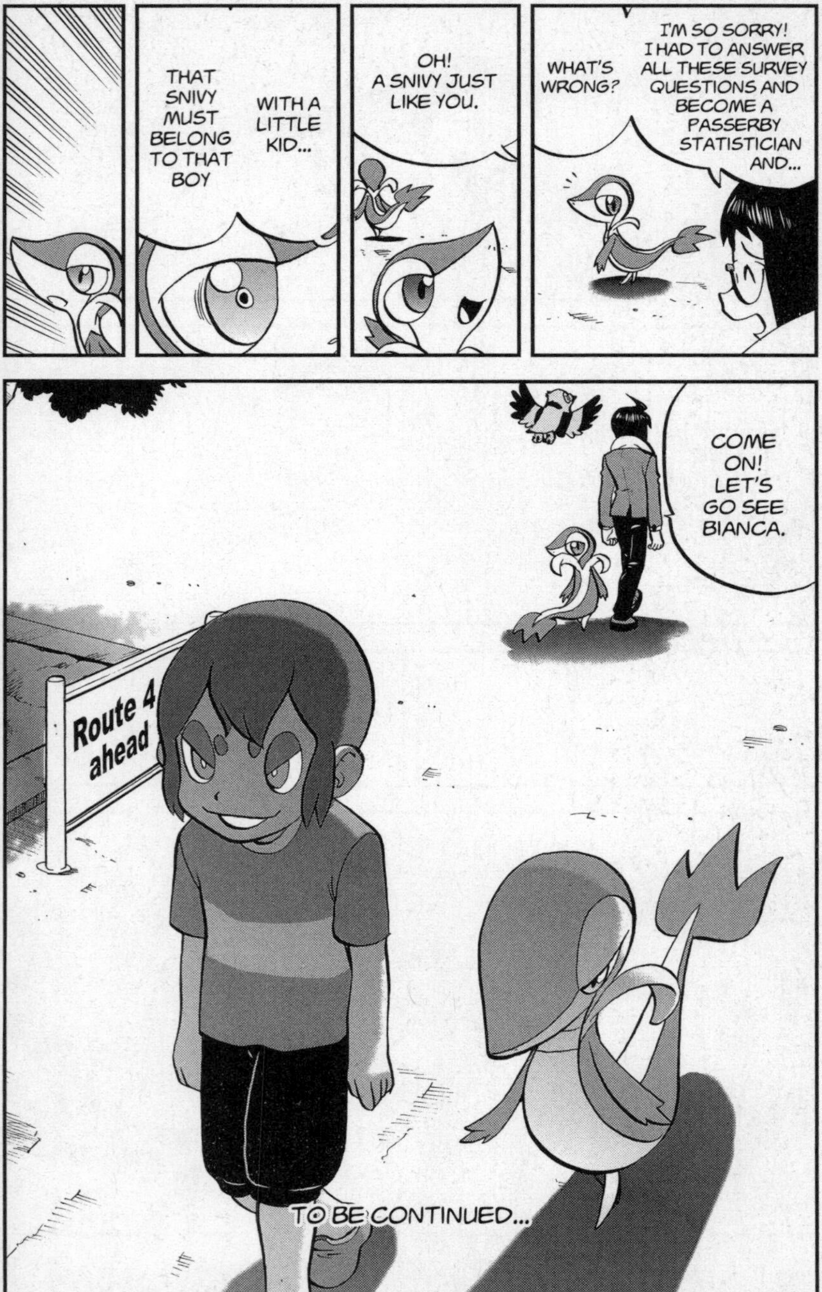
I'M SO SORRY! I HAD TO ANSWER ALL THESE SURVEY QUESTIONS AND BECOME A PASSERBY STATISTICIAN AND...
WHAT'S WRONG?
OH! A SNIVY JUST LIKE YOU.
THAT SNIVY MUST BELONG TO THAT BOY
WITH A LITTLE KID...
COME ON! LET'S GO SEE BIANCA.
Route 4 ahead
TO BE CONTINUED...

TO BE
CONTINUED

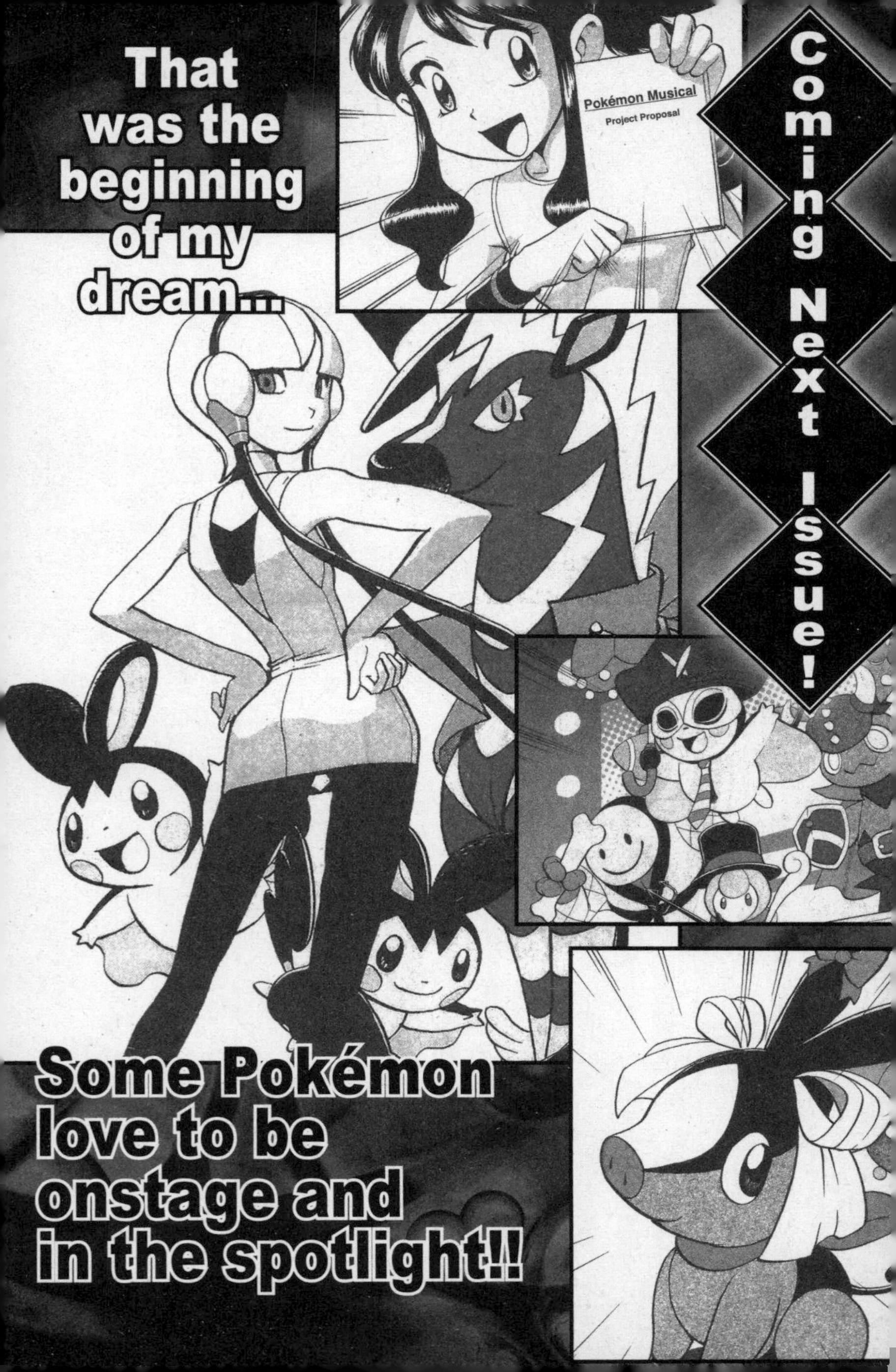
Coming Next Issue!
Pokémon Musical
Project Proposal
That was the beginning of my dream...
Some Pokémon love to be onstage and in the spotlight!!

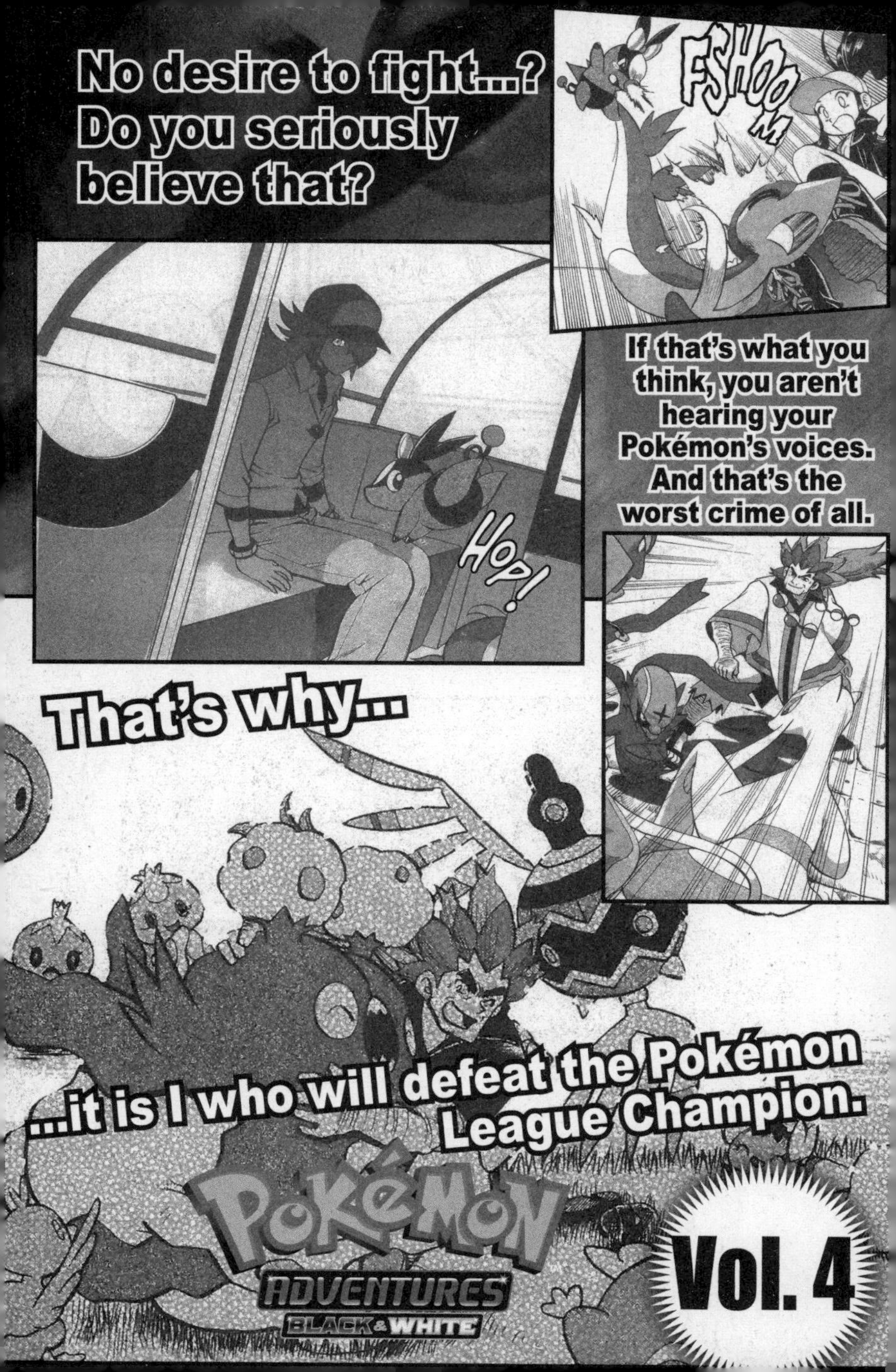
FSHOOOM
No desire to fight...? Do you seriously believe that?
If that's what you think, you aren't hearing your Pokémon's voices. And that's the worst crime of all.
HOP!
That's why...
...it is I who will defeat the Pokémon League Champion.
POKÉMON ADVENTURES BLACK & WHITE
Vol. 4

Special Feature

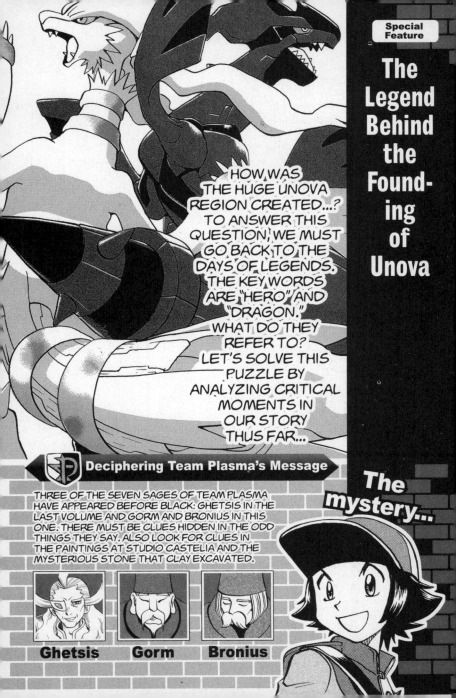

The Legend Behind the Founding of Unova

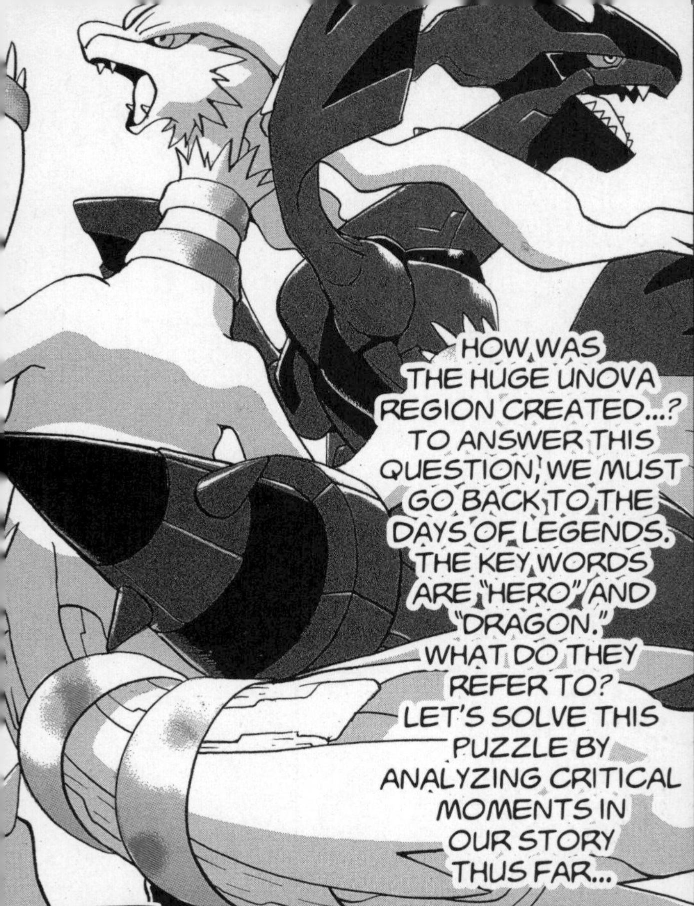

HOW WAS THE HUGE UNOVA REGION CREATED...? TO ANSWER THIS QUESTION, WE MUST GO BACK TO THE DAYS OF LEGENDS. THE KEY WORDS ARE "HERO" AND "DRAGON." WHAT DO THEY REFER TO? LET'S SOLVE THIS PUZZLE BY ANALYZING CRITICAL MOMENTS IN OUR STORY THUS FAR...

Deciphering Team Plasma's Message

THREE OF THE SEVEN SAGES OF TEAM PLASMA HAVE APPEARED BEFORE BLACK: GHETSIS IN THE LAST VOLUME AND GORM AND BRONIUS IN THIS ONE. THERE MUST BE CLUES HIDDEN IN THE ODD THINGS THEY SAY. ALSO LOOK FOR CLUES IN THE PAINTINGS AT STUDIO CASTELIA AND THE MYSTERIOUS STONE THAT CLAY EXCAVATED.

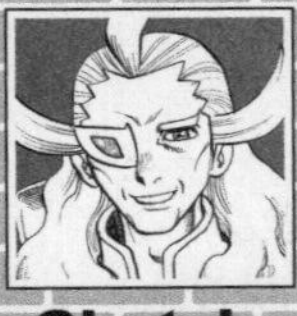

Ghetsis

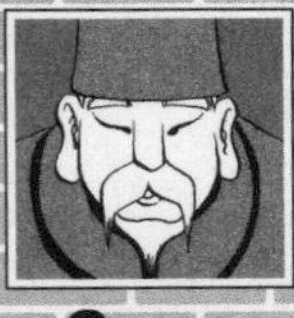

Gorm

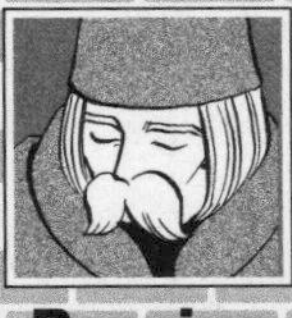

Bronius

The mystery...

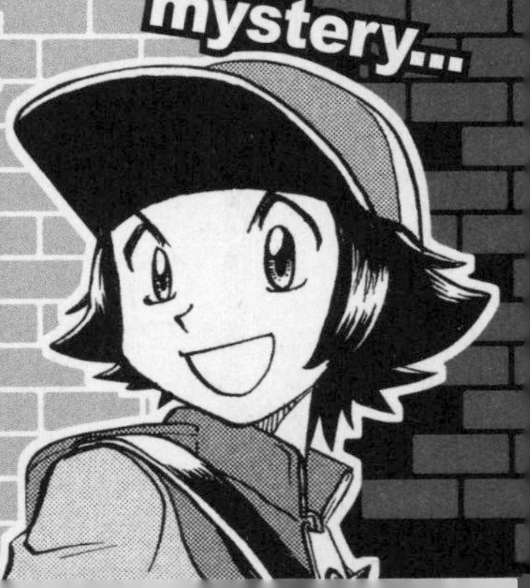

Clue 1

Hero

TEAM PLASMA KEEPS MENTIONING A "HERO." ACCORDING TO LEGEND, THIS PERSON WILL GUIDE OTHERS. TEAM PLASMA DREAMS OF LIBERATING POKÉMON FROM PEOPLE. COULD IT BE THAT N, THEIR KING, IS THE HERO THEY SPEAK OF?

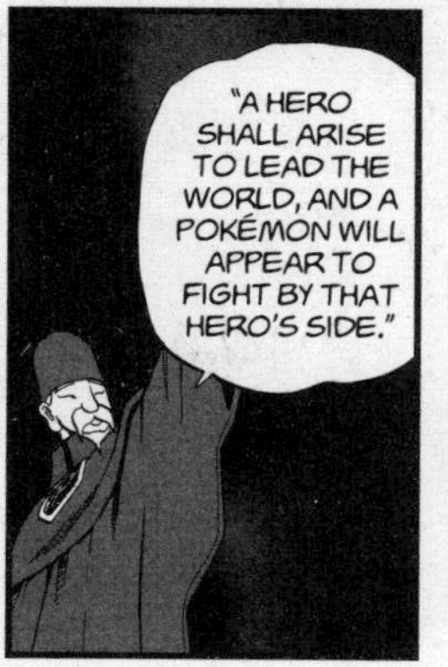
"A HERO SHALL ARISE TO LEAD THE WORLD, AND A POKÉMON WILL APPEAR TO FIGHT BY THAT HERO'S SIDE."

➡ A POKÉMON THAT WILL AID THE HERO? IS TEAM PLASMA AFTER THIS POKÉMON?

⬇ EVERYTHING TEAM PLASMA DOES IS FOR THEIR HERO, AND THIS IS THEIR EXCUSE FOR EVERYTHING THEY DO. HOW DISTURBING...

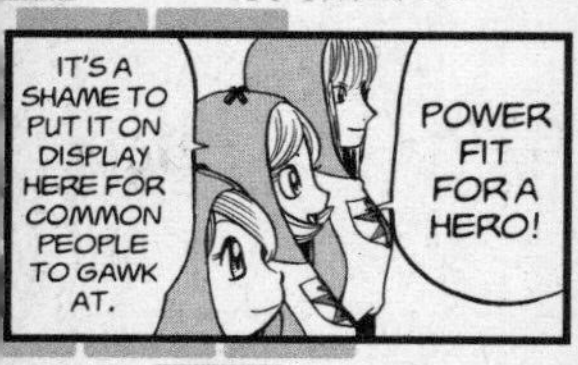
POWER FIT FOR A HERO!
IT'S A SHAME TO PUT IT ON DISPLAY HERE FOR COMMON PEOPLE TO GAWK AT.

Clue 2

Revive

WHEN TALKING ABOUT THE FOUNDING OF UNOVA, BRONIUS SPOKE OF "BRINGING BACK" SOMETHING. TEAM PLASMA APPARENTLY NEEDS WHATEVER THIS THING IS TO BRING THE PEOPLE OF UNOVA TOGETHER SOMEHOW. WHAT IS IT THEY'RE TRYING TO BRING BACK...?

HE USED THE TERM "BLACK LIGHTNING BOLT" AS WELL AS "HERO." ⬅ ⬇

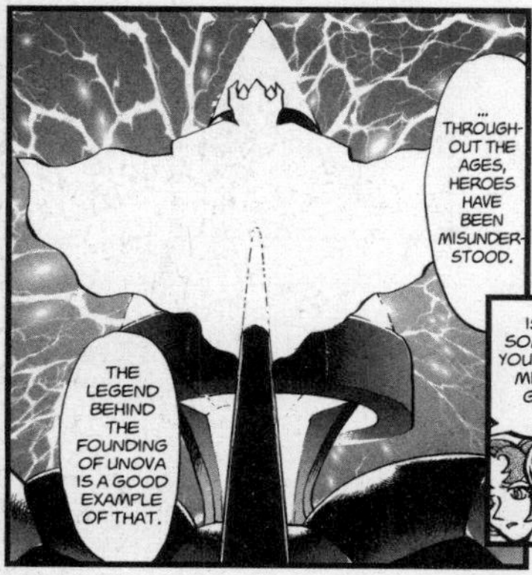
... THROUGHOUT THE AGES, HEROES HAVE BEEN MISUNDERSTOOD.
THE LEGEND BEHIND THE FOUNDING OF UNOVA IS A GOOD EXAMPLE OF THAT.

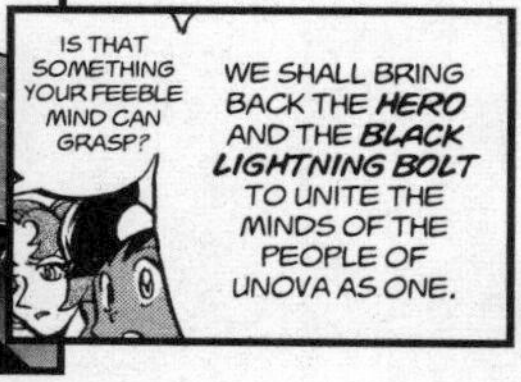
WE SHALL BRING BACK THE ***HERO*** AND THE ***BLACK LIGHTNING BOLT*** TO UNITE THE MINDS OF THE PEOPLE OF UNOVA AS ONE.
IS THAT SOMETHING YOUR FEEBLE MIND CAN GRASP?

Clue 3

Dragon-type Pokémon Fossil

TEAM PLASMA STOLE THE DRAGON-TYPE POKÉMON FOSSIL FROM THE NACRENE MUSEUM. DOES THIS HAVE SOMETHING TO DO WITH WHAT BRONIUS WANTS TO "BRING BACK"?

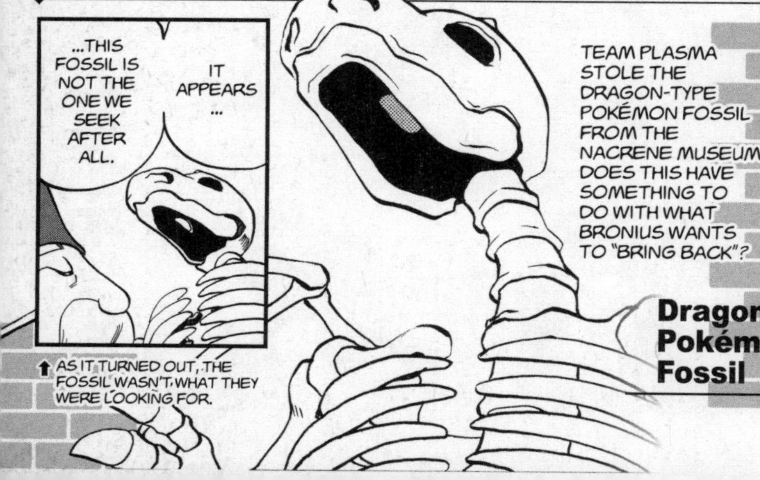
IT APPEARS ...
...THIS FOSSIL IS NOT THE ONE WE SEEK AFTER ALL.

⬆ AS IT TURNED OUT, THE FOSSIL WASN'T WHAT THEY WERE LOOKING FOR.

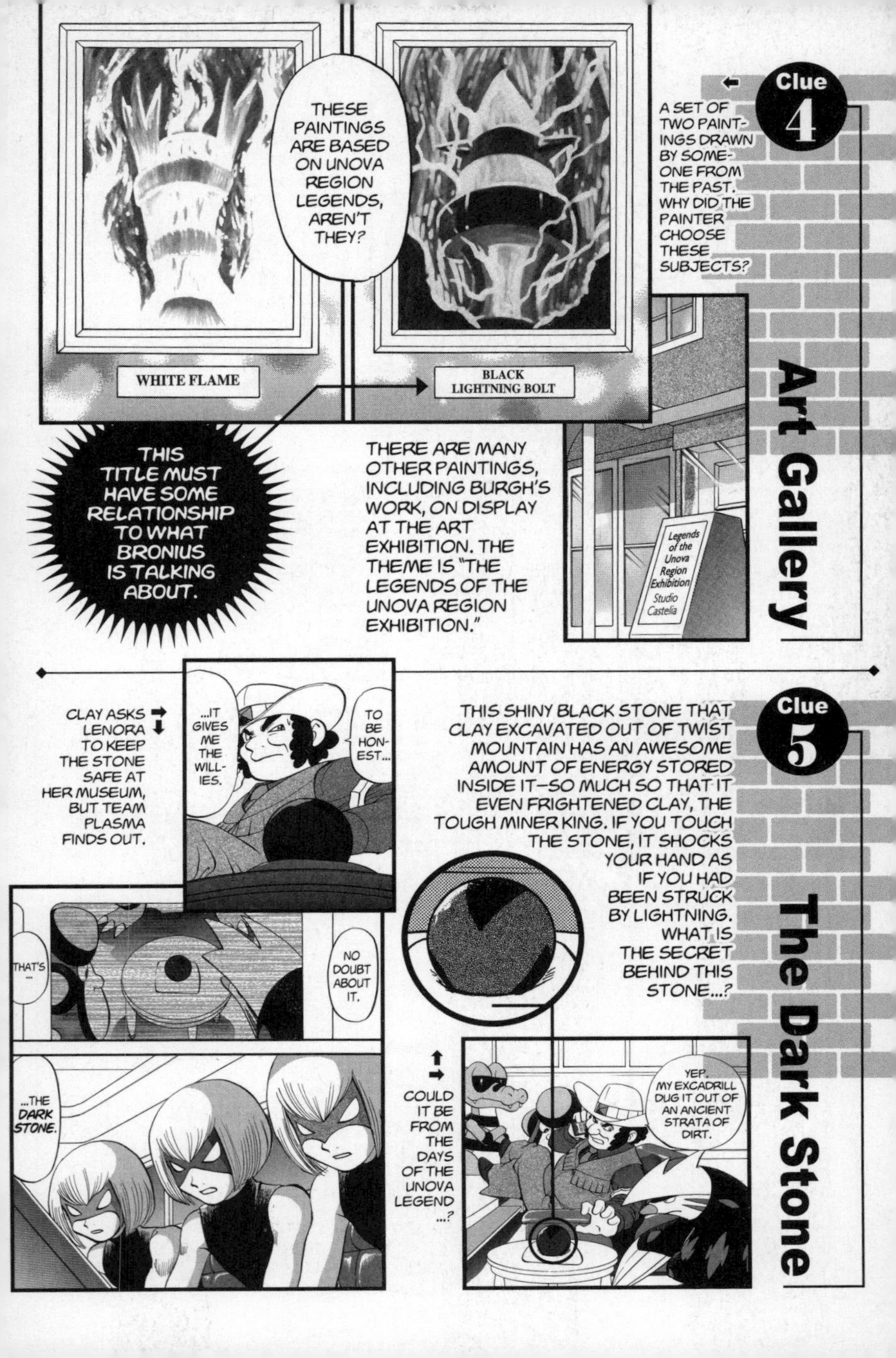
Clue 4
A SET OF TWO PAINT-INGS DRAWN BY SOME-ONE FROM THE PAST. WHY DID THE PAINTER CHOOSE THESE SUBJECTS?
Art Gallery
THESE PAINTINGS ARE BASED ON UNOVA REGION LEGENDS, AREN'T THEY?
BLACK LIGHTNING BOLT
WHITE FLAME
Legends of the Unova Region Exhibition Studio Castelia
THERE ARE MANY OTHER PAINTINGS, INCLUDING BURGH'S WORK, ON DISPLAY AT THE ART EXHIBITION. THE THEME IS "THE LEGENDS OF THE UNOVA REGION EXHIBITION."
THIS TITLE MUST HAVE SOME RELATIONSHIP TO WHAT BRONIUS IS TALKING ABOUT.
Clue 5
The Dark Stone
THIS SHINY BLACK STONE THAT CLAY EXCAVATED OUT OF TWIST MOUNTAIN HAS AN AWESOME AMOUNT OF ENERGY STORED INSIDE IT—SO MUCH SO THAT IT EVEN FRIGHTENED CLAY, THE TOUGH MINER KING. IF YOU TOUCH THE STONE, IT SHOCKS YOUR HAND AS IF YOU HAD BEEN STRUCK BY LIGHTNING. WHAT IS THE SECRET BEHIND THIS STONE...?
TO BE HON-EST...
...IT GIVES ME THE WILL-IES.
CLAY ASKS LENORA TO KEEP THE STONE SAFE AT HER MUSEUM, BUT TEAM PLASMA FINDS OUT.
NO DOUBT ABOUT IT.
THAT'S...
YEP. MY EXCADRILL DUG IT OUT OF AN ANCIENT STRATA OF DIRT.
COULD IT BE FROM THE DAYS OF THE UNOVA LEGEND...?
...THE DARK STONE.

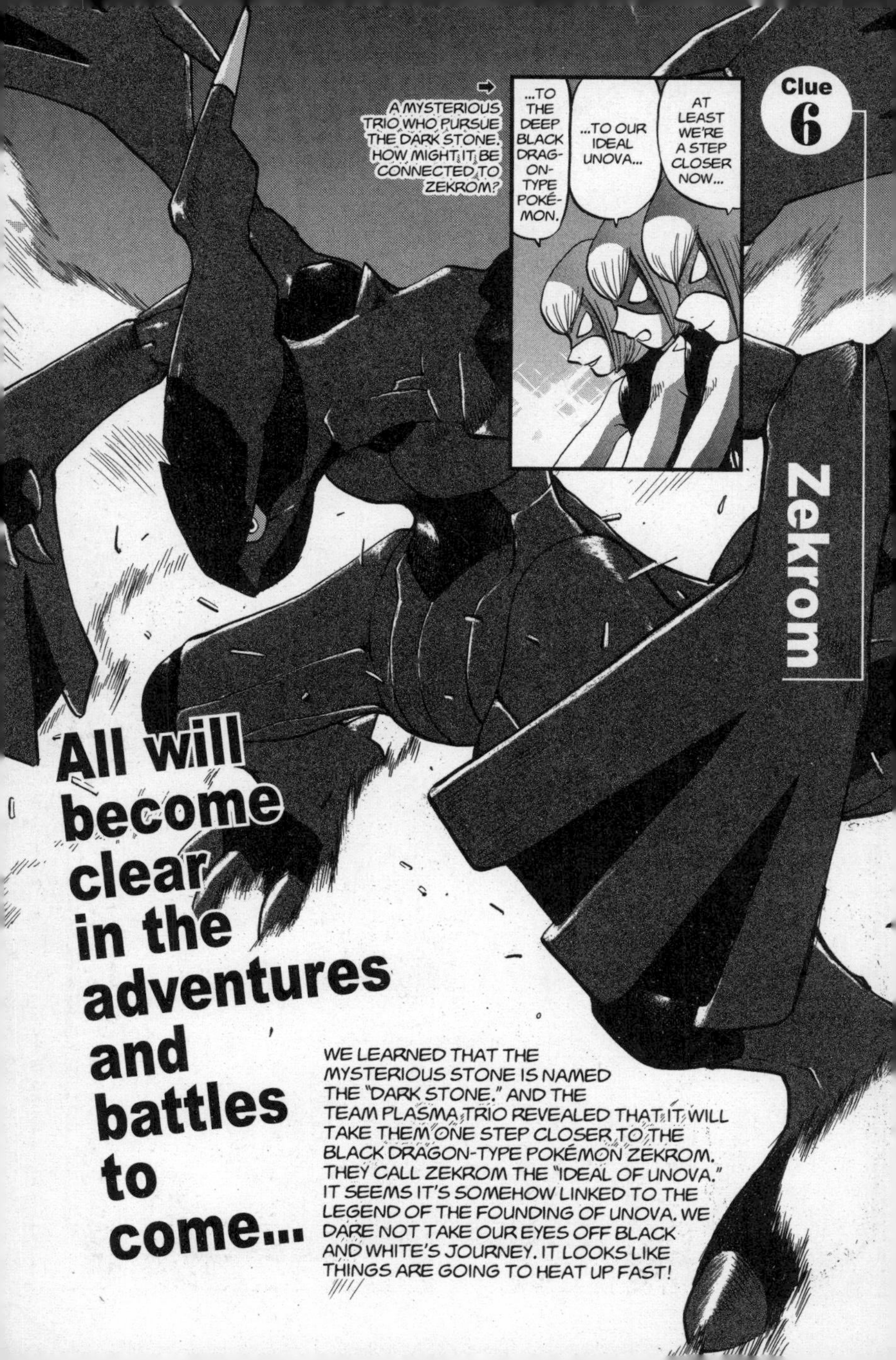
Clue 6
Zekrom
AT LEAST WE'RE A STEP CLOSER NOW...
...TO OUR IDEAL UNOVA...
...TO THE DEEP BLACK DRAGON-TYPE POKÉMON.
A MYSTERIOUS TRIO WHO PURSUE THE DARK STONE. HOW MIGHT IT BE CONNECTED TO ZEKROM?
All will become clear in the adventures and battles to come...
WE LEARNED THAT THE MYSTERIOUS STONE IS NAMED THE "DARK STONE." AND THE TEAM PLASMA TRIO REVEALED THAT IT WILL TAKE THEM ONE STEP CLOSER TO THE BLACK DRAGON-TYPE POKÉMON ZEKROM. THEY CALL ZEKROM THE "IDEAL OF UNOVA." IT SEEMS IT'S SOMEHOW LINKED TO THE LEGEND OF THE FOUNDING OF UNOVA. WE DARE NOT TAKE OUR EYES OFF BLACK AND WHITE'S JOURNEY. IT LOOKS LIKE THINGS ARE GOING TO HEAT UP FAST!

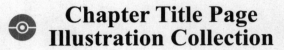

Chapter Title Page Illustration Collection

Presenting title page illustrations originally drawn for some of the chapters of *Pokémon Black and White* when they were first published in Japanese children's magazines *Pokémon Fan* and *Corocoro Ichiban!*.

Let's take a look back at Black and White's journey in pictures...

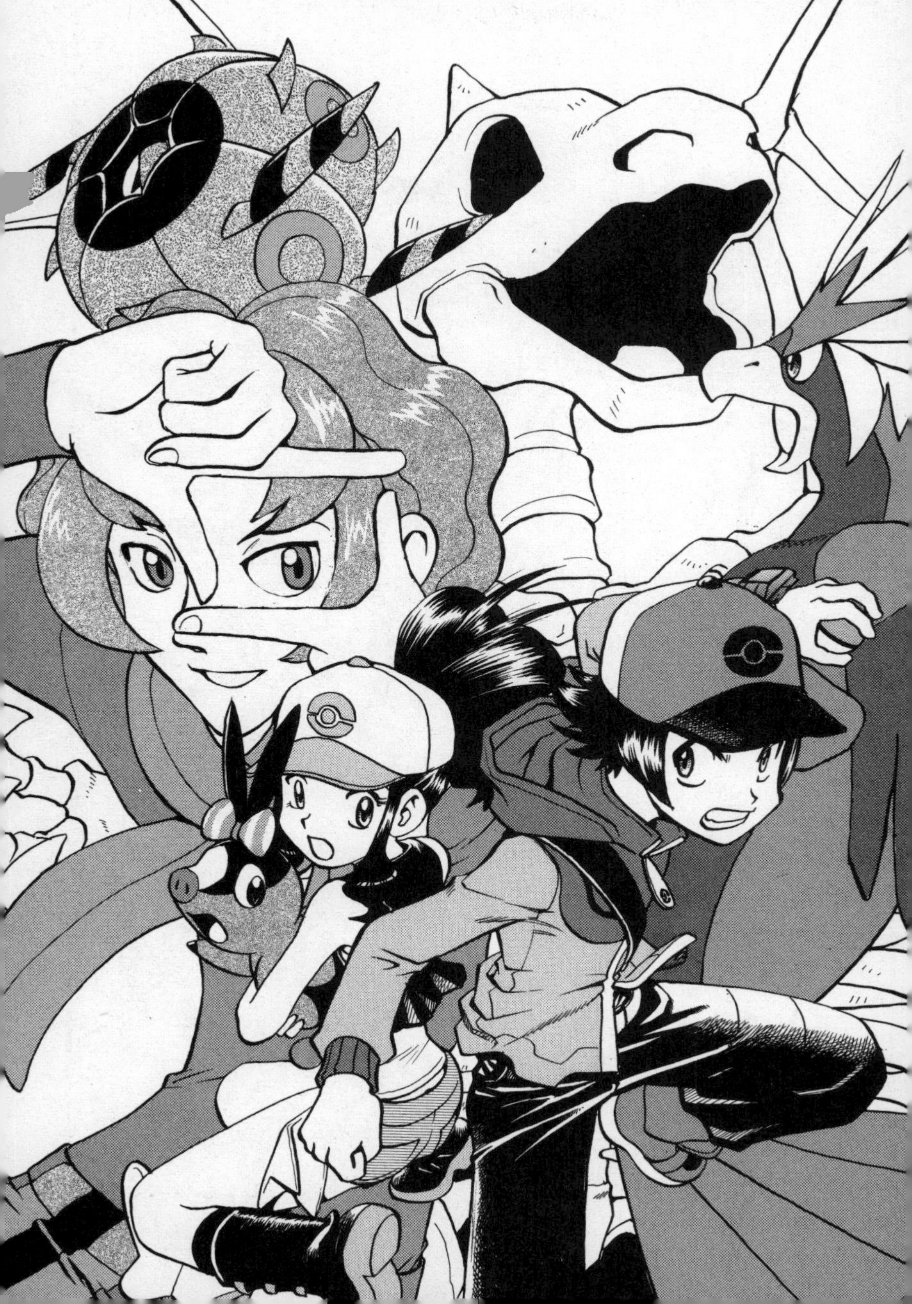

Pokémon Fan, Issue 16

Corocoro Ichiban!
August 2011 Issue

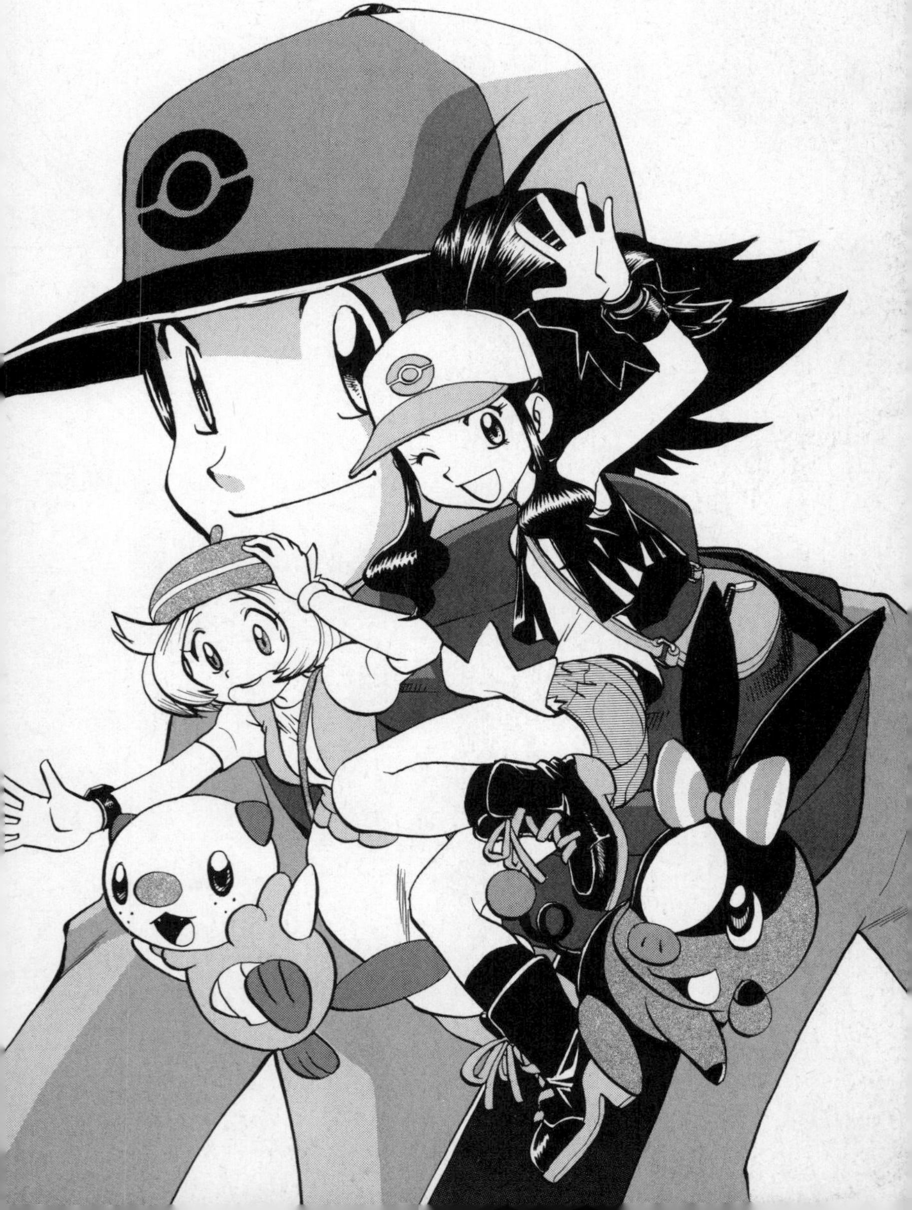

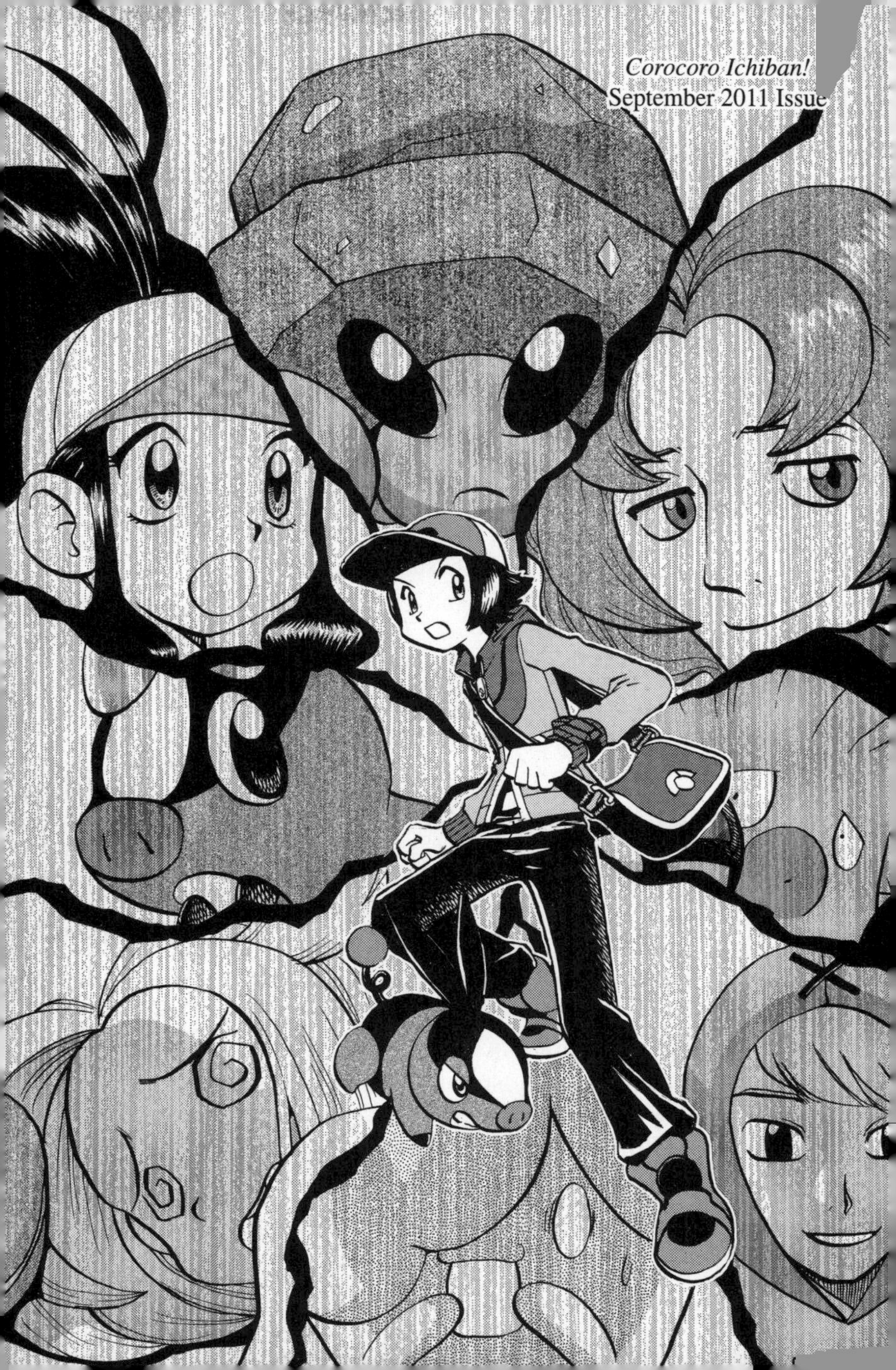

Corocoro Ichiban!
September 2011 Issue

Message from
Hidenori Kusaka

Since I began working on this series, I haven't taken part in an autograph session. I have the artist do that while I stand quietly behind the chain and watch. That way I can better observe our fans. But recently, I've had a bit of a change of heart, and I've started to appear before our fans myself...although I'm still pretty shy about it. On the plus side, the warmth and connection I feel when I shake a fan's hand inspires and motivates me. I'm very grateful for that. (´ ▽ `)ﾉ

Message from
Satoshi Yamamoto

From Nacrene City to Skyarrow Bridge and then to Castelia City... The story moves from one setting to the next, so it's full of chance meetings and leave-takings. This is the 45th volume of the *Pokémon Adventures* series! Countless characters have appeared in it already! I want the bit parts to be especially memorable, though. It's a fun challenge finding ways to differentiate them so that readers don't think to themselves, "Hey, haven't I seen this character somewhere before...?"

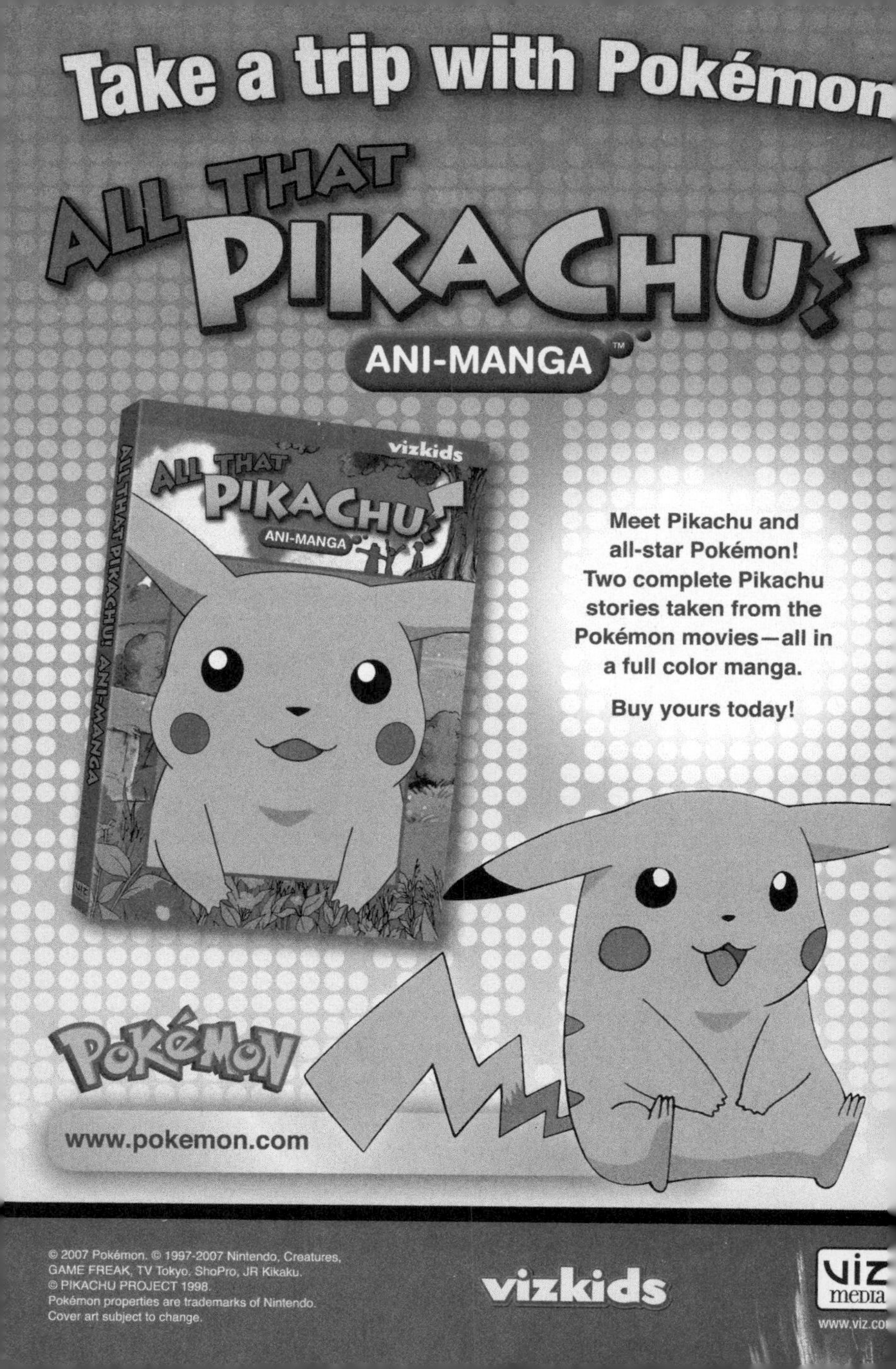

Take a trip with Pokémon
ALL THAT PIKACHU!
ANI-MANGA™
vizkids
ALL THAT PIKACHU!
ANI-MANGA
ALL THAT PIKACHU! ANI-MANGA
Meet Pikachu and all-star Pokémon! Two complete Pikachu stories taken from the Pokémon movies—all in a full color manga.
Buy yours today!
POKéMON
www.pokemon.com
© 2007 Pokémon. © 1997-2007 Nintendo, Creatures, GAME FREAK, TV Tokyo, ShoPro, JR Kikaku. © PIKACHU PROJECT 1998. Pokémon properties are trademarks of Nintendo. Cover art subject to change.
vizkids
VIZ media
www.viz.com

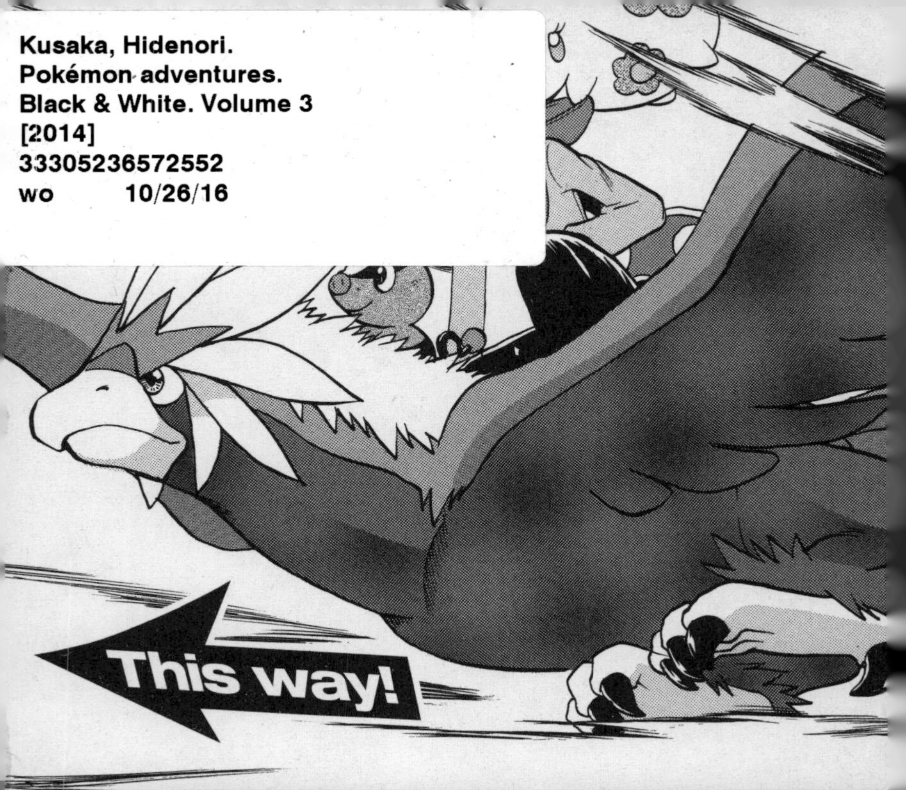
This way!

THIS IS THE END OF THIS GRAPHIC NOVEL!

To properly enjoy this VIZ Media graphic novel, please turn it around and begin reading from right to left.

This book has been printed in the original Japanese format in order to preserve the orientation of the original artwork.

Have fun with it!

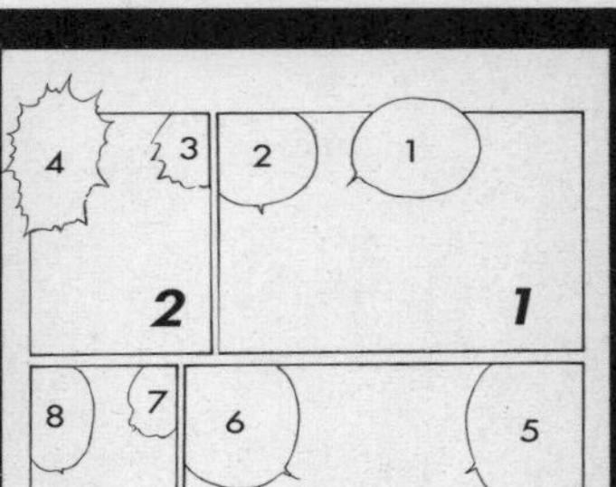
1
2
3
4
1
2
5
6
7
8
3
4
9
5

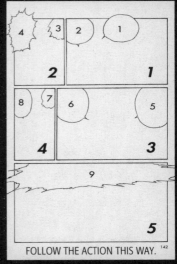

FOLLOW THE ACTION THIS WAY.